LEGACY

**A STORY OF HOPE
FOR A TIME OF ENVIRONMENTAL CRISIS**

Joanne Poyourow

This book contains references to the valued work of hundreds of people and organizations. These references are intended to cultivate further awareness and appreciation for these world-changing ideas, and to encourage *Legacy* readers to seek out the underlying nonfiction materials. While it has not been possible nor practical to notify hundreds of innovators of the reference to their work, an exhaustive search was done to determine whether previously published material included in this book required permission to reprint. If any required acknowledgments have been omitted, I apologize and, if notified, will correct such omission in subsequent editions.

Permissions begin on page 375 and are considered a continuation of the copyright page.

"Legacy," by Joanne Poyourow. ISBN 1-58939-789-4.

This book is dedicated to my children,
J.J.P. and H.J.P.

and to your cousins and friends,
to the children of Los Angeles,
to the children of the world
and your children's children

because we have to leave you a better legacy than this.

TABLE OF CONTENTS

LEGACY

MAY 2105

"Forget seven generations ..."

Arissa arched one eyebrow in amusement as the scrawled handwriting conveyed its fury across more than a century. She extracted the ribbon-bound packet of letters from the dusty box and moved to the window to read more.

Something weighty and metal slipped out from between the letters: a large gold locket, circular rather than the usual heart-shaped, with an etched design that artistically suggested the continents of the globe. It looked vaguely familiar. Arissa turned it in her hand until she realized where she had seen it before, so many times. *Great-Grandma Tia always wore this on a long gold chain. She never would show me what was inside, no matter how much I begged.*

Arissa carefully pried open the locket. Inside were a few dusty bits which looked like they might once have been ordinary grasses. Puzzled, she snapped the locket shut and dropped it next to a tiny antique crystal dish on the table beside her. The locket made a dull clink against the dish as if it weren't meant to be there.

She pulled the ribbon off the bundle of letters, threaded the locket onto it, and tied the ribbon around her neck. The locket felt comforting against her skin: strengthening, purposeful.

Satisfied, she returned to the letters, to reread the words which had been directed to Tia:

> Forget 'seven generations,' this planet's heating up,
> the oceans are rising, the forests are being razed,
> and still it's gas guzzling SUV's, let's drill the
> Arctic National Wildlife Refuge, and gimme more
> disposable commodities. Junk and waste. We're
> devastating the earth. With the way things are
> going, there won't *be* any grandchildren!

Ah, Cassandra, but someone was listening.

Arissa gazed out the bronze solar-efficient paned window of her Los Angeles eco-village unit. A flock of tiny sparrows twittered gaily among the grey green leaves of the fruit laden feijoa bushes, clearing them of insects. The soft voices of the day's Community Reapers Committee drifted in the window as the workers made their way snip-clip through the common grounds, harvesting for dinner from the diverse species and varieties of the water-efficient garden. Her eyes turned to the clear sky, free of smog and pollutants, and her thoughts ran beyond, to the decreasing carbon dioxide concentrations in the atmosphere.

Arissa fingered the locket at her throat, thinking of life back in Tia's days: noisy, filthy automobiles, crowded roadways, chemically poisoned foods, overfilled landfills, and nations that refused to work together toward the benefit of the planet and its people.

A group of children ran laughing down the garden path, mixed ages, boys and girls, in delighted tumult. A dark haired eight year old boy separated from the crowd and flew through Arissa's doorway. He paused to hug Arissa briefly, his intense brown eyes flashing merriment, then dashed into the depths of their home.

'There won't be any grandchildren.' Arissa grinned as her thoughts returned to the letter. She tallied on her fingers: *Cassandra, Tia, Grandma, Mom, me ... count Saffi, and my Janus is the seventh generation.*

The Permaculture Flower

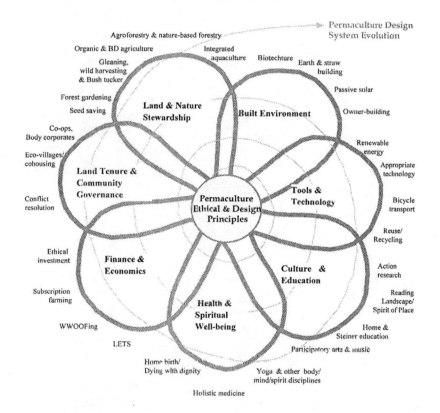

PART ONE

We must be willing to get rid of the life we've planned, so as to have the life that is waiting for us. The old skin has to be shed before the new one can come.

Joseph Campbell

CHAPTER 1:

VORACIOUS

EARLY SPRING, 2002

Tia pushed back from her desk, away from the pile of glossy corporate reports. She stood and stretched her long legs, moving to the window. Smoggy haze blurred the narrow slice of Los Angeles visible between the office buildings. In the tiny courtyard below her, unnaturally green grass outlined perfect geometry amid the line of manicured ficus trees, always the same, day in and day out, year round. Her mind jumped to the ever-changing elder trees two counties away at Coyote Creek and tears pricked her eyes. She turned from the window abruptly.

Returning to her desk, she tried to continue with the reports. Their words and figures merged meaninglessly together as her vision blurred. *Focus!* She wiped her eyes in irritation.

She fiddled with the few pink message slips that had accumulated during her lunch hour. The client. *Probably wants this report, can't return that one yet.* Doug. *Later, after his board meeting. Besides, he doesn't understand.*

A partially drafted email beckoned from her computer screen.

… and just like that he is gone. No time for goodbyes, no 'I love you Tia,' just gone forever. Forever is such a crazy long time. The police found fragments of a pipe bomb …

She sobbed, a tight silent gasp, unable to contain it any longer. Elbows on the reports, her head in her hands, her tears dripped long stains down the sleeves of her silk blouse.

Give up and take a walk.

Grabbing her purse and jacket, she stumbled to the elevator. As the car descended she automatically checked her appearance in the chrome panels. *Thin, that gym membership is paying off.* She smoothed her straight light-brown hair, then turned away at the sight of her face, her eyes puffy from crying. *Next year thirty, right now I really look it.* She tugged at the uncomfortable waistband in her tailored designer skirt.

Noisy, jostling, frenzied, the city streets were hardly the place for a calming walk. Tia coughed in exhaust fumes as a particularly obnoxious limousine rounded the corner in front of her. A pigeon swooped low as the limo accelerated out of the turn. A quiet thump, and the dead bird hit the sidewalk at her feet.

Get me out of here!

Her distracted pace slowed outside a gleaming chrome and glass doorway. Serenity and quiet beckoned within: a bookstore, a big chain one. Entering, she automatically browsed the aisles, not registering much of anything, but the smell of newsprint and fresh bindings calmed her. She sank into the stillness of a cushiony chair and wiped her tears, just now realizing she was still crying.

Titles from the shelves around her came into focus: *The Heat Is On ... The Next One Hundred Years ... Worldwatch Institute State of the World.* She recognized these titles from her parents' bookshelves.

Daddy, she thought, and the tears welled up again. As if to bring him nearer, she reached for a familiar looking book, then clutched it to her chest. Another. And another. Rocking slightly in the chair, her tears fell in earnest.

(2.)

To: valleybloom@ovi.com
Sahara – First day back to work since I saw you at the memorial service. Work was awful. I lasted about half a day. Went to a bookstore and bought a bunch of those old environment books my parents read. Crazy. I don't usually read that stuff. I miss him more than I can bear. Call your dad tonight and tell him you love him, you just never know how long you've got.

Tia sent the email. Sahara of all people would understand.

I'm too far away, here in the city. Mom always says so, but tonight even I can feel it.

Tia listlessly paced her apartment. There wasn't much to pace, from one room into the next. She turned on the stereo, then almost instantly switched it off. She ran a finger along the long line of bookshelves, straightening books already impeccably tidy and too clean to merit a dusting. At the bookend a smiling photo of her parents was heartbreaking to see; she turned it face down. Wandering into the kitchen, she checked the fridge, then closed it again, she wasn't hungry. Even the view of the channel, glistening through the trees, couldn't hold her interest.

Her foot tipped the bag of new books. Bending to straighten them, she changed her mind, picked up the stack and headed for the couch to curl in her favorite corner nook. The cat came running, purred and nestled in a ball on Tia's feet. Tia adjusted the lamp and began to read.

(3.)

"Mom, I've been doing some reading ... kind of different stuff for me, I picked up a bunch of books like Dad used to have," Tia said cautiously into the phone. *Oh, I wish I hadn't mentioned him, please don't talk about him, I can't bear it.* She paced her office as she anxiously waited for Cassandra's response.

"You mean you bought them? You could borrow his copies from here, or use the library – you do have libraries down there, don't you? Don't feed the consumerist machine! I'm sorry honey, what were you saying?" Cassandra sounded as disoriented as Tia felt.

Relieved that her mother had launched on the tangent, Tia's voice was more solid this time. "I've been up all night, reading about – well – the environment, all the things happening. It's even bigger than you'd told me."

"You're reading that stuff *now*? You never had any interest all these years, just wanted to be a big-deals corporate executive type!"

We can't even talk about this, Tia sighed, *let alone what's right between us!*

"Mom ..." she began again.

"I've been trying to tell you about these things for ages!" Cassandra interrupted. "You have to read the real stuff, check out who the authors are. Filter it. There's lots of crap science out there, but then there are the real facts. The U.S. politicians these days are subsidizing the garbage studies. That way they can support their oil agenda. Don't read anything EPA, you can't trust them, political pressures have distorted their 'studies' for years." She was on a roll now.

"Read current things, from the EU, Australia, India, international. Get the real picture. Start with something solid, like the Worldwatch reports. Union of Concerned Scientists, or the IPCC – that's the Intergovernmental Panel on Climate Change, they're good too. Honey, why are you doing this now, of all times?"

"I don't know. I guess it felt like it'd bring him closer." Tia answered lamely. "I kind of got into it for him, and then, I got *into* it. Now I want to learn more."

"I tell you what, honey, I'll pack up some books we have around here and ship them to you. That'll get you off on the right foot. Oh, Sahara's just driving up, she's taking me to the doctor's to have these dressings changed. I've got to go – take care, honey."

Tia pressed the phone into the cradle, a little too firmly. She had a sudden image of her mother's thickly bandaged arms and hands. *Don't think about it. If you start, you might never stop.*

She returned to the pile of dull corporate reports. Two weeks ago these had been hot, urgent, enticing. But now – words formed in her mind that sounded suspiciously like something her mother might say: *those despoiling raiders.*

Yikes, these are my clients, my career, even my friends. What's getting into me?

(4.)

Tia's reading took on a life of its own. The footnotes of one book pointed her to another. She devoured them in every spare moment.

She learned about the greenhouse effect, how the buildup of carbon dioxide (CO_2) and certain other gasses in our atmosphere are trapping the sun's radiation, causing the earth's temperatures to rise. International scientists agree that this phenomenon is accelerating due to human activities, particularly the burning of fossil fuels. Forests can be carbon sinks, she read, absorbing the CO_2 emissions and reducing the radiation trapping effect. Yet forests are being razed worldwide at a horrendous rate. She perused Intergovernmental Panel on Climate Change scenarios, which indicated that, in order to stabilize the CO_2 levels, world emissions of greenhouse gasses must come under control before the year 2040.

She studied temperature projections, which anticipate the planet warming several degrees overall this century. Several degrees didn't sound like much, until she read how the increase won't be evenly distributed, with some areas warming considerably and others less so. She read the projections of mega-droughts, which will dwarf the U.S. Dustbowl of the 1930s. Rainfall reallocations, similar to the temperature rise, will be disproportionate.

Tia learned about rising sea levels, brought on by melting polar ice caps, together with molecular expansion. These rising sea levels will soon cover heavily populated parts of Bangladesh, one of the world's poorest countries, already experiencing food production problems. Sea level rise will also jeopardize the Netherlands, the Nile Delta, Florida, Louisiana, and much of the Carolina coastline. Climate change will dramatically affect the El Niño phenomenon, bringing more frequent and fiercer storms from the Pacific.

Tia read about glacial ice shrinkage, wildlife habitat destruction, and decreases in species diversity worldwide. And she read about the Kyoto Protocol, one of the world's first efforts to create an agreement between nations in attempt to solve some of these global problems.[1]

We're right on the edge of what's possible – we have to act now! If we wait, it might all be too late! The urgency drove her to pace the floor of her apartment in agitation. Even the physical motion did little to calm her frantic feelings.

The more she read, the more she began to feel estranged from her typical city lifestyle. Her new insight made her raw to the daily evidence of consumerism, material waste, pollution and excess. It suddenly felt like everything she did or touched was making it worse.

She now knew about CO_2 emissions, but she relied on her car to get to work. She'd read about destructive agricultural practices, soils and aquifer depletion, but she still needed to eat, and biodynamic products were hard to find. She had to use computers and electricity in her work, despite the power plant issues. She lived in an apartment, so installing solar wasn't an option for her.

The problems were now clear to her but she couldn't figure out what to do about them. With her heightened awareness, she felt like a destroyer.

(5.)

The hot parking garage was packed with lunchtime crowds. Tia sat in her Lexus SUV, impatiently waiting for a parking space. *Come on, come on, I have to get in and out of here and back to work.* She drummed her manicured fingernails on the steering wheel.

As she dashed through the mall's entrance corridor, her cell phone warbled. She looked down to note the caller's i.d., and nearly collided with another shopper.

"Oh, I'm sorry Ma'am ... wait, Doug ... yeah, I'm here. I just slammed into some poor lady. I'm just going into the mall ... sure, dinner ... after the gym? Okay, say 7:30." Stuffing the phone into her purse, she rounded the corner.

This enormous luxury mall had been Tia's regular lunchtime haunt for years, but today the opulent shopping scene struck her as never before.

The glittering array was like a shock wave, hitting her full in the chest, an overwhelming view of *Stuff.*

The sheer number of items on display ... dresses ... shoes ... jewelry ... perfume ... *How could we possibly need so much?* ... dishes … linens ... *The mind-boggling quantity of items!* ... toys ... electronics ... *The vast amount of resources taken to manufacture, package, ship all of this!*

She gasped, stepping backward, twisting her ankle in her fashion heels. She winced in pain. *Stupid shoes.* Wrenching them off her feet, she looked down and was horrified. In her twisted perception the shoes became gleaming fragments of the decadent shopping scene around her. *I'm part of it! I'm feeding the vast consumption machine!*

(6.)

Tia met Doug for dinner at a chic little cafe, twinkling with white Christmas lights out of season. The tiny lights, reflecting off polished silverware and sleek chrome furniture, multiplied to infinity, causing Tia to think of United Nations population projections.

An up-and-coming executive, Doug Montgomery at thirty-two was athletic and solidly built, with reddish blond hair which was already threatening to recede. He was impeccably groomed in his high-end department store attire.

"I'll have the blackened Chilean Seabass," Doug said to the waiter.

"Overfishing, bycatch, habitat damage ..." Tia murmured.

"What?"

"Never mind."

Doug completed with the waiter and turned on Tia. "What has gotten into you lately? What was that nonsense?"

"Well, I was reading about the Chilean Seabass. They live at least forty years and breed late in life. The Monterey Bay Aquarium lists them as 'Avoid' on their Seafood Watch list."[2]

"What a bunch of rot! You're sounding more like Cassandra every day!"

"Actually, I've been reading more of her books, she shipped another box to me this week."

"Hold on now, she's always had some pretty wild ideas."

"I don't find them quite so wild anymore."

"What's with you? Ever since your father's death ..."

"Murder, you mean." Tia interrupted.

"Whatever."

"It's certainly not 'whatever'! That's exactly the point! My father was murdered because the project he was working on threatened big corporate money. So they sent their thugs ..."

"What!? Don't even go there!"

"I have to go there, it's true!"

"Blatant unproven slander aside, these are your clients you're talking about, mine too! Corporate America, for God's sake! This is what runs the economy, runs the country, runs the world! Sure, they don't always do things perfectly like in Cassandra's pretty little eco dream-world."

"Murder is a far cry from not-quite-perfect! Murdering my dad because he had invented something that would totally outmode their mass-produced, disposable, bulk-consumer ..."

"You can't say that! This is what feeds you, these corporations pay your salary, put this food on this table!" He gestured to the salads, now arriving.

"Un huh, pesticide-laden, grown by downtrodden impoverished families in Mexico and further warping the trade deficit ..."

"You know too fucking much!" he sounded sickened. "What is happening to you?"

"I'm waking up." Tia said it almost as much to herself as to him.

"You can't damn it, and at the same time still take it as your livelihood," he began.

"That's the dichotomy I have to change," Tia realized aloud. "I'm caught in-between. I see the problem, but I'm also part of the problem, and I don't know how to break out of it."

"Look, if you're headed down Cassandra's path ..." He hadn't quite worked it up into a threat.

"No, I plan to make my own path."

"That's what I'm taking about. Up until your father's death, I thought we were walking the same path – together," he tried.

"I don't think we are, anymore," Tia looked away, across the restaurant.

"Fine. I get the picture. Fine." He flicked imaginary lint off the cuff of his immaculate dry-cleaned shirt.

Then he raised his steely blue eyes to hers. "I love you. Or, I love what I thought was you. I thought we were headed for a life together. But now I don't know. You're like a snake that's shedding its skin ..."

He broke off; the metaphor wasn't working out quite like he'd intended.

With sudden fury he slammed his fist into the table, sloshing the water glasses. He muttered a coarse profanity at life in general, pushed back his chair and marched out of the restaurant without another glance at Tia.

The waiter brought the entree. Tia sat staring soberly at Doug's cooling plate of Chilean Seabass. *Waste*. She looked around her at the tables of Los Angeles' finest, chattering gaily. Wisps of conversation about fashion and shopping, movies and business deals, spun around her in a dizzying mist.

Through the window, she saw Doug paying the valet and climbing into his Lincoln Navigator. *I think I'll get a Prius*, some odd cold part of her made a mental note. Doug's departure merely added to the massive dullness sitting so heavily somewhere between her heart and stomach.

She flipped open her cell phone and rang Sahara.

(7.)

Tia slapped John Jeavons' book *How To Grow More Vegetables* face down on the couch and walked to the balcony to ruefully survey her work. Her cat trotted over, meowing, to rub against her legs.

Sahara had suggested it, a little garden on the balcony, claiming it would be fun, relaxing, centering. Tia wasn't so sure about that centering bit, but she had eagerly shopped the warehouse store for pots, seeds and planting mix, and run to the bookstore for the titles Sahara recommended. Too bad she hadn't read first and planted second!

The pots were altogether too small, they'd limit root expansion, require vast quantities of water, or else dry out in the summer sun. The warehouse store potting soil was far from organic, it was pre-laced with petroleum-based fertilizer. Peas and lettuce craved cool weather, not the oncoming summer heat. Tomatoes should be tall and flowering at this time of year, not freshly seeded. Maybe the beans would do all right, but then, they were hybrid seed ...

(8.)

"Look what I've got!" Edie Bela gleefully scampered into Tia's office, rustling a small white paper bag. She opened the two pink boxes inside and laid out mounds of paper napkins, fast-talking all the while. "The flakiest pastries in LA – from that new French bakery by my place. Let's go down to the mall for lunch. I want to exchange that apricot shirt I bought – I don't like the neckline anymore." Edie picked pieces off her pastry with her fingers, her motions careful and awkward to preserve her perfect manicure.

Tia gulped. Her last visit to the mall had left such an impression that she hadn't been back. "Well ..."

"Or did you have other plans?"

"I was going to grab a salad at the place downstairs and ... read," Tia admitted.

"Read!" Edie scoffed. "What's all this reading lately? Okay, then how about tonight. I'm meeting Jim down at that cute little café on Wilshire, maybe catch a movie. Call Doug, we can all go together like usual, Doug's vehicle is big enough for all of us. You know, Jim test drove a Navigator last week but I'll bet he's going to get the new Expedition. I think he's trying to get a bigger one than Doug!" Edie smirked suggestively.

"We – uh – broke up."

"No way! What did you do that for? He was perfect! Professional, good looking, big house, *successful*." She drew the word out. "He's going to be a partner in that business you know. Why did you break up with him?"

Tia looked at Edie, energetic and cute, her outfit the latest fashionable melon color, ever so slightly clashing with her streaked hair. Edie, whose conversation rarely ventured deeper than her boyfriend's Jacuzzi. "We just have different views on life."

"What's that supposed to mean? I thought you were going to marry the guy." Edie shot her a piercing look. "Hey, did he dump you?"

Tia didn't answer.

Edie nodded her head knowingly. "Ah, honey, best thing for a broken heart: let's go shopping!"

(9.)

"You know too fucking much." Doug's parting barb echoed in Tia's head. Wasn't that the crux of it.

Certainly she missed Doug in her life. She missed the shared outings, and the physical intimacy of a relationship. But as the days passed she realized she didn't much miss Doug himself.

He had said snake-shedding-its-skin, but she felt more like some odd little caterpillar, who used to devour things all day long. Now she was entering the chrysalis phase, and the caterpillar body was curling, shriveling.

"You know too fucking much." She was messing with the unquestionable in their society, breaking the Code. The story of 'The Emperor's New Clothes' echoed to her from childhood. So long as no one mentioned the obvious, society could carry on, pretending the problems didn't exist. She had dared to explore the treason, and Doug couldn't bear the magnitude of it.

Doug lived wholeheartedly in that sparkling elite world. And for a time, she had to admit, she had too. Her life with Doug was part of some glamorous dream she had yearned for and cherished, once upon a time. But that dream was slipping away, it didn't fit anymore, not with her newfound knowledge.

(10.)

"Playing in the dirt," as Tia jokingly called it to herself and to Sahara, was incredibly soothing to the turmoil within. Since that disastrous initial foray, Tia's skill at tending her little balcony garden had vastly improved. Now in mid-summer, the beans were finishing. Tia tied up a long branch from one of the heirloom tomato plants Sahara had shipped, then peered into her vermicompost bin. Amazing – the worms turned kitchen scraps into powerful plant nutrition in a scant two months. She harvested a purple striped tomato and moved into the kitchen.[3]

Nail brushes just don't do it. She sighed, ruefully looking at her broken fingernails under the running water. Was it a mere months ago that she had taken such pride in an immaculate porcelain manicure? Now perhaps her nails revealed best her inner journey.

(11.)

"Air conditioners! Their recommendation for global warming is that we make better use of air conditioners!"

In a single sentence Tia could tell that this phone call was yet another typical Cassandra rant.

"Our infamous State Department issued a report on climate change and that's exactly what those idiots said. Head in the sand, that's what they are."

"Right, Mom," Tia was only half listening, continuing to work the figures for the client report on her desk.

"Attorneys General from eleven states wrote a letter in protest. It's absolutely ridiculous that the global warming issue in the U.S. has to be handled on a piecemeal basis when we could be participating in an international cohesive approach, like the Kyoto Protocol!"

The frustrated anger in Cassandra's voice twisted to anguish.

"This is exactly the kind of thing that would so enrage Rick."

Tia couldn't hear her mother anymore; the sob that raked Tia was all-encompassing: *the environment ... Daddy ... our civilization.*

(12.)

"Westside Community Gardens," the sign read, but Tia felt like Alice, alive with Wonderland discoveries. Sunflowers in a rainbow of varieties waved over unique and individual plots. Beans, artichokes, corn, nasturtiums.

She entered the office, if you could call it that. A tiny trailer, its interior completely filled by a basic desk and water cooler, heaped with dusty paperwork and old seed packets.

"I'm Tia Chandler. My name came up in the waiting list ..."

"Tia, hi, I'm Jana Damek. Welcome to the gardens." Jana stood up carefully in the tiny space, extending her hand. She was almost taller than Tia and looked to be of similar age. Broad shouldered and tanned, her brown eyes were friendly and welcoming. She wore her dark hair in a long braid trailing from beneath her crushed straw sunhat. She flipped through a disheveled wirebound notebook. "Ah, plot K32. Let me show you."

Jana strode down the path, blithely weaving between pole bean tendrils, drooping sunflowers, cascading lavender bushes. The smell of sun-drenched moist earth and plant life made a heady mix with the intense early autumn heat. Jana offered a continuous tour. "The hose access is over here. We don't provide the hoses, so you can bring your own or borrow from a neighbor. Hi, Mrs. Springsteen!" Her greetings of other gardeners punctuated her commentary. "We hold regular classes at the Theatre. There's a schedule on the board outside the office." She was delightfully warm and seemed to know everyone by name. Tia was already beginning to like her. "Here's your plot."

Tia was unprepared for the rush of emotion of that first glimpse. Her own plot. Its deep brown earth beckoned in possibilities.

Okay, the cynic in her said, *you have a lot of work to do. The fence needs to be propped up, the dirt looks compacted, there are leftover skeletal plants from the last gardener ... but, my own plot!*

Tia recalled her little garden as a child at Coyote Creek, planting bean seeds at her mother's side. A child in Wonderland she was again today, she had certainly fallen through the rabbit hole.

Impulsively she bent down and burrowed her fingers in the damp earth. *Reality.* The cool soil was calming and centering.

Jana was moving away now, to the summons of another gardener.

"Oh, thanks!" Tia called after her, weakly.

Jana turned back to wave, with a warm smile that embraced Tia, all this growing stuff, the other gardeners, life's wonder in general. Tia eagerly soaked it up, at the same time wondering: *Could I ever smile like that?*

(13.)

Tia sat in a board meeting, twirling her gold mechanical pencil idly as the client's CEO, Mr. Ansel, droned on. She crossed her legs and felt the run in her nylon unravel a few stitches more. *Gardening hands don't go with nylons*, she chuckled to herself. Mr. Ansel was talking stock prices now, anticipating steady value increases across the next five years.

A young assistant from his company, blond haired with thick plastic glasses, raised his hand like a schoolboy.

"Yes?" barked the CEO.

"Do your price projections reflect the market projections of Robert Prechter?" the young assistant's voice was shy but clear.

"Who?" Mr. Ansel sounded quite irritated now.

"Robert Prechter. He calculates that we've just passed a major market peak." The young man glanced at his papers, "a grand supercycle wave."

"Oh, that doomsday guy the Wall Street Journal dredges up on market down days? Don't waste my time!" Mr. Ansel snapped, returning to his glowing forecast.

The young assistant took the rebuke silently. He pushed his glasses back on his nose and stared at his notes. Across the conference table Tia could see that the shapes of the charts on his pages were dramatically different from the ones the CEO was presenting.

Tia lost track of what Mr. Ansel was saying. Her daydreams on the word 'Supercycle' flowed to the idea of growth cycles. Last night she had been studying systems of rotational planting in which legume crops, like peas and beans, are planted immediately following nutrient-demanding crops like squash and lettuce. The legumes capture nitrogen for other crops to use, part of the biodynamic method of building the soil.

The meeting broke up, and Tia found herself in the elevator with the young assistant. "Tia Chandler, from Roberts & Warner."

"Hi, I'm Carl Farren, the junior economist. Assistant to Mr. Sharis in Finance."

Tia indulged her curiosity. "If you don't have plans for lunch, I'd love to hear more about those Prechter waves."

The chain restaurant served a steady stream of local businessmen and secretaries celebrating birthdays. Tia and Carl eventually received a table.

"Robert Prechter's theories are about the natural repetition of waves, using Fibonacci mathematics, like the calculation of the curve of the Nautilus shell," Carl began. "When the Wall Street Journal reports the market is moving up or down, that action, plotted on a chart, makes a pattern. The patterns follow a basic wave structure, like a 5-part zigzag. There's a certain predictability to the overall structure.

"All markets are emotionally driven. When people are optimistic and hopeful, that drives the markets up. Then at some point a few people worry that values have gone too high and these few sell. The market begins to cool off. People get pessimistic, values ease back, more people sell to claim their profits. Values come down. A few people get excited over this bargain opportunity and jump in to buy. Enthusiasm builds, and values are driven upward again. These emotional cycles repeat and the cycles become visible patterns on the charts."

Carl opened his hefty briefcase nearly upsetting a water glass which Tia rescued just in time. He pulled out thick financial market books and hand-annotated charts. The fiery cover of *Conquer the Crash* blazed at Tia, an alarmingly similar image to the cover of the climate crisis book *The Heat is On* from her table at home.

"Prechter's analyses reveal we've just passed a major crest. He figures we're in the early stages of a market crash. A big one."

Tia's stomach lurched. "Like 1929?"

"Bigger, a lot bigger."

Tia picked up Carl's hand labeled charts. He pressed his glasses back on his nose and began explaining the finer points of wave formations. "The third wave is the most powerful ..."

(14.)

Carl invited Tia to lunch a few days later. They met at a chain restaurant, the sort that serves bland Americanized food and calls it

French. Although Tia knew right away that he was not her type romantically, she enjoyed their economic discussions and their friendship grew.

"Imagine – Los Angeles like Las Vegas in summer!" Carl exclaimed, gesturing to the Union of Concerned Scientists report on the table.[4] "If the Sierra Nevada snow pack shifts, our huge aqueducts will lie empty. Just think of all the water rights renegotiations – those will affect Arizona and Mexico too!"

"Look at the rainfall section," Tia replied morosely. "There will be very little water to negotiate over."

Carl paged deeper into the report. "With sea level rise over the next decade or so, plus stronger El Niño formations, wow, our winter storms are going to be incredible around here!"

"We'll have to rebuild our seawalls. Places up and down the coast, like Manhattan Beach, the Marina and Malibu will flood like crazy." Tia added her gloomy thoughts. "What will happen to the unstable governments in South America when all this gets very real?"

"You know, you should meet some friends of mine. They're into this climate change stuff too. You could say they do the 'economics of the environment.'" He chuckled. "We're all getting together next Tuesday night."

He paused, then added shyly, "If you'd like to go, I'll pick you up."

(15.)

That weekend, Tia broke ground in her garden plot. Although she had read a bit about the benefits of no-till methods, soil patterns revealed considerable soil compaction. Tia began the backbreaking job of double-digging her plot.

Jana and an older gentleman gardener stopped by to chat.

"When I came out from the East in the '50s," he said, "one thing I missed were the cloud formations. We used to have so many different cloud formations there, and here nothing."

He gazed at the afternoon sky. "Now we have them here. Things are changing, big things. Well, see you around." He ambled down the path.

Jana's eyes met Tia's as if they were echoing the same ominous thought: *Global Warming.*

Tia hid the panic feeling rising inside her by plunging her pitchfork perhaps too deep into the soil.

"There are a few of us who get together once in a while to talk about the environment. Maybe you'd like to join us sometime," Jana began quietly.

Tia's mind jolted alive at the thought of a community of environmentalists. The thrill of this prospect collided suddenly within her with the tide of rising panic. *I can't do it. I can't bear sitting through discussions of further irreversible devastation in the state of the planet!* Grappling with the intense feelings, she bent further over her garden, wresting the pitchfork from a lump of clay.

"We'll be at the Venice library community room, 7:30 on Tuesday night."

"Sorry, I have a conflict," Tia dodged. She wiped the sweat from her brow. This September heat was intense. Amazing how she was never aware of this in her air conditioned office.

"Oh well, maybe some other time." Jana moved off to greet other gardeners.

(16.)

Global Warming, Supercycle market crashes, sea levels rising, glacial melting, rainforest and ecosystem destruction, wildlife species extinction ... what more? It was all so overwhelming. So very, very real.

The gloom and doom cries from her reading began to echo in Tia's head as she went about her day – driving on the freeway, quiet moments in her office, doing the laundry at home.

The busy civilized life around her seemed to zip along in complete denial of it all. *Daily, the freeway is packed with cars belching toxic pollutants and greenhouse gasses. The T.V. sings advertisements for 'disposable' products which we don't need, which deplete our resources and then end up in our landfills. People pour in and out of warehouse stores buying, buying, buying as if there were nothing going on.*

Maybe it's not so much denial, as utter hopelessness. Maybe they've tried, but the set of problems facing us – it's overwhelming! And all interrelated. The complexity is bewildering. It's such a huge set of problems, maybe no one else knows where to begin either!

She'd read things like *50 Simple Things You Can Do to Save the Earth*, but the suggestions felt so infinitesimal. With General Motors rolling out more SUVs every waking moment, and the President's oil cronies pushing to drill the Arctic National Wildlife Refuge, "Reusing envelopes" seemed pathetic by comparison.[5]

And still they won't ratify the Kyoto Protocol.
What was one small person to do?

CHAPTER 2:

POSSIBILITIES

SPRING – SUMMER 2002

Tia parked her car outside the Venice library and sat for a moment before getting out. Usually confident at all sorts of meetings, she couldn't explain this nervousness and hesitation. Moreover, she couldn't figure out why she had been drawn to decline Carl's invitation, and find her way unannounced to Jana's meeting.

She smoothed her organic cotton skirt, its breathable natural feel a tactile reminder of the changes in her world, so unlike the tailored dry-clean-only skirts she had worn to the office most of her career.

As she entered the stark community room, she met with a shocked greeting.

"Tia! I thought you had another appointment?" It was Carl.

"Uh, this was the meeting you invited me to?"

Embarrassed at being caught in the fib, but more than that, her stomach tightened as she realized now why she had attempted to choose Jana's invitation over Carl's. *I was yearning for low key. I don't want to deal with the politics, the higher-mindedness. Global problems, I can't bear to think that big! Darn, I thought Jana's would be simpler themes, gardening, recycling.* She managed a weak smile.

Carl seemed to interpret the smile as an apology. "Well, I'm glad that you're here." He guided her by the arm to introduce the few people in the room. She shivered. *I should have brought a sweater for the air conditioning.* She looked around for Jana, but Jana was clearly missing.

"This is Steve Vernados, one of our co-founders, he's an environmentally-conscious builder. Benton Tremain, meet Tia Chandler. Ben's interest is city planning. In his 'day job' he works for the county."

Steve was tall, his broad muscular shoulders filling out his casual t-shirt. Sandy-haired with a hint of red, his tanned face carried a good natured welcoming grin. Ben, by contrast, was heavy set, round and black, and quite a bit older than Tia.

"Day job?" she questioned the odd phrase.

"Oh, that's Carl's private joke among us. We have to pay the rent. For most of us, the save-the-world environmental crusade doesn't do that, quite yet. The monetary world has yet to catch up. But we're always hopeful!" Ben's lightheartedness was catching. Tia's mood picked up a bit.

A tall good-looking man to whom she had not yet been introduced began to call the meeting to order. They found chairs, Carl still glued to Tia's side. She found herself mesmerized by the leader's voice of command; although he was not the evening's speaker, he obviously held the respect of the dozen or so others present. Out of the corner of her eye, Tia saw Jana slip in the door.

The topic was Paul Hawken's book *Natural Capitalism*. About half the attendees had read it, and they willingly shared its ideas.

"Capital," Steve opened the discussion. "Think of it like 'accumulated wealth.' Hawken describes four types of capital: human capital, financial capital, manufactured capital and natural capital.

"Financial capital, that's pretty simple: cash and investments.

"Manufactured capital, that's machines, tools, factories, things we've built.

"Human capital – labor, intelligence, culture and organization – it doesn't get recorded well in traditional financial statements. Businesses track intellectual property and copyrights to a limited extent, but for the most part, human capital is left out of the system.

"The fourth one is natural capital. That's the biggie: natural resources and ecosystems.

"Hawken's point is that in today's business world our models and accounting calculations totally omit natural and human capital. That's where we run into trouble, marginalizing people and devastating our environment. Just think: if a business had to show on their financial statements the true cost to the world's ecosystems of polluting the Mississippi, or copper strip mine tailings, business decisions would be made very differently. If all the real costs were recorded, things like oil production and nuclear power would look a whole lot less attractive. When natural and human capital are unaccounted for, they get taken for granted."

The tall leader broke in. "Hawken fleshed out his theories with many examples in which the modern day business world actually is getting it right. However, despite all he says he doesn't really lay out a plan. How do we implement massive changes like these? How do we take these things from delightful niche examples out to the societal mainstream? That's one of the things we have to figure out."

There was a barrage of agreement, and many tangents were brought up.

At the break, Tia found Jana.

"I'm thrilled that you made it – what do you think so far?" Jana twinkled.

Tia's head was swimming with the ideas of the evening. Her brain attempted to formulate a reply, but Jana's attention was pulled away as the group leader came to her side.

"Jana, check in with Steve about the next session before you leave," he commanded.

Jana was tall, but the man was taller still. Jana grinned. "May I introduce my brother: Ari Damek, Tia Chandler."

There was a certain family resemblance. Straight dark hair, tanned complexion, chiseled cheekbones, and those same intensely rich dark brown eyes. Ari carried himself with a confidence that said it didn't matter what he was wearing, he'd look good in anything.

"Welcome." It hardly sounded like a greeting. One dark piercing glance at Tia, and abruptly he turned away to some other management task.

"Never mind him," Jana said brightly. "You have to get to know him. Let's get some cookies before they're all gone."

The meeting resumed with Steve leading the discussion. As much as she had tried to avoid 'higher-minded ideas,' Tia found herself drawn into the circle, and she was soon contributing actively.

"What about the Genuine Progress Indicator, the GPI?" Tia offered. "It's a substitute proposed for the Gross National Product. Each of these try to measure the economic progress of our society. They are how the politicians and economists gauge whether our economy is growing or not.

"As a measure of true well-being that people really feel, the GPI is a much better match. It includes many more items which Americans actually experience in their daily lives. GPI includes the value of items like household and volunteer work. GPI is reduced for costs to our well-being, like crime, divorce, resource depletion, pollution, and long-term environmental damage.

"Gross National Product – the one our financial industry and politicians use – treats the costs of social decay and natural disasters as economic gain. GNP would lead us to believe we are living better with these things. The GNP spiked noticeably, for instance, with the Enron scam legal expenditures and the cleanup of the Exxon Valdez oil spill!"

"Yes," Ari joined her, "when you graph both GNP and GPI together, while GNP has been claiming a steady rise, GPI has basically been flat since the 70's. People haven't felt much better off." Tia felt

Ari's eyes on her. Heat rose to her cheeks as Steve continued the discussion.

Later, as part of a discussion of consumerism, Carl brought up the Prechter waves. "I think the market crash will take care of a lot of the excess," he ventured. The responses revealed that many in the circle did not share his doomsday forecast of a coming Great Depression.

But Ari picked up the thread. "David Holmgren's energy curve, from his book *Permaculture*, exactly coincides with Prechter's forecast. Holmgren illustrates the rise of energy consumption with a bell curve, a very steep tall skinny one, that reaches its peak just about now and then goes into sharp decline.

"Prechter similarly predicts a major peak in the economic market charts just about now. It's eerie how two thinkers from dramatically contrasted disciplines come up with similarly shaped curves, and the same timeline for peak and declines."

That touched off quite a debate. Tia sat back in amazement, taking in the interplay of minds alive grappling with world problems.

She found herself watching Ari much more than the discussion flow warranted. He was animated in the discussion, gesturing dramatically with long arms to bring home his points. He leaned forward debating an issue, his broad shoulders strong without being too muscular. Now leaning back in his chair stroking his smooth chin, his long legs stretched out before him as he contemplated a point made by Steve.

Ari seemed interested in every topic, and seemed to contribute knowledgeably to most. Tia was intrigued by his expressed views. He conveyed great confidence, and, Tia decided, he was quite handsome. His casual attire was impeccably tidy; his elegance came not from garment selection but from presence. Glancing up, he caught her look and returned it with interest.

As the meeting wrapped up, and they put away chairs, it seemed like Carl was edging toward an invitation. Tia tried to avoid him, hanging with Jana. Someone grabbed her elbow.

"Let's go get a coffee." It was Ari.

Tia turned, and melted under the directness of those deeply dark brown eyes. "Sure," she stammered. She just had to look away. Out of the corner of her eye, she saw Jana smiling as she lifted the last chair into place.

(2.)

They walked to the local coffee cafe, a narrow little nook of a place, with rough cut wood and dark colors, a style that could be retro 70's, or could simply have been neglected since then and only recently dusted off. It was fairly full, with a jostling intellectual crowd, even at this late hour.

Ari selected the fair trade, shade grown label, Tia couldn't help but notice. They sat down awkwardly at a too-tiny table.

"Chandler. I've heard that name around environmental circles." he began.

"Perhaps my father. He was an inventor." Tia replied, staring at the steam swirling from her cup. She just couldn't meet those eyes.

"Orrick Chandler?"

She nodded.

"Amazing man!"

She looked up at him in surprise.

"I'm so sorry about your loss. I read about it in the energy media." Gone was the gruffness of the meeting, he truly conveyed sympathy.

Tia could feel the prickle of tears beginning. She wanted to look away, but she couldn't break this gaze. His brown eyes held her, eyes rich with passion for life. In that moment she knew: here was a man who – once he set his sights on something – got what he wanted, a man of confidence in his own abilities, a man of intention. And that intention, together with a bit of curiosity and amusement, was currently trained on her. The realization made her tremble inside.

"I was following his research – photoremediation. Bombard radioactive waste with gamma rays and it renders the waste stable![6] Incredible! Your father truly was a brilliant mind. I was appalled at what happened. Murder!" He shook his head. "How are you handling it?"

Tia stammered something useless, but he continued.

"And the batteries – designed to last twenty-five years. Imagine the waste stream reduction! They've really suppressed knowledge of his work. It's hard to get ahold of his research papers, even. Since his company still holds the patents, they'll likely continue ... that is, if they have anyone with the guts to market it, now." He looked away darkly. The spell was broken.

Tia looked down at the table. This was not what she wanted to talk about. But she didn't trust her voice just now to begin a different subject. An uneasy silence settled over the two of them.

"What did you think of the meeting?" Ari tried. "You seemed to fit right in."

"It was fascinating." Tia was glad for the help out of that space. "I hadn't read that book, but I had read a great article about it ..." she trailed off and glanced at him, just realizing who had written the article.

"You've seen my work, then," he said with a bit of quiet pride.

"Yes. It's really thoughtful. Really thorough." She kicked herself for getting shy right now.

But this was an opportunity to quiz the author of that brilliant article. She cleared her throat nervously. "When you wrote about your 'Transformation Wave' theory, how does that fit into say, the Prechter waves?" Tia almost said 'Carl's theories,' but she really didn't want to bring up Carl right now.

"Well, like I said in tonight's meeting, it's eerie how Holmgren's projected peak in energy consumption coincides with Prechter's economic market peak. Each thinker shows a significant 'crash' right after that peak. But I think neither of their diagrams addresses something Hawken's been saying about the rise of groups dealing with social and environmental issues.

"Hawken points out that these groups – NGO's and other groups – are small, not centralized, and well outside the mainstream. There's a tremendous grassroots ground surge in environmentalism and social change, that seems hell-bent on redirecting our societal consciousness." Ari leaned back in his chair in contemplative conversation, quite at ease now. "This is the 'Transformation Wave' I was envisioning as I wrote that article. We're in the initial stages of the rise on the bell curve of an entirely new way of thinking in our society.[7]

"Think of the emotions of a market. The environmental and social change groups are at the point where a few people are on board, but the mainstream hasn't yet caught up the enthusiasm. It's not really evident, you have to know where to look to see it. It's not in the widespread media.

"Hawken nailed it when he said the movement's coming from too many very small sources for the media to take much notice. The huge corporations still control the major press. That's why the major press is still so consumerist.

"But look around you. Particularly in this area of the country, it's all around you: organics, recycling, solar, wildlife conservation, wind power out in Palm Springs. Remember, we're in LA, on the coast. The coasts lead the country: they're several years, maybe decades ahead in most trends. When you see the mainstream press beginning to acknowledge this environmental upsurge, you'll know it's major and it's very real. It's the tip of the iceberg, there is so much behind it.

"I think these social and environmental change groups are steadily on the rise, despite the political suppression and prior to any economic crashes. Presidents will come and go, Prechter's economic markets may crest and break, but the mechanisms are already in place for another 'wave' of something altogether new."

It was comforting to hear his views, so different from Cassandra's doomsday tirades.

"And that 'something new' is us," he continued. His gesture seemed to take in the meeting just held. "We're all part of it, we're what's driving it. Little groups like ours, here and there, tucked away in cities across the country and around the world."

Tia felt she could hardly be rolled into that 'us,' she felt like such a newbie.

"So how did you hear about the meeting tonight?" he asked.

She shared her tale. Her father's death, her reading journey, even her garden trials, since his sister was so much a part of that. She found herself telling not just the highlights of the story, but quite a bit of her inner turmoil as well.

Ari seemed quite interested. They compared notes on her reading, he laughed at her garden mistakes, but he was quite serious when she explained the double invitation to the same meeting.

"It's more than a coincidence, you know. It came from two sources you trusted. You know something's right for you when it comes at you like that." he said quietly.

She looked at him in astonishment. He had put into words something she had felt but had not named in the rush of the evening's events. The rest of her tale came tumbling out of her mouth before she could stop it, her realization upon stepping into the meeting room that evening. "I was yearning for something simpler, something low key. I don't want to deal with the politics, I can't bear to think that big!"

She clapped her hand to her mouth, she hadn't meant to share all that.

Ari leaned forward across the tiny table, inches from her face. *He is a very large man!* He gently took her hand from across her mouth, and held it in both of his. Looking directly into her eyes, he spoke very carefully, very firmly.

"Thinkers. It's going to take thinkers and doers – not mindless followers – to solve the problems we face. You cannot escape it. You're too intelligent. You cannot close your mind to it, now that you have learned what we're up against. Come with us, work with us."

He was referring to her reading and the environmental discussions, she knew, but it felt like he was inviting her to something oh so very different.

She could feel his warm breath on her cheek, she could see every speck of color in those rich dark eyes. The deep aroma of coffee swirled around them.

He released her hand and eased back in his chair, staring across the coffee bar. "We have our next meeting in three weeks. Jana's going to tell us about the Permaculture movement out of Australia and New Zealand."

He stole a glance at her as he said it. Tia felt he wanted to catch her reaction. She already knew she wouldn't miss it for the world. And she was certain that this was written clearly across her face.

He stood to leave, and held out his hand to help her to her feet, as if she were some sort of grand royalty. He didn't release her immediately, guiding her through the still-crowded café. As he walked her back to her car his shoulder brushed warmly against hers.

(3.)

Sahara, I met this really great guy last night ...

Tia deleted the message unfinished, unsent. It made her evening sound so trivial, so soap-opera-ish. *You can't capture moments like these in emails!*

She went about her workday, but between the heady content of last evening's meeting discussion, and the private moments with Ari, her head was spinning.

She daydreamed blissfully about his deep brown eyes, his intense focus, that little lock of hair that wouldn't stay brushed back that drifted onto his forehead. Her hand tingled at the memory of his hands around hers.

The mere idea of a building wave of environmental restoration was mind-boggling. How thrilling it would be if she were lucky enough to see such changes unfold during her lifetime.

Around midday, recalling Ben's words, she realized, *this is my day job. It pays the rent. But something big is changing in me. What next? That part's not yet clear.*

(4.)

It had been another warm late summer day, so after work Tia went to water her community garden plot. Instantly, Jana appeared on the path.

"Well, how'd it go?" Jana had a considerable twinkle in her eye.

Tia looked up over the hose spray and pretended she didn't hear, but her face was crimson.

"Aha! I thought so!" Jana was clearly delighted. "I haven't ever seen him like that." Her amusement at her brother was evident.

Tia felt trapped. Did she dare talk about it with Jana, his sister? But Jana seemed to do plenty of talking.

"When I saw him this morning, he could do nothing but quiz me about you. How long had I known you, what did I know about you. You made quite some impression, girl!" Jana grinned over the fence.

"I've never met anyone like him," Tia admitted quietly. That was enough to launch Jana again.

"Well, when are you going to see him again? Are you coming to our next meeting? I'm going to be the speaker, you know. I'll be sharing ideas from my tour of New Zealand ... maybe we could do dinner beforehand. No, a threesome wouldn't be right. Let me think on it." Jana clearly wanted to force the issue.

"No, that's all right," Tia murmured in a tone of passive decline.

Jana did a double take. "You're not interested in him?"

"No, no, that's not what I meant at all!" Tia exclaimed, blushing all over again.

"Yeah! I thought so!" Jana danced away in delight.

(5.)

Tia didn't hear from Ari all week. As yet a second week crawled by, she gave up hope of hearing from him again before the next meeting. Since that first day, she hadn't seen Jana either. Tia had been to the gardens, but Jana seemed to have different hours.

Mid-way through the third week she returned from a client meeting to find a phone message slip on her desk. Ari Damek, with a phone number. It felt so out-of-place here in her corporate office, almost a sacrilege to the themes of their meeting. She waited until she got home that evening to return the call.

"Ari? It's Tia," she said cautiously. She didn't want to sound too eager.

"Tia – I would have called sooner, but I've been out of town."

Tia's alarm bells went off. Was this some lame cover? She suddenly realized how little she knew about this guy.

"To where did you travel?" She phrased it with intentional formality.

"Bonn – I'll tell you about it when I see you. Do you have plans for dinner?"

"Tonight!?"

"But of course."

They met at a small Thai restaurant near the beach in Playa del Rey. As the waiter brought menus, Ari told Tia about the low elevation of many parts of Thailand, and the population that will be displaced with the sea level rise in the next few decades.

"What were you doing in Bonn, of all places?" she asked when chance presented itself.

"Executive Board meeting," he said offhandedly, studying the menu.

"For what company?"

"Company?" He looked at her as if she had five heads. "The U.S. Delegation, of course."

She realized she'd missed something very big here. "And what do you do for them?"

He laughed. "You don't even know what I do! I guess we never got to that part last time." He leaned back into his chair and stretched out his long legs, looking almost arrogantly at ease.

"The Executive Board of the Clean Development Mechanism, United Nations Framework Convention on Climate Change. Quite an obtuse mouthful, isn't it? That's why we just say Executive Board or CDM. It's one of the teams developing the implementation plan for the Kyoto Protocol. The CDM meets in Bonn annually."

Yikes, is this for real? How on earth did I stumble upon this?

"I'm a 'change agent.' I make things happen. In practical terms that means I'm a consultant, a networker, an organizer. My specialty is alternative energy technology and climate change but I branch out a bit – the article you read and our little group being prime examples."

"A change agent?"

He grinned. "A 'maker of change.' I spread ideas around, get the connections flowing, get key people focused in the right direction."

His tone became quite sober. "My personal mission is quite simply 'saving the earth.' Turning the destructive environmental tide, fostering recovery from the damage that we have done to the earth, so there's a planet left when it's time to turn it over to our children and grandchildren."

"Do you have any children?" she asked quietly.

"No ..." he glanced at her briefly and then looked away. "Not yet, anyway."

He looked down at the table, turning a fork in his fingers. "My office looks down on an elementary school playground. Those little kids ... those kids are my inspiration. I don't know them personally, but I see those kids and say to myself: we have to hand them a better legacy than this!"

"Oh," she gasped. She'd never heard anyone talk like this. She felt she had just glimpsed the deepest inner workings of this man. Humbled in the presence of such intention, such purpose, she felt honored to be at his table.

He cleared the emotion from his throat. "I'm here in LA for a bit and then I head off to Johannesburg for a very different kind of international event, the World Summit on Sustainable Development. Although I'll be giving a presentation on the status of the emissions negotiations, the Summit is about Sustainability."

Their dinner arrived and conversation turned to other subjects including the local group meetings.

"Steve and I started it not that long ago. We're just a loose affiliation of people around LA who are all trying to accomplish the same thing, waging the same battle, toward a Sustainable future. We work together, redefining the way our city runs. Business, transportation, utilities, education – we have high hopes for it all, although you'll find our approaches and our areas of focus are vastly different.

"Sometimes we swap leads, but, particularly in these rough political times, we mostly support each other in our parallel courses. Typically, someone's had a victory on a day when someone else has had a rough go. There are times when this journey gets really challenging and it's good to know you're not alone." He looked at her as if to gauge her reaction to this.

I have felt so alone in this journey, she wanted to cry out. *How do you do it? How do you stay in this day in and day out? How do you keep all the bad news from getting to you?* That too-familiar panic was rising in her again, the panic brought on by her reading about the multifold crisis closing in upon the planet. She swallowed deeply and changed abruptly to easier subjects.

"Ari. Is that short for anything?"

"No," he replied, still watching her intently.

Did he see my panic? Oh, no, he definitely did!

"...but since you're asking there must be more to yours."

"Hestia," she wrinkled her nose in distaste. "After the Roman goddess of hearth and home."

"Goddess of hearth and home," he repeated with a contemplative smile, "with gorgeous green eyes."

Tia turned crimson.

He paid the check, then extended his hand to help her up. Hand in hand they left the restaurant and strolled in the pleasant evening. The moon was three days before full, Tia noted, thinking of her garden planting calendar. The few restaurants yielded quickly to waterfront condos along the channel. The sidewalk became bike path and stretched out toward the water.

The moon and the sea beckoned, and they found themselves on the path atop the breakwater at the channel. The wind off the ocean was chill and damp, and Tia shivered. Ari took off his thick wool jacket and settled it around her slender shoulders. The jacket warmed her with his body heat.

He hadn't released her shoulders, and drew her toward him in a tender embrace, pressing her head to his heart. She sighed in the closeness of his body against hers, and slipped her arms around his trim waist.

She felt his cheek nuzzle the top of her head and she turned up to meet him. His deep brown eyes gazed intently into hers for a long moment's connection, then he slowly leaned down and met her lips.

(6.)

Business at the office delayed Tia, and she arrived at the meeting later than her preferred early. Carl seemed to have been watching for her arrival and was over to greet her before she had found a chair.

"Hey, I – uh – haven't seen you around much lately," he began, stumbling over his words.

Tia busied herself with selecting her chair and settling her purse. "I've had a lot going on ..."

Ari strode across the room.

"Carl," he directed, "Jana needs the chairs set up in a circle this time."

Ari looked to Tia affectionately. His hand was warm upon her shoulder in a brief gentle caress. "Hi."

She met his gaze with a tender smile.

Carl looked from one to the other of them, first in confusion, then in realization. He opened his mouth as if to speak, closed it again, and covered by beginning to move chairs.

Tia had been looking forward to Jana's presentation on Permaculture. This, Tia thought, would be the gardening topic she had reckoned on hearing at that first meeting. But she was in for a surprise.

"Permaculture – the term comes from 'permanent' plus 'agriculture' – is a design system that started in the mid 70s with Bill Mollison and David Holmgren," Jana began. There were a few new faces in the audience this week.

"I say 'design system' because it includes a lot more than just the agriculture in its name. It's more about permanent or Sustainable culture. A Sustainable culture is one consciously designed so that it can continue to give us the food and resources we need through future generations without depleting the environment.

"Permaculture starts with the idea of Observation – study your site, observe nature's cycles, its truisms. Then base your design upon what you learn. These truisms run so deep that they could as easily be applied to layout of a site and selection of a crop, as to selection of a waste disposal method, or creation of a community network.

"Tonight I wanted to share with you a small part of the system of Permaculture Ethics that David Holmgren created." Jana distributed a diagram that looked a bit like an elementary school child's drawing of a daisy.

"This is Holmgren's Permaculture Flower. This Flower diagram is great for describing the panorama of life we experience within a city or a community. The seven petals are labeled with different areas of life: Land & Nature Stewardship, Built Environment, Tools & Technology, Culture & Education, Health & Spiritual Well-being, Finance & Economics, and Land Tenure & Community Governance. Outside the petals, Holmgren lists the more familiar disciplines which fall into each category.

"Now, it's clear that our society is operating at a full-tilt, totally unsustainable level of operations in all seven of these petals. In reforming society toward Sustainability, our job is to move each of these areas of life forward toward the goal. How do we go about it?

"First, pick your petal: what is it that you like to do, where do your passions and talents lie? Where do you have knowledge and contacts and wisdom? Start there. Think about your chosen area, its environmental and social impact. How effectively does it use natural capital? Human capital? Where could improvements be made? This is your personal beginning in the campaign toward Sustainability.

"Think about our little circle," Jana gestured to the assembled group, "don't we represent many of these Petals? I'll bet we cover just about all of them with the knowledge base in this room. That said, how specifically do we progress toward Sustainability within each petal, thus within the Flower as a whole?"

The group broke into noisy discussion and Jana stepped back to allow the process to unfold. With marker in hand, she captured ideas on the board at the front of the room.

Tia stared at the diagram in her hand. She had lived virtually all of her professional career within the "Finance & Economics" petal, far from Sustainably. Her mother's career path was within "Land & Nature Stewardship," and she was certainly striving for a Sustainable future. Her father had been "Tools & Technology," most definitely. "Health & Spiritual Well-being" encompassed everyday living, but achieving Sustainability? *I'm having a tough time finding organic vegetables, for goodness sake!*

She glanced across the circle at Ari, who was engaged in lively discussion with a new member. *Saving the earth, he told me. Yikes, is he trying to do all of these things at once?* The magnitude of the undertaking was staggering.

Jana brought the group back to order, gesturing. "I had us set up in a circle for a reason today: We are this Flower. You are a part of a much greater whole. Each of you, by your talents, specialties and creativity, represents one or more of the petals.[8]

"And this list," she gestured to the board where she had listed participant comments, "is our common agenda. These are the things we need to accomplish in order to progress toward Sustainability in this city. It's a big list.

"Taken as a whole, this list could appear daunting: land, air, finance, social causes, politics. But if each of us selects one small part to devote our efforts to, if each of us works toward making Sustainable change within our chosen petal, just look at the enormity of the transformation we can achieve. 'We,' the people in this room, plus 'we,' the greater numbers outside this room. Remember: the whole is far greater than the sum of its parts."

(7.)

"Your presentation of that Flower was great!" Tia approached Jana.

"Thanks!" Jana bubbled with her success. "Holmgren created the diagram. It hooked me when I heard about it, and I knew it would get this group talking!"

She continued in a more conspirational undertone. "But don't waste your time with me, I'll see you sometime this week." She gestured across the room toward her brother. "He's leaving for South Africa in the morning."

"Oh," Tia gasped in dismay, looking over at Ari.

Carl had engaged Ari in a heated discussion. At least, Carl was fired up about it; Ari looked bored. Ari caught Tia's glance, collected his jacket and pulled away from Carl.

"Want to grab a coffee? I haven't much time." Ari checked his watch. "I have a 7 am flight to connect to Johannesburg and I have to get over to the Westwood office tonight to pick up some documents before I go."

"Bye, have a safe trip," Jana called to him fondly.

"Won't I see you later?" he asked.

"Nope, I'll be turning in early."

He squeezed his sister's forearm. "Ok, bye then. Take care." His eyes were suddenly serious, watching Jana.

Turning to leave, Ari slipped his arm around Tia's shoulders. They walked the few brief blocks to the little coffee place.

"You and Jana live together?" she asked.

"We live in a house about a mile from here with two other roommates."

"And your office is in Westwood?"

"No, the delegate I'm working for is there. My own office is over in Culver City. No eco-setup, but I really like the building. I like how the architect experimented with unexpected materials. I have high hopes that one day we'll see such exploration and artistic achievement in the green building movement.

"I just heard about an architect in Holland who constructs 'organic' buildings that sound incredible. They integrate natural materials, light, plants, water. They apparently evolve and change all day long as the sunlight angles in differently. I plan to see one of them next time I'm over there."

They settled into the same little table as last time. Ari slid his chair around so that they sat shoulder to shoulder.

Tia reached out to stroke his hand on the table. One finger was knobby and bent at an odd angle. "What did you do to it?"

He curled his fist to hide it. "Let's not talk about that."

She looked at him but he wouldn't meet her eyes. Puzzled, she tried a different subject. "Jana showed you this Permaculture Ethics stuff before?"

"Yes, it's her area of specialty. I'd heard Mollison's side of things, but she sought out Holmgren's."

"Their theories are different? I thought they were the cofounders of Permaculture."

"Holmgren and Mollison worked together briefly years ago. Mollison codified Permaculture design trainings. Holmgren put the concepts to work on his property in Australia, and recently published a book outlining his philosophy. They're both remarkable innovators with ideas that can help transform the world. Yet followers sometimes bicker over who does Permaculture better.

"The point is, no one single approach is going to work for all scenarios. The world needs both of them, Holmgren and Mollison. And we need John Jeavons and Alan Chadwick and Masanobu Fukuoka and a few hundred more. We need a diversity of techniques to solve the myriad of problems our civilization has gotten ourselves into.[9]

"The danger zone is when one of us thinks we have the one idea that will save the world – one technology, or one sweeping theory. At that point we begin to stifle the other ideas coming up, which means that some problems will be left unresolved. A hole in the dike that holds back disaster. And that hole, that unresolved problem, leaves all of us exposed to jeopardy when we're talking about CO_2 and CFC emission controls, population statistics, and more. We can't shut down solutions. We must remain open to the fullest possibilities."

Possibilities, she breathed softly.

Perhaps he was thinking the same thing. He wrapped his arm around her. As she rested her head upon his shoulder she felt his lips brushing her forehead.

(8.)

The Westside Community Garden Theatre was a semicircle of eucalyptus trunk segments in a dirt open space, with a suggestion of a firepit in a circle of stones. The Garden Talk speaker this evening was an older woman named Millie, whom Tia had often seen around the gardens.

"Soils are the topic tonight. Soils, not dirt! Dirt is that stuff kids play in and get messy, it's a catch-all term for whatever miscellany got left behind that nobody wanted. Soil, good healthy soil, now that's another thing altogether.

"Good soil is porous – it has air pockets in it. That means you can't stomp about on it, nor run over it with tractors and compact it. Don't drown it with too much water. Those roots have got to breathe! Good soil has different ratios of sand or loam, but most of all it has lots of organic material. Bits of matter that used to be living stuff: compost, mulch, those kinds of things.

"Good soil is *alive*!" her eyes sparkled. "It's full of earthworms, bugs, and nematodes, good and bad, duking it out in there. It's got living things in it that we can't even see, except with microscopes. Things like mycorrhizal fungae, algae, bacteria, all linked together in symbiotic relationship, raising healthy plants.

"Now, how well do you think all these living things do if you go and dump a bunch of *petrochemicals* on them? Why, they up and die, of course! You no longer have living soil, you have *dead dirt!*

"Now, I want you to think about those T.V. pictures you see of the farmlands of America, recall the images." She began working the crowd, pointing and drawing out responses. "A huge tractor, yes, doing what? Plowing. Did I hear 'compacting the soil porosity'? What about 'destroying the mychorizae'?

"Other pictures. The sprays – yes, the sprays! What do you think they're spraying? Let me ask you this: if you were trying to grow things in dead dirt ... Yes, you'd need *fertilizer*, and *lots of it!* And where does that fertilizer come from? If you said petroleum, you get a prize. And if you're trying to grow plants in dead dirt and spraying it with lots of 'plant drug' chemicals, will they be vibrant healthy plants? Not on your life! They're weakened and susceptible to insect pests. Let's spray some more!

"Sprays, let's talk about sprays. The other thing they spray for is weeds. Now it's darn 'inconvenient' to only spray weedkiller when the field is fallow. Wouldn't it be easier to spray for weeds when the weeds are growing up between the corn? Well, if we take our corn into a very *scientific* laboratory, they can alter the genes, to make genetically modified corn. Now when we spray our fields with the weedkiller, it kills the weeds and doesn't affect the corn! But oops, when we spray that weedkiller, and the Monarch butterfly larvae eat the weed leaves that have spray on them, half of them die, and the survivors grow up stunted. And our beneficial insects, you know what those are – good bugs, the gardeners' friend, they're affected too. The familiar ladybug, the lacewing, the honeybee and all his other pollinator friends ... virtually unnoticeable, but they keep the whole ecosystem going, they are part of the whole food chain. We have less birds, because there are less bugs for them to eat. So the GMOs mess all that up.[10]

"But what about Farmer Jones who gets wise to all this and says, no thank you, I don't want to grow this GMO stuff anymore, I'll go back to the good old-fashioned varieties. Let me tell you: corn is wind-pollinated. That means those long silky tassels catch pollen blown in the breezes. Farmer John who opted out of GMOs has his field across the highway from Farmer Techno who grows GMOs. A breeze kicks up, a little swirly one. Now all those corn tassels are being pollinated in both our farmers' fields. By what? By pollen from both GMO and old-fashioned corn – the wind does not sort the pollen out, folks! Then Monsanto Corporation in its infinite power comes down and tests the corn of our Farmer Jones and declares his corn harvest, and the seed he saved for next year, shows evidence of Monsanto's patented GMO genes in it. They accuse him of growing their patented product without paying them royalties, and they sue him. He was doing his best to remain with traditional varieties!

"The point being, this GMO stuff is insidious, it cannot be contained."

(9.)

"Millie's a funny one," Jana mused as she and Tia climbed into Tia's Prius and spun off to get dinner. "I set a topic and she starts there. Sometimes she drifts far afield, but it's always interesting stuff."

"So what have you been working on lately? Is this community garden work your vocation or avocation?"

Jana laughed. "It's really both. I work for the city so it's steady employment. I really like the job, I like the concept of the garden, and I like the people I meet there. But then I have my other projects. I teach a bit, I write quite a bit, and I'm helping set up community gardens through the inner city areas. I work with Esperanza – have you met her? No, I guess not. She doesn't come to our meetings very often, she's too busy. Our projects encourage people to take back the neighborhoods, to really embrace them."

Their conversation flew easily and rapidly across a myriad of subjects.

"I heard you and Ari live in a house near the library? What about your family?"

"Yes, he owns a house over on the edge of Venice. You should come by sometime and see my garden. Our parents are gone now. Mom died two years ago. My dad died almost ten years ago, when I was seventeen. Ari was twenty-four. That was a really hard time. When Dad died Ari threw himself into a mad fit of activity. It was around then that he discovered the environmental stuff and got so serious about it."

"Jana, remember that Permaculture Flower you showed us – all those different petals? Do you think Ari's trying to do it all himself? I mean, every one of those petals?"

Jana threw back her head and laughed. "I never thought of it that way. Maybe he is! Really though, I'll bet he thinks if he builds up the networks, like our little circle, and similar in other cities, and works on the global situation ..." She stopped. "Listen to me: 'and-and-and'! I think you may have a point there! He's been striving for the superhuman trophy for almost a decade. That's just how he is."

(10.)

To: tchand@aol.com
The Summit is not going well. All my recommendations for firm targets regarding transition to renewable energy sources such as wind and solar, have been welcomed by the EU but shot down by my own country's delegation. In addition, and perhaps more appalling, is the effort by U.S. delegates to dissuade passage of Kyoto. It's incredible, but certain people who were rallying for the Treaty have changed their tune. It is quite disheartening to those of us who are fighting for it. As the saying goes, 'These are the times that try men's souls.' Who said that anyway? I'm having a rough time personally. A.

Ari's emails were getting less frequent and more despairing as the week stretched on. Tia kept writing to him, but she felt helpless as far as what to say.

To: adamek@LAglobalsolutions.net
Ari – I'm sorry that things are so tough for you. I've seen news reports about the lack of progress at the Summit. The international news sources provide a lot more detail than our U.S. ones. The quote you sent is from Thomas Paine. It is from a U.S. Revolutionary era pamphlet. We eventually won the Revolution, you know. If it will be any help to you, I could pick you up at the airport. It isn't far for me. Tia

She yearned to say far more, to pour her heart out. But his terse tone did not allow her an entry point.

To: tchand@aol.com
8:37 pm, Bradley Terminal, don't bother to come in. I'll come out to the curb by baggage claim.

There was no more to his reply.

(11.)

In accordance with his directions, Tia met Ari at curbside in front of the terminal. He greeted her with a cursory kiss and then she spun her Prius in silent acceleration out into the traffic parade.

"Thanks for picking me up like this." Ari said rather dully.

"No problem. I didn't know if you would have a car parked here."

"I don't own one." He stared distractedly out the window.

Tia gaped at him but he didn't turn around. She tried again. "Have you had dinner? Should we stop somewhere?"

"Yes, that would be fine."

"I had such high hopes for this Summit," he said heavily. "A World Summit on Sustainability, for heaven's sake, and nothing real came of it. Or rather, the same old roadblocks halted it. This Summit, Rio+10, was the tenth anniversary of the landmark Rio Earth Summit. The topic should have been Sustainability. The reality was, most nations merely brought their same emissions negotiation and World Trade Organization grievances to this Sustainability forum."

As she maneuvered her little car, Tia slid her hand across his forearm in a gentle hug.

"We experienced the same powerful nations exerting multinational pressure as we do in the climate control conferences. Because I'm a consultant, I have quite a bit of latitude, I'm not strictly bound to the U.S. delegation. But it is still crushing to see the country of my birth and citizenship actively trying to circumvent efforts to develop binding international rules, going so against the grain of my beliefs of where the world needs to head.

"The U.S. delegation was totally unwilling to get down to specifics. In fact, certain members of our delegation actively campaigned against concrete targets. One in particular, she..."

He straightened a little, and drew a deep breath. His voice sounded tight as he changed course. "I need to tell you about this woman," he began.

Tia stiffened. She didn't have a good feeling about this.

"Lori Fordon. She's an assistant delegate in the UNFCCC meetings now. In Germany, two years ago, we were both consultants, we were working together, we were champions of the Kyoto treaty. And we had a little thing going."

Tia knew he had to have a past, but she dreaded knowing about it.

"I ended that last year."

He cleared his throat to go on.

What more could there be? Her stomach turned leaden.

"This week in Johannesburg she was out to win me over. All over me. She used all her tricks to draw me to her side." He ran his fingers through his hair, sighing deeply. "And in the end she certainly triumphed, she got what she wanted ..." He slowly shook his head at the memory.

Tia recoiled from him, trying to cover by clenching the steering wheel.

Oh no, he's still sleeping with her! It's still going on, and I'm falling right in the middle of it all! Tia could hardly keep the car on the road.

"It was Lori who actively campaigned the U.S. delegation, to assure that the U.S. sidestepped any form of binding agreements. No binding commitments! No concrete numbers, no limits, all to be voluntary! I just can't understand it, how someone can be so passionate about something, and then just change sides like that."

I have been a fool. Of course, it figures. He's a jet setter, he travels the world, he's darn good-looking, why didn't I realize he'd have women at every stop? Oh, I have been such a little fool!

"On second thought, I'm really tired, I'll just drop you at your place."

Ari gave her a puzzled look. "Okay," he paused, "then you'll need to make a left at that signal..."

CHAPTER 3:

TIME TO CHOOSE

AUTUMN 2002

"Voluntary Partnerships!?" Cassandra shouted through the phone. Tia held the receiver three inches away from her ear. "What are they thinking!? They're not thinking, that's what!" Cassandra was carrying on both halves of the debate just fine all by herself.

"The original Kyoto Protocol called for firm limitations on emissions. Now the U.S. delegation in their infinite wisdom, hear my sarcasm, is trying to change it to 'voluntary partnerships.' They're not thinking about anything except their obscene oil profits ..."

Every vicious sentence tore into Tia like a personal assault.

U.S. delegation ... it could very well have been Lori who coined that phrase Mom's harping on ... Kyoto Protocol ... Oh, Ari! I can't get you out of my mind.

Cassandra's political rants didn't typically bother Tia, but this one was torture. International debates sounded so distant in a news sound bite, but suddenly the participants were all too real.

Mom, do you realize that there is plenty of thinking and wisdom on that team? One tall, dark eyed man, to whom I may have lost my heart...

... and then there's some woman named Lori, who has his bed.

I can't take any more!

"Mom, I have to go now." Tia hung up the phone abruptly.

Cassandra clearly wasn't done yet, as her letter, arriving two days later, carried on in the same vein:

> "... Forget 'seven generations,' this planet's heating
> up, the oceans are rising, the forests are being razed,
> and still it's gas guzzling SUV's, let's drill the
> Arctic National Wildlife Refuge, and gimme more
> disposable commodities! Junk and waste! We're
> devastating the earth! With the way things are
> going, there won't *be* any grandchildren!"

(2.)

Perhaps it was the client's last minute phone call, or perhaps it was attributable to the knot in her stomach, but Tia arrived late to the meeting. She slid into a chair near the door.

"Four meetings ago," Carl was facilitating this evening, "we heard how members of Sustainable Seattle set up the organization that fostered an increase in Sustainability-focused activities in their area."

Tia looked around to get her bearings. More new faces, attendance was increasing. Ari sat, as usual, in the front row. Jana flashed a grin from the center of the crowd.

"I think this group needs a name and a focus," Carl continued. "We'll soon be promoting it to a wider circle. I propose that we call ourselves Sustainable Los Angeles."

"If we do that, don't we have to follow Sustainable Seattle's guidelines?" Ben asked.

"We discussed setting up our own guidelines, and they were not exact matches for those of Sustainable Seattle," reminded Steve.

"What if we changed it around, so it's close but not exact? Like LA Sustainable or something." Carl suggested.

"But who would want to 'sustain' what we've got: overcrowded freeways, urban sprawl, pollution, inner city problems, no green space!" Ben sputtered. "We need to focus on 'restoring' not just 'sustaining.'"

"The name should convey what we're striving for," Ari's voice resonated from the front of the room. Tia didn't dare look at him.

"It should inspire new traditions for our people," added a petite Hispanic woman from the back of the room.

Words came unbidden into Tia's mind: *'I see those kids and say to myself: we have to hand them a better legacy than this!'* She jumped to her feet.

"Legacy LA!" she called out.

"It's perfect!" Ben's voice boomed out.

After the meeting, Tia slipped into the crowd around Ben, to catch the news of his new job.

"I'm now with MTA, mass transit. Finally, there's real interest in my comprehensive plan for light rail in LA!"

"You've been hoping to get that position for quite some time. Congratulations!" Steve clapped Ben on the shoulder.

Although she could feel Ari's eyes following her, Tia steadfastly resisted returning the glance. Carl approached her and made small talk.

Seeing Jana and Steve nearby, Tia tried to be animated in her responses, but her heart followed Ari around the room. As Ari worked his way over to her, she hastily gathered her purse and turned to leave. He stepped between her and the door.

"Do you have time for a cup of coffee?" he invited with a warm smile.

"No thanks, not tonight." Phrasing it as indifferently as she could muster, she brushed by him and fled.

(3.)

"Girlfriend, what the heck are you doing?" Jana was hanging over the fence of Tia's community garden plot.

"What do you mean?" Tia pretended innocence.

"I heard you at the meeting, giving him the brush off. I thought things were going great between you two."

Tia could feel the sting of tears beginning; she blinked them back and swallowed hard. She tried to hold the tremor out of her voice, but a hint of it remained. "He ..." she faltered, "he has someone else, overseas."

There. It's out. I've actually said it.

"No! Really?"

"He told me. He meets up with her when he travels." Tia's misery was evident.

"Wow, I didn't know of anything since Bonn a year ago." Jana seemed intrigued.

"He saw her on his trip to Johannesburg."

"Strange that I never heard anything about it."

"He tells you everything?"

"No, of course he doesn't!"

∽

Two days later, Tia's secretary buzzed, "Ari Damek, line two."

"Please, tell him I'm in a meeting."

Tia put down her pen and pushed back from her desk. Ari's uniquely intense look came back to her so clearly, the memory of him inches away in the coffee cafe, his kisses at the breakwater and after the last Legacy LA meeting. She thought of their talks and how alive he made her feel, how passionate he was about his causes.

But I can't do it. Not when he has her. I won't be part of his worldwide harem.

(4.)

As Tia was driving home from work one evening, Ari's words echoed back to her. *"We have to hand them a better legacy than this."*

An overwhelming feeling of awe for him rushed over her. She thought of his focus, his purposefulness, his passion for this Sustainability crusade. She realized that everything she knew about him all revolved around it. His 'mission,' he called it. *He's a great man. I've never met anyone like him.*

Integrity. All the pieces adding up to one whole. He has such high integrity. It seemed like each new thing she learned about him was like another puzzle piece snapping into place. All put together they made a solid arrow in a single clear direction.

All the pieces ... except one.

(5.)

Before she knew it, another Legacy LA meeting arrived on the calendar.

"Tia," Ben greeted her. "Have you met Matthew Goodman? Tia Chandler. Matthew's new to the group. He's an attorney."

Matthew was slim, of medium height, with an air of the finer things in life. His suit, so at odds with the casual attire of others in the room, was of exquisite texture and tailoring. He was the picture of refinement and financial success.

"And?" Tia asked with an expectant smile.

Ben turned to Matthew with a chuckle. "Tia's discovered there's an 'and' for most of us here. We each wear multiple hats in this environmental campaign."

"*And* I've been doing some legal work for Esperanza Chavez and a community garden fighting eviction." Matthew joined in.

Even as Tia learned more about Matthew's project, her every sense was painfully aware of Ari as he circulated through the room.

Steve called the meeting to order. Tia hurried to take a seat, and Jana dashed over to sit beside her, taking the aisle.

"Tonight we're going to hear from Dr. Ari Damek about Sustainability."

Tia's stomach did a flip. *Oh no! He's the speaker. Listening to him, watching him, I can't bear it!* She thought of leaving, but even as she made the decision, Jana stretched out her long legs, blocking Tia's exit.

Already she could hear his familiar voice; it reached out and surrounded her as if in embrace.

"There are several hot words that get tossed around the environmental circles these days." He went to the board and wrote: Restoration ... Sustainability ... Conservation. He then heaved a conference chair up on top of the table at the front of the room.

"We're going to try a little demonstration here tonight. A little demonstration on two levels. We have one level on the chair seat up high, and the second on the tabletop level below.

"Let's call this chair seat the ecological balance we had on earth at, say, the beginning of the Industrial Revolution." Ari pulled out a card that read 'Ecological Balance' and stood it on the chair.

Next he produced a long ruler and a small toy ball. He propped the ruler in a steep downward slope between the chair seat and the table surface below.

"Here we are at Ecological Balance." He held up the toy ball, then put it on the chair seat. "And along comes the Industrial Revolution."

Zip! He released the ball and it zoomed down the ruler ramp and across the room. Steve and Carl laughingly went diving under chairs to retrieve it.

"There we go: that's what we've done with the atmosphere, we've degraded it."

Zip! Another ball from his pocket flew down the ramp. Again Steve went to get it.

"That's what we've done with soils. Aquifers. Fresh water. Rainforests." Zip! Zip!

"How many of these things do you have?" Steve sputtered. The audience chuckled at the action.

"Ok, you get the point." Ari gestured for Steve to put the balls on the tabletop.

Ari now pointed to the tabletop level.

"So here we sit Today, with an ecosystem that is, shall we say, somewhat 'downhill' from where our ancestors began." Another sign, labeled 'Today,' appeared down on the tabletop.

"Along comes the Green movement. Going to save the earth."

Hearing his voice pronounce this phrase made Tia's heart ache.

"Sustainability. It has become a big buzz word. What does it mean? Well, entire international delegations have spent weeks trying to agree upon a definition," he grimaced, "but they're still no closer. The point being, Sustainability can mean a wide variety of things, and can mean different things to different listeners. Most definitions have something to do with balance: the inputs equaling the outputs, the flow is balanced. The things we use are taken out of the planet no faster than the planet can make more. That could be timber forests, fresh water, soil particles, clean air ...[11]

"Now, there are several problems with this Sustainability concept. For instance:

"We're sitting at Today," he pointed to the table surface, "and we're using the word Sustainability. Let me show you Sustainable."

He snatched up the ruler, held it flat and level in front of his face and placed a ball upon it. With exquisite care he rolled the ball back and forth balanced upon the ruler. The audience clapped at his circus trick, so he took a bow, hamming it up in the role of clown.

"In its ideal attained form, Sustainable is a stable, closed loop. I held my demonstration up high so you could see my balancing trick, but we're really operating down at the Today table top level."

He smacked the ruler down on the table surface and plopped the ball upon it.

"If we try to achieve Sustainability right now, today, then we're stuck down here in a degraded system." He hit the table top with the palm of his hand.

"But what about our ecosystem? The playing field for Sustainable existence is up at Ecological Balance." He gently motioned to the higher chair seat level.

He took up his ruler and rebuilt his slanted ramp between table and chair seat, then took a ball and mimed its marching up the ramp to the chair seat.

"To get to our Sustainability playing field, we need to climb.

"That," he declared, "is Restoration. Restoring our environment to a point where we are able to exist Sustainably.[12]

"Now, there's a big catch. Or maybe two. One is this: we get partway to our goal ..."

Marching the ball halfway up the ruler ramp, he released it, and it shot down under Ben's chair.

"It is a lot easier to slide back down into familiar patterns than to keep on striving for the changes it's going to take.

"Secondly, Restoration means a climb. It means we must make much bigger changes in society. Many mainstream and reactionary people are having a hard enough time wrapping their brains around the idea of Sustainability, let alone the steeper climb of Restoration.

"I have one more up there on the board: Conservation. Actually, this buzzword was popular before folks started talking up Sustainability. Conservation looks like this."

He took one ball off by itself and cuddled it tenderly in his palms. "Save the El Segundo Blue Butterfly!" he called out, imitating an activists' rally.

"You'll note I'm nowhere near Ecological Balance. I've really isolated the item I'm ostensibly trying to preserve. That's why conservation efforts don't usually pan out the way the organizers had hoped. The species fail to flourish, the habitat deteriorates when they're out of connection with the larger ecosystem.

"So, where does this leave us?"

He placed all the balls back on the Today tabletop with the ruler in slant position.

"Ben, come up here. Carl. Steve. Jana."

As each came to the front of the room he orchestrated them marching separate balls up the ruler ramp from Today toward Ecological Balance.

"Restoration is not something any one of us can do alone. We need you, and you..." he began flinging extra balls into the audience, "...and you, and you ..."

Running out of trinkets to toss, Ari spun around. In a dramatic grand finale gesture, like the Uncle Sam recruitment poster, he thrust out his arm and pointed directly at Tia.

"We need you!"

Caught up in the drama of the presentation, his dark eyes were fierce fire that blazed into hers.

The audience burst into wild applause. Ari's arm dropped, but his eyes remained locked with Tia's until people rising to their feet blocked her view.

Tia sat, stunned. *This guy, he's incredible. He just doesn't quit!* Her heart was aching, pounding in her throat. She put her head in her hands, feeling weak and trembly. *Oh, damn it, he really gets to me!*

At the commotion of people around her beginning to leave, she looked up. Steve was talking earnestly to Jana. Ari had packed up his props and was headed out. As he reached the main door, he paused and half turned toward Tia.

Their eyes met again. Gone was the fire of the presentation, gone was the captivating smile. His face was sober. He slowly turned away and left the room.

Tears welled up in Tia's eyes. She grabbed her purse and fled through the side door toward the parking lot. Running to her car, she fumbled her keys in the dark.

"Tia!"

She heard Jana calling her name. She opened her car door.

"Tia, wait up!"

Jana caught up to her. A big sob wrenched Tia, and she leaned on the roof of her car and cried. Jana stood at her side, hand on Tia's shoulder.

"Tia, oh, girlfriend, I hate to see this. You're all torn up over this. You know, I've seen it, he is too."

Sure, he's disappointed he can't add another to his collection, most likely.

"Tia, give it up, go to him!"

Not when she's in the picture. Tia shook her head miserably.

"At least talk with him!"

"He just walked out of there without a word!" Tia gestured back toward the community room.

"Of course he did! You gave him the royal brush off, last meeting!"

And again tonight, I suppose.

"The ball's in your court, lady. If it's going to happen, you've got to go for it."

(6.)

Edie slumped into the upholstered visitor's chair of Tia's office. She set a styrofoam cup of coffee in front of Tia, careful not to spill her own. "Man, these shoes are killing me." She peeled off one of her strappy high heels.

The coffee smelled harsh, of sitting too long over the warmer. Edie opened packets of artificial sweetener and creamer and dumped them into hers.

"How can you stand that fake stuff?" Tia asked, grimacing.

"Hate it." Edie shrugged, stirring her coffee idly, the plastic stir stick held in awkwardly stiffened fingers to avoid her nails. "Jim wants to go to Vail next month, a whole bunch of us, but my credit card's maxed out. Have you paid off that Maui trip yet? I haven't." Edie peered at Tia over the rim of her cup. "You know, you look terrible. Really pale. You should go to the spa, get a massage or something, pamper yourself."

"I'm okay." She didn't feel it.

Slicing the edge of her cup with her sparkling fingernails, Edie continued slyly. "I saw Doug this week."

"So?"

"He bought a boat. Big one, to look good in front of his Marina house." Edie squinted her heavily lined eyelids. "He asked about you."

"Terrific." Tia's voice was flat.

"Still no interest, huh? Fight musta been pretty bad." Edie's nails flicked the array of pink phone message slips on Tia's desk. "Who's this Ari Damek? That's not a client. Two messages, wait, is that three?"

Tia snatched the message slips away, turning crimson.

"Ah, you're dating him?"

"No!"

"I get it, he was a one-nighter!" Edie grinned smugly.

No, I was almost his one-nighter. Tia swallowed hard. The last thing she wanted to do was cry in front of Edie.

"Hot Quacamoles, girl! I didn't know you did that kind of thing! Well, it's clear you have little time for poor old Doug. I have half a mind to dump Jim and go for Doug myself. Mr. Big Business, that guy's going to do something with his life!"

Edie rose to go, dropping stir stick and sweetener packet scraps into her almost untouched cup of coffee. "There's a shoe sale at Nordstrom's, starts tomorrow – want to go with me?"

That guy's going to do something with his life.

Tia shook her head to get rid of Edie before the tears hit.

(7.)

It was sunset along the breakwater. The wind was chill, and Tia pulled her knees up under her chin, becoming a small huddled ball of humanity atop the rocks. She found herself drawn here often, to watch the current of the channel sweep the rocks and to think.

Choices, she thought today, *it's all about choices. If we could only make better choices. Wiser, greener choices. Our money is a vote. We can vote for the least-cost mass-produced warehouse goods. Or we can vote for greener choices, the organics, the fledgling biodynamics, the Priuses versus the Hummers of the marketplace. Our spending choices are one way we can support this drive toward Sustainability.*

But greener consumer choices aren't all of it, her mind argued. In the physical waves against the rocks around her she saw again the shopping mall wave of Stuff. *The sheer volume we consume! We have become accustomed to taking, buying, using so much.*

But if the goods were more durable, less disposable, would we take less of them?

The volume is what drives the economy, she argued. *It creates jobs to make all that Stuff.*

Really? Jobs for humans or 'jobs' for factory machines?

'Thinkers. It's going to take thinkers and doers to solve the problems we face.'

I need another mind to pull it apart with. And I know precisely which mind.

The oncoming tide of water around her matched the returning tide of heartache. It seemed she could only push it away for short moments. *I knew him for such a brief time, yet he continues to affect me this much.*

His focus, his drive to bring something better to the world – it was a feeling she was just beginning to recognize in herself. *My life needs to be about something more than just everyday existence. There has to be some little petal of the Flower to which I can contribute, it doesn't have to be global causes ...*

Global causes ...

Saving the earth ...

Oh Ari, haven't you picked the ultimate mission! I want it too.

I want you too.

A flash of an image came over her, of dark eyes blazing fierce fire, Ari pointing, "We need you!"

I can't just let him slip away, I can't!

Tia wandered back up the breakwater path, back toward civilization. She thought of dark eyes, an incredible force of personality. *Choices.*

I've never met anyone even remotely like him. Choices.

Tears stung the corners of her eyes. *Choices.*

I choose a life that has him in it.

International harem, if that's how it has to be, so be it.

As she got closer to the buildings, she opened her cell phone and dialed his number. Recording. She hung up without leaving a message.

When she got home, she went to her laptop.

> To: adamek@LAglobalsolutions.net
> I tried to call but got your recording. Maybe we could get together for a coffee?

His response was in her inbox when she awoke:

> To: tchand@aol.com
> Regretfully, I'm in New Delhi at the moment. Perhaps upon my return.

Her stomach sank. *New Delhi! Oh, this is going to be difficult! But at least he responded. Ok, Tia, if it's going to happen, you have to pull it together and make it happen.* She sighed deeply and began to type.

> To: adamek@LAglobalsolutions.net
> Your presentation at Legacy LA was breathtaking, it took my breath away. Particularly the finale. I'm very sorry we didn't get together while you were in LA. How is New Delhi, I presume you're at the UNFCCC Conference? I can't find much about it on the internet.

She almost deleted it, she felt perhaps it revealed too much. Instead, she closed her eyes and hit "send."

His reply arrived within the hour.

> To: tchand@aol.com
> The Delhi Conference (yes, it's the UNFCCC) is frustrating and has yielded little progress. The discussion has unfortunately boiled down to 'you make your move first.' Rich, developed nations, both those that have ratified the Protocol and those that haven't, are pressuring the poorer, undeveloped nations to reduce emissions first. The U.S. delegation, for its part, has claimed Protocol terms will mean job losses. How come our policy makers can't see that adjustment to Protocol terms will create jobs?

'You make your move first'? Yes, that's what I'm trying to do. Before she left for the office, she wrote again.

> To: adamek@LAglobalsolutions.net
> I'm so sorry it isn't going well there. How very disappointing. For you, and for the world. I just wish they would wake up and realize it! Please keep up the good fight. We need you.

We need you. I want you. I love you.

Oh! That's what you, too, said to me in the meeting. I just now understood it. You shouted your declaration, in front of all those people!

When she arrived home, there was a message waiting.

> To: tchand@aol.com
> It's primarily the United States whom we have to
> wake up. Someday I'll figure out how to do it.
> Thanks for the encouragement. I'll keep fighting for
> you. This Delhi Conference ends tomorrow.

Tia's eyes widened, staring at his words on the screen. She took a deep breath and sent off another message, but didn't expect a response due to the time difference.

> To: adamek@LAglobalsolutions.net
> When do you return to LA? May I make dinner for
> you?

By bedtime, she had received his answer, from halfway around the world.

> To: tchand@aol.com
> I come in to LA on Tuesday. I'll see you Tuesday
> night.

(8.)

Tia looked around her apartment, all was ready.

Dinner was simmering on the stove. She had considered the menu carefully. Ari was, after all, an international traveler, so he must have sampled many interesting cuisines. She discarded the idea of Indian food since he was just arriving from New Delhi.

It needed to be a menu that was showy but not too demanding, particularly one that needed little in the way of last minute touches. She finally settled upon Persian cuisine, from one of her favorite cookbooks. A fresh herb khoresh (stew), a deluxe polow (rice), her favorite version of the traditional yogurt and cucumber, and a rice pudding with rosewater for dessert.

She looked in the mirror to check her appearance. Tonight she had selected a flowy skirt, with a top that was lower cut than the usual office styles he'd seen her wear. It showed off her figure quite nicely. She brushed her hair and arranged it loosely around her shoulders. She looked soft and pretty. The doorbell rang.

As she opened the door, their eyes met and held. Tia's heart was tight in her chest, she could barely breathe. *Oh, I'd forgotten the intensity of that look!* She felt a rush of warmth through her body and her knees felt weak.

Suddenly realizing they were just standing in the doorway, staring, she blinked and stammered something vague. At that exact moment he tried to fill the silence, and they talked across each other.

Tia giggled, Ari cleared his throat. "Hi."

He handed her an armload of flowers, blush roses in a mixed bouquet. He had also brought wine. Her cat came running to check out the newcomer. They moved to the kitchen, to vases and wine glasses. Tia felt his eyes roll over her; he didn't miss her neckline.

He poured the wine and they clinked glasses. "To new beginnings," he said. Their eyes met again over the glasses.

He put his glass down and pulled her into his arms. "I missed you." He kissed her, slowly, deliciously, and she felt her desire for him surge through her body. She pulled away gently. *I can't do this. Not yet.*

"So how was your trip?" She nervously fussed with the flowers. *Why did I say that, he already told me in emails!*

Ari leaned in the kitchen doorway, his long body wedged in the frame, effectively holding her captive in her own kitchen. He fiddled with his wine glass as he spoke. "There really seem to be three main agendas that countries are bringing to these talks. One major area is ecological effectiveness, as in 'let's get the environmental job done.' The EU and the Alliance of Small Island Nations push for this, because they are the ones who are beginning to feel the real physical impact of rising sea levels.

"A second area of concern has been called Social Justice and Equity. Poorer developing nations want to industrialize, as the richer countries have already done. These developing nations claim their right to use their resources to improve their standard of living. They don't want to be penalized for current greenhouse gas buildups, which are attributable to the industrial history of the wealthy developed nations.

"The third area of concern is the only one that seems to get any press in the U.S.: economic effectiveness: 'Can we make money off it.' Because of the U.S. position in the world, the issue of economic effectiveness has completely eclipsed the other two areas of concern."

She began arranging the dinner on the plates. It did look impressive. The rice, with bits of lentil, date and strips of caramelized onions, was a marvel of textures. The khoresh looked positively exotic, pureed dark green herbs atop lamb pieces. The cucumber was a bit plain-looking, but did balance the plate. A sprig of cilantro helped a lot.

From his doorway vantage point Ari paused in his conversation. For a long moment he simply stared at the plate in her hand.

"I'm at a loss for words."

Oh no, he doesn't like it. It's too weird. Maybe I should have just made a steak.

"You've really gone all out, here. Tell me about it."

She told him the names of the various dishes, with highlights of the ingredients list. But Ari wasn't looking at the plate, his eyes were on her.

They moved to the table. She debated whether to bring out candles, but decided against it, the atmosphere was charged enough already.

"Wow, you are one impressive cook, this is delicious!"

"Thanks," she murmured, looking down and away, unable to meet his eyes. Her heart was pounding, to the point that she could barely eat.

"You were telling me about your Conference," she tried to get him back on his topic. He went willingly.

"In Delhi the rich nations were pushing that emissions reduction targets be imposed on poorer developing nations, which disregards their social justice and equity concerns. In the past it was understood that the wealthier nations would assist poorer undeveloped nations to access cleaner technology. This was affirmed in Johannesburg but no real action has been taken to support this process."

He ran a fingertip gently up her arm. She smiled at him, but slipped away.

"Overall, though, I couldn't get much accomplished. At least, not what I'd hoped. Not that I was surprised, after the atmosphere at the Summit two months ago. We still have no solid commitments ..."

"Was she in New Delhi?" Tia blurted out, and immediately wished she hadn't said it. *But I have to know!*

"Who?"

Is he playing it dumb?

"Lori."

"Of course."

"You saw her again. Like in Johannesburg."

"Oh yes." He said it with definite emphasis and raised his eyebrow.

Tia's sharp intake of breath was audible. She closed her eyes as tears welled up.

"So then you see her at all these conferences?" Tia's voice was choked.

"Certainly."

"So then it's not over between you." She almost whispered it in stunned defeat.

"Between us? The relationship you mean?" His voice became barely controlled fury. "That was over, done, a year ago at Bonn, when she made it her agenda to undermine Kyoto! She's a traitor to all I am fighting for! When the U.S. team refused to return to the table last year at Bonn, she sided with them. I went on to the Bonn Conference, together with the other nations of the world!"

Tears were streaming down Tia's cheeks now. "But after Johannesburg, you said she ..."

He interrupted, his dark eyes blazing, his tone complete disgust. "In Johannesburg she created one hell of a debate, right in the middle of the damn session! She was all over me when I wouldn't back down. I was pushing for concrete emissions caps, but in the end she got exactly what she was after: no emissions limits, no ..."

He paused as a look of realization came over his face. His tone changed abruptly. "Oh, Tia, you thought ... oh God, no!" He shook his head violently.

"Come over here, you." He stood and reached across the table to draw her up to his embrace. "Look, I don't know how this got so mixed up."

He brushed her hair back with his hand. "In Delhi, in Johannesburg, here in LA, you are the one who's been on my mind. Tia, there's no one else." With a gentle touch of his hand he raised her chin and kissed her cheek. When he reached her lips she could taste the salt of her own tears.

There's no one else!

And for me, there can be no one else but you. She nestled into his chest.

"Get your coat, let's take a walk along that water I saw out there."

Tia's apartment in Marina del Rey was near the channel. They strolled the railed footpath along the rock barrier, holding each other close.

"Isn't this near where we were that other evening?" he asked.

"That was right across the way."

They walked over to the railing and paused to look at the sea. The waves of the incoming tide swept the rocks of the breakwater, the current deep and blackened in the orange glow of the street lamps. The mammoth rocks of the breakwater, polished by years of these waves, became hopelessly tiny in the face of the ocean's forces.

At the sheer power of the water the chill of Tia's so-familiar fears welled up inside her. *Sea levels rising, El Niño on the rampage, global warming.* The raw fear grew within her and she tried to swallow it back down.

"How do you do it?" she whispered. "How do you keep going? How do you keep your spirits up in the midst of this crisis?" She wasn't sure whether she had voiced these thoughts aloud.

But somehow he understood her. He leaned back against the railing, pulling her against him into his warm embrace. He stroked her hair as he spoke.

"How do I keep going? I keep going because I have to. I'm driven to. It's something I committed myself to, about ten years ago.

"I started out very much like you. Stuck in one life and growing into another. I was working in conventional fuels but then I became aware of the environmental issues and global warming. This is what I decided to make my life be about.

"Once I made that decision, once I threw my heart and my best efforts after it, there was just no going back. Once I took action, it took on a life of its own. Having such a focus, a purpose, well, it simplifies things, it makes my decisions easier.

"It doesn't make the challenges go away, nor the disappointments. It doesn't ease the pain of losing. But my commitment makes it certain that after that loss, I'll pick myself up, dust myself off, and get back to work.

"Bonn last year, when my own country declared Kyoto dead, was one of those losses for me. Johannesburg also, when Sustainability went out the window in the face of political clamoring. But I'm getting over it, going on.

"I think you asked, not so much to see what keeps me going, as to discover what'll keep you going. I can't tell you that, you'll have to discover it for yourself. Reach beyond your job, beyond your garden, beyond your self and your family, to some greater cause. The way to the answer is to ask yourself: what do I believe in, what do I want to make my life be about?"[13]

'He's been striving for the superhuman trophy for more than a decade.' Jana's words came back to her.

Ah, but it looks great on him! Tia decided.

"Ari, in the Legacy LA meeting, when you pointed to me, you were trying to tell me this, weren't you?"

"Yes ... yes I was." He cleared his throat. "This ... among other things."

Tia reached up and found his lips. It began as a long slow kiss, tender and exploring. *... for the unsaid messages, for the wisdom of your words tonight, for your dedication, your focus, your passion ... for your desire ... and my own ...*

"We're taking this indoors," he said in a husky voice when at last they broke away. Pressing her body against his, he guided her back to the path. The sea wind was getting colder now, but somehow it didn't matter to them.

Back in her living room, Tia paused in latching the door. She could feel Ari's body heat as he stood behind her. Then he grasped her shoulders, turning her to meet him. His hand was in her hair, his mouth on hers, their desire rekindled. He stripped off her coat, his hands traveling her body. Through the fabric of his shirt, the muscles of his chest felt firm and full beneath her palms.

He paused, his dark eyes fierce fire as they gazed into hers. She met his look fully, no longer running from all that she saw there: his passion, his desire, his intention. Her eyes answered back. *I love you. I want you.* He traced her bare skin at the open neckline, slipping in to caress her breast. She took his hand and lead him into her bedroom.

(9.)

The next morning, Tia awakened to the early sunshine, Ari sleeping beside her, skin to skin. She lay breathing in the delicious warmth of his presence. He stirred in his sleep and rolled over. Resisting the impulse to stroke his rumpled hair, she tenderly watched the rise and fall of his bare chest; he was resting so peacefully.

After a while, she slipped silently out of bed and pulled on a silk robe. She made the coffee and stole a bite of last night's neglected rice pudding dessert, then leaned at her window frame watching the gulls circling the channel.

Sea levels rising, global warming, species extinction. She felt the stifling panic rising within her. *If multinational delegations can't stop this, what can?* She took a deep breath but it did nothing to soothe her.

She heard Ari approaching behind her. "Good morning, ready for the new day?" he asked brightly, draping his arms over her shoulders. She could feel every bit of his naked body against hers through the thin silk robe.

"You can see part of the ocean and the channel from here," he observed.

"You can see the waves lashing the shore," she countered. "Imagine them with higher sea levels. And intense El Niño storms.

"It haunts me," she confessed. "Everything I look at: the shopping malls, the freeways, war on the evening news. They're not stopping, it just goes on and on. People buy more gas guzzlers, and WalMart keeps opening stores. I feel so helpless …"

"Don't ever use that word."

He spun her around to face him, taking her hands in his. His expression was serious but his eyes were brilliantly alive. "Tia, because you comprehend the changes our civilization must make, because you glimpse what lies before us if we don't change course, you have a job to do.

"You can't remain on the sidelines. It'll drive you crazy with fear and worry. Or else, you'll try to blind yourself to it, and shut down a part of your innermost self. The only way out of this is by doing, by stepping out into the lead to help transform this society as you realize it must.

"It's time for you to choose your place, to select what you want to do. What problem do you want to embrace? What issue do you want to devote yourself to? It's time to act."

"I'm afraid," she replied quietly.

How strange my voice sounds, it does not tremble. And then she realized in astonishment, *I don't fear taking action, nearly so much as I fear the consequences if we don't act!*

"The point is not whether you're afraid, but what you *do* with your fear. Do you permit it to stop you? Or do you acknowledge it and go on, anyhow, and do what you must do."

"You have incredible courage," he murmured in her ear.

She moaned softly, running her hands down his naked body. He untied her robe and slipped it off her shoulders. It fell to the floor, a discarded shimmering silken skin.

(10.)

'It's time for you to choose.' Alone in her apartment two days later, Ari's words mingled with words from the article Tia was reading:

> I take a look at the world and say, What's the most
> creative way I can think of to change this for the
> better? And how does that match up with what I'm
> good at, and what I love to do?

On the notebook beside her she sketched the Permaculture Flower. She casually listed ideas at points around the Flower: books she had read, positive solutions she had heard.

It struck her how, while many of her books had conveyed her mother's doomsday tone, the Legacy LA gatherings had not.

The Legacy LA meetings were a regular message of hope and possibilities, a place where she could meet others who worked in hope and possibilities, even as she read websites which ran scrolling counters of species extinction and rainforest acreage laid barren; even as her mailbox brought news of wildlife devastation, AIDS epidemics, horrifying social injustices; even as vehicles on the street outside and power plants elsewhere in the state released further CO_2 molecules to float upwards to the upper atmosphere.

We need beacons of hope. Not to say the job is done, not by a long shot, but to say we have to keep on trying. The bad news is so staggering. It is too easy to succumb to despair. It is too easy to say 'enough!' and shut down. The problems are not going away. And they will certainly not go away if we ignore them, nor if we get overwhelmed by them and frozen into inaction.

She thought of Ari's 'Transformation Wave' concept. *How many people really see this wave beginning? It's nearly invisible. They must feel so alone in their striving to make a difference. I worked hard these past months to find it, to get beyond Mom's doomsday news, to news of possibilities.*

She looked down at the annotated diagram in her notebook. *The least I can do is share this list with others.*

She pulled open her laptop and began to format a webpage.

PART TWO

Never doubt that a small group of thoughtful, committed citizens can change the world. Indeed, it's the only thing that ever has.

Margaret Meade

CHAPTER 4:

THOUGHTFUL

2002-2005

"Mom, this is Ari." Tia held her breath.

"Mrs. Chandler," Ari extended his hand.

"Oh, no, I'm Cassandra!" She bypassed his handshake to give him a warm hug.

They looked odd together, Ari tall, lean and dark; Cassandra not even reaching his shoulder, plump and pastel, unbound and flowing, from her long grey hair to her ethnic-print dress.

Coyote Creek was small compared to other farms in the rustic Ojai valley community, yet it always felt spacious to Tia after the close quarters of LA. The house was a low sprawling ranch style house, fronted by a curved gravel drive with native sycamores and Toyon. Now, at Thanksgiving, the sycamores were nearly bare of leaves, and the Toyon were showing promise of their breathtaking red berries.

There was a certain deep satisfaction in re-entering her childhood home. Tia sighed, feeling its habitual security surround her. And then she remembered. Something fragile crumbled deep inside. *It will never, ever be the same.* The tears welled up, but she swallowed them down and tried to carry off a smile.

They gathered in the family room, where Cassandra offered limeade, then bustled into the kitchen. *The curtains are closed in here, how odd. Mom usually prefers natural daylight.*

Tia opened the curtains broadly. And froze. The picture window perfectly framed the stark concrete pad where the workshop had once stood. Tia gasped and whisked the curtains shut. She leaned against the wall, her heart thumping.

It will never be the same.

Ari moved over to her. "Should we take a walk? You're very pale."

"Let's get out of here. I'll show you Mom's gardens." Tia staggered from the room.

Once out in the sunshine, Tia brightened up considerably. "We moved here when I was really tiny, I can't even remember times before Coyote Creek." She took Ari's hand and lead him into a tall grove of eucalyptus trees nearby. "My friend Sahara and I used to play here. Her folks' place is just up the road." Tia scrambled up a tree onto a low branch and sat, swinging her feet gaily.

"All you need are pigtails; I get the picture." Ari laughed.

Tia rained seed pods down upon him, jumped down and chased him. He spun around and caught her, tumbling with her to the ground amid the pungent eucalyptus leaves. The world smelled like bruised eucalyptus and fresh earth. He rolled across her and kissed her leisurely, tenderly.

"I love you, Tia." His dark eyes were rich and warm.

"I love you, too." She delighted to see Ari, usually so serious, relaxing into such playfulness.

She next showed him the creek. "It looks dry at this time of year, you only see water flow for a short while after a rain. But look." With a stick she dug down in what appeared to be dry creek bottom. Sure enough, a few inches down it was damp. "The water continues to flow in an underground creek," she explained.

"In the early spring all these elders are in blossom." She gestured to the drooping trees around them. "It smells heavenly."

They moved along to Cassandra's experimental fields. "Over here is Mom's real focus. Drylands agriculture. All organic. She's growing Native American vegetable varieties from the Southwestern and Mexican deserts. She saves the seed, carefully selecting for ultimate attributes. Over the years, generation after generation, she's developing varieties which are highly productive without chemical support, and are tolerant of extremely low water conditions."[14]

The site of the workshop seemed to contain magnetic forces – as much as Tia tried to shy away from it, they just seemed to keep heading back in that direction. Finally, she surrendered, and they walked there solemnly.

"You miss him very much," Ari said quietly.

"Yes." *It's all too raw and new.*

"He must have been very special. I wish I'd known him." Ari didn't even finish his sentence, and she was sobbing uncontrollably against his chest. He held her tightly and stroked her hair.

Later, Tia found Ari alone in the family room, holding aside the curtain, gazing out at the workshop's barren pad. Her stricken face begged the question.

Ari cleared his throat. "Have you ever considered planting a tree there?"

Cassandra loved his idea.

❧

"Sahara!" Tia ran to the driveway to greet her friend. "It's been so long! And Jeffrey – oh, you have grown! Sahara, let me introduce Ari, Ari Damek."

Sahara was Tia's age, twenty-nine, but short and plump. She had grey-blue eyes and short hair that had a tendency to curl gently.

Ari reached out to greet Sahara, but hesitated as a four year old boy steadfastly blocked his path, hands on hips.

"Who are you?" Jeffrey demanded.

Ari crouched down on one knee until he was eye to eye with the boy, and extended his hand to Jeffrey instead of his mother. They shook, with exaggerated high spirits. "Pleased to meet you!"

"He'll be your friend for life after that," commented Sahara.

"Where's Wendell?"

"He's off on another – tour – for want of a better word." The sadness and weariness were wrapped up in Sahara's tone.

Sahara and Tia joined Cassandra in the kitchen. Through the big window over the sink, they could see Ari outside, swinging Jeffrey in wide circles. The squeals of delight brightened the trio of women.

"That one's a keeper, Tia," Sahara teased. "He'll make a good father!"

Tia blushed deeply.

"Tsk, tsk, in front of her mother no less!" Cassandra laughed.

After dinner, Sahara and Tia took a private stroll away from the group, out past the workshop.

"So, this Ari, what's he like?" Sahara wasted no time.

"He's a lot like Dad, really focused, immersed in his intellectual stuff."

"Yes, I noticed he likes to talk!"

Tia giggled. "He talks more when he's nervous. But I like it. He puts such different ideas together."

"Does he live with you?"

"Not really. Sort of. He has a house. And he travels a lot."

"Tia, it's a lonely life with these travelers." Her voice trembled.

"Wendell's gone that much?"

"It's not how much he's gone, it's become an issue of when he's gone. Life gets stressful, money gets tight and suddenly he gets an itch for another roaming expedition. 'Seeking inspiration' he calls it. Supposedly gets material for his music.

"It's been really tough this time, Jeffrey's been a handful. But I keep busy. I'm restructuring Mom and Dad's old farm. I've been inspired by the work your mom is doing, but I really want to explore the biodynamic concepts. They take the organics a giant step further. Everything is based upon your soil. Grow the soil and the soil will provide you with crops. I'm experimenting with growing my own carbon crops, plants specifically selected to be composted back into the soil.[15] And I'm learning about seedsaving from your mom. In this way, the entire cycle, from seeds to fertilizer, is all captured on the plot of land. It's a much more Sustainable way of producing crops. But I wanted to hear about this guy, not talk about me!"

"Ari's travels aren't spontaneous like Wendell's, they're very scheduled, sometimes years into the future. He mostly works at meetings about greenhouse gas emissions control – you know – the Kyoto Protocol. But occasionally he goes to other international sessions about Sustainability."

"They have those?"

"Sure they do. There was one in Rio in 1992, a World Summit on Sustainability. It was apparently quite a big deal, they always refer to it. Another of these Sustainability meetings was held in Johannesburg this year, but it sounds like it wasn't nearly as much of a success."[16]

"I didn't know there was any world effort in the direction of Sustainability."

"Sounds to me like they're still trying to get it figured out, but yes, they meet."

"What about the rest of life, children, things like that?"

"He made it clear on our first date that he'd like to have kids. We haven't talked about it really, but I can't imagine he'd want a big family, he has such strong views about Sustainable living."

"That's okay with you?"

"Sure, I like the Sustainability ideas. I don't know how we get there from here, from this lifestyle."

"Especially the way you city folk live!" Sahara's laugh was part grimace.

They passed the experimental fields and reached the creek. Tia soaked up the sunshine, the fields, the elders. "I wish there were a way to bring all this down into the cities."

"Maybe you'll figure out a way."

"That sounds like something he might say to me."

"So he's it," Sahara looked at Tia knowingly, "your soulmate?"

Tia's heart thumped in her throat at the word.

"Why yes, I think he is."

﹁

Before the weekend was over, Cassandra acquired a small tree by barter.

"It's an oak, honey," she told Tia, "a California native scrub oak, because Orrick means 'strong like an oak.' It should do fine for years with very little water."

Tia noticed that her mother's eyes were red rimmed, even though she was smiling now. Hesitantly slipping her arms around her mother's shoulders, and feeling rather awkward, Tia gave her a gentle hug.

Ari dug the hole and the three carefully planted the tree.

Burying her bare hands in the soil around the little tree, Cassandra sighed deeply. Her long unbound grey hair shielded her face, but Tia felt sure she was crying. "He was such a kind man, peaceable. He loved to tinker with his inventions and projects. Often he'd come home from the corporate lab and go straight out here to the workshop. I'd bring his dinner out just to be with him. He would be lost in the thoughts of his formula, he might not have much to say. If he did talk about his work it was all calculations and molecular equations, it was quite above my head.

"We lived under such a shadow of fear those final years. There were threats, multiple threats. There had been trumped up legal charges and stolen patents to slow his progress. They were trying to hold back his work, it threatened major corporate money. Then he learned that government scientists have known the photoremediation concept for years and have taken no action to implement it." Cassandra lapsed into silence.

"I'm astounded by the magnitude of what Rick discovered," Ari said after a while. "And saddened how few people know of it, the knowledge has been so completely suppressed.

"How many people realize that nuclear waste could be a non-issue? That it is possible to neutralize it, rather than attempting to store it for tens of thousands of years. And moreover, that the process of neutralizing it can be a power-generating operation.

"How many other innovators must there be out there, whose discoveries can solve major world problems, yet we know nothing of them. The knowledge might still be in experimental phases, or not yet spread to the mainstream, or may even be actively suppressed. I'm confident that the solutions exist, thus the possibilities exist, for restoring major ecosystems and guiding human life to a Sustainable existence on the planet."[17]

Tia remained silent. She remembered as a small girl visiting her dad in his workshop. She looked out over the naked workshop foundation. Its exterior had resembled an old antique barn. Inside, it had been an efficient modern lab, her father's happy little lair for working out his latest theories.

Tia remembered arriving from LA the day of the explosion, the twisted burned-out wreckage, the shards of wood and glass and metal, the police barrier lines, the questions that never seemed to end. And the horror of her mother's bandaged arms and hands, her hair singed from her efforts to claw her way into the burning workshop. The now-empty workshop pad seemed to mimic and mock the desperate empty feeling in Tia's heart.

How does Mom continue with this vast emptiness?

There was something here, tangible, in the intertwined lives of Rick and Cassandra. He with his fantastic solutions for the most toxic waste humankind had ever produced. She with her love of growing things, and her drive to be ready for the impending climate changes. There was something powerful that linked these two, that Tia couldn't quite name. Tia suddenly felt that although she knew them so well, she also hardly knew them at all.

She looked at Ari, resting tall and proud on the shovel. *What is it that links us? It's much more than infatuation or passion, habits or lifestyle. Yet I feel no closer to naming it.*

(2.)

"What have you done with my brother?" Jana teased, as members gathered before the Legacy LA meeting. "It's a rare night he spends at the Venice house anymore!"

Tia grinned in answer, wiggling her eyebrows suggestively. "What about you, Jana, when's it going to be your turn?"

Jana turned ashen, the tease drained from her face.

"Never mind, bad joke, I shouldn't have started it," Jana snapped. Her face was closed to all discussion as she abruptly turned away and found a seat deep within the crowd.

What the heck did I say? Tia wondered.

As Steve called the meeting to order, Tia moved to her now-habitual chair at Ari's side. Other audience members blocked her view of Jana.

"Tonight I'm going to tell you how new ideas get spread, from the inventor, out to the mainstream population." Steve began his presentation.

"Say, an inventor creates an idea. This could be a product, like solar panels; a technique, like recycling; or a theory, like natural capital. It's a great idea, but this guy's an inventor, he's really technical, and he's not very good at sharing it with people.

"That's why he needs the Change Agent. The Change Agent's special talent is translating that idea to something which others can understand. He hears about the innovator's new idea. He understands the inventor's techno-talk, but he has the art of persuasion. Our Change Agent goes out and tells folks about the idea."

At the mention of Change Agents, Tia slid her hand down Ari's forearm and intertwined her fingers with his.

"Now, a good Change Agent doesn't go out and address everyone he meets. If he wants to be really effective, he targets specific people: people who will be receptive to the new idea, but usually people who are also leaders within a group or a company, the ones Madison Avenue calls the 'early adopters.' Alan AtKisson calls them Transformers.[18]

"The Transformers are the ones who 'transform' the mainstream. By the Transformer's mere adoption of the new idea, technique or product, the idea becomes safer, more approachable, as mainstream folks see it put into action. As in electricity, the Transformer tones down the 'voltage' of the idea, making it a little less radical, more palatable and accessible to the mainstream.

"Reactionaries are those who actively resist the adoption of the new idea. Think of the tobacco company executive who knows his product is going to lose revenues if this 'no smoking in public buildings' idea goes mainstream.

"The last one I'll speak about tonight is the Iconoclast. These are the ones who stage the protests against the evils of the status quo. They can be pretty useful in keeping the Reactionaries busy. But it is important to note that the Iconoclasts tend to be nay-sayers, not idea-generators. Their energy is focused on stopping, rather than creating something new.

"What thrills me about working with this group," Steve gestured to the entire gathering, "is we seem to harbor very few nay-sayers. Here at Legacy LA we gather a lot of Transformers and Change Agents. We're not necessarily the inventors, and we're not activists in the sense of an Iconoclast staging political protests. Our membership consists of the people who seek out new ideas and incorporate these new ideas into the fabric of society.

"We are the change makers, who adopt features of sustainable living ahead of the crowd. We massage the solutions into practicality, and we model them for others to see. We show the mainstream, through our actions and our everyday living, that environmental change is possible, it is enticing, it is fun, and it is desirable.

"Thank you, each of you, for taking part in these changes. Together we are building a positive Legacy for LA!"

After Steve's presentation, as Tia waited for Ari to finish his rounds of conversations, she helped Steve and Jana stack chairs. Jana was still brooding, and slid away from Tia's efforts to connect with her.

Tia crossed the room to get a far off chair. Turning around with chair in hand, she saw Steve talking closely with Jana. He extended his hand to Jana's shoulder, then with a violent movement, Jana shook him off and stalked out of the room.

(3.)

Tia didn't realize that when Ari moved in, so many extra people would come too. Tia learned to prepare dinners for three or four as a matter of course.

Jana was a frequent and welcome visitor. Tia and Jana had been casual friends before, but now they were developing a new level of closeness.

Carl dropped in often. His economic discussions with Ari typically carried very late into the night. After Carl's departures, Tia would fall asleep to the sound of Ari's agitated pacing.

Steve's almost constant presence usually meant stimulating conversation. As Ari's sounding board, or bearing new ideas from his own pursuits, Steve's views seemed perfect complement to Ari's.

This early summer evening, Steve stretched out in Tia's living room chair looking quite at home. The cat hopped onto Steve's lap and curled into a ball, purring loudly. Tia curled up against Ari on the couch, partially on his lap, the purrs in her imagination reflected in the flirtatious smile she flashed up at Ari.

"Big Business versus Deep Green," Ari began. "I've long thought that this was the core of the environmental change deadlock, the reason that society persists in the old ways, despite awareness of climate change and other issues.

"Big Business locks heads with Deep Green. Big Business wants progress, development, growth, linear ascent. Deep Green preaches for us to use less, cut back, restrict, conserve, small is beautiful."

"Stated that way, there's no solution!" Tia observed in horror.

"Big Business is momentum, forward motion, a driving machine going places. It gets things done. Adrenaline, competition, excitement, enticing invitations with fascinating new things. A few of the businessmen are leaders; many of them are just a blind pack of followers.

"The energy of the Deep Greens is markedly different: the brakes are on, it's a shrinking inward, a bucket of cold water on the thrill of it all.

"What if the environmentalists, rather than attempting to *halt* Business, stepped in as the vision makers, deciding to inspire rather than resist. 'Here's where we need to go: restoration, environmental harmony, Sustainable development. Apply that famous American ingenuity to it!' What if, rather than putting on the brakes, the environmentalists directed and focused the innovation and forward-motion energy of Business?"

Steve raised a tawny eyebrow. "Do you really think that's possible?" The doubt was heavy in his words.

"Do I think it's possible for Deep Green to *halt* Big Business? No. I don't think they have a hope in hell. The momentum of Big Business is just too strong. And Big Business will never embrace the 'cut back and sacrifice' aspect of the Deep Green philosophy.

"Do I think it's possible to focus and inspire Business, to ride on their coattails, to move forward on their energy and momentum? I think it's a lot more realistic.

"David Holmgren is probably right, the future logically has to be an 'energy descent.' But I'm not at all certain that an energy descent has to mean mass misery. We can actively engage the business leaders and the entrepreneurs, inspire them to get involved in the design of a more Sustainable future. Who knows, they may take us wonderful places the Deep Greens never dreamed possible.[19]

Steve's response was sarcastic, almost bitter. "Yeah, we just need a few good Change Agents to translate the environmental message into something that directs Business in that direction."

"Yes," Ari said reflectively. "I just have to figure out how to convey the message."

Tia tended to side with Steve, it sounded impossible. Yet Ari was so sure of himself with clear eyed confidence. His powerful belief was contagious. She slipped her arm through his.

(4.)

Christmas holidays, Tia and Ari again visited Coyote Creek. They took a walk in the cool winter sun. The creek was trickling as runoff from the November rains continued. Sycamores overhead were naked and lacy against the sky. Tia settled in on a warm sunshiny rock to watch the creek. Ari explored a few yards upstream, poking at rocks and picking at grasses as he meandered.

He wandered back, hands in pockets, idly kicking small stones with his shoe. "I think Carl's old theories have been right, I think we may be in for rough years ahead. With Kyoto in the balance, I'll still be traveling a lot. The environmental effort is probably going to get tougher with the economic times. It's not going to be easy."

He stopped in front of her and cleared his throat, "Tia, we're strong, you and I. We're strong together."

As he said this he held out his hand and helped her to her feet, atop her rock. For once, she was looking down at him, a half a head taller than he. Those intense dark brown eyes gazed up at hers, connecting deeply, lingering a long tender moment.

"Tia, will you marry me?"

"Yes," she replied with a delighted smile.

"This," he pulled a tiny object from his pocket, "is made from the grasses that spring from the earth of your homeland. I give you this as a symbol of our commitment, and a symbol of our joint purpose."

Onto her finger he slipped a delicate ring he had carefully woven from the creek grasses.

"Goddess of my hearth and home," he whispered.

With a playful bounce he lifted her down from her pedestal, down to his embrace and further, as they dropped to roll joyfully together in the tall winter grass.

(5.)

> We try to live lightly on the land in a culture where
> that's impossible. ...

Isn't that the truth!

Tia curled in an armchair in the apartment, her faithful lap-cat purring in position atop her feet, reading Donella Meadows' collection of essays, *The Global Citizen.*

Just try planning a wedding – even a small one – in this culture, with a view to living lightly on the earth!

> ... But we have lightened up about our own
> compromises and those of others. We do our best,
> we're always willing to try to do better, and we're
> still major transgressors on the ecosystems and

resources of the planet. We're a lot more tolerant of
our fellow transgressors than we used to be. ...

*Even as I try to refine my habits, try to incorporate greener ways,
I still feel the tug of guilt for those habits where I have not yet broken
with the mainstream culture, a perpetual sense of 'glass is half empty.'*
*Instead, it's time to celebrate that which I have changed, those
areas where I have made my life greener.*

... As a child in the middle-class Midwest, I lived
out of a subconscious sense of *abundance*. That
sense permits security, innovation, generosity, and
joy. But it can also harbor insensitivity, greed, and
waste. After returning from India, I lived out of a
sense of *scarcity*. That is fine when it fosters
stewardship, simplicity, and frugality, but not when
it leads to grimness, intolerance, and separation
from one's fellows. Now I try to base my life on the
idea of *sufficiency* – there is just enough of
everything for everyone and not one bit more. ...

*Sufficiency. A good word. A satisfying feeling. How does one
create a wedding – so typically a luxury event – with a sense of
Sufficiency?*
We're well on our way, she realized.
She had shifted the emphasis from that typical focus on luxury
bridal couture and Rococo details. Together with her closest women
friends, Sahara, Jana and others, she was weaving her personal
creation.
The ceremony itself would be in a public gardens, with nature
surrounding them as they said their vows. The reception would be small,
intimate, loving, full of meaning. The food was to be homemade by friends,
each one folding her love into the dish. Sahara would bake the cake.
Tia and Ari asked that in lieu of gifts, donations be made to
Greenpeace, the Sierra Club or Esperanza's inner city youth project. A
friend of Sahara's was handcrafting Tia's dress, from cotton grown in
Cassandra and Sahara's fields. Tia's flowers would come from the
downtown community gardens run by Esperanza's project.
There really was little need for more.

... There is enough for generosity but not waste,
enough for security but not hoarding. Or, as Gandhi

said, enough for everyone's need, but not for everyone's greed.

(6.)

Tia stood in the lobby of the luxurious downtown restaurant. The client and his banker had just said their goodbyes. Tia handed the valet her ticket then reached for her briefcase.

Suddenly large beefy hands grabbed her shoulders from behind. She spun around.

Doug. Tia's heart pounded from the scare.

"Tia! How have you been doing? I haven't seen you around. Haven't seen you at the gym."

"I let my membership lapse."

"What have you been up to?"

"I've been busy enough."

"Business has been good for me. Let's go have a drink and catch up on things." His hand returned to her shoulder.

Doug's tailored business attire was of the latest refined fashionable cut and color, his Italian leather shoes uncreased and gleaming. A fat gold watch flashed on his wrist.

Removing his hand from her shoulder, Tia turned away. *When will this valet get here?*

"Doug, I've moved on to other things. And I'm seeing someone else. Actually, we're engaged."

Doug grabbed Tia's left hand, his thumb rolling over her ring finger – no ring.

"Nice try," he looked at her pointedly. "But I get the message."

He turned on his heel and disappeared toward the bar.

(7.)

Hestia Rae Chandler
And
Ari Ziven Damek
invite you to share in their joy
as they exchange marriage vows
and begin their new life together
Saturday, April 10th, 2004

(8.)

"Some deal, getting married all the way up in Santa Barbara, and leaving old friends out of it!" Edie sounded only a little bit miffed. "But then, it's not like we've exactly *met* this marvelous guy." She fingered the small framed photograph of Ari on Tia's desk.

"Well, he travels a lot ..."

How to explain this politely? Ari and Edie didn't even speak the same language.

Edie looked at Tia with eyebrows arched. "You haven't even asked what I've been up to, you've been so wrapped up in wedding bliss."

"So spill it."

"Jim is history, I have a new love! He's blue-eyed, and gloriously successful, you've met him a few times before ..." Edie stretched out across Tia's desk. "And the master bedroom at that big Marina house is pretty fine!"

"What!?"

"Yep, Doug!" Edie danced away. "I'm with Doug now! You were crazy, girl, to give him up. Enjoy your ho-hum life with Mr. No-name, I have the glamorous Mr. Doug Montgomery."

(9.)

"They've ratified Kyoto!" Ari called triumphantly as he flew in the apartment door one evening in late October. "The Russians have ratified Kyoto!" He swept Tia up in his arms and twirled her around the room.

"Oh Ari, how thrilling!"

"We hoped they might, they made promises, but now it's official! This is cause for celebration!" He rummaged through the cabinet, selected a bottle of wine and opened it.

"But the U.S. still hasn't ratified?"

"No, we haven't. But today is a huge message to U.S. policymakers: the world is going forward with this Treaty, with or without you. Your tantrums are no longer effective. All the blockading, all the U.S. positioning and heavy politicking has come to nothing.

He raised his glass in toast. "To international progress!" His dark eyes were alive with excitement.

"Now, the United States is on the outside, looking in. The inner circle has been formed by the countries who have ratified, and the U.S. has not made itself part of that number."

"But won't the treaty be ineffective without the U.S. on board?"

"The mere fact that enough countries have ratified – all the developed countries except the U.S. and Australia now – makes it clear that this is the direction of the future. U.S. businesses are listening. Even if policymakers refuse to support the Treaty, it is coming into vogue. Businesses are already creating their first Sustainability plans. Congress has several times considered bills which would impose Kyoto-style emissions limitations upon U.S. businesses – potential U.S. federal laws, even though we are not subject to any international commitment."

"I didn't know it had gone before Congress."

"There have been several versions over the years. The most recent attempt was almost a year ago, the McCain-Lieberman Climate Stewardship Act. That measure failed, but it was important because it was a bi-partisan effort, showing that U.S. legislators are getting closer to coming together around this issue."[20]

"So how will the Russian Ratification affect your Buenos Aires Conference?" She watched him tenderly over the rim of her glass.

"I'm sure it will generate a tremendous amount of excitement. Countries have made ratification announcements just prior to other Conferences and those were thrilling. But Russia's ratification is much more significant in that it's the last one needed to put the Treaty into effect, to create a binding international law.

"Beyond Buenos Aires, the next step comes in a mere eight years – 2012. That's when Kyoto expires, and by that time we need to hash out the terms for the treaty that succeeds Kyoto."

He said 'we.' Oh no, he's planning to participate in negotiations for 2012! More travel, even more time away! She stood silently spinning her ring – his mother's wedding ring – so new to her finger.

"Someday, we'll have an international treaty that includes Factor 10," he continued.

And will he be involved in that one too? She tried to cover by moving to the window to look out at the view.

"Isn't that a huge step? Factor 10? The U.S. hasn't even accepted the mild emissions limit of Kyoto," she said dully.

And I haven't quite accepted this perpetual traveling! Oh, please don't go, she thought, knowing all the while that he would and he had to.

We need him to, she tried to persuade herself.

"Factor 10 is about resource productivity; Kyoto is about emissions. In some ways similar, but emissions are much more specific, they're only a small subset of resource productivity. Resource productivity is how productively you are using your resources: how much waste – how much garbage, heat, ecological impact – are you generating as you use the resource for your desired purpose. Emissions are one part of that list of inefficiencies."

He began pacing the room in his excitement.

"Think back to Hawken's four kinds of capital. At present the U.S. is totally focused on making financial and manufactured capital productive: Get good rates of return on your money. Build more efficient factory machines. Run your employee team with cut-throat efficiency.

"But we are terribly inefficient when it comes to natural capital. As in, say, our use of petroleum, our water supply. We generate tremendous amounts of waste and pollution, which are resource inefficiencies.

"The Factor 10 concept challenges industrialized countries to increase their current resource productivity by a Factor of 10, to be ten times more productive in using our resources than we are today.[21] There's also an intermediate step, Factor 4, which is the same concept but a different magnitude.

"We all acknowledge that the Kyoto Protocol is a weakened, watered down document. But we must remember, it is our first step, it is our first major international treaty to address the environment. You always need an entry point, a 'foot in the door.'

"An international treaty built around Factor 10 terms would cause countries and their businesses to look at much more than just emissions. It would cause us to look at waste disposal, agricultural practices, natural resource use, and a myriad of other eco-efficient solutions." He came to join her at the window.

He's always thinking light years beyond the rest of us!

"Do you think the world is ready for this yet?" she asked.

"Kyoto was drafted in 1997. Today marks seven years it took to reach the status of a binding international treaty. No, the world's not ready for Factor 10 today. But striving to write it into a treaty will take years, and bringing that treaty into force ..."

"You're thinking in terms of decades!" Her amazement slipped out into speech.

He wrapped his arms around her tightly, pressing her body to his. "No, Tia, darling, I'm thinking in terms of generations."

"The world needs thinkers like you on that team," she whispered.

She felt his deep sigh of contentment, he was holding her that tightly. He kissed her hair, then down the long line of her neck. She purred softly. He lead her to their bedroom, where he slowly stripped her of her clothing, one piece at a time, leaving trails of kisses as her body was revealed.

(10.)

"How was Buenos Aires?" Their little car zipped along the cloverleaf exiting the airport.

"More of the same." Ari grimaced.

"There was next to nothing about it on the news." Tia said quietly.

"I could have guessed." The disgust was thick in his voice. "Imagine, lack of news coverage in the U.S., particularly when this Conference follows so closely on the heels of the Russian ratification, plus lack of willingness in the U.S. to negotiate the major issues that divide developed and undeveloped nations. Hey, where are you going, you missed the turn. Home's that way."

"There's something I want to do on the way home," she smiled mysteriously as she turned off the main highway onto the fast double-lane boulevard that cut across the Ballona Wetlands.

Amid the non-native iceplant invading the reeds alongside the road, fast food drink cups floated. A lone heron glided overhead. SUVs in macabre array sped by them: Expedition, Tahoe, Yukon.

Each model year they get bigger.

"Do you think they'll ever get it?" she asked.

"I hope so." It wasn't clear that he was speaking of the same thing but the sentiment still applied.

Even the model names are a mockery.

An Excursion whizzed by with a bumper sticker reading 'Save Ballona.' She suddenly felt quite ill.

We rally to save a small patch of degraded land, a rare wildflower, a single species, but we can't manage to rally to prevent global warming. The heating of the planet will kill those birds and butterflies too! The nausea was now much stronger. She drew her hand across her face.

"Are you okay?"

Tia nodded as she maneuvered the car into a parking space on a narrow street near the beach.

"Come on, we're going for a walk." She smiled bravely.

"This is down near that breakwater ..."

"Yup." She linked her hand with his.

In the bright winter sunshine they walked out onto the breakwater.

"It was a tough week," Ari continued. "The U.S. and Saudi Arabian delegations worked side by side, basically throwing a wrench in the negotiations wherever possible. The highlight of it all, if you can call it that, was when the Saudis demanded compensation for lost revenues as the world moves away from oil consumption. Isn't that the ultimate?" His voice trembled in fury.

She reached her destination and stopped, gripping his arm to halt his wild pace.

He looked down at her, then glanced around at the scenery. "I remember this path, we were right here on one of our first dates." He gathered her into his arms and kissed her the way he had them.

She took his hand and placed it across her belly. "Ari, we're going to have a baby."

"Uh, wow ..." His eyes were wide, his face devoid of any smile. "I mean, that's great."

"Ari, what's the matter? You're not happy? We were trying ..."

He sighed deeply, running his hand through his hair. "Tia, it's wonderful. It's ... aw, shit." He wrapped her in an enormous bear hug. "Of course I'm thrilled. I just have to get used to the idea. And ..."

"And? What, Ari?"

"What kind of life will this child have? We've gotten nowhere on implementation, nowhere on temperature stabilization, the environment's a mess, but, oh wow, a child! Our child! Oh Tia, this is wonderful!" This time she could hear the smile in his voice.

"This is our Russian Ratification baby," she smiled, referring to that particular night.

"Kyoto. We'll call the baby Kyoto!" He laughed in delight, squeezing her again.

She relaxed into his strong arms, thinking of his efforts in Buenos Aires. Her heart filled with long ago words: '... *saving the earth ... so that there's a planet left when it's time to turn it over to our children and grandchildren.'*

What sort of a world will you face, my little one?

(11.)

"Have you heard, General Motors is crushing all the EV1 electric cars they produced?" Steve flopped into the armchair in the Damek's apartment. "This was the first truly clean car manufactured by a U.S. automaker."

"My mom camped out at a protest at the GM plant in Burbank." Still feeling a bit green in mid-pregnancy, Tia curled beside Ari on the couch. "GM took all the EV1's back from the public and is systematically destroying them."

"Why would they do that?" Ari asked. "Any electric car technology beats the fossil fuel driven models they're producing now."

"That's precisely it. GM won't give a decent reason," Steve responded. "Most of the vehicles were leased to the public. At the expiration of the leases GM simply took them back."

"My mom swears the silence on motive, together with the fact they're destroying what could otherwise become a collector's item, points to a Big Conspiracy," Tia smirked.

"Cassandra might have a point there," Steve replied. "The official reason GM gives is that the production run was so small – 1,000 vehicles – that they don't have parts available and that's a safety issue. I don't buy it. There are plenty of fine collector cars that are made in small batches and no one's out crushing those. The Bugatti Veyron is made in production runs of 300. No one's crushing small-run Ferraris or Alpha Romeos.

"There's been no mention of mechanical difficulties nor technical issues still needing to be worked out. The users loved the vehicles. It's not about liability either, since people have tried to buy the remaining EV1's from GM, but GM has refused, even when offered legal releases from warranty or liability.

"GM claims their hybrids and hydrogen-powered fuel cell models will replace the EV1, but those models remain linked to the oil industry, whereas the EV1 had the potential to be fully independent of oil. I think that's what it all boils down to: the ties to the oil industry. The EV1 was a truly viable solution to get us off oil."[22]

(12.)

Edie flounced into Tia's office, slammed her hands onto the desk atop all the papers, narrowly missing the coffee mug. She leaned over, her broad grin inches from Tia's nose. "Notice anything different?"

"New lipstick?"

"No, my hands, silly!"

A huge diamond, well over a carat, gleamed on Edie's hand. Edie danced around the room, admiring it, the smile never leaving her face.

"Wow, so you and Doug are getting married."

"The wedding's going to be really big: wedding party of ten, flowers, dresses, limousine, ballroom and band, all the finery. We'll be registered at Gearys of course. Guest list from here to Tuesday. But sorry, Tia, you're not on it." Edie spun out of the office.

(13.)

The rainy season of 2004-5 came as a surprise to most, the second rainiest in LA's recorded history. A tornado touched down in Ladera Heights, ripping the roof from one house and damaging several others. The heavy rains on city hardscapes flooded streets and filled stormdrains, washing out to the ocean, sweeping with them toxic pollutants from roadways. The city had no ability to capture any of the water bounty into aqueducts or water storage facilities.

That winter season, the Pacific Northwest suffered from record high temperatures, receiving less than a third of their typical snowpack. Farmers in Arizona were forced to sell their cattle when drought-stricken landscapes yielded insufficient grass. It was the sixth year of drought in the Northern Rockies and high plains. Weather monitoring systems revealed severe conditions across the northwestern quarter of the continental United States.

Yet climate scientists considered 2005 to be only a "mild" El Niño year.

The following summer a Class 5 hurricane – the largest possible on storm severity indexes – hit New Orleans. Thousands lost their lives. Massive portions of the city were flooded. Damage in the Gulf states was beyond comprehension. The previous year an unprecedented four hurricanes had hit the Florida area. And studies by National Oceanic and Atmospheric Administration scientists predicted that the strongest hurricanes in current times would be surpassed by even stronger storms as global temperatures increased in the decades to come.

(14.)

"Carl Farren, line four," the secretary announced over the intercom.

Tia looked up from the client spreadsheet in surprise. Carl hadn't called her in ages.

"Tia, it's Carl." He sounded hushed, even conspirational.

"What's up?" Her mind drifted back to the spreadsheet.

"I don't know how to say this, but I want to make sure you're all right. The Prechter waves – they're cresting – the market's going to crash."

An icy chill washed over her. It was hard to hear such doomsday news confirmed.

"Yes, Carl, I've been watching." She paused. "Like you taught me. Thanks."

"You've seen it? The third wave down?"

"Yes, I've been charting it."

"Have you pulled out?"

"Maybe a bit early. I pulled our stuff out two weeks ago."

"Yeah, me too. Uh, I've been ... wanting to call you."

"Thanks for thinking of us, Carl."

Tia clicked the connection, her hand still resting on the phone. *Yes, we've pulled out, but that is small comfort.*

She knew from the Prechter wave calculations that the drop would be extreme. She couldn't even imagine what collateral impact the crash might have in other areas of the economy. She felt as if they sat at the crest of the roller coaster, facing the way down. *It's still scary, it still drops the pit of your stomach, even if you can see the tracks.*

(15.)

The Legacy LA meeting the week after the market crash, like most gatherings at that time, was solemn. People huddled in small groups before the lecture, comparing notes.

Carl walked around with a smug little smile lingering at the corner of his mouth. So many in the group had doubted his forecasts.

Ben had listened to Carl. Ben didn't mind sharing that he had pulled his personal savings out of the market with plenty of time, although he had little ability to control his retirement account which was held by the city and was likely lost.

Jana was oblivious to most of the market discussions. It was clear that she and Esperanza gave the market little thought, they weren't involved.

Steve looked gravely concerned. Although he stated he had lost nothing in the crash, his ongoing business as a builder was dependent upon the affluence of others.

"Lots of people are panicking." Ari preferred the overview, without revealing his own story. "Most have lost their life savings. All the retirement benefits the baby boomers counted on aren't worth diddly. Firms are closing too. Luckily, the banks are holding fast, it looks like the protections created in the 1930's are working so far. Either way, it's quite a different world we're facing. Like 1929."

Matthew was chalky and staring. When his story began to trickle out, the group quieted and listened.

"One of my clients shot himself this morning. I can't believe it. He had everything tied up in the stock market, fully leveraged. He just couldn't face the losses. He ended his life instead." Matthew shook his head slowly at the horror of it.

"What about you? How did you fare?" someone asked.

"It's bad, really bad. I've been really hard hit. My 401k retirement is wiped out, all my savings are gone, my kid's college fund too. I wasn't in as deep as some, I guess it could have been worse. I'm not totally upside down yet, but I'm going to have to unload my house really quickly. I can't cope with that mortgage when I have no resources. Cancelled the leases on the Beemer and the Mercedes this morning. I pray that I'll keep my job so that my family can eat."

He looked so odd standing there in his finely tailored suit with all the fancy accessories, admitting he was virtually penniless.

"I never thought ... I never thought this could happen. Carl's theories were just too out-there. No one else was pulling out, in fact people were trying to figure out how to put more in! So I stayed in with the others."

A mindless follower, caught in the midst of the pack, following one behind the other, last week dashing over a cliff.

Tia thought about the phone call from Carl. How fortunate they were that Carl had taught them to read the markets. So many people had lost in this crash. She heaved a huge sigh. Despite the finality with which Matthew seemed to be taking it, the crash didn't seem to be over yet, just resting on the way down.

I was a follower too, not all that long ago. Somehow I pulled myself out of that mentality.

'Thinkers. It's going to take thinkers and doers to solve the problems we face.'

Her mind turned from stock market crashes to ecological nightmares. *Will we go over the cliff on that one too?*

(16.)

Jana invited herself to the apartment for dinner, now a frequent occurrence. Today she brought a rich vegetarian chili to share, bright with the year's first peppers.

Midmeal, Ari put his fork down. "Ladies, I've decided to sell the Venice house."

Jana gasped. Ari ignored her.

"I've been talking with Carl, and I suspect the real estate market will fall apart sometime soon. I think I'll pull out of it for a while.

"Meanwhile, I've been looking at places. This one-bedroom apartment of Tia's just won't work anymore once the baby begins to grow.

"There's a section in Santa Monica where we could rent a little duplex." He looked at Tia. "We could live in one place and perhaps Jana would share the other with a roommate. We could still have the community atmosphere of the Venice place. Tia, that way Jana would be nearby to help you with the baby, when I'm traveling.

"The place I'm thinking of — you two creative green thumbs will have quite a fun time redoing the garden." Ari smiled at them with deep affection.

～

The building turned out to be a triplex under remodeling, totally vacant. To Tia and Jana's delight, Ari cut a deal with the owner and the landscaping was left unfinished. Jana decided to take her unit alone, and Matthew Goodman and his family agreed to take the remaining unit.

The Goodman family met them at the triplex. The building was a one-story, situated on a large lot, the two-bedroom units to left and right, with a smaller unit set back in-between. The property was bordered by a low wooden fence.

"I talked the owner into selecting energy efficient appliances and hot water heaters," Ari said to Matthew. "I wish I could persuade the guy to try solar."

"Did you have solar on your house?" Matthew asked.

"The Venice place? A limited array, experimental really. Some day I'll have a place we'll really do up right!"

Mark Goodman was an active three year old, and delighted in running circles around the construction debris.

"Do you think he'll stay out of the garden?" Tia asked Jana in undertone.

"Do you think that one will?" Jana laughed and pointed to Tia's belly, well rounded now at six months pregnant.

Shannon Goodman was rather short and almost plump, with short curly sandy-colored hair. Her pregnancy, a month behind Tia's, was just becoming obvious. From the beginning she declared herself to be no gardener, but assured them she'd more than make up for it as a cook. Jana immediately set out to work drawing up plans for the garden.

"Open space for the children to romp, fruit trees, and of course vegetables. I wish I could include chickens, but that might be a bit over the top!" Jana chuckled at her own joke. "I thought about a food forest, but I'll settle for fruit trees with guilds beneath."

"I'm afraid you'll have to translate that for me," sighed Shannon.

Tia explained, since Jana had bounded back to her plans. "In a forest, you'd find plants growing at several layers: a canopy of tall trees, shrubbery layers, and understory layers. You might even have vines running through the trees. A food forest tries to copy this layering system using food-bearing plants: fruit trees, grapevines, vegetables, herbs, for example.

"Guilds are groups of plants that benefit each other. Perhaps they concentrate soil nutrients for each other, or attract beneficial insects like pollinators. By planting them together, you maximize these benefits for the better health of your crops without needing to resort to chemicals.[23]

"I think what Jana's trying to do is to replicate what happens within an ecosystem – each element of the system supports the others in some way. Guilds and food forests are both ways to create a more balanced, more sustainable cycle that yields food for humans."

(17.)

When Shannon's family arrived, Jana and Tia went over to help her unpack.

"I don't even know where to begin," Shannon sighed deeply as she opened and closed empty cupboards surveying the layout. "We're coming out of a five-bedroom house. We have way too much stuff for a two-bedroom apartment.

"Mark, is that a good place to climb?" Shannon called aside to a grinning Mark, who clambered down from the mountain of boxes and ran outside.

"I meant to go through it, pare it down some," Shannon said, gesturing at the vast numbers of boxes, "but there wasn't time with the house sale, I've been too tired with my pregnancy, and, well, it was just too hard to do. I can't let go of it, it's like these things are all we have, all we'll ever have now, after all that's happened!"

Shannon began to cry softly. "It's so hard. I always thought life would be like some great crescendo where you start off small, poor, learning. You get your feet on the ground, get established, and then things get better and better.

"This is all so backwards, what has happened to us – it's like we've jumped back to the starting place again when we're supposed to be in the middle and climbing. Bingo – here we are back at this earlier point, but saddled with the kids and the responsibilities and the expectations of that middle point." She wiped her tears. "Sorry about that little outburst, I just feel so mixed up these days." Shannon's voice still trembled.

"It sounds terribly hard," Jana said consolingly. "I never gave it much thought. I've never had much material Stuff – never wanted it bad enough to pursue it, I guess. But it must really be hard to want it, strive for it, get it, and then lose it."

"The funny thing is," Shannon said reflectively, "I never really craved it, it just came our way out of Matthew's success. And then, well, you get used to having it." Shannon opened a box. "We might as well get started."

Jana and Shannon worked in the kitchen while Tia unpacked books nearby.

"Fascinating titles you have here: *Nourishing Traditions, Your Healthy Child,* herbal remedies ..." Tia poured through them as she filled the bookshelves.

"Oh, if you see anything you like you're welcome to borrow it. A lot of them are things I discovered when Mark was born. I began learning how the preservatives and the agricultural toxins in our food affect children in particular because children are sensitive and small in size. But in my reading I realized those things aren't good for any of us! So I started buying organic and biodynamic and changed my cooking style to eliminate processed foods.

"More recently I realized that our mainstream medical system is oriented towards treating symptoms using medications and surgery. I've been learning about nutrition and herbs and ways to treat the whole body rather than just the symptoms. I've been working to build up my family's health so that we rarely need to resort to MD's. It's another form of Sustainability – sustaining one's health."[24]

"Wow, I'm impressed," Tia said. "How did you do all this?"

"First, I learned. I read a lot. I would find one book that seemed to make solid points, and then read books referred to by that author. Once I began to learn, I started putting it into practice, little by little. I'd try a new recipe here, a new technique there. Over time I've been building up a repertoire of recipes, techniques, remedies. It doesn't happen overnight, I've been at it for several years – well, since Mark's been with us. It's the kind of thing where you're never 'done,' the process is always unfolding.

"And now – a garden! I'm delighted because I don't know anything about growing plants. I always bought my produce and herbs.

The idea of cooking produce that's this fresh out of the garden – wow! I just can't wait."[25]

(18.)

"We're closing more than half our offices," Mr. Warner continued, "this entire location. With the economy, clients have cut way back, and they've cut back on the services ..."

Tia heard very little of what he was saying. The words washed over her; she felt like she was in a small capsule of numbness, immobile, the sea of change cresting and swirling over her. She rose to her feet. She hardly felt Mr. Warner's handshake, her body going mechanically through the long-cultivated motions of good manners upon departure. His parting words didn't even register.

She made it down the hall to her office, closed the door and leaned against it. *Almost five years. Over. Done. Just like that.* Rational thought wasn't processing amid these swirling currents of strangeness. The door felt solid behind her and she stretched out to press more fully against it. Consciousness was returning.

Her phone rang with an irritating buzz. She merely stared at the accompanying flashing red button. *How odd that the buzzing sound and flashing light are out of sync*, she thought. She fixated on the pulse of that tiny red light. *Out of sync, out of sync, I have become out of sync with this lifestyle. It's been in process for a very long time. And now it is final, it has come to an end.* The heartbeat of the little red light stopped.

She could hear others in the office suite, moving about their day. *They don't know yet.* Tia wondered how Edie would take the layoff.

In response to her prolonged stillness, the baby began kicking. She put a hand on her belly to feel her little one. She sighed deeply and moved away from the door. *Perhaps it is all just as well, but that doesn't make it any easier.*

She moved to her desk and pulled out her purse. The end of the month, Mr. Warner had said. *Time enough to deal with all this.* She looked around the small office. Her eyes stopped on the picture of Ari. She picked it up and slipped it into her purse. Somehow it had never really belonged here, he had never really belonged here.

And there was the crux of it. She moved to the window and looked out at the view. The never-changing ficus trees were visible off to one side. Their artificial greenness, the manicured lawn, the blue light fluorescent, the lifeless air from the air conditioning, she felt the flatness of it all.

She hugged her purse to her, sensing Ari's photo inside. A warmth came over her, a sense of fullness at the life she lead outside this dead office: Ari, their life together, Jana, Shannon, Steve, Legacy LA, the gardens at the triplex just taking root, and now, the baby. Growing things. Sunshine, and rain, and seasons. Contrasts. A slight smile graced her face.

She had a sense of being on the edge of a great divide. It had begun small, but in these few short years, it had deepened and broadened within her heart. A hairline fissure, now become the Grand Canyon. No longer would she have to do a daily broad-jump across it to come into this deadened atmosphere.

She breathed deeply. *Everything happens for a reason.* The baby began stirring again. *My life will become more whole without this job, integral.*

She stood taller now, a weight lifted from her shoulders. She turned to the door, and left the office.

CHAPTER 5:

COMMITTED

2005-2011

Ari was stretched out on the sofa, with four week old Annis sound asleep, a tiny bundle on his chest. "Isn't she wonderful? I take so much delight in just being with her, simply, like this. And yet ...

"Tia, times are changing. Since the U.S. will likely go to the Montreal Conference this December in observer-only status, there's not much I can accomplish as a part of the U.S. team. We may even be barred from participation in some of the side sessions." He sighed deeply. "It pains me greatly to have to do this, but it is not in my nature to just sit on the sidelines. I need to go where I can accomplish something real. Tia, I've been entertaining offers from other countries to go as consultant for their teams of delegates."

Tia gasped but Ari continued, grimly. "A brain-drain is happening, I'm not the only one. All the prime thinkers, the best minds, are jumping ship from the U.S. team. It's as if, with the current U.S. anti-environment political mindset, together with the U.S. refusal to budge even after last November's Russian ratification put the Protocol in force, the deep thinkers have given up on U.S. ratification.

"Following Buenos Aires, the Kyoto countries are proceeding forward. The world is determined to make progress, regardless of whether the U.S. decides to come on board. Basically the world is not going to be swayed by U.S. bullying and blockading.

"So, I've decided to leave the U.S. delegation. It's really hard to do this, it feels like an abandonment of my country. In part I worry that without our efforts, the efforts of the erstwhile U.S. team, ratification may never come about in this country. But on the other hand the clock keeps ticking. 2040 is the date, calculated by the Intergovernmental Panel on Climate Change, by which we must succeed in reducing the volume of emissions. Otherwise we stand little chance of stabilizing planetary temperature increases.[26]

"I feel a duty to a larger entity than my country. I feel a duty to the world, to the children of the world." He stroked sleeping Annis' tiny head. "Having this little one here ... every time I hold her it's a reminder. There is no time to waste on positioning and blaming. We must get on with operations now. We must get implementation well under way.

"And after that, after this Conference ... I'd like to join the team that is forming to create the 2012 treaty, the treaty that will succeed the Kyoto Protocol. I've said before that Kyoto is merely an opening play. Everyone on board is striving to beat the targets, to reduce emissions as much as possible, not stopping at the required level. I think the 2012 agreement will really be something to behold. And I want to be part of it."

He looked at Tia solemnly with those deep dark intense eyes. "I know what this means to you and to Annis. She'll be seven before that 2012 treaty is written, and I may be absent for much of her growing." He drew his hand across his face, sighing deeply.

Tears stung Tia's eyes.

Gone!? For years into the future? For years as our daughter grows? This isn't how life's supposed to go! This isn't how I thought it would be!

Oh, Ari, I know you're the traveler, you always have been. I know your work takes you around the globe. It always has. But that knowledge doesn't help the heartache!

Oh, how I thought it'd be different – some sort of Norman Rockwell cottage I suppose, rosy cheeked children gathered round, you and me together.

The tears began to flow in earnest now.

But that doesn't fit with who you are, who we are. She sobbed. *That dream doesn't fit with this world around us, this world in crisis, this world in desperate need of big changes. Consciousness shifts, like you're trying to bring about, my darling.*

"Consciousness shifts ... mean letting go of some big dreams! It's too big. I can't do it!" She fell to her knees at his side, and sobbed on his shoulder alongside Annis. "The cost of being a change agent of this magnitude is so impossibly high!"

When her tears had quieted, he gently turned her face to his and kissed her tenderly. "Tia, darling, the cost is high, but the payoff is even higher. For her," he patted Annis' fat cloth diaper, "and for her grandchildren."

(2.)

The faces of the Westside affluent communities changed, discretely. Following the market crash, certain individuals simply "moved away" from the better neighborhoods. There were few buyers and plenty of sellers. In the changeover of ownership, real estate values plateaued and began slipping.

The trickle down of corporate upset became evident as overextended chain stores made sweeping decisions to close locations. WalMart, which had cast aside generations of small businesses in its push for expansion, now simply pulled out of many communities, citing "corporate consolidation." In an effort to remain competitive, Costco, Target and other corporate giants were forced to do the same. Faded "for lease" signs, shabby paint, and boarded windows became a common sight around town.

People had to buy their food and necessaries somewhere, thus the few locally owned independent businesses which had survived the WalMart invasions found their fortunes turned. With the dissolution of the chain branches, city dwellers turned inward, to their neighborhoods, to farmers' markets, family-run corner stores, resale shops and home businesses for their survival supplies. Because these independents had flexibility with regards to purchasing – they weren't locked into corporate brand names – goods were adequately supplied, even though the specific brand names shifted frequently.

Small businesses which had previously existed with the purpose of being "alternative" or "green" had never been able to plug into the big-time corporate world and now found they were only marginally affected by its crumbling. As the buyers turned to small locally owned businesses, these green businesses similarly experienced increased volume.

Buyers too felt the pinch, as jobs became more precious and the effects of corporate downsizing began to be felt. Consumers were more careful with their dollars. They bought less, and bought wiser. Wild, careless consumerism was changing.

(3.)

The day before Ari's departure for Europe, Tia and Ari took a walk along the channel path, six month old Annis babbling happily in the backpack frame on Ari's shoulders.

Tia eyed the father-daughter pair with affection. "What was your father like? You rarely talk about him."

"He was devoted, a hard worker. He was an engineer for Standard Oil. Worked on new products, the ground work for what became today's alternative fuels. I wanted to be just like him. I went to college, and got a job at Exxon to follow in his footsteps."

"You worked for Exxon?"

He smirked. "For a short while. I got myself fired."

She looked at him in amazement.

"In the aftermath of the Exxon Valdez, I made a few speeches. I wasn't exactly discrete."

"I can imagine!" She laughed.

"It wasn't funny then. My dad was furious. How was I going to build a career? I was unemployed so I started back to school, and then my dad had his stroke. He was bedridden, helpless, for seven months before he died. Couldn't talk, couldn't feed himself. Hideous." He shivered. "He was such a proud man, so able. 'Heal the world,' he'd tell us, that was our duty in life.

"I learned about the environmental issues while doing my post-grad work. He and I would debate until late at night." He shook his head. "I was very hard on him for working for the oil companies. He defended it, saying cheaper power made a better life possible for people. Better life? With all the toxins and pollutants I was learning about? And then he was struck down, trapped in that useless body, unable to contribute to society. I could see it in his eyes, it was torture for him. For both of us.

"When he died it was a very dark time for us. Jana ... Mom was useless to stop her." He paused, massaging his hand, pressing his crippled finger as if he could straighten it, staring out at the sea.

"Does it hurt?" she gestured to his hand.

"She was really hurt. I took her home, got an apartment for the two of us so I could keep an eye on her. Got her a job, back on her feet."

"You mean your mom?"

He glanced at her. "No, Jana. Look, I don't want to talk about this."

He stared out over the sea, his face dark and troubled, still massaging that hand. Annis had fallen asleep in the backpack, slumped sideways, drooling over the frame, the picture of vulnerability.

(4.)

Los Angeles was technically a desert. In normal years rain fell in storms between the months of November and March; the rest of the year, not a drop of rain fell for seven months straight. In the city's abundant gardens and landscapes, every bit of green foliage visible from late May through early November was irrigated. Daily irrigation was necessary in the case of lawn grasses, whereas non-native flowers and shrubs might be watered weekly.

Most of this irrigation was done with sprinklers, which cast the misted water into the breeze, losing much of it to evaporation or to waste upon the sidewalks and streets. And virtually all of this irrigation was done with fresh potable water; only the occasional progressive city building used reclaimed water at some recently renovated site. Fresh potable water for the city of Los Angeles came from hundreds of miles away – from the eastern Sierra Nevada Mountains via the Owens River Valley, and from the Colorado River.

(5.)

Sunshine brought out the scent of the dusty lavenders and peppery nasturtiums as Tia and Steve sat in the shade of the orange tree. The heat felt like summer temperatures – it was hard to believe the calendar read April.

Eight month old Annis reached for a snail, as Tia's quick fingers pried a pebble from Peter's grasp. Four year old Mark prowled the garden border looking for pillbugs, releasing his finds to crawl on Steve's knee, while Steve pounded nails into a stool he was crafting for Mark.

"Tia, I need a partner," Steve began. "Ari and I used to work together to run Legacy LA. Since he's been overseas, I've been scrapping by on my own. But with my own travel schedule to support Sustainability groups in other cities, well, the group deserves better than a half a leader. If you would partner me, I know that Ari's influence would still be felt in the group."

Ari had forecast this, so Tia was ready with her answer. "Sure Steve, I'm with you. How can I help?"

Steve smiled his gratitude. "Well, one thing that is becoming an issue is our meeting space, we're quickly outgrowing it. Oddly enough, it seems as though, despite unemployment, people are looking for places to volunteer and contribute. We're getting more new members with every meeting."

"It makes sense," Tia said. "So many of our Sustainability ideas are skills, conservation techniques, or a shift in choices: they don't necessarily require significant spending."

Steve reached for another nail. "The other thing to tackle is our meeting topics. "For the next meeting, I've lined up a speaker from Oasis Systems, about using greywater.[27] I had thought I'd include a representative from the City of El Segundo, because I learned they use reclaimed water to irrigate their median landscaping. But when I researched a little deeper I found that El Segundo works with the West Basin Municipal Water District out of Carson. That should be an entire meeting's topic on its own. West Basin efforts include a pilot desalinization project at the El Segundo Power Plant, and several reclaimed water projects."

Mark cruised by, to release three more pillbugs upon Steve's knee. Steve poked at them in amusement, chasing them down the leg of his jeans.

"One of these days I'd like to get TreePeople back in here. We haven't had them speak since they did those sustainability-focused Demonstration Houses under their T.R.E.E.S. program. Quite inspiring, a lot like what I do … that is, when I have work." His jaw tensed.

"Andy Lipkis and TreePeople have been such a major force for decades, in restoring LA's urban forest." Tia tried to fill the sudden silence. "Steve, I have a pretty radical idea for a meeting..."

"You forget what we're doing here. Legacy LA's pretty radical by definition."

"What about a session on the power of Vision? Steven Covey presented it pretty well in his book *First Things First*."

"Wow, what an idea! Who could we get to lead it? I think it'd be best if it were someone who knows our group."

"I know who should lead it."

Tia and Steve looked at each other. "Ari," they said together.

"Not Ari." A voice came from the garden bed. Evidently Jana had been listening to the entire discussion. Standing up and brushing the dirt from her hands, she addressed Tia.

"You and Ari."

"Me?"

"My brother might be pretty good at drafting a vision, and he'd be great at guiding this group to forming one. But you, you're the one who's great at holding a vision, believing in it, making it come alive."

"Whatever do you mean? I haven't done anything except raising babies, since the website ..."

"Which now runs how many dozen pages?" Jana debated.

"Really all I've done is support Ari and you guys," Tia protested.

"By being our sounding board..." Steve put in.

"Our shoulder to cry on ..." Jana added.

"... and reminding us why we're doing this ..."

"...believing it's possible ..."

"...even when we've left off believing in ourselves."

Little Annis began to whimper. Slipping Annis into the baby sling to nurse her, Tia carried Peter over to Shannon's.[28]

As Tia crossed back to her own unit, she could see Steve still talking with Jana. Jana was poised to run from him at any moment.

(6.)

In the early days, when Ari was working with the U.S. delegation, while his travel schedule had been considerable, there had at least been times when he would be home in LA. Now that he was affiliated with the EU, he was absent far more than he was home. His schedule was particularly grueling in that he was assigned to a liaison team between the EU and other international delegations. Thus he spent the better part of his time globe-hopping, spending a scant week here or there.

"I'm sorry I woke you again, but I won't have time later to talk. It's incredibly exhausting," Ari admitted on the international cell to Tia. "No sooner do I land and adjust to a time zone, have a few meetings, then I'm off to the next place.

"What a life: working to put in place a greenhouse gas emissions treaty, but spending half my time on these airplanes which are horrific in their emissions.[29] A very dark irony. It really eats at me."

"I'm sorry it's so exhausting for you. We miss you very much." She longed to hug him. "Here's something that might cheer you. Congressman Rafferty has spoken out again against Kyoto, and if you read between the lines it sounds like he wants to keep the U.S. out of any post-2012 agreement as well ..."

"This is supposed to cheer me?" he broke in.

"Wait, let me finish. An interesting thing is happening. You told me that these environmental issues must be solved by both top-down legislation and grassroots effort – Kyoto is top-down for most countries of the world, but here in the U.S. it's looking more and more like it will be a grassroots achievement."

"Well, all the top-down solutions on greenhouse gasses in the U.S. certainly haven't come to fruition. Our short-sighted policymakers pulled out of the international treaty. The Lieberman-McCain Act was defeated at the federal level. I did hear some individual states are getting in the act." Ari sounded so weary of the U.S. scene.

"Then you know about the Regional Greenhouse Gas Initiative? The Northeast and mid-Atlantic states have come together, nine of them. Three more are close to being on board. Nine others have some form of greenhouse gas legislation or have action plans."[30]

"Wait a second, where are you getting this?"

"I've been making a list," Tia laughed, "specifically to tell you about it."

"You nutcase, I love you."

Tia could hear his grin.

"That's twenty states I've found – nearly half – have some sort of concrete commitment to reducing greenhouse gas emissions.

"At yet another layer down, the Mayor of Seattle began a campaign at the city level. At this point he's completely surpassed his stated goal of 140 cities committed to the 'intent and spirit of Kyoto,' as he calls it.[31] So, Ari, the Kyoto Protocol is happening in the U.S., it's just happening a little differently."

"But the cities effort isn't actual legislation. And the California law is being contested in court by the Alliance of Automobile Manufacturers." Ari seemed determined to see the glass as half-empty.

"Ari, it's peoples' declarations, it's the peoples' mandate. The intent of it will filter up the political food chain, I'm sure of it. The message will get through."

"I sure hope you're right."

(7.)

Tia sat on the edge of her bed gathering ice blocks and washcloths from the bedcovers, tucking the blankets around the tiny sleeping form. Two year old Annis gave an occasional sob as she slept. Tia bent to hug her, sending reassurances into that tiny subconscious. She smoothed Annis' damp dark hair back from the nasty wound on her forehead. It was a surface wound, more brushburn than cut, but the size of the swelling was enough to make a mother's heart stop.

It had been a freak playground accident. Cement block wall, loose sand on concrete, slick soled children's shoes, Annis running with Mark and Peter. It had all happened so fast, Tia wasn't sure what actually happened. The blood had been terrifying; it made the injury seem far worse than it turned out to be.

Tia felt the aching chill that follows when adrenaline action is done. A deep breath, and then the tears came. Tears of relief that Annis would be all right, everything was now fine. Tears for her own unrealized fears in those moments of panic. Tears free to flow now, for fears unexpressed then ... *a head injury ... Annis could have ...* Tia didn't even dare name the horrors.

Annis was sleeping soundly now as Tia bent to grasp her tiny hand. *Oh Ari, you are so far away for times like these.* Trembling, Tia ached for his supportive hugs even as she resented the fact that she'd had to go it alone.

It's all left to me.

Suddenly the floodgates were opened.

How dare you!? You've dumped it all on my shoulders!

You're off tilting windmills in all these foreign places leaving me to cope with the details, leaving me to clean up all the garbage of our joint life. You flit off on your jet planes without a care in the world but your so-important Treaty!

What about us? It's not just those damned schoolchildren, we're your family. We need you too!

She cried as if her heart would break from it all – the cooped up anger, the strain of the worry, the guilt she felt at resenting him.

I'm being so selfish. He's not tilting windmills, it's not a ridiculous fight! It's my fight too. I believe in it, it's for all of us.

But the logical response did little to salve the pain of his absence.

It's so hard to remain supportive!

Annis sighed in her sleep and rolled over. Tia tucked her in again.

Life is so fragile, she thought, stroking Annis' precious little cheek. *There are so many dangers, so many opportunities for peril. It's much harder to keep something alive than to kill it.*

She thought of Ari's battle for the earth's ecosystems. *It's much harder to keep the planet alive than to kill it.*

(8.)

To: adamek@LAglobalsolutions.net
Ari – We, each of the tenants, have been served with notification that the bank has foreclosed on the landlord. Thus, our little complex here may soon slip out of our grasp. I'm not sure what to do, whether to look for a new place. Annis says 'Hi' to Daddy – .wav sound file attached. All my love, Tia

To: tdamek@LAglobalsolutions.net
Tia – I really believe we're in the best of all possible worlds on this foreclosure issue. The bank won't kick us out so long as we continue paying our rent. With the real estate values plunging, and so much for sale on the market, I doubt they'll find a buyer for their loan amount anytime in the near future. Recall, this owner had refinanced the

property at maximum value in order to do the remodel before we moved in. So, sit tight, it's going to be a wild ride. Manilla is lonely, I miss you and Annis very much. Thank you for the recording of her laughter, I will treasure it as I travel. Hugs and kisses to all. A.

(9.)

The room was packed. Rather than the usual verbal call for organization, at the appropriate hour Ari stood at elegant attention, in command of the room. The crowd settled and quieted. He chose a low, even tone for this presentation, a tone that wrapped the room and drew the audience closer.

"We're going to do something a little different at tonight's meeting.

"Many of you have children. Others of you hope to have children. Some of you already have grandkids. Tonight I invite you to think out to the adulthood of these special young people in your lives, out to the point at which your sons, daughters, nieces, nephews are having children of their own. Think about the life that next generation of children will lead.

"What will life in LA be like? What are your most optimistic hopes? In your personal area of specialty, what new developments do you hope will become mainstream?

"Tonight we're going to capture this dream. We're going to bring it alive in our collective imagination, share it with others, and capture some aspects of it on paper.

"Let's journey forward to the city of LA, at the half-way point in this century, 2050.

"What is life like? What does it feel like? What things are part of the everyday? What problems have been solved?" Ari began drawing responses from the crowd. Tia and Jana wrote them on flip charts.

No freeway traffic ...workable mass transit ... no litter ... greywater systems ... no more homeless ... food for everyone ... meaningful employment for all ... peace in the inner city ...

Tia stepped in. "What are your fears? Let's get these up here. Or rather, state your fear's opposite, in terms of a positive outcome."

... no nuclear threats ... no gangs ... no global warming ...

"We're getting quite a list up here," Ari segued as the responses tapered off. "Which of these things up here are essential? Which items fall into an 'it would be nice' category? We want to sort out the less important aspects. We're clarifying the core of our dream, and we'll trust that the details will fall into line however they're meant to be. We also need to proofread for items that aren't fully within our power to change.

"From my area of specialty, for instance, we can't exactly achieve 'no global warming,' since it has already begun. If this Vision was for the entire planet, 'stabilize global warming' might be an appropriate statement. However since we initially defined this list to be LA-centric, I question whether global warming is fully within our power." He drew a line through the item on the board.

Tia looked at him in astonishment.

She thought back to the Permaculture Flower, and how the most realistic solutions to global warming were within the Governance petal, Ari's chosen course of action. She rested her hand gently on his arm.

"Ari, although the list is LA-centric, you're part of Legacy LA, and the Treaty to control global warming is the project you're working on. I think the vision should include 'we are doing all within our power to stabilize global warming.'"

A dark wave washed across Ari's face. He wouldn't look at her, carrying on with the presentation as if nothing had happened.

"Now it's time to commit it to paper. I intentionally did not say 'write it down.' If we were doing this formally, we'd refine our language at this point to assure that it reflects specifically the outcome we desire."

Tia picked up here. "When a dream is still inside you, locked up deep in your mind, you work on it alone. But when you bring it out, write it down, share it, something magical happens. You expand your resources. Others begin to help you. When a friend knows your dream her eyes are then open and on the lookout for things in her life that might help you. Thus you are expanding your turf as far as life's little coincidences coming your way.

"As we go through life we are always manifesting outcomes. Others respond to our attitudes and our demeanor as well as our actions. If we do not consciously choose how we present ourselves, our subconscious will choose for us. Without a conscious plan, our presentation is haphazard and unfocused. And so are our results.

"By holding a clear Vision, we are choosing, or programming, what we want to manifest. When all we put out to the world is coordinated around a unified focus, we increase our chances of getting the outcome we want.[32]

"I propose that we ask a few members to refine the lists we have made tonight, to bring it into a clear, unified form, to define the outcome we want for LA 2050."

The meeting broke up rather quietly, quite different than the typical general clatter. It was hard to judge whether they had pulled it off, or whether they had pitched it beyond the crowd.

Ari seemed self-involved. He wasn't talking to people, even though he hadn't connected with most of the Legacy LA members for quite some time due to his travel. Perhaps it sat oddly with him too.

⤚

Once home, Ari remained in a dark mood. He sat in front of his laptop, as if to work, but Tia could see he wasn't writing, he was staring into space.

"Ari, what's up?"

"Your comment at the meeting is eating at me. 'We are doing all within our power.' Why did you do that?" his eyes were dark and cold.

"It surprised me that you, of all people, would take global warming off the list. It felt like you were removing it, not so much because it didn't fit, but because you didn't think it was achievable."

He turned sharply away from her. She felt pressed to go on.

"Ari, I believe in you, I believe in the efforts you are putting into this Treaty. Even if it doesn't feel like progress at the moment, it's still happening, the conferences continue, the world is still trying."

"No, it doesn't feel like progress!" he exploded, pounding the table with his fist. "The U.S. absolutely refuses to come on board, endorsing non-cooperation. It's all falling apart. We're going no place fast, the calendar pages keep flying toward 2040 and we haven't done a damn thing to truly cut emissions! We can talk until we're blue in the face, but all the treaties in the world won't make a bit of difference if we can't get the biggest problem nation on board. And it's my own fucking country!"

He abruptly flung himself to his feet. For a moment it looked like he was going to punch something more, but he grabbed his fist with his other hand. He swung around to tower over Tia, his face dark and furious.

"And I don't need you throwing this in my face in front of a hundred people!"

Tears pricked her eyes at the shock of his fury. She moved to hug him, but he pushed her away roughly and slammed out of the apartment.

Ari didn't return until the wee hours of the morning. She heard him enter the apartment but he did not come to bed; he spent the night alone on the couch.

He said little in the morning, offering no explanation for the night before. He looked haggard, and wouldn't meet her eyes. In stony silence he took two year old Annis to the park for an outing.

He'll be leaving for Milan in the morning! Tia realized. Her heart ached at the thought of him departing for weeks in such a mood, leaving such a feeling of estrangement. The whole episode was eating at her, she couldn't figure out precisely how it had gone so wrong. She prepared a big dinner, some of his favorite dishes, for his last night home before departure.

Later that afternoon, Jana brought Annis in. "Wow, Ari's in quite a mood! Steve stopped by, and then they went off together. No, they didn't say when they'd be back."

Dinnertime came and went, and still he did not reappear. Tia sadly put away the leftovers of what she had hoped could be a warm family gathering. She bathed Annis and put her to bed. Tia tried to remain awake, reading, but fell asleep on her book with the light still on. Around two in the morning she awakened, but all was stillness; Ari was not in the apartment.

What have I done to him? He's carrying this, I'm carrying this, and where is the resolution? She cried herself to sleep.

He returned early in the morning to pack his bags for Milan. He said nothing to her beyond that necessary for his packing.

By the time Annis awakened, Ari's bags were lined up in the kitchen, ready to go. For Annis he had warm hugs and kisses, as she bade Daddy a tearful goodbye. The contrast made Tia's pain even greater.

"Ari, please, I'm sorry..."

He glanced at her with stony eyes, his face pinched and grey. Then he turned away, speaking to her while looking out the window. His voice was strained and it trembled a bit.

"Look, some of this I just need to sort out for myself. You can't do it for me. I have to go now." He picked up his bags and moved through the door.

No! Don't leave like this! Tears streaming down her cheeks, she ran to him and tried to hug him. He hesitated a moment to tolerate it, still holding his bags. Then he turned and was gone.

(10.)

"And then he just turned and left!" Tia was crying so hard that the phone was slippery. Already she had a headache. "Oh, Sahara, what have I done?"

Sahara patiently listened, not adding much except encouragement for Tia to spill the entire story. When Tia had finished, and was just a sodden lump on the end of the phone, Sahara took a deep breath and began.

"Well, it certainly sounds like something was eating at him. I'll bet you stepped right in the middle of it with your comment in the meeting. But yikes, Tia, you had to do it in a public forum, in front of his peers? You kicked him when he was down, onstage."

Tia gasped.

"You have to remember, from everything you've told me about him, this guy *is* his mission. You can never question that."

"I didn't think I was questioning it, I thought I was supporting it!"

"You highlighted the fact that *he* was questioning it, and you did it in public."

"Oh, Sahara, you're so right! But what now? I won't see him for a month! What can I possibly do?"

"Love him. Simply. Completely. Remember, he's out there hurting, from the pain of his own inner demons."

Oh Ari! Her arms ached to soothe him and try to make it all better.

"Tia, you fell in love with him once upon a time. But now comes the real test. Let your commitment guide you, it will help you with your decisions."

"He said something like that to me once, about himself and his sense of purpose."

"This isn't any different. Commitment is commitment. When you're really committed to something – a relationship, or something like he is to his life work – when you trust that commitment, and allow it to be powerful, it'll be clear which actions are right and which are not. And meanwhile, you have to release all this turmoil you're carrying."

Tia remembered the feeling of his body standing so stiff on the pathway, not even putting his bags down when she tried to hug him, then pulling away, the fabric of his sleeve slipping through her very fingers. She pressed her hands to her face. The knot in her stomach was intense. Her sob sounded like a hiccup.

"Let it go, Tia, feel it," Sahara coaxed. "Shout it out, pound on something, write about it, whatever it takes to get it out of your system and let it go. Cleanse that part of your heart and move on.

"Look, I know how it is – Wendell's gone a lot of the time too. When he's home that's the only time we have together. If I spent all that time staying pissed at him, Tia, we'd never have any good times!

"So let's try it: if you're truly committed to sustaining your marriage and to supporting that mission of his, what do you need to do right now?"

"Send him my love and support as if nothing ever happened."

"Bingo."

"But how? I can't! It's a lie, because all this garbage *did* happen!"

"I'm not saying to swallow the hurt, you have to release it. But it isn't going to help your marriage to release it at *him*. Tell *me* about it, or Jana, or Cassandra, cry on our shoulders, rant and rave with us, but send your love to him. Remember your commitment to this marriage and let that guide you to do what will sustain it.

"This stuff isn't fashionable, not in this disposable, I-want society. Most shrinks and women's shows won't tell you to look to your commitment; they'll tell you the guy was a jerk, look out for yourself, 'stick up for your rights.' But honestly, looking out to protect your rights doesn't sustain a relationship through the tough times. For a sustained relationship, it's no longer about 'rights,' it's about the greater good."

"Rights, greater good, suddenly you sound like you're talking about Ari's work again – the U.S. looking out for its own selfish interests rather than committing to the good of humanity."

"Precisely! I told you, it's not that much different. If we make a commitment to self-interests, that's what will guide our decisions, and guess what we'll get? But if we reach beyond our self-interests, and commit to something bigger, if we trust that commitment to guide our decisions – ooh, the power we wield to bring change in this world!"

❧

Jana dropped by the apartment to return a soup pot. Tia was sitting at the kitchen table, phone in her lap, head in her hands.

"Hey Tia – wow, are you okay?"

"Not exactly, I have a wicked headache." Tia looked up.

Jana recoiled at the sight of Tia's face, puffy and red from crying. "You look horrible! What's the matter, girlfriend?"

Tia burst into tears all over again. "It's Ari," she sobbed.

"Yeah, he was really in a fit yesterday, wasn't he?"

"No, I mean, well, I think I did a terrible thing in that meeting."

"The meeting? What does that have to do with it?"

"The vision meeting, when I told him to put global warming back on the board. Sahara says I kicked him when he was down."

"Oh, he was down alright, you should have heard him yesterday at my place with Steve. I don't know what it has to do with the meeting though. Ari's crazy with worry that somehow all his negotiations are about to fall through."

"What!? What do you mean?"

"He was stomping around my place ranting about the whole world going to hell, didn't you hear him through the wall? It's a wonder they didn't hear him in Orange County."

"Why would he say that?"

"I'm not quite sure, I missed a good part of it – the quiet part! He didn't tell you?"

"No, he didn't tell me anything. He blew up at me, night before last. I thought it was something I did."

"Girlfriend, I'm sure this isn't about you. You just happened to be there when he blew. Even if you did something that triggered it, you can't go carrying it and letting it upset you, it's clear that he had other things on his mind. Look, he can be a real jerk sometimes, Tia. He's got his own life to lead, good, bad and ugly. Give him the space to rattle around in."

Little Annis came in from the bedroom, rubbing her eyes.

"Hey, look who just woke up from her nap! Come give Auntie Jana a hug. Let's make a nice cup of peppermint tea for your mommy and then we'll take her out of here and go to..."

"Beee," Annis declared.

"Good idea, the beach. We can all take a walk there."

❧

While Annis and Jana played chase up and down the path, Tia found her way down to her favorite spot at the breakwater. Settling onto her rock, she pulled a notebook from her purse, and wrote furiously for several pages. Then with much difficulty in the sea breeze she burned the pages, releasing their contents to the winds.

She thought of her parents and how rarely she had seen them disagree. Her thoughts turned to her mother and her dedication to drylands agriculture, how for decades she hadn't faltered, even when the naysayers told her she was crazy. *Mom kept at it, she allowed her commitment to guide her.*

As for Ari, he's always been so completely on-track, this doubting is so different for him.

A sudden gust of icy wind buffeted Tia. The ocean swells of deep grey mirrored the oncoming banks of dark clouds. She clenched her teeth and drew her inadequate sweater around her.

Will the world ever reach agreement? Will they be able to control the emissions? Ari, my darling, I hope you can be successful. The future of the planet is riding on this.

Tia huddled tiny against the rocks, in the midst of the storm's mounting strength. She heard Annis' thin voice from far down the breakwater path. The wind took the words away; all Tia caught was the high-pitched tone. It felt to be a chilling glimpse into Ari's view of life: *our children, fragile voices amid the oncoming forces of the storm.*

(11.)

That afternoon the storm rolled in. Dark clouds brought premature evening, and by nightfall the gale was in full force.

"She's asleep now." Tia said, returning to the kitchen from Annis' room.

"Let's hope another round of thunder doesn't come soon," Jana said. "I'll bet that's what woke her last time."

The wind howled and drove rain sideways to clatter on the windows.

"This storm is really something," Jana continued. "Another one of those 50 year storms, the newscast says. Seems like we're getting 50 year storms every two or three years anymore. Record rainfall in 2005 and now this, just three years later. Seems hard to believe the forecasts of megadroughts, doesn't it?"

"Remember, the rainfall will be redistributed. The megadroughts are underway up north."

"I hope Steve's all right, he's crazy to drive here in this stuff." Jana worried.

The electricity flickered, browned and renewed. Tia automatically pulled out candles, matches, flashlights.

"You like him, don't you." Tia stated it softly. It wasn't really a question.

Jana's eyes looked like those of a trapped wild thing. "We're ... we're just friends, nothing more," she stammered, picking at the wax of a candle. She quickly changed the subject. "Esperanza wants us to open our gardens here as a teaching facility. There are so many people who want what we have, yet don't know how to get there. We've become an example, an inspiration to others."

"Why all this push for edible landscaping?"

"It's not just edible landscaping. It's the gardens, the cooking, the doing-it-ourselves. It's a whole way of being. People have lost it, yet we've brought it alive, right here." Jana's gesture included the entire triplex and gardens. "People have fallen out of the habit of doing things hands-on. We have become a society of packaged materials and kits, where all the pieces are purchased. The reeducation will be in getting people back in touch with their creativity and resourcefulness, persuading them to roll up their sleeves and get dirty.

"Edible landscaping gets people back in touch with the land. We need to reengage them in the earth, touching it, surrounding themselves with its cycles. Whenever we go through weeks on end where our food comes out of boxes and plastic packages, weeks on end when we go from air conditioned office to freeway automobile to isolated urban residence, we become estranged, we literally 'lose touch' with our connection to this planet.

"Once people lose that connection, it's easy to forget natural capital, it's easy to focus solely on the artificial realm of humans, it's easy to get into taking and raping the planet. We lose touch with the fact that a part of us is part of the planet."[33]

A huge thunderclap rattled the building causing Annis to whimper from the bedroom. Tia hurried to settle her. From Annis' side in the bedroom, Tia heard the sound of the door slamming and Jana's relieved gasp, footsteps, and then silence.

Annis drifted back into uneasy sleep and Tia went out to rejoin the adults. She rounded the corner to the kitchen, but instantly jumped back into the hall.

Steve and Jana were standing in the kitchen, in full embrace, quite engaged in a passionate kiss.

Yes! Finally, he got through to her! Tia leaned against the wall in the darkened hall, waiting, waiting, for some sign of conversation in the room beyond. *How many years has it been?*

Then Tia's happiness for her friends was completely overcome by aching for Ari. *Darling, I love you. I wish you were here. I wish we hadn't parted so!* She drifted back to their early dating days, the feel of his touch, the press of his lips, the memories of their first night together.

Then she chilled at the thought of his furious glare the night of the vision meeting. She remembered how he hadn't even put down his bags to bid her goodbye. The dull aching of this dreadful separation welled up and became tears. She pressed her cheek against the cool plaster wall as she had so often pressed her face to his strong chest.

I'll send him an email tonight, she decided.

Another thunderclap, the house electricity flickered and died. Inky darkness settled over all. Tia heard Jana's infectious giggle – come to think of it, it had been quite some time since Jana had laughed around Steve.

"Tia put candles on the table," Jana said softly.

Tia heard scuffling and the sound of a match being struck.

"I like this mood lighting," Steve's voice was low and husky.

Tia tiptoed back down the hall to her room leaving the newfound lovers to themselves. With the power outage there would be no emails tonight. Alone in the darkness, she cried herself to sleep.

(12.)

At the Santa Monica triplex, Jana lost a heavily laden orange tree to the storm winds. Huddled in storm channels throughout the city, a dozen or more homeless lost their lives in the storm water runoffs. A hundred others succumbed to the diseases of exposure.

In Westside boutique markets, shoppers bemoaned "temporary" shortages of certain accustomed products. Children in impoverished areas around the city hoped in vain that today perhaps there might be two meals, when yesterday there was only one.

Citizens in wealthy areas stepped up Neighborhood Watch programs, and private security services experienced a business boom. Downtown businesses hired a unique niche business to use riot-control water cannons to blast the homeless from business parking lots and storefront niches. This was not "newsworthy," however, so in the absence of media highlight, the practice was easily ignored by the affluent.

(13.)

To: adamek@LAglobalsolutions.net

Ari, darling, I hope your plane made it out before the storm clouds. This rainy season has really been something, 2005 revisited. We were without electricity for 24 hours. By the way, Jana and Steve seem to have broken through the barrier – I caught them in our kitchen, now clearly more than 'just friends.' I hope Milan is going as well as can be expected; you gave every indication that you did not expect great things from this session. Annis sends her hugs. All my love, Tia

In the days that followed, she sent three more emails with various home news in the same general tone before he responded to a one of them.

> To: tdamek@LAglobalsolutions.net
> Milan sucks. Negotiations are stalemated. The world is going to hell.

> To: adamek@LAglobalsolutions.net
> Ari, darling, my heart goes out to you, I'm sorry the negotiations are going so poorly. Jana had said you were upset about the lack of progress. There is no news of it in the press, even in international online. I do hope the tide will turn soon. Somehow, it will happen. Love, Tia

> To: tdamek@LAglobalsolutions.net
> At least Jana was listening! Italy is planning to pull out of Kyoto upon expiration. They will not renew. This fractures the EU unity and when combined with U.S. bullheadedness may be the end of any hope for an international accord. You don't see any press on it currently because this is OLD NEWS, it happened before I was in LA!

So that's it. That is what he's been carrying! Ooh, but his tone stings.

> To: adamek@LAglobalsolutions.net
> Ari, darling, I'm so sorry to hear about Italy. The news must have been crushing to you as it is to me. We just must keep on believing that enough countries will stay in to maintain the quorum. I send my hugs, over the seas. Love, Tia

> To: tdamek@LAglobalsolutions.net
> Between Italy and the U.S. we're at a standstill internationally. It's pretty much hopeless. If any 2012 agreement survives all this crap, it will be very much the same as Kyoto has been, a mild cap and trade agreement, even the proposed terms aren't

much more strict. At this rate, we will never
achieve the IPCC's 2040 mark. Fuck the future,
they're all saying. Fordon has been on the warpath
again. I'm ready to quit it all.

It was raw, but at least he was communicating again. Tia reread
his message. His despair was heart-wrenching.

On sudden inspiration, she grabbed their digital camera and drove
to Culver City, to a certain schoolyard where his old office had been.
Approximating the angle from his old window, she took several photos
of the children at play. She sent the playground pictures, together with
a photo of Annis, to Ari's address, with a one-line message:

We need you.

Tia didn't hear from him for three days. She felt certain she'd
made a huge mistake, and yearned to call back that message.

To: tdamek@LAglobalsolutions.net
Tia – Thank you for the photos. I have had them
open on my laptop as inspiration through 3 days of
hell-inspired meetings. Fordon has now gone back
to DC, the UNFCCC belatedly decided to impose
Montreal members-only rules on this session, which
bumps the U.S. out of it. Italy continues to
participate, it feels like they are hanging by a
thread. Annis is beautiful. She looks so much like
you. A.

Tia cried every time she read it, which was just about every hour.

To: adamek@LAglobalsolutions.net
Ari, darling, I love you. Threads are a good thing,
pull them snug and take another stitch. It will all
come together. I miss you terribly. See Annis and
new kitty in attached photo. Love, Tia.

To: tdamek@LAglobalsolutions.net
Tia – Your 'other stitch' just arrived – China is
making suggestions they will come aboard! China,
of all places, aboard the emissions treaty! I cannot
believe it. We are all so thrilled! I'm very busy

here, yet can't wait to get home to all my 'kittens,' both new and long-favorites. A.

To: adamek@LAglobalsolutions.net
Ari: prrrrrr, this kitty can't wait to snuggle with you. All my love, Tia

To: tdamek@LAglobalsolutions.net
Tia – hold that thought another 72 hours. A.

(14.)

Nervously picking at her fingernails, Tia waited with Annis at the airport security barrier. The first passengers began emerging, tourists and grandparents.

Then Tia saw him, half a head taller than all the rest, coat in hand, efficiency carryon and laptop case slung over his shoulder, his easy stride so comfortable amid the airport chaos. As he reached the queue for security clearance, their eyes met. He scarcely broke the connection as he maneuvered through the jostling crowd at the checkpoint.

Annis loosened Tia's hand and ran to Ari as soon as he was clear of security. Ari scooped her up, spinning her around, Annis shrieking with glee.

Their spinning and giggling paused and Ari's eyes caught Tia's again. *The fire, the purpose, the intention, the unsaid messages, it's all still there. Four years hasn't diminished it one bit. In fact, it's intensified.* She ran to him.

One hand still holding Annis, Ari grabbed Tia with his free arm, crushing her body against his. His kiss seemed desperate to make up for lost time, feeling like greeting, forgiveness, yearning and passion all at once.

Annis' giggles bade them to part. Tia felt limp, tingly and breathless.

"I'll never leave like that again," he whispered.

(15.)

The small auditorium was at fire marshal capacity as Ari began to speak. "Steve has asked me to give you an update on the international climate control negotiations.

"First of all, where are we? The Kyoto Protocol is a binding Treaty between more than 155 nations. It came into effect back in 2005."

Ari arranged 'nations' Steve, Esperanza and Ben at one side of the stage and handed them a sign labeled 'Kyoto Protocol.' Jana stood alone at the other side of the stage waving a tiny U.S. flag. Ari pointed to her as he continued.

"The United States has refused to be a part of the Kyoto Protocol. This is worrisome because ..."

Jana struck a match and lit a cigarette. Several audience members gasped, as smoking in public places was illegal.

"When she smokes that cigarette, it ruins the clean air for all of us. Similarly with greenhouse emissions: when one country persists in excess emissions, it devastates the environment for all.

"If the international community has no legal recourse because she's not party to the treaty, then she can do whatever she pleases, and to hell with the rest of us. If however, we have an international treaty that is legally binding, we can enforce upon her to stop."

Jana put out the cigarette.

"Now you see the importance of getting the United States on board the treaty."

The team put down their props and readied for the next exercise.

Ari continued. "The Kyoto Protocol is about to expire. We're working diligently on a new treaty to be its successor, trying to work out several major issues.

"Say I have four kids." He gestured to the four people onstage. "I'm a generous dad. As my kids reach their teens, I give each one a set of ten movie passes."

He handed ticket booklets to Jana and Steve, skipping Ben and Esperanza.

"The younger ones aren't ready for them yet." Ari explained.

"Along comes Mom Kyoto Protocol, who limits how many movies each kid can see in a given month." Tia stepped forward and took some tickets away from Jana and from Steve.

"My younger kids are clamoring." Ari narrated.

"Hey, what about us?" Ben hammed it up.

"We want to go to the movies too!" said Esperanza.

"You're not ready yet." Ari said to them firmly.

"When I grow up will I get to go to ten movies?" Esperanza asked.

"No, each of you may only see two movies per month," replied Tia.

"But they got ten when they became teens, why won't we get ten when we do?" wailed Ben.

"Because we didn't have limits then and now we do. You only get two." Tia answered.

"I have a right to ten! They got to go to ten movies all this time. It's not fair!" Ben stomped his foot and whined.

Steve snapped right back, "If I'm limited to two, there's no way you get more than two, even when you grow up. Talk about not fair!"

Ari summed it up. "That, folks, is the dispute currently going on between the nations of the world. Our 'teens' are the developed nations – like the U.S. and the EU. The younger kids are the underdeveloped nations such as those in South America, Africa and the small island nations. The underdeveloped nations resist emissions caps because they feel it is unjust at this point in their blossoming development.

"Now, I believe the solutions to our environmental crisis are only going to be solved with multiple approaches. Top-down, like the Kyoto Protocol, plus grassroots, like the work each of you are doing. Simultaneously. We must attack the environmental problems from all sides.

"Your work, here in your neighborhoods, in this city, in this state, is vital to the restructuring of our society, whether you're working to save the virgin forests in Siskiyou or to save the Ballona Wetlands, whether you're campaigning for light rail or bicycle lanes, whether you're working with inner city schoolchildren or the problems of the homeless. All of these pursuits are helping to solve the problems we face. These environmental and social changes are being made here in LA, in Seattle, in Pittsburg, in the United Nations, in cities around the globe. Together we can make it happen. Thank you for all you are doing."

Matthew approached Ari after the presentation.

"Here we're all worried about the U.S. being Jana with the cigarette – what about China? I heard they have no caps at all!"

"I worry that we're getting to a point where we blame China for the world's environmental problems in an effort to avoid changing our own destructive habits!" Ari exclaimed, then settled into the discussion.

"China's one of the nations that Ben represented in the skit – too 'young' or undeveloped to get an emissions cap. But there's an interesting thing going on in China. On one hand we hear horrifying projections of the amount of world oil resources they may use in the coming decade. On the other hand we see them coming to the table with plans for the environment on a voluntary basis. Now that the Kyoto Protocol is international law, and we have an international awareness of the greenhouse gas situation and other environmental issues, my bet is that we'll see China deciding to out-compete other nations in the environmental field as well. Both in manufacturing – solar panels and wind turbines, and Japan's Clean Air Vehicles – and in things like emissions.

"I'm willing to bet China will opt for clean development for competitive reasons, so that they won't have to bear the costs of retrenching in a post-Kyoto world, and so that their manufacturing processes will already be highly competitive on the cutting edge of technology. Regardless of the reasons, I think we're going to see great environmental news coming out of China in the near future."

(16.)

"Service economies – they solve both the natural and human capital issues," Carl said. Carl and Steve relaxed with Ari on the stairs of the apartment. "Dow Chemical and Interface Carpet have been doing it for years." Their voices carried through the screen door into the kitchen where Tia sat mending Annis' playclothes.

"The issue with Big Business' transition to many green ideas is a problem of control of the resource, and of income stream," Carl continued. "With oil, the corporations control the resource, from start to finish. They control extraction, refining, distribution, and there are profits to be made all along the way. With something like solar energy the corporations don't control the sun.

"All they can profit from is the initial manufacture and sale of that panel. There's no income stream. For oil, they keep getting paid whenever we need more energy. For that solar panel, once they've made the panel, the transaction is complete – there's no way to reap ongoing profits. This is why the mega-corps have so little interest in supporting solar. Profits. Or lack of them."

"By contrast, we have the service economies," Ari prompted.

"Dow Chemical found that rather than selling your factory gallons of chemical solvent, they could sell 'dissolving services.' Dow owns the chemical and they send out a team who perform the service you need done."

"How is this better?" Steve asked.

"From a natural capital viewpoint, it's better because the chemical is reused – Dow discovered it could be repurified and reused fifty to one hundred times. We've kept the toxic chemicals out of the waste stream. Plus there's less of it toxically manufactured.

"From a human capital standpoint, the dissolving services team means jobs. So here's a case where what's good for business is good for the environment."[34]

"It's an interesting solution for the Transition time," Ari said contemplatively.

"What do you mean, Transition?" Carl sounded a bit defensive.

"Well it works in the cross-over period, while we still have toxic elements of our old-style life to contend with. But long term, as we move into a truly Sustainable human existence, will we really need or even want the toxic chemicals?"

Annis whimpered and Tia went to attend to her. When she returned, Carl had departed and Steve and Ari were talking quietly beyond the screen.

"I'm going to ask her to marry me."

"Have you yet?"

"Not yet, waiting for my time. I've waited for her for years, what's a bit more?"

(17.)

"Tonight's Legacy LA meeting is quite special," Jana introduced with a big grin. "It's a mother-daughter show: Cassandra Chandler and our own Tia Damek!"

"Steinbeck, *Grapes of Wrath* ... massive dust storms ..." Tia began. "Step back in time, into a Dorothea Lange photograph. The Dust Bowls which our country experienced during the 1930's were brought on by a mere half-decade of diverted rainfall.

"Climate change projections are forecasting shifts in rainfall patterns which may last several decades. They're called Megadroughts."

Tia gestured to a map she had on display. "In their best case scenario, the Union of Concerned Scientists expects Sierra Nevada snowpack in the next three decades to decrease to three-quarters of what we are accustomed to. And in their best case scenario, they expect the snowpack by 2100 to be a mere third of what we have now.

"You'll notice I'm not even mentioning the worst case scenarios.

"Imagine this, together with the increased temperatures brought on by global warming, in our Central Valley, where we grow one-fourth of our country's food.

Cassandra took over. "Lettuce, carrots, broccoli, zucchini, corn, beans, all the typical vegetables you buy at the supermarket. The industrial varieties of these vegetables require a lot of water in order to produce a crop. In the past, Native Americans did not have access to the huge water projects and irrigation systems we have today. They raised their food crops from diverse varieties which would yield well even with lower water availability.

"Right now, most of our vegetables come from genetically similar material. A green bean in a supermarket in Los Angeles looks just like a green bean in a supermarket in New York. They're mass-produced hybrids, with very little diversity. If you look back a scant few generations, you'll discover that beans come in all shapes and sizes, colors and patterns. They're beautiful."

Cassandra opened a cloth napkin on the table at the front of the room, allowing multicolored heirloom beans to rain through her fingers. Tia distributed handfuls to audience members to pass around.

"The differences are not just in their appearances," Cassandra continued. "Some of these beans yield early in the season, others are late producers. Some do better in cooler temperatures, others prefer intense heat. Some put up with greater salinity levels in the soil, others are resistant to viruses and may be more durable in times of stress.

"Climate change will bring great differences to the massive fields where we produce our food crops. Some of these changes we can anticipate. Other changes will surprise us. Plant diseases, plant pests, we cannot possibly guess the full extent of what we, and our food plants, will have to cope with. If we move into this vast unknown with single varieties of the food crops we are accustomed to consuming, our food supply is in grave jeopardy. We need an insurance policy for uncertain times. We need flexibility. By building options into our system, we create possibilities for survival.

"For almost two decades I have been working with seeds developed by Native Americans in the desert Southwest and Mexican deserts. I have been building a genetic bank of diverse varieties, with particular emphasis on those which do well under drought stress. I'm building that insurance policy.

"Let me change course and talk about desertification – the deterioration of land caused by erosion and poor land management practices. Wind or water erosion can remove topsoil. Stripping land barren of vegetation can expose it to these forces unnecessarily, like the Dust Bowl of the 1930's.

"Desertification is a serious issue in arid areas of Africa, Asia and South America. Overexploitation such as deforestation, overgrazing, removal of native plants, and salt saturation decrease the land's ability to grow crops.

"The temperature increases of global warming increase the rate of nutrient loss from the earth's soils. If we do not manage our land resources wisely, as we enter this era of higher global and local temperatures, desertification will become a pressing issue right here in the U.S., in the Great Plains states and in California's Central Valley.

"Soil erosion is already a problem. Modern agricultural methods have already cost Iowa more than half of its arable topsoil. This occurred due to modern mechanized farming techniques. One source said our soil is being literally strip-mined. Our civilization risks running out of soil before we run out of oil.

"Additionally, we're not using our soil as the asset it could be. Use of wise land management practices could achieve what is called carbon sequestration, the recapture of carbon molecules back into the soils of the planet. Experts estimate that 5%-15% of global greenhouse gas emissions could be recaptured each year using soil sequestration.[35]

"What can we do? Sustainable farming practices are the answer. Water and nutrients management, no-till farming, composting, mulching, use of legumes, water harvesting, agroforestry, and wisdom about use of chemicals. Wisdom in land management practices can help to solve climate change, desertification and biodiversity issues."

As Cassandra and Tia packed their materials, Jana and Esperanza approached.

"I can't stay," Tia said, "Shannon has Annis. Why don't you come over to our place?"

Esperanza's focus was clearly elsewhere. "Who's that good-looking guy over there? Do you know him?"

"Oh, Xavier, Ari knows him," Tia said.

Jana eyed Tia and nodded.

"Come on, I'll introduce you before I leave," Tia took the hint.

"Reuse," Xavier declared to another member as Tia approached with Esperanza. "Reuse and Rebuy. Moving toward Sustainability these will be much more important than Recycling. Reusing objects in their current form, and transferring those objects between users, without the energy input to recast and reform them in any recycling process."[36]

"Xavier, I'd like you to meet ..." Tia began.

Xavier swung around. He caught sight of Esperanza and didn't even notice Tia's presence.

"...Esperanza Chavez," Tia finished, to what she was sure were deaf ears.

"Xavier Navarro, at your service." Xavier's and Esperanza's eyes were locked.

"Recycling?" Esperanza asked.

"Yes, I run a recycling operation in Sun Valley," Xavier's pride was visible. "I have plans to bring it up a notch, recycle more goods here within the city footprint, reduce the waste going unused to landfills. A highly sophisticated sorting process, networked with manufacturers to supply raw materials."

Tia grinned and walked away.

⁓

At the triplex, Tia laid out extra teacups, knowing well that where Jana was, Steve was soon to follow.

Jana entered the apartment with a basket of herbs, giggling, with a laughing Steve draped around her. The talk flowed easily with such a bountiful garden right outside the door.

"Jana, you've done such a great job in designing this garden. It's the perfect merging of aesthetic beauty and functionality."[37] Cassandra said.

"I was trying for something that looked a bit English country, yet provided our herbs and as many vegetables as I could reasonably fit in," Jana smiled happily. "I would have added more if I didn't need to save room for the kids!

"You see, with the unique common living situation we have here, we can blur the lines where there would otherwise be fences. It becomes one larger piece of property rather than several postage stamps. Less land becomes more: more efficiency plus a feeling of more spaciousness. Yet because the grounds contain just our three-unit insular group, we still retain privacy from the outside world. It's a concept Esperanza and I yearned to try in the inner city." Jana grinned as Esperanza belatedly joined the party.

"In the inner city it wouldn't work very well," Esperanza picked up the conversation, "because the families aren't well matched. Typically we have an apartment building that is distinctly separate from the garden plot, so the sense of 'ownership' just isn't there. So there we stick more to the Community Garden concept."

"We're just about to start a small class series here, to teach others how to do this," Jana said proudly.

"Why not offer it through Parks and Rec? You could reach more people that way," Cassandra asked.

"There's no funding for it, I tried," Esperanza said sadly.

"Tia and I are going to try offering it here at the triplex, on a barter system," Jana finished.

"I wish Sahara could see this. Her land is laid out using the biointensive concepts of Alan Chadwick." Cassandra explained to the group. "It ends up being a lot more farm-like, with little of the quaint cottage beauty that Jana's put in here. I have this sense that there could be a cross-pollination." Everyone chuckled at her pun.

"So let's see," Steve summed it all up, "we have Permaculture, biointensive, drylands techniques, community gardens, am I missing any? I just can't help but think that somewhere in here is a new solution, the wave of the future."

"There goes Steve, trying to market it!" teased Jana. Steve already had his arm around her but this was an excuse for an extra hug.

Esperanza got a far away look in her eyes. "You know, my mind keeps going back to the camps ..."

"The homeless camps?"

"Precisely. Somehow in all this, we have to find a way to help the people in those camps."

(18.)

To: adamek@LAglobalsolutions.net
Ari – Last night a band of homeless jumped the fence and raided Jana's garden – she is heartbroken. They took all the fruit from the trees, and in the process trampled quite a bit of her precious 'understory.' I guess they didn't recognize the food value in unharvested vegetables because they really didn't steal much besides the fruit. All the same, it still feels like a significant invasion to our snug little compound. Matthew is furiously declaring that the fence needs to be taller. He and Steve are going to do it themselves. Tia

To: tdamek@LAglobalsolutions.net
Tia – I am outraged that people would come into our yard, despite the fence. I'm glad everyone is safe. Matthew and Steve's construction project sounds like the way to go, unless we resort to an armed camp. I wish I were there to participate. Brussels is altogether too far away from LA. A.

(19.)

"Esperanza had a new idea this week," Jana told Tia as they planted out chard seedlings together. Three year olds Annis and Peter played nearby. She wants us to get together with Ben on it. The idea came to her when our garden was raided. She wants to make a proposal to the Parks Department to place edible landscaping in the city's parks and greenbelts.

"She hopes to get the Urban Forestry program involved. They have a replacement schedule for park trees and she wants to get citrus and other edible species into the list of replacement trees. The catch is, there might not be any funding, with Depression cutbacks. So she may try to integrate independent organizations like TreePeople."[38]

"Wow, that lady never stops trying to change the face of LA!" Tia exclaimed. "I think it's a great idea. Citrus is evergreen, it maintains park appearances, it's low maintenance with respect to pruning. A standard size tree casts a decent shadow for their shade tree requirements, and since most of their park space is lawns, irrigation would already be in place. In a year or so, the trees will be bearing food for people.

"Species like feijoas – some people call them pineapple guavas – would work in median strips where there's little water. They would still bear fruit even in drought and higher temperatures. We'll have to help her with a plant list. I'll ask Mom for more ideas."

Shannon came out to the garden with six year old Mark.

"Lessons are done for the day!" she announced.

"How's that going?" Tia asked, tucking slug collars around the seedlings.

"Homeschooling works great for us. I like to say that my kids attend the best private school I can afford. The teacher-to-student ratio is 1:2!" Shannon chuckled at her own joke.

"I need to learn more about it," Tia said. "The school options in these days are appalling."

"I'd be happy to loan you some materials to get started. Some of my favorites to begin with are the works of John Holt. Then there's a classic by John Taylor Gatto, where he reveals the hidden agendas of our school system; basically, it's to develop placid Mainstreamers."

"Hardly a place to grow Transformers and Change Agents!"

"Precisely my thinking. In this time more than any other, we need to be raising thinkers, because there's no way we can solve all these cumulative environmental issues during our generation. We're doing future generations a huge disservice to raise our children as Mainstreamers or worse yet, Reactionaries."

"I think Ari might like this approach."

(20.)

"This is just like 2004!" Cassandra ranted over the phone to Tia. "I'm watching the Election '08 results come in on the TV. It's just like 2004, with the red states and the blue states! All the central and southern states are carrying Rafferty!"

"Of course, Mom, Bush in 2004 carried those same areas. At least Rafferty's not in the pocket of the oil companies."

"But he's from Big Business, that will hardly be any better."

"Well maybe he'll leave the Arctic National Wildlife Refuge alone," Tia said hopefully.

"He doesn't seem likely to be any less rigidly opposed to Kyoto. It still looks like it's going to be a darn long time before we reach U.S. ratification!"

(21.)

Tia looked around her comfortable little home, the kids playing happily in the bountiful sunny garden. In the midst of this it was easy to lose track of the world outside, where the economy was in turmoil.

With business layoffs and closures since the market crash, many families were seeing 'changed circumstances,' as they now called it. In the affluent areas of the city, foreclosed homes became abandoned and boarded up, their erstwhile owners moving to a succession of smaller and cheaper rentals in less desirable areas. Many families were without jobs, limited in food and basic necessities. Those who still held jobs worried they might soon become unemployed. Employers reduced wages to levels unheard of for decades. Times were bleak and getting bleaker.

Disheartened by the cascading economy, for the first time in half a century people began returning to the churches, at first a trickle and then in large numbers, seeking solace and answers in their hopelessness. The post-World War II trend to the self-sufficient humanistic stance seemed to have passed its peak. People returned in droves to matters of the spirit. The pulpits of the U.S. regained the position they hadn't held for decades, a leadership of the hearts of the people.

Speaking with Jana and Esperanza, who regularly made trips downtown, drove home the reality. The numbers of homeless in the streets of LA were increasing at an alarming rate. In the 1930s they were called 'hobos' or 'Oakies,' depending upon the area of the country and the particular source of their condition. In the 2000s they were known as 'homeless'; the euphemism rolled off the tongue with a more benign feel. Regardless of which term you chose, it still referred to people huddled in sub-animal existence on the streets, out of money, out of hope.

In the past they had been mostly men, but now that the shelters were overfilled it was quite normal to see entire families. They often scavenged in packs, which was quite frightening.

Long ago, Carl had shown Tia the forecast of the economic crash. *We're living it now, or rather, most of this city, most of this country, is living it now.*

Yet Tia had an almost tactile sense of a movement growing, a movement being borne upward to a new way of being, a way of living in harmony with the earth rather than in domination over it. It wasn't an economic thing. In fact, many of the deepest manifestations of this harmony involved nothing economic whatsoever.

Jana and Tia's garden class for barter had been a huge success. Legacy LA was growing by leaps and bounds. Every meeting there were more reports of new projects, new ideas, further progress made. She thought of their colleagues in other cities around the country, the groups that Steve and others were nurturing. Seattle Mayor Greg Nickels' dream of 141 cities adopting Kyoto was a gross underestimation – nearly every major U.S. city was on board the 'Green Team' now.

Ari's Transformation Wave ... it feels like we're riding that wave.

Cities, and now States were awakening to the possibility that greening the U.S. might be an industry in itself – a much-needed assist to the dismal economy. It was happening internationally as well, Tia knew this from her internet research.

Around the globe, the Change Agents and the Transformers are getting in place.

(22.)

Tia stretched in the wide bed at the apartment, a space disturbingly large for her lone slim body. Two months it had been this time, two full moon cycles without a visit home. She lay remembering the feel of Ari's lips on hers, his hands traveling her body, his lovemaking. *Damn it, I'm married to a memory.* She spun her wedding ring, then worked it off her finger. She stared at her naked hand, the memory of the ring visible in the indentation on her skin. Somehow it felt more appropriate. She put the ring on her nightstand and flicked it with her nail. It skittered and tumbled down behind the furniture. Tia groaned silently.

Again she stared at the ring impression on her hand. *Marriage.* She snorted. *This isn't what I signed up for.* The whirlwind of their dating days spun in her memory. The sunny mornings in her Marina apartment, waking to Ari in bed beside her, a stark contrast to the chill reality of the empty space beside her now. Her laugh was bitter. *I worried about international harems back then.*

Her eyes widened in realization. *The meetings, the Treaties, they hold him. I get the crumbs, the occasional tryst.* She flopped over on her back and her tears rolled down into her ears. *Let the damn ring stay behind the nightstand.*

His hugs. Wrapped in his great arms it feels like everything will be okay. No problem is too big, no dream impossible. Her ears felt sticky from the tears. She tried to dry her face with the sleeve of her nightgown.

Four year old Annis padded in, sleepily clutching a green stuffed dog. Tia wrapped her in the blankets and cuddled her. Annis had cried when Ari left, was weepy for a day or so, but now she hardly seemed to notice his absence. This time the length of the trip exceeded her time concept; checking off squares on a calendar had become meaningless. *What will she remember of him from her childhood?* Tia rocked Annis in her arms. *We need you too, Ari.*

Annis was now waking and wriggled out of Tia's grasp. She chattered happily, playing with Tia's fingers. Annis touched the ring finger. "Where's your ring, Mommy?" The question was almost panicked.

"It fell behind the nightstand."

Annis scrambled to retrieve it and replace it on Tia's hand, then smiled happily. Proper order had been restored.

(23.)

Steve opened the Legacy LA meeting. "Tonight we'll hear from Matthew Goodman on the issue of Faith-Based Environmentalism."

Matthew's posture had changed. *He looks humble,* Tia realized. He still wore the same expensive suits, but it was now clear that these were the same expensive suits, rather than representatives from a continuous flow – the suits were now showing unmistakable signs of wear.

"Steve asked me to give this talk some years ago, and somehow I never had the time. As many of you know, I have recently had the gift of considerable time. And that has allowed me to contemplate many of life's issues.

"Environmentalists and Religious Thinkers. Sound like polar opposites? Not necessarily, as I'd like to show you tonight.

"In a 1967 essay, historian Lynn White presented the inflammatory view that our ecological crisis has its underpinnings in Christian attitudes of man's relationship with nature. White declared that 'we shall continue to have a worsening ecologic crisis until we reject the Christian axiom that nature has no reason for existence save to serve man.' Sierra Club Executive Director Carl Pope suggests that interpretation of the White essay convinced an entire generation of western environmentalists that religion is the root of our environmental problem, and caused a parting of the ways between environmentalists and religious thinkers.[39]

"Now, I have studied the White essay, and perhaps my views can be attributed to the rose-colored lenses of our time, as contrasted with the views of 1967, but I find some interesting points in there. White states that 'more science and more technology are not going to get us out of the present ecologic crisis until we find a new religion, or rethink our old one.'

"My point tonight is that, in the intervening years since White wrote, that rethinking *has* taken place, and is *still* taking place, within nearly every major religion.

"Consider this quotation: 'Simplicity, moderation and discipline, as well as a spirit of sacrifice, must become part of everyday life, lest all suffer the negative consequences of the careless habits of a few.' Sound like a Southern Hemisphere delegation to the United Nations? No, that was Pope John Paul II.

"'To continue to walk the current path of ecological destruction is not only folly; it is sin.' That warning is from the National Council of Churches, not from the WorldWatch Institute.

"This 1992 statement by the Head of the Holy See Delegation to the United Nations Conference in Rio is almost the antithesis of White's 1967 comments: 'The Creator has placed the human beings at the center of creation, making them the responsible stewards, not the exploiting despots, of the world around them.' It certainly reveals how much progress the religious communities have made since 1967. It is time to acknowledge that the Transformation Wave is happening within religious communities too.

"In 1986 representatives of five major world religions – Buddhism, Christianity, Hinduism, Islam and Judaism – met in Assisi, Italy. They published the Assisi Declarations, opening the discussion within religions for how to implement an earth-care ethic. That discussion has continued.

"Interfaith organizations have been formed, such as the National Religious Partnership for the Environment, whose membership organizations include the United States Catholic Conference, the National Council of Churches of Christ, the Evangelical Environmental Network and the Coalition on the Environment and Jewish Life.

"The World Council of Churches, a fellowship of more than 340 Christian churches spanning more than 120 countries on all continents, has had a WCC Climate Change Programme since 1988.

"In 2005, The National Council of Churches published an Open Letter about the sacredness of the earth. This organization encompasses Protestant, Anglican, Orthodox, historic African American and Living Peace faith groups.

"Within the Evangelical communities there is also an environmentally-conscious direction, under the umbrella of Creation Care. In late 2004 The National Association of Evangelicals adopted a document entitled 'For the Health of the Nation: and Evangelical Call to Civic Action' which included the statement 'We are not the owners of creation, but its stewards, summoned by God to "watch over and care for it." This implies the principle of sustainability: our uses of the Earth must be designed to conserve and renew the Earth rather than to deplete or destroy it.'

"The Catholics published 'Renewing the Earth: An Invitation to Reflection and Action on Environment in Light of Catholic Social Teaching' in 1991. As part of this document they highlight the concept that 'the ecological problem is intimately connected to justice for the poor.' The Catholics promote education and authentic development policies, particularly for underdeveloped countries. When you think about it, education and development policies are the heart of a truly Sustainable change, as contrasted with a mandated, externally forced, unsustainable change. This topic is one I will defer to another forum, but let me suffice to say that care for our environment and social causes are clearly interconnected.

"Within the American Jewish movements we find concepts taking hold such as *Shomrei Adamah* – loosely translated as Guardians of the Earth – and eco-kosher. It is kosher to bring your own mug to drink coffee at this gathering, while a single-use styrofoam cup isn't kosher. I could go into other major religions but we have time constraints here tonight.[40]

"Gary Gardner made the point that 'a major challenge of our civilization is to reintegrate our societal heart and head, to reestablish spirituality as partner in dialogue with science.' That partnership is precisely what I feel we must cultivate. In forming any good partnership one must begin by extending respect and trust to our prospective partners.

"Organized religions represent powerful Transformers and Change Agents in guiding the Mainstream. 'The task set before us is unprecedented, intricate, complex. No single solution will be adequate to the task.' As Dr. Damek, one of our fearless founders, has told us so many times, it's going to take a multitude of solutions and a multitude of approaches to solve the crises facing us.

"Gary Gardner points out that the European 'scientific focus on writing an objective story about *what is* was achieved largely without reference to the emotive story of *what ought to be*, a traditional strength of religion.'

"Right now, we are at a crossroads, where we have realized how far we have strayed from 'what ought to be' with respect to the earth's resources. What better partner for environmentalists to have at this point in time, than organizations who have long made it their specialty to invoke 'what ought to be.'"

∽

After Matthew's talk, Tia overheard Esperanza speaking with another Legacy LA member. "When the Oakies came to California in huge numbers in the 1940s and there was so little work to be had, they were in camps too, just like the homeless of today. There were terrible battles over enrolling the Oakies' children in the regular school system."

"I can only imagine – the local Californians must have really objected."

"They certainly did. Leo Hart was the Kern County superintendent of education. He started a new public school just for the kids of the Oakies called Weedpatch School. All he had to work with was an empty government lot and donated materials. Weedpatch became do-it-yourself at its finest. The kids became the work force, building the structures, thus learning construction techniques. They were the cafeteria workers, learning cooking and other skills. They kept farm animals and gardened on the premises, yielding food for the cafeteria. Part of each day was remedial academics and part was practical skills."

"Wasn't that the kind of segregation that people fought so hard to abolish in the 1960s?"

"On the contrary, we could use some of this hands-on training today! The kids emerged from Weedpatch with fierce pride and incredible motivation. Many went on to become leaders in California communities."

(24.)

"Will Steve be over as usual? I'll have Annis set the table," Tia said as she laid out leeks, radish greens and turnips for the soup.

"Steve? Yes, I guess always, now." Jana chopped the leeks fiercely, haphazardly, her movements while cooking unusually crisp.

Tia tried to make conversation. "Where did you two go? You were gone for three days. Someplace fun I hope."

"Steve will tell you later." Jana seemed determined to shut down, so Tia let it drop.

Ari arrived home from a meeting downtown. Five year old Annis instantly glued herself to his side, clamoring for his attention. He grimaced at her breathless stories of antics with Mark and Peter, checking his watch and looking out the window for Steve.

When Steve ambled in a few minutes later, they all sat down to eat. Annis told a lengthy tale of a mud puddle she, Mark and Peter had dug that day. Surprisingly, Jana had no comment about the presence of a mud puddle amidst her precious garden.

When Annis had finished her story, Steve looked to Jana. "Do you want to tell them?" He looked radiant.

"No." Jana answered flatly.

"Okay, so I will." Steve made a grand gesture like a game show host. "Let me present the new Mrs. Steve Vernados!"

Tia screamed with delight, running to hug Jana. Annis sat looking between the adults as if at a tennis match, not comprehending.

"Well, congratulations to the both of you!" Ari sat back in his chair with an amused little smile. "Married ... after all these years ..."

Annis understood it this time, dropped her fork and danced around the kitchen. "Auntie Jana's getting married! Auntie Jana's getting married!"

"Annis, please stop that," Jana looked like she was going to cry. "It's not *getting* married, it's *got* married." She turned to Steve. "And that is not my name."

"You mean we missed the wedding?" Annis' disappointment was evident.

"You know, Annis, Jana, I think we should have a celebration." Tia tried to soothe them.

"I don't want a party." The bride was sullen. "Not about this."

"No party? Pleeease Auntie Jana?"

"Annis, stop it!" This time Jana's tone was quite sharp. Wide eyed, Annis ran from the room.

Everybody was at loss for words, the dynamic in the room felt so off. Tears welled up in Jana's eyes.

"I don't get it. What's the matter?" Tia asked.

"I think she might never have married me." Steve wrapped his arms around Jana in a bear hug. Jana tried half-heartedly to push him away but he didn't release her. "I've asked her to, I don't know how many times. She might have held out on me forever, except..."

Jana's tears spilled over. "I'm sort of pregnant."

"You don't want the baby?" Tia asked in hushed tones, eyes on the doorway in lookout for Annis.

"That's not it at all!" Steve laughed, "It's me! She's been running from me since the day I met her!"

At this, Jana pressed her hands to her face and shook her head in denial, still crying. Steve looked down at her on his shoulder and kissed her hair with clear affection. Jana curled one hand up around his neck, and buried her face deeper in his shoulder, if that were possible.

Tia glanced at Ari. He was staring at his hand, flexing it repeatedly.

Tia turned back to Jana. "But you love him, don't you?" The answer was clear for all to see.

Ari reached for Tia's arm in a gesture of restraint. "Tia, give her some space, she'll get used to it."

He turned to his sister. "Time to let go of the history. Steve's a great guy, can't you see that? He's been steady as can be for almost eight years. Let him love you, for God's sake!"

"You're choking me, woman," Steve said with an affectionate grimace, peeling Jana's hand off his neck. He shifted her on his shoulder so he could kiss her, deeply, lovingly.

Tia heard a rustle at the door. Annis peeked around the doorframe, grinning widely at the sight of Jana and Steve kissing.

(25.)

A few days later, Steve came over for coffee. After some good-natured kidding of the bridegroom, Ari turned to their typical political bantering.

"With 2009 now upon us, what do you think about our vehicle situation?" Ari asked Steve as they sat down at the Damek kitchen table.

"Well, the California law which restricts greenhouse gas emissions on new vehicles is now coming into effect," Steve said.

"Wasn't that challenged in the courts?" Tia asked, looking up from the parsnips she was scrubbing.

"Back in 2004-2005, yes it was. The Alliance of Automobile Manufacturers, including DaimlerChrysler, GM and Ford, joined the American International Automobile Dealers and tried to overturn the law. They claimed the law was a covert way of regulating fuel economy. But it stood up in court, and will become effective for vehicles manufactured after 2009."[41] Steve explained.

"What does fuel economy have to do with it?" sputtered Tia. "Greenhouse gas legislation is about what comes out, not what goes in!"

"Shows you where the mainstream thinking is," Steve replied.

"You mean they don't know one end from the other?"

"Well, that too!" Steve laughed. "But I meant that the mainstream thinking is still with fuel economy. The automakers act like this trend is a revisit of the 1970's gas crunch when we switched from huge vehicles to the lightweight little imports. Our U.S. automakers don't get it, that this time it's about an altogether different issue, the greenhouse emissions. Sure, better fuel economy will help – less fuel burned means somewhat less emissions – but carbon is carbon. Retaining the focus on fuel economy means the automakers aren't striving to invent technology for the Zero Emissions Vehicles we wish they could produce.

"Going back to Ari's original question, unfortunately there's not much new technology out there since that law was passed in 2002. The fuel cells we have available are still flawed. The Depression times hit the Research and Development in this area pretty hard.

"You see, a fuel cell is a storage unit like a battery. You have to put the energy into it. That energy needs to come from someplace. When you refer to fuel cells, you should think of the fuel cell as 'in concert with' the power source. Unfortunately, the oil and gas industry wants the power source to come from them. Right now 95% of our generated hydrogen is produced by conventional hydrocarbon fuels, like oil and coal. So while the fuel cell vehicle itself might be touted as Zero Emissions, the fact of the matter is, when the energy that goes into that fuel cell comes from fossil fuels all you've really done is outsource the energy production to your off-site power plant. The vehicle may be Zero Emissions but the entire system is not, you've externalized the bad news.

"To meet the 2009 requirement in California, automakers are begrudgingly producing hybrids, like Tia's old Prius. The fun news is, they've developed a wider variety of body styles to fit that hybrid engine, but there haven't been many changes to its inner workings since the early 2000's.

"The demand for huge boats like the Hummer and the Excursion declined significantly with the Depression times, but most of those outrageous 2005-2006 models are still on the road, still emitting greenhouse gasses and other pollutants."

"Outrageous?"

"I get furious every time I think about it. Automakers actually added weight to the Hummer, Suburban, Tahoe and Excursion and a few other trucks in order to push them over the 8500 pound mark, to utilize a loophole and qualify for lower fuel economy under the federal CAFE standards. Can you believe such waste? The Sierra Club nicknamed the Excursion the 'Valdez.'

"But some things are changing. The U.S. Postal Service has ordered some fuel cell vehicles for its fleet. UPS and FedEx have been testing fuel cell vehicles since 2004, and are now increasing their fleet percentages of fuel cells and hybrids.[42]

"Rocky Mountain Institute, an environmental activist group, hopes that their idea of a truly clean air, Zero Emissions, lightweight carbon vehicle, will one day happen."

"On the subject of hoping," Ari segued, "how has the Sustainability effort been going in the other cities you've been working with?"

"I haven't been able to afford much travel lately, but I've been keeping up with my groups by phone," Steve replied. "We've gotten great response, the groups are growing by leaps and bounds, just like here in LA.

"You've already heard about Sustainable San Francisco, I'm sure. Sustainable Monterey Bay is well underway with plans for a series of Transit Eco-Villages linked by rail. I'm working with the Santa Barbara Permaculture Network, as well as groups in Oakland, Long Beach and

San Diego. My next big push will be into Orange County, where there hasn't been much organization around the Sustainability concept."[43]

Ari's face became serious. "And how's the work situation?"

Steve looked away. "Pretty desperate. I'm absolutely cracked to take on a wife and a kid right now, but what the hell was I to do? Good times will come again. Meanwhile I get a little piecework here and there."

"If you need any …"

"No." Steve interrupted, forcefully. "We'll do okay." His sudden smile wiped away the grim expression. "After all these years, she's actually my *wife*." His voice had a quality of magic about it.

(26.)

"Tia, we've done it." Calling from Moscow, Ari sounded exhausted. "The agreement is drafted. Now it's a matter of getting it ratified."

"Ari, you don't sound very thrilled," Tia noted cautiously.

"I'm too tired to be thrilled. I've been in too many cities in the last week to count. Plus the agreement itself – called the Moscow Treaty – is lackluster. It's basically Kyoto with slightly stricter emissions cap figures. It retains all the flaws of Kyoto – the complexity, the emissions trading, the unfairness of target reaches."

"So if the agreement is written, and ratification begins, then ..." *Please, say you're coming home, please!*

"Well, they'll not formally declare it 'drafted' until after the MOP meeting here in Moscow next week, but we back-room pens have completed our work." He hesitated.

"Tia, the EU is sending me to Washington for a year to try to round up influence there. I'm going to go with it. At least when I'm in the U.S. I can get home a little more often. I'm headed to DC next week, but I will arrange to swing through LA even though it's not exactly on the way."

(27.)

Jana delivered at home one December evening, in the middle of one of the more spectacular thunderstorms in recent memory. The midwife and Tia were in attendance. One might say Steve was there, in body; he was clearly off on a cloud, he was so excited. Yet when the baby crowned, he was solidly present, and with skilled hands the midwife guided Steve to catch his newborn son.[44]

Tia hadn't witnessed a birth before, Annis' birth having been her only experience. It was transporting to behold. One minute there were four people in the room, and then miraculously there were five. When Tia's turn came to hold the newborn, now bundled in a towel all scrunchy and red, her thoughts ran far beyond the immediate.

It's a woman's role to open and receive, and with what we receive, our bodies reform it, and nurture it, and bring forth a new life. A miraculous transformation.

A bolt of lightning cut the sky, and thunder rattled the windows.

It's a woman's role to open and receive. The climate change. The ecological crisis. You cannot close yourself to it. Open your heart and receive it. And Transform it. Make of it a new life. Birth it. Suckle it, nurture it, feed it, and teach it to stand on its own. A new life: a new lifestyle, a new take on society, a new future. Related to, but distinctly different from its origins.

A sudden torrent of rain demanded attention. Still holding the newborn, Tia peeked around the window drapes. The orange streetlamps gave the storm a haunting fiery-world color.

She looked down to the wrinkled face of the new person in her arms. *What will your life be like? What will life be like when you hold your newborn child?*

(28.)

The 2010-2011 storm season arrived early, with a severity that lashed the Southland with front after front in a matter of days. News reports of flash floods, mudslides and sandbag brigades were daily fare. A sizeable chunk of the Santa Monica pier was lost to the waves and high tides claimed several more of Malibu's beachfront homes.

Floodwaters tore through storm channels, flushing out the homeless huddled beneath overpasses in shelter from the rains. The winds tore apart cardboard shelters and ripped into makeshift tents. The extensive death counts were carefully concealed by the news media, but just about everyone knew someone who had volunteered in the relief efforts. Stories of horror and suffering spread through the city, stories magnified by lack of concrete facts, worsened by the silence of the press and the general population's refusal to acknowledge the crisis.

The gap between 'haves' and 'have nots' within the city was becoming greater with every passing month. Conservative governments declared on one hand that there was no money to fund social programs, that private relief would handle it, while on the other hand disavowing that there was a problem and that the problem was growing. Churches and private charities were strapped trying to handle the mind-boggling demand, amid the Depression economics which had erstwhile donors holding tightly to their funds. The contribution stream was drying up, even as the need grew more desperate.

The El Niño phenomenon affects a wide area of the Pacific rim. While the U.S. Pacific Coast and Southern states received excess rains, southern Mexico, Latin America and the coast of South America received searing drought. The fisheries off Peru deteriorated. Amid crop failures and fears of uprisings in those countries, a trickle of the wealthy and the educated began the migration, and the numbers soon grew. The United States, long a world symbol of possibilities, was the destination, and immigrants ran the border in droves.

Homeland Security was called in, and further demands were made on military Reserves already hard hit by call-ups for the Middle East wars. Many felt it was a subtle distinction, border defense versus undeclared war. Most of the immigrants were unarmed, faced with the unanswerable choice between running U.S. guns and remaining amid disease, civil upheaval and starvation in their countries of origin.

Those that penetrated the border guard made their way to the large cities, and LA was a major stopping place. As the makeshift tent camps swelled with the immigrants, the bands of scavenging homeless grew in number and in desperation. The wealthy areas of the city fought back with armed private patrols. Many Westside communities closed street entrances and became gated. LA's communities condensed further into insular pockets.

(29.)

Tia awakened to the first chirp of Ari's phone amid the strangeness of the hotel room, Ari nestled against her, naked from the night before. He awoke to the second ring.

"Hello? Yes, Senator." Ari was on his feet in an instant, pulling on his pants and moving to the little table where his papers and laptop were spread. He stretched out in a chair, his attention already deep in international affairs.

Tia propped herself on an elbow and watched him fondly. It wasn't often that she joined him on his travels. In the early years there had been her job to consider, and then baby Annis. Later had come the overseas years, when he was switching countries too quickly for even his jet set spirit.

He'd phoned her last week, however. "Tia, come to DC for the weekend, I have a light schedule, only one gathering I must attend."

It had been a whirlwind of a weekend thus far, a time to bask in being lovers rather than parents, a time of museums, sightseeing and restaurants, a very different life from her LA everyday.

Ari was active in his discussion. Tia hadn't much idea what they were talking about, she wasn't really listening. The long line of his body hypnotized her, now stretched out, now animated searching for a data point amid his paperwork, now pacing the room as he got riled up over the issue. At forty-two, his body was lean and muscular.

He clicked his phone closed and flopped on the bed beside her, atop the covers, still half-dressed. His face was alert and alive, his eyes sparkling with excitement.

"Senator Alden's been drafting a greenhouse gas bill – dusting off the Lieberman-McCain effort. The timing's probably much better for it now that Kyoto's binding on the international scene. Also, many U.S. states and businesses are already actively on board. They'll drive it, rather than Resist it. The business competitiveness issue of five years ago is moot now. There are some concerns with the shape of the economy but I think we need the influx of new industry this will stimulate.

"The big news is that Diamont seems interested. If Alden can get him on board, he has tremendous influence. At that point it'll be another bi-partisan effort and stands a really good chance. You'll meet Alden at the party tonight."

Tia watched the long line of his shoulders, his muscles smooth as he propped himself on one elbow to talk. "Who else will I meet at the party tonight? Tell me about the tall, good-looking handsome ones." She crawled across the bed to kiss him, the blankets slipping down, revealing her body.

His eyes widened and he drew back from her embraces, slowly sitting up on the bed. "Shit, I didn't think about this. Tia, you need to know, Lori Fordon will likely be at that party too."

A chill ran through her.

"There's nothing to worry about," he said, but his voice was tense.

The sparkle had gone out of the morning. She pulled at the blankets to cover herself, but they were now caught beneath Ari's arm.

He looked over at her, her face now tight and closed, her chin quivering. "Tia, it was a long time ago."

"It feels like it never ended."

"That's because of the politics. She took the side of the U.S. She's become a red-white-and-blue patriot, touting the company line the whole damn way without thinking. She's forgotten what used to really matter to her. We used to be on the same side, fighting for the good of the world."

"Before Johannesburg?"

"Long before that. March 2001. That's when the United States declared it would not join the countries of the world in the Kyoto Protocol. And that's when Lori Fordon took the side of the U.S., turning her back on all the world is trying to do to bring emissions under control and keep global warming in check. Now we're just fighting each other. And getting nothing accomplished." Now it was his face that was tight and resigned.

"After I broke it off with her, it was like she formed a vendetta. Every time she could, she would attack me, every chance to cause a debate in the formal scene. I simply avoided her everywhere else. Tia, I want you to be ready, I don't know what kind of fireworks she's going to pull tonight."

Tia sat in the middle of the bed, a huddled lump, naked under the blankets. She missed Annis terribly; it had only been two days, but the longest separation since her birth. Lares felt very far away. Suddenly, Tia desperately wanted to go home.

Ari crawled over to her. Lifting her chin with his finger he kissed her gently. It did nothing to lift her spirits. "Come on, let's go get some breakfast."

∽

For the party that evening, Tia chose a simple dress of black silk. It wasn't tight, but it certainly flattered her slender figure, with a neckline that was just a hint of reveal without an awkward plunge. *Looking darn good for thirty-seven*, the mirror told her; this raised her confidence one small notch. She arranged her hair loosely around her shoulders, then slipped on now-unfamiliar high heels.

Ari looked sensational in his dark suit – in California he didn't dress up like this. He stood tall, his self-assurance radiating through his well-tailored clothes. At his temples a scant few hairs of silver now proclaimed 'distinguished,' a look he wore very well.

His dark eyes rolled down the line of her body with obvious liking. After six years of marriage it felt delicious to be received like this. She stood a little taller and smiled flirtatiously, savoring the moment. Ari offered her his arm in jovial formality and they were off.

The tower suite clearly belonged to another lifestyle than hers. Stark white and glass, modern art of obvious prestige, wide windows overlooking the Potomac. The energy amongst the guests was at once strange and off-putting. Accustomed to the warm candor of her LA eco-circle, the primping and positioning of these people was obvious to Tia, and she didn't like it. She looked around more closely at the women – they were all wearing white. Clearly black was quite out of fashion in DC this year.

Ari found them drinks and escorted Tia partially around the room making some introductions. She recognized many names from his conversations and from the media. Over Ari's shoulder she noticed a woman in a red dress, staring at them. Ari was now guiding Tia to the next grouping. She looked back at the woman and their eyes connected. Tia could feel the ice in that stare.

"Senator Alden, this is my wife, Tia Damek," Ari was saying.

Tia swung around.

Barry Alden was tall – statuesque, even. Scarcely older than Ari, with sandy colored hair and clean Ivy-League appearance, he carried himself with the same confidence that Ari did. The Senator was pleasant enough, yet there was an air of too-little-time as other guests clamored for his recognition. The Senator politely excused himself, taking Ari's elbow and pulling him aside for a more serious exchange.

Knowing that Ari would be working this event, Tia let him go. She took a deep breath, feeling like the gazelle, hunted. The red dress materialized at her side.

The woman was dazzling in her closely fitted couture dress, extravagant diamond earrings, careful makeup, and impeccably coiffed salon-darkened hair. She was of Tia's height and of graceful build. The scent of expensive perfume followed her gestures. She smiled with formal graciousness and extended a hand.

"I don't believe we've met. I'm Lori Fordon, U.S. Delegate to the UNFCCC." Lori paused, clearly expecting her name to have impact.

Copying Ari's habit, Tia pulled her shoulders back and drew herself up to her full height. She looked Lori in the eye.

"Tia Damek."

That'd be Mrs. *Damek to you, sweetie.*

Lori glanced over Tia, clearly taking inventory. Tia could feel the ice down her back and willed her knees not to tremble.

"I know Ari." Lori's grey eyes were stony, her carriage flawless. A beauty queen's cultivated smile fixed itself upon her face.

"Yes, I believe you do." Tia's voice came out quietly, and calmed her with its strength.

"I work with him."

"No, you work against him."

"I protect the interests of the United States." Lori sounded imperial.

"My husband is fighting for the benefit of the world."

"He's abandoned his country," Lori's voice was carefully measured but her eyes and jaw were granite hard. "He's campaigning for others, against the U.S."

"No, you've abandoned what you know is right." The knot in Tia's stomach burst open; she couldn't believe these words came out of her mouth.

"Don't feed me his lines," Lori hissed. Tia thought she imagined it, or perhaps the corner of Lori's exquisite mouth wobbled, just for a moment.

"Maybe that's just what you need to hear right now, his lines."

"Not from you." Lori's delivery was a dagger thrust.

A sudden image of Annis' gleeful little face appeared in Tia's mind, and they were precisely Ari's words that came to her lips.

"Ms. Fordon, what is it that really matters to you? What are you fighting for?"

A tiny muscle moved beside Lori's eye.

The words seemed to flow through Tia. "You know, there are millions of little kids out there who are trusting you. They're trusting that you're here fighting to make a better world for them."

The color drained from Lori's face. She still held herself as elegantly as ever. She opened her mouth halfway as if to reply, then turned on her heel and disappeared into the crowd.

Tia watched her go, a little disappointed; she felt she had just gotten started.

Ari instantly appeared at Tia's elbow. "I was with Alden. I can't believe that she would single you out like that. Are you okay?"

"I did all right for myself," Tia said, the energy and determination still in her voice.

He looked at her for a long moment, clearly processing this strange response. His dark eyes flitted to where the red dress had been, and then returned to Tia, his focus suddenly rich and direct. A small smile appeared on his face.

"You amaze me," he said simply. "I don't know how you do it." His eyes connected with hers for a long moment. The party seemed suspended in time. "I have one more person I want to talk with," his fingers graced the skin of her shoulder and her bare neck in a way that made her tingle, "and then we'll go back to the hotel."

She formed a little kiss in his direction. After a long pause, he turned away into the crowd in search of his political quarry. Tia watched Ari's elegant figure part the crowd and sighed, savoring the anticipation their little flirtation had awakened in her. Out of the corner of her eye, she caught the flash of a bright red dress, fleeing the party.

(30.)

"A convention on Sustainable development? Tia, you're crazy! We're in the middle of a damned Depression!" Steve was looking quite grey these days; he hadn't had a job in months.

"Matthew found a Foundation which will underwrite it financially. Just look at all the people who are interested in the Sustainability movement, the numbers are growing at a phenomenal rate." Tia gestured around the auditorium where the Legacy LA meeting was breaking up.

Indeed, even though they had moved the meetings to larger quarters, the numbers of attendees had similarly increased. There were downsides to this: all aspects of the meeting now had to be on microphone.

"Yeah, at some point we've got to figure out how to get smaller circles going so that we can bring back the discussion interplay." Steve's conversation drifted to the meeting format, but Tia brought him back.

"We could showcase green innovations and Sustainable ideas. If we could manage free admission, many people would attend just for something to do, and it would spread the word that much further."

Steve seemed to consider the idea. "You know, if we put in a conference type schedule, we could hold the discussion forums at the same time as your convention showcase. Which building were you thinking of? Veterans Memorial?"

"Oh, not at all. I was thinking of an open air forum. Perhaps El Dorado Park or Kenneth Hahn in Baldwin Hills. The exhibits could be in tents, the discussion circles out in fresh air. I think that would be much more appropriate to the subject material!"

Steve's face was beginning to come alive. "Hey, instead of the cold and corporate sounding 'Conference' or 'Convention,' we could call it a Fair, with the lightheartedness of that old Renaissance Faire. The Sustainability transition is a Renaissance, after all!"

Tia's delight was clear. "The LA Future Fair! We don't even need to say 'Sustainable' because we already know that's the only way our future can be!"

(31.)

Ari called from Washington, his voice sounding shaken. "Tia, I just had the most unusual meeting ... with Lori Fordon."

Tia's heart skipped a beat.

"She said ... she said she is switching sides on Kyoto. I still can't believe it. She's going to push for U.S. ratification, and asked for my help.

"She referred to this reversal as political and personal suicide, I don't quite understand what that meant, but she said she just had to do it.

"Tia," he paused, "she said it was something you said to her at that party, something I used to tell her, years ago, and you reminded her, got her to thinking differently. Tia, whatever you said to her, thank you!"

(32.)

Mainstream media made no mention of it, but in 2011 a group of world leaders quietly and humbly assembled. Representatives from Buddhism, Christianity, Hinduism, Islam and Judaism, gathered to discuss world environmental and social issues. These dignitaries met in Christchurch, New Zealand where they boarded a ship that took them past the crumbling Ross Ice Shelf of Antarctica.

In clear contrast to the 2002 Earth Charter and its Ark of Hope, the 2011 Ross gathering emerged from the general session with a short and simple two line statement of mutual respect and clear hope for peace and understanding between peoples.

Rather than a single homogenized document about the relationship of religion to world issues, which risked being meaningless to all and offensive to some, individual religious leaders in breakout retreats each produced statements specific to their belief. The statements were as different and diverse as the peoples they represented. Yet each contained its own soulfelt beauty, and a powerful commitment to changing the earthly lifestyle of humanity.

(33.)

"Tia! The Senate just passed the Alden-Diamont Bill!" Ari nearly shouted through the phone in his excitement.

"Oh, Ari, that's thrilling!"

"It was close, but we made it! Rafferty's conceded, he'll sign it."

"So now the terms of Kyoto will become U.S. law, even if we don't ratify?"

"Yes, even if we don't ratify the international treaty. If it's federal law, it'll still be binding, the United States will have to adjust to emissions management thinking."

"It's really no different than if we had ratified."

"I wouldn't say that, but in the end it should have a similar effect. Regardless of whether by federal or international law, U.S. emissions won't go uncontrolled, as was feared when Bush rejected Kyoto."

"So does this mean your job there is done?"

"Not exactly." He was calmer now. "There's still quite a bit to work out with respect to the trading schemes. The U.S. hopes to integrate its federal trading system with the international one.

"It would be great to get the U.S. on board Kyoto because then we'd be party to the world negotiations. But I think that's not likely to happen. The main agenda now is to get the U.S. on board the post-2012 agreement. And the chances right now, right after the Alden-Diamont bill, are probably not good politically. So I think I'll come home for a while..."

Tia shrieked with joy.

CHAPTER 6:

NO LONGER A SMALL GROUP

2011-2018

"'Poverty is the greatest polluter of the environment.'" Esperanza was the speaker at tonight's Legacy LA meeting. Petite, lively and pretty, she captivated the large crowd. "Indira Gandhi said that in 1973. Unfortunately, it is no less true today, almost forty years later.

"As environmentalists, we may think our battle is solely about ecosystems and natural capital. I beg to differ. Social causes and environmentalism are irrefutably linked. We cannot bring one issue to Sustainability without solving the other simultaneously. We cannot create a pretty little system for West LA and disregard South Central and East LA. We cannot solve global warming without taking into account the poverty which drives indigenous people to clear rain forests in favor of cash crops. A Sustainable environment must include solutions for education, literacy, labor rights, women's rights, justice.

"Here in the U.S. we have adopted an unstated policy of 'take care of your own.' I'm asking you to stretch your definition of 'your own' by a few billion. 6.9 billion to give a rough estimate. Every man, woman and child on the planet is part of this issue.

"It's easier to visualize Sustainability and resource productivity when we speak of say, a timber forest. If we see heaps of scrap materials, and barren stripped acreage, there are clearly inefficiencies in the system. We're not using the resource – the timber forest – as productively as we can. If we log material more quickly than the earth can regrow it, we are clearly acting in an irresponsible and unsustainable manner.

"When we marginalize people – when we cast aside certain groups of individuals, certain populations, or whole nations – we are not acting in a Sustainable manner; we are compounding the problem. When we have large segments of the population unemployed or underemployed, we are not being efficient.

"Poverty drives people to act from desperation rather than from responsibility. A desperate people will do anything to put food in the mouths of their children, even if that action is not in the interest of global causes. It is up to us to act from responsibility, to reach out, to solve these problems, to assist people in rising out of poverty and desperation as part of our plan of Sustainability.

"It has become popular in the wealthy countries of the Northern Hemisphere to blame our global environmental problems on population growth. Specifically, to point fingers at the underdeveloped countries of the Southern Hemisphere and say: if they didn't have so many babies, we wouldn't be in this mess.[45]

"I invite you to take a hard look at per capita consumption. A child born in the wealthy developed countries consumes fifty times more world resources than a child born in developing countries. In terms of per capita share of world resources, the U.S. population currently consumes more than five times our Sustainable share of world resources. So while total world population does indeed remain a concern, the real issue is horrifically unsustainable consumption practices, particularly in the wealthy countries of the Northern Hemisphere.

"'It is manifestly unjust that a privileged few should continue to accumulate excess goods, squandering available resources, while masses of people are living in conditions of misery at the very lowest level of subsistence.'

"We must change the ways of society, *para los niños*, for the children of the world."

⤟

After the presentation, as Tia moved through the crowd, she passed Carl, talking with a member she did not recognize. "I'm a lecturer at USC now, School of Business. I teach Natural Capitalism and Market Trends."

"Oh, Carl, congratulations! I hadn't heard." Tia interrupted them.

"Hey, Tia, meet Al Chapman. I knew him through the marketing department back at my old firm."

"I wish I could say I was a professor like Carl here! Currently I'm just an unemployed theorist." Al grinned broadly as if it were all a big joke.

"Tia, did you hear about the new AICPA guidelines?" Carl asked.

"The who?" asked Al.

"The American Institute of Certified Public Accountants, they determine the standards for how the financial statements of U.S. companies are prepared," Carl explained.

"I know they were under pressure to draft guidelines on the reporting of greenhouse gas emissions, particularly after the passage of the Alden-Diamont bill," Tia replied. "I think they were trying to figure out Sustainability reporting as well."[46]

"They just issued new guidelines which require companies to disclose the status of the company's greenhouse gas emissions in their financial statement footnotes. This is to be measured according to 'federal standards,' which just so happen to equate to Kyoto Protocol measurement standards." Carl sounded delighted.

"So now, companies can be compared to one another based upon at least one aspect of their impact on the environment," Tia said. "This is the first major step toward financial statement reporting of aspects of Natural Capital."

(2.)

Ari stretched out in the spring sunshine on the apartment steps, while Tia filled a basket with some of the year's last snowpeas from the garden. Steve joined them, toddler Seth at his heels.

"Steve and his shadow!" Ari grinned.

"Yes, he insists on being with me wherever I go," Steve said with proud delight. "So, Damek, now that you're in LA for a while, what's the next project going to be? Are you going to edge in on our LA Future Fair?"

"If I'm lucky, I'll be in town for your Fair, but I'm not going to count on it. The Fair is for you and Tia to manage. I have a few other things up my sleeve. Ben's coming by in a bit to go over his rail plan, I'm going to help him get it through City Hall. On another, I'm going to need your construction services. How's your workload?"

"Nonexistent, in this economy." Steve grimaced. The shadow of worry was clear around his eyes these days.

"I've been talking with Carl and I think that's about to change, perhaps after the election. Meanwhile," Ari paused and looked at Tia, a twinkle in his eye, "I think it's time for me to get back into the real estate market. I think it's time to buy a house."

"Oh, Ari!" Tia flew out of the garden to fling herself into his arms with unrestrained joy. Ari laughed, a deep laugh full of satisfaction with life.

Steve looked downcast. "So, that'll mean the end of this comfy little complex." He looked around the garden.

Tia drew a sharp breath. *Ari, I don't think Steve can afford to leave here!*

"Matthew told me last night his legal work has dried up. They are planning to move to San Diego to join Shannon's family," Ari said to Steve. "So that just leaves you and Jana. I had it in mind that we might join this new de-mansionizing trend. Perhaps we could find a bigger house and reconfigure it for our two families."

Steve's eyes widened. "Jana would love that."

Tia sighed. *Ari sees it.*

"I would love that," Tia nestled herself deeper against Ari's neck.

Ari absentmindedly played with her hair as he spoke. "In this economy, there are lots of choices. So many properties foreclosed and boarded up. The prices represent incredible deals.

"With the Depression needs, so many families doubled up or took in relatives that most of the single-family zoning regulations are now pointless. I think it's high time to overturn them. Rather than spreading civilization further at the edges of our city, we should be redeveloping the less efficient land use we already have within the bounds, particularly in areas within reach of future mass transit. Some of the least efficient are these sprawling luxury neighborhoods where only one family uses a quarter acre in the center of the city."

"Hi everyone! Hey, what a greeting committee!" Ben walked up the path.

As Ari moved to make room for Ben on the step, Tia disentangled herself from Ari's embrace.

"No need to break that up on my account – it looked pretty cozy!" Ben kidded them. Tia blushed and returned to her garden work, righting the basket she had spilled in her dash to Ari. Little Seth found a snowpea amidst the thyme plants.

"Is this the Olmsted plan?" Steve asked.

"Olmsted-inspired, you mean." Ben laughed. "Frederick Law Olmsted designed before 1900. Places like New York's Central Park, Niagara Falls and Yosemite."

"Yosemite? That's wilderness!" Steve exclaimed.

Ben chuckled. "Actually, it's not. It's a planted and managed forest. A lot of people don't realize this. Olmsted laid out roads and paths to make public access possible. He designed them to direct the visitor's gaze to elements in the scenery. His objective was 'the contemplation of natural scenes of an impressive character.'

"Olmsted also did urban spaces, where he tried to bring the advantages of natural scenery to those who could not travel.

"His sons laid out the plan for Seattle's park system. Their goal was to locate a park or a playground within one half mile of every home in Seattle."[47]

"Wow, I doubt any areas around here can equal that!" Steve said.

"Perhaps Santa Monica, Beverly Hills or El Segundo, but certainly not LA proper," Tia replied from the garden.

"The Olmsted Brothers' idea was explored for the city of LA in the 1930s," Ben continued. "My associates and I recently got a grant from the John Randolph Haynes Foundation,[48] and during these slow times we have been working with these ideas.

"We've put together a comprehensive plan of rail systems for the Greater LA Area. The light rail and Metrolink we have today is so basic I can't even describe it as a skeletal system – there is so much more to be done. Our plan threads together the various neighborhood pockets. In addition to the present Metro lines built in the late 1990s and early 2000s, our plan includes extensive rail additions throughout the area.[49]

"Bus lines will radiate outward like spokes from the rail station stops. There will be a clean-fueled jitney cab which will circulate through the neighborhood around each station. The station areas and line easements are landscaped Olmstead-style into parks, community gardens and managed wildlands with native plants.

"When the Olmsted Brothers created the Seattle plan they emphasized implementing it quickly, so that desirable sites could be obtained at prices affordable to the city. It occurred to me this morning that we're in exactly the same boat, right now in LA."

"With bargain prices on real estate, you mean," Ari concurred.

"Exactly. While we already have easements on a few of these parcels, now's the prime time for the city to snap up the additional lots it needs in order to put the transit system together. The plan's on file. It's time to begin it."

Ben's comprehensive Plan for a Los Angeles Sustainable Environment came to be known as PLASE, a nickname which suited Ben just fine.

(3.)

"Ari, what happened in that meeting, the one in DC with Lori?" The thought had been nagging at Tia for days, since Ari's phone call, since his return to LA, and now it came bursting out of her.

Ari stiffened and returned the tangerine to his breakfast plate. "She said she's going to support the treaty," he said slowly.

"And ..."

"And what?" He wouldn't meet her eyes.

"Ari, I have to hear it, it's eating at me."

"All right. She called and wanted to meet. I was busy reviewing a report for Alden's staff, I didn't have time for her usual shenanigans."

"Usual shenanigans!" Tia's eyebrows shot up.

"Political posturing." He drew the phrase out. "This time she was different, quiet, not her typical fire and brimstone. She … Tia, this gets into old history."

"Right now it's not sounding very much like it's history!"

"She started talking about old times, long before I met you. Tia, I broke it off with her, she wouldn't have ended it, she was still …" he paused, then cleared his throat. "It seems like somehow she has now realized, all these years later, the mistakes she made. Realized how far she has gotten off track from what she believed in."

"What did she believe in?"

"In the old days, everything for her was about the children. She loved children. Funny that she doesn't have any. Out of the blue she asked if I had pictures of my kids."

Leave my daughter out of this!

"On my cell I had that one of Annis in the garden. Fordon looked at it and started crying. It was then that she told me she was switching sides." He shook his head. "This is going to kill her politically, it's a huge shift. I just don't understand why she did it."

He stopped and looked over at Tia. "What did you say to her?"

"N-nothing."

"She said it was you." He brought the full intensity of those dark eyes to bear on her.

Tia rose and started washing dishes at the sink. Lori's face appeared in front of her, gasping for a comeback, shutting down and turning tail.

"Tia? Tia, I've been working on this woman for years with no results. You see her at a party for twenty seconds and she flips sides."

Tia spun around to face him, grabbing the counter behind her for support. "I told her … that children out there trust her to make the right decisions."

His eyes widened. He rested his forehead in his hand and stared at the floor. "Of all the things …"

"What? What did I say?"

His dark eyes returned to hers. "As a child, Lori never felt she had an adult she could trust; she was raised by an endless flow of hired help. She's the daughter of an Ambassador and a Texas millionaire. She tried to shed it all at one point, that's when I met her. She wanted to do something for the world, to make a difference.

"Well, you certainly stirred things up. It should be exciting, whatever happens next. You know, that Alden-Diamont bill just passed. I wonder ... I wouldn't be surprised if she bent the ear of some Senator on that one."

(4.)

The closing of WalMarts and other chain stores, the resultant blossoming of neighborhood stores and businesses, the boarded up and abandoned properties throughout the area, and the sealing and gating of Westside affluent neighborhoods, would seem to be distinctly separate events. Yet all lead to a turning inward of neighborhoods, both affluent and ethnic, creating a more insular feel in a city which had long been spread too far afield into suburbia.

LA's development was a story of urban sprawl, a bursting outward from the developed city cores in continuous pursuit of new space. Unlike cities such as New York and San Francisco, in LA there were no waterways to contain the horizontal development and redirect it to vertical. So, unlike New York and San Francisco, where transit systems could be plotted within relatively easy access of desired destinations, the haphazard suburban history of LA had always meant that potential riders and prospective transport had never been realistically close. Mass transit had been explored before for LA, unsuccessfully.

But this time it was different.

The neighborhood pockets forming throughout the city created the perfect segue into the PLASE plan. Suddenly LA had what other cities had long had: destinations, rather than sprawl, for bus service, subway and light rail.

Abandoned properties falling through the tangled web of multiple foreclosures and escheating to the State opened spaces within the cityscape, spaces unheard of in erstwhile crowded LA, spaces much needed to reintroduce Olmstead's 'advantages of natural beauty.'

(5.)

The house was a rambling one-story in the Brentwood area. It, along with several others in the once posh neighborhood, was boarded up with landscaping brown from desertion. Its U-shaped layout included spacious public rooms – living room, kitchen, dining room, office – and two wings of smaller rooms, which would make perfect suites for the two families.

While Ari negotiated escrows and zoning in an era of infrequent real estate transactions, Jana, Tia and Steve debated construction and garden plans. It was a delightful time of dreaming and anticipation, sitting around the Damek kitchen table. All three talked at once in their excitement.

"I'll put french doors on the hallway of each wing, so that each family has a small private area away from the common." Steve was already deep into planning his construction effort. "The large common rooms will be perfect for sharing. In fact, the office that's already there is large enough for all four of us to use interchangeably – we wouldn't all tend to use it at the same time anyway. I'll make built-in furniture for the desks and computer stations."

"The huge kitchen will be great for six." Tia had come to enjoy cooking for a crowd in the days of sharing at the triplex.

"Plus company – you just know we'll have plenty!" Jana joined in. "You might recall, the group that became Legacy LA grew out of gatherings we used to have in the living room at the Venice house!"

"That was well before my time," Tia laughed.

"Not for the second go-round – it'll be right under your nose, girlfriend! Remember who you're married to, Mr. Organizer himself!"

A giggling six year old Annis chased Seth through the kitchen and out to the garden.

Steve continued outlining his plans. "I'll reconfigure the plumbing, to separate greywater from black. We'll keep the greywater from kitchen preparation, laundry and showers and process it on the property, draining it through filtration beds, perhaps onto fruit trees. I'll configure the drain lines so that at some point down the line we'll have the option of blackwater treatment – composting toilets and the like – but for now we'll let that go to the city sewers.

"Ari wants solar. I'm not sure if he wants to get completely off the grid and use batteries, or whether he wants to engage in buyback with the power companies. Either one's an option as far as I'm concerned. The solar panels we'll need will cover a mere fraction of the roof surface, so whatever he decides will work from the construction angle."

"I've been over the property, observing grading, wind, sun angles," Jana said with excitement. "We'll install swales to cache rainwater for those storms we do receive. The driveway will be crushed rock so that any rains we get will add to the water table rather than to the storm drains."

"Are you following the T.R.E.E.S. Planbook to create mini-watersheds?"[50] Tia asked.

"Somewhat ... with a few touches of my own, of course!" Jana grinned.

"Thinking of trees, will we be able to save those mature trees on the property?" Tia asked.

"During the abandonment, many of them suffered from drought and subsequent pest invasions. I'll have a tree surgeon prune them and see what we can save but it'll likely be wiser to remove several, putting in native species and food-bearing ones. I'll set up a schedule of phase-out so that we are never without canopy and shade cover, but we can gradually convert to a wiser selection of species.

"I'll redo the gardens, of course, with all that I have learned at the triplex. I'm thinking of having an area with benches so we could have an outdoor classroom – to teach this stuff right from our own premises!" Jana replied.

"Oh, Jana, can we finally have those chickens?" Tia teased.

"You bet. I'll start some research on the breeds right away! The kids will love raising them!"

Ari returned from his appointments downtown. He lounged in the kitchen doorframe, watching the trio pouring over plans.

"You're all thinking much too small," he said.

Tia heard mischief in his voice.

"What do you mean, too small, I'm regrading a quarter of the property!" Steve flashed defensive.

Ari strode over to the plans unfurled on the table. Picking up Jana's pencil, he marked big slashes across parts of the drawings. "This property boundary wall has to go, and this one. The swales will need rethinking, and all the landscape areas. The solar capacity's inadequate, the greywater layout, because ..." he looked at Tia, "...I just bought two of them."

"You what!?" Tia was the first to find her voice.

"Actually, we should do the plans for three – Carl likes the idea and is picking up one also. All adjoining."

"Ari, these are $1 to 3 million properties," Tia worried.

"They were. In the old days. Now they can't find anyone to take them. The former owner's cars likely cost him more than that second house cost me. You saw how many places over there are boarded up. I could have had more if I'd been willing to finance them, but I wouldn't do that in this economy.

"It's a legal nightmare. I called Matthew up from San Diego to work on it. The banks that held the properties in foreclosure have folded themselves. Carl's property may even have escheated to the State. I'll let Carl and Matthew figure that one out. My extra one was being sold at auction. There are no buyers out there, no one can afford to maintain these huge arks.

"The market crashes wiped out much of the upper middle class – most people were so heavily leveraged they couldn't escape it. Plummeting values took them upside down. There aren't too many people around now with the cash to buy these big places. The few buyers are going for the lower priced smaller houses."

"Slow down, Damek," Steve interrupted. "Where do you get the cash to buy two mansions? Venice didn't net you that much."

Ari paused and looked at Steve, considering. "Venice yielded a decent amount, I'd held it through that wild appreciation. But then ... I shorted the stock market crash."

"Holy shit." Steve was speechless. Even Jana looked stunned.

Ari continued blithely. "I put in a bid on a lark, put down what I thought was an absurdly low figure. Turns out I was the only bidder and they took it!" He shrugged. "I still can't believe it."

"You son of a ..." Steve shook his head slowly.

"Ari, what are we going to do with three houses?" Tia was still worrying.

He shot her that you've-got-five-heads look. "More of the same, of course! A whole complex. It's an opportunity to get more people involved, to really create a new direction in housing in LA. You have three main houses, each with a three- or four-car garage, plus two guest houses, all to make over just as you've been doing. These properties which used to be reserved for three families should house nine or more families when we get done with them."

"We can spread the landscape layout across all the properties?" Jana was already back to the plans.

"Of course. It's just around an acre, an insane amount of land in the middle of the city! I figured on one overall plan, across the entire parcel. No walls, just like you did here at the triplex. It should feel quite spacious."

"Wow, I can really make a zone 5 now!" Jana was delighted. "I can't wait to get back out there, to observe the site at these new properties!"

"Zone 5?"

"Permaculture zone. In Permaculture layout, you think in concentric circles from the main area of use – for example, the houses. The area closest to the house, the Permaculturists call Zone 1. This is where they put all the high-intensity tasks and plantings, like seedlings which need daily watering. Think of efficiency of motion: you pass them every day as you move around your home, so you notice what they need, and you hardly lift a finger to get to them.

"Further out in your concentric circles, you put things you use less and less often, like semi-intensely cultivated vegetables in zone 2 and minimal care orchards in zone 3.

"Zone 5 is the outer circle, and in an ideal situation, this is where you put wildlands, woods, wildlife refuges, and things like that. You leave these areas to the wild things, yet you 'reap' from them in observation and inspiration."[51]

(6.)

"Ben, thanks so much for stepping in like this on the spur of the moment," Tia said, as they sat down at the Damek's kitchen table. "Steve suddenly has his hands full."

"Yeah, I heard Ari gave him a little project." Ben chuckled. "So where did you guys leave it?"

"We've confirmed the site – the Kenneth Hahn Recreation Area."

"That's a terraced park going up the hillside, right?"

"Yes. We'll take the knoll of the hill for the main exhibits. We can put the discussion circles on tiers further down."

"In tents, I presume?"

"Ideally yes, but I haven't arranged for those yet."

Ben made a note on his handheld.

"I can handle the food!" Ben rubbed his ample stomach. "I'm a qualified expert."

"You might check with Shannon. She might have some leads."

"Exhibits? Are they all arranged?"

"Many are." She referred to her clipboard. "We have fuel cell vehicles, a biodiesel exhibit, the Department of Water and Power's Green Power program.[52] There will be classes on composting, edible landscaping, barter networks, greywater."

"Ooh, I want to see this one: Mass-Transit Plan for a Los Angeles Sustainable Environment," Ben clowned, running his finger down the list to his own name as presenter.

Tia grinned. "I'm sure you'll do a fine job with it. Hey, let me get Annis and we'll drive up to the site – she'll enjoy running around and you can see the layout."

(7.)

"Immersion. It's the best way to teach languages and it's the best way to teach greener living." Lauren Tilford began her 'Growing Sustainably-Minded Adults' lecture at the LA Future Fair. Lauren was tall, maternal and feminine, with shoulder-length brunette hair. Tia felt particularly drawn to this topic, out of all the options on the schedule.

"When we teach babies language, we teach by immersion: the spoken word surrounds them, day in and day out. Their basic needs are dependent upon communicating in that language.

"Similarly, immersion seems to me to be the best and easiest way to raise people who will behave in a greener, or more Sustainable manner. Surround them with Sustainability, day in and day out, as much Sustainability as we can manage.[53]

"In a typical school setting, the kids are surrounded by a peer group. Who has the latest fashion shoes? Who has the latest electronic toy? What did you get for Christmas? What outings have you consumed lately? A hierarchical society defined by consumerism, much the same as the hierarchical society of consumption we adults experience in mainstream adult social circles and the business world.

"It is challenging to establish green ethics in our youngsters. The societal pressure is everywhere, even within the esoteric walls of a Waldorf school. This societal pressure, the defining of one's self in comparison with others, seems to be part of the human condition within groups. So it strikes me that the thing to do is, surround yourself and your child with the right group – immerse yourselves in Green.

"Look at the success that a generation of schools have had teaching Recycling. We now have a populace where the seed of Recycling has already been planted. Certainly we have further to go with it, but we have achieved a generation that doesn't bat an eye at separating glass and aluminum from general garbage. The concept is already instilled. That colored barrel with the triangle does not need explanation any more. Education is working.

"How then do we reform other aspects of society? Some ideas:

"School busses and school district vehicles – what if they were all Clean Air Vehicles, rather than belching that raunchy stuff? If school busses were the cleanest, sleekest, contemporary models available, then busses would become attractive, and mass transit would be instilled in minds-in-formation as a desirable and attractive option over mom and dad's fossil-fuel-burning road hog.[54]

"Water wisdom – what if school grounds and city buildings were landscaped attractively in local native plants and low water plantings, called xeriscaping. This aesthetic would become the norm. The same with greywater irrigation, and the habits of dividing greywater versus blackwater wastes. If children grow up surrounded by it, the concept is not new, and will be assimilated into the fabric of society as these children grow and make their life choices.

"Solar power. Green buildings. Health supportive foods. And consumer choices, that's a big one.[55]

"Already I have seen websites devoted to greener September back-to-schools. But directing consumer choice is perhaps our most challenging issue, as educators and as parents. Consumerism is all around us, from the clothes we wear, to the music we listen to, the volume of material we devour. How do we immerse our children – the adults of the next generation – in to anything other than *more* when we presently live in a 'more' culture?

"Number One: Be it. Live it yourselves, live greener values, greener practices within your family home: Simple Living, less Stuff, green products, Sufficiency, an inner sense of well-being. The way to transform future generations is to begin the process now, instill it as the norm in their growing years. To do that, we as parents must make the uncomfortable changes – because all change is by human nature uncomfortable – in our lives, modeling this for our children.

"Number Two: *Do* with them. Teach hands-on skills. Get their hands in contact with the earth. Grow a garden of edible fruits and vegetables so that they can learn to nurture living plants, and eat the product of their labors. Teach them how to repair household items. If you don't know how, learn, and let them see you learning. Teach them how to cook, from paring fresh vegetables, on through to a finished dish for the family table. Take them to community service projects and wildlands cleanup events. Seek social outreach projects that are kid-appropriate. Take them in small groups – ones and twos – out to natural spaces, our wilder parks, just to be in the bosom of the planet, removed from the city confines created by man. Listen, smell, observe together.

"Number Three: Talk with them. Explain these things to your kids as you do them. As you take out the recycling, celebrate that this bucket is that much more we can divert from our landfills and why this is important. Explain to them the idea of limited world resources. Explain to them why mass-transit, or these alternatively fueled vehicles on display up the hill here today, are preferable to the gasoline-fueled internal combustion engine. Explain to them the concept of renewable energy sources as contrasted with nonrenewables. Let them know why it is preferable to choose a reusable container for their bag lunches rather than a disposable plastic baggie. Put them in charge of carrying the reusable canvas bags to market, and explain to them why it is wiser. Take them to farmer's markets, let them see the health of the bounty before them, let them talk with the growers, have them taste-test a fruit grown to ripeness locally versus a supermarket fruit preharvested and warehouse ripened during shipping and storage. Take them to local businesses where they meet the vendors, as contrasted with warehouse chain stores where the hourly clerks feel no connection to the product for sale. Read to them about Sustainable lifestyles. I have a booklist at the back of the room. In short, immerse them in Sustainable whys.

"Number Four: Peer selection. The social set with which our family chooses to surround itself is environmentally conscious. The adults are making a valiant effort to bring eco-practices into their family lives. Imagine, a circle of families where Reuse is the norm and New is unusual. Where leads on consignment stores and Freecycle are a typical topic of conversation. Where books and clothes and toys are regularly passed along to the next available user. Where the menu that is in the lunchboxes and on the birthday party tables of your kids' friends consists of biodynamic and organic foods.

"Imagine attending a nine year old's birthday party where the birthday child says: come to play and celebrate, and instead of a present, I have enough stuff, please join our family in making a donation to Heifer International.[56] Heifer is a charity which gives live farm animals – chickens, goats, cows – to families in poverty-stricken foreign countries. And when one family in the circle begins it, the fashion spreads; soon Green and Giving become the norm. Immersion.

"I'm not claiming sainthood here, this isn't about perfection. We're each on a journey, toward this future called Sustainable. For each of us the journey will look different. One person may have solved some Sustainability issues by replacing a lawn with native plants, while her neighbor traded the SUV for a hybrid. The xeriscape success can't beat herself up for not achieving a greener transport, nor should the hybrid family berate themselves for not yet achieving water-wisdom. We each phase-in different elements at different times.

"This means that each of us is simultaneously sitting at multiple locations along a continuum from 'quite sustainable' to 'outrageously unsustainable.'

"The trick is, to find peace with being simultaneously at those multiple degrees of attainment. Donella Meadows was one thinker who aired thoughts on finding peace with less-than-perfection as we move toward living greener in the midst of a consumer society.

"Arthur Waskow encourages us to release the single-standard, on-off, black-white barricade of *forbidden* versus *acceptable*. He recommends thinking of it as a constantly moving standard in which the test is: Are we constantly doing what is more respectful, less damaging to the earth than we did last year?

"A constantly moving standard of more respectful, less damaging: if we can immerse our growing minds in this sole concept, we will have made major headway in preparing future generations to live more Sustainably than we presently do.

"Thank you, for caring enough about future generations to join in this exploration."

◆

After the lecture, Tia headed over to Cassandra's exhibit. Cassandra was talking with an older man, bearded, short and round. As Tia approached the table, Cassandra laughed, and nudged the man in a lingering, playful sort of way.

Tia's eyes widened in astonishment.

The man's hand came to rest on Cassandra's plump upper arm.

"Tia!" Cassandra's voice still held laughter.

"Mom, the Fair will be closing for the day, in about half an hour." Tia said coolly, looking from Cassandra to the man and back.

"Tia, this is Wade Cooper. Wade, my daughter Hestia Damek. She's one of the organizers of this Fair."

And you didn't mention who he is.

"I guess I'd better pack up my exhibit too," Wade said, moving apart from Cassandra.

"He invents rainwater cachement and water storage units," Cassandra explained as Wade ambled off.

"How long have you known him, Mom?"

Cassandra tried to look matter-of-fact. "We met last year when I went up through the Central Valley." She looked away, smiling at the memory.

She's acting like she's twenty, rather than sixty.

"You're lovers." Tia's voice was hard.

Cassandra looked up at her daughter with soft eyes.

"Tia, your dad died just over ten years ago. I'm still very much alive." Cassandra brushed her hair back, and on her arms Tia saw again the glowing white scars.

Tears pricked the corners of Tia's eyes. She turned away so that her mother couldn't see her face.

"Life moves on, honey. Wade's a wonderful man. He's very kind, and easy going. No one will ever replace Rick. Ever. It's just... different. I hope you can get to know him."

Daddy, all the pieces of our lives you've missed. You've never held your grandchild. You never had a chance to meet Ari. I have changed so much, Daddy, would you even recognize me now?

In the distance Tia could see Wade waiting under a tree for Cassandra.

"Mom, go to him, he's waiting for you." Tia swallowed hard. "And bring him along when you come by for dinner later."

(8.)

Tia crossed the Fair amid thinning crowds in search of Ari. As she passed the automobile exhibits, a vaguely familiar figure emerged from the tents.

"Tia? Wow, I hardly recognized you. What's it been? Five – no, eight years?"

"Hi Doug." Tia smiled. She felt strangely sorry for him.

The years had not been kind to him. His once-athletic body was now soft with excess weight, his hair greyed and thinning. His complexion had lost its vigor, and the worries of stress showed across his brow. He still selected stylish clothes, although it was evident that his budget was now quite changed.

"Tia, you look … beautiful."

Shocked at his choice of words – she never thought of herself as beautiful – she considered how her appearance had changed. She was still slim, and she now wore her hair long and unbound like her mother. A few strands of natural grey graced it. For her Fair duties, she was carrying her efficiency clipboard, which contrasted oddly with her flowy print skirt and artistically hand-knit top.

Doug's eyes flitted from her face to her left hand and back.

"So you're still married," he said. "Did he drag you here? My girlfriend was begging to come." He made a disparaging face.

"I'm the Coordinator of the Fair."

Doug's face registered shock. "Sheesh, Tia, you really did go Cassandra on me!"

Tia sighed. *Such a chasm.* She chose instead to twist his remark.

"Oh, yes, Cassandra's here, I just left her exhibit."

"Man, what is this world coming to?" he muttered. "So I guess that tells me what you've been up to."

"And you, Doug?" She asked more from politeness than from real interest.

"Well, I'm rebuilding the business. We lost it all in the stock market crash, you know."

"Oh, I didn't know."

"When the market crashed, well that was a dreadful time. The company was totally upside down. Personally, I lost everything, I was all-out leveraged. Lost my Marina house, lost the Mar Vista rental property, even went B.K."

Bankrupt! Tia was shocked. *Doug? Brazenly successful Doug, bankrupt?*

"Now I'm rebuilding it, this time on my own, no partners. It's been tough, in this economy, but there's always some little project that needs to get off the ground. My operations are a lot smaller now than they used to be. But I'm doing okay."

A young woman in her mid-twenties with breathtaking Middle Eastern features approached Doug and draped herself on his arm. Tia's mouth dropped open.

"Layla, meet Tia."

"What about Edie?" Tia whispered.

"Oh, she divorced me quick as could be when the market fell."

Doug's eyes lingered on Tia as he and Layla turned to go.

(9.)

Tia found Ari at the computer exhibit, turning a miniscule gadget covetously in his hand.

"It's the Sliver," Ari announced in an awed voice. He clicked it and it slid smoothly open, telescoping to double its original size. "Voice recognition. No need for a keyboard. Man, I want one of these things." Ari was loathe to put it back on the table. "Look at the size of it! Powerful enough to replace my laptop, yet it slips in my pocket."

Sleek and flat, it scarcely filled Tia's palm.

"Clean chip technology," the vendor said proudly. "The Sliver's not quite ready for production yet, we're still working on the screen. But this one ..."

The vendor pulled out a larger fist-sized device. "It's a first-generation 4C. That stands for Clean Compact Communications Center. It's a phone, wireless web access, and some light computer capabilities. But the big difference is, it uses clean chips and components. We're trying to do everything with low-impact materials now. None of the lead chips of the old days, and its innards are made so they can easily be disassembled for repair or recycling.

"There have historically been several problems with the electronics industry. One issue has been the toxic elements: lead, and some other components of the early 2000's style screens. Those elements were why people at the turn of the century had such a tough time disposing of their old components – they were toxic waste in the landfills. Not to mention, significant toxicity during manufacture.[57] But Americans didn't worry too much about that part, because the manufacturing-end pollution was mostly in underdeveloped countries overseas.

"Another big issue in the old days was planned obsolescence. In the drive to move more product for greater corporate profits, the manufacturers designed devices to wear out quickly, or to require replacement rather than accept repair. We try not to build them like that anymore!

"Still another issue with the old computers, cell phones, handhelds, media devices, was the multitude of materials. You couldn't just drop them in a recycling bin, there were way too many different things inside there to make recycling realistic. The automobile manufacturers had the same problem, by the way.

"Now our waste stream friends have become far more sophisticated, with advanced technologies for sorting and processing the various types of materials. I had a great meeting with a guy here, Xavier Navarro. He has some incredibly innovative ideas – he's apparently just waiting for the city to nibble with interest."

"Yes, we know Xavier." Tia smiled, her eyes on Ari.

Ari was still caressing the Sliver device. He finally placed it in the vendor's hands rather than surrender it to the impersonal table.

"You let me know when they're available."

"Certainly, Mr. Damek."

It's so different to see Ari wanting that Sliver device. It's so rare that he shows interest in a consumer thing. A line from an old novel popped into her head: *'the wealth of selection, not of accumulation.'*

Before the market crash, our society was so clearly about wealth of accumulation. 'More, more, gimme more.' The shopping mall tidal wave image flashed through her mind.

Does transitioning to a more Sustainable society mean we can no longer have the things we crave, like Ari and his Sliver?

Perhaps, and not necessarily.

As a society we have an aching within. We pile goods into shopping bags and haul them home in search of that emotional thrill. The fleeting thrill of the new in attempts to cover the desperate emptiness of ennui.

If instead we sought to bring deeper meaning to our lives – purpose, spirit – we could fill that hunger with real value.[58]

Wealth of selection. It's much more than just buying cleaner, greener products. It's the full heart of Sufficiency.

(10.)

Jana named the complex the Lares project. "It stands for Los Angeles Restoration and Sustainability," Jana declared proudly. "The

Lares were Ancient Roman spirits who, if you took care of them, protected the home."

The three main houses each became two-family units. Two of them were shared premises like the Damek's. The other was split into a simple duplex. The two guest houses yielded additional family units.

Only a portion of one four-car garage was retained for vehicles. Two of the garages were remodeled into dwelling units. These conversions freed up not only the additional structures, but also the land which had previously been lengthy curving driveways. Shared vehicle 'car resources' were included as part of the community, and to his delight Steve was given free reign to find the cleanest, greenest vehicles he could. A mini-electric Neighborhood Vehicle was perfect for errands within the Brentwood neighborhood pocket. An experimental fuel cell vehicle and a contemporary hybrid rounded out the fleet.[59] Bus service was just a short walk from the corner of the complex for other journeys through the city.

The other portion of the sole remaining garage became a community room and classroom, Jana anticipating the interest they had experienced in their work at the triplex gardens.

Jana had laid out gardens based on Permaculture zones. Fortunately, she began her plans while Steve was still planning the reconstruction effort, because the combination resulted in a turning-inside-out of the houses. Where the old mansions had focused toward lengthy circular driveways and streets, Jana and Steve reoriented the focal point of each building toward the main central garden between the houses. Large solar-efficient paned French doors opened onto patios or decks. These now became the 'front' of the homes, facing toward the little community rather than focusing on automobiles.

High-intensity Permaculture zones 1 and 2, for herbs, seedlings and tender care vegetables were located in the center of the complex, between the houses. The lower-intensity zone 3, for orchards, composting, and greywater processing reed beds, and zone 5 with native plants for wildlife, ringed the complex in what had previously been the 'front yards' of the mansions.

Jana's chickens lived in portable domed enclosures which were moved to follow the harvest in a scheduled rotation, thus avoiding an unpleasant permanent poultry yard on the property. In this way the chickens assisted in the cycle of breaking down garden debris and distributing compost.[60]

Steve was able to achieve a fine architectural appearance with very little in the way of new resources. Virtually all the luxury finishes of the previous owners remained, including the beautiful wood flooring and the wide windows looking out to where Jana's gardens would soon flourish. Steve retained the upscale kitchen in its entirety, as changes there were nearly all behind-the-scenes. Timber, doors, and many other pieces were acquired from a buddy of Steve's who ran a salvage operation, warehousing the pieces for reuse.

Steve included all the energy saving ideas the families had yearned to try at the triplex: ultra-efficient hot water heaters, appliances and refrigerators; water efficient showerheads; energy-efficient lighting. Wood for built-in furniture was carefully selected to exclude tropical woods, using wood from sources certified by the Forest Stewardship Council.[61]

Jana brought in a lively young friend of hers, Verity Pearce, a petite, gutsy, vivacious blonde in her mid-twenties. Verity worked with Carl and Matthew on the community agreements and financial arrangements, setting up a Community Land Trust and CoHousing agreements. They were a solid team, plus it was soon clear that Verity and Carl were developing more than just a working relationship.

(11.)

President Rafferty, after backing down from the conflict begun by Bush in Iraq, announced that he would not be running for a second term in 2012. The wide field in both parties came down to two strong candidates: Senator Alvin MacKay, whose background included Texas oil, and Governor John Elliott, who made no effort to conceal his strong religious stance.

The media, in their usual pre-election muckraking zeal, discovered articles written by Elliott early in his career, proclaiming the religious duty to steward the environment. Coming on the heels of the Alden-Diamont bill, this was headline news.

Until the MacKay reports came in.

In the midst of a political environment influenced heavily by a religious trend that had only intensified over the past decade, the press dramatically unveiled clear evidence of MacKay's ten-year extramarital affair. Details of the affair were splayed across headlines daily, from receipts for diamond earrings, to compromising photos.

The Other Woman at the center of this whirlwind was stunningly photogenic, and amazingly cooperative with the press ... one Ms. Lori Fordon.

Ms. Fordon lingered for photo ops whenever she was seen in public, posing at a ribbon-cutting ceremony for a CDM-registered hydroelectric project in Rio Blanco, at an anti-oil rally in Washington, outside a wind power conference in Denver. To the discerning reader of her press clippings, the backdrops of her scandal were as well selected as her glamorous wardrobe. The press adored her and capitalized on the contrast between her dark past and her noble causes.

MacKay went down in flames, and like a phoenix from those very flames, Lori Fordon rose to become a household name; a figure of mystery, sophistication, intriguing complexity, and raw power.

(12.)

In the Lares project, there were so many details to work out, that Tia soon found herself learning about construction, large scale landscaping, zoning, finance, community land trusts and mutual housing associations, helping Ari and Steve coordinate various aspects of the project.

One day at the construction site, Ari pulled Tia aside. Slipping his 4C into his pocket he lead her out to a portion of the garden-to-be.

"I need you to keep the project afloat. I'm going to Barcelona next month. I just received the call that confirms it."

Tia laughed aloud, from the shock and the ridiculousness of it.

"It's the next World Conference on Sustainable Development, successor to the Johannesburg conference I attended when we first met. I want to be there. This gathering could be more effective on world Sustainability issues than the UNFCCC meetings, now that Kyoto is settled as an international mandate."

"Will you go with the U.S. delegation?"

Please, don't pull another foreign affiliation!

Ari's expression was grim. "There is no U.S. delegation. The U.S. is boycotting the Conference, citing Depression economics. I've been talking with a few associates who want to be there as badly as I do. We've tried the official route, it didn't work. So we're going anyhow, on our own, ostensibly just to participate in the vendor side events. Basically, we're going to crash the party. We'll have no official capacity to participate in the actual negotiations, but I can't bear not to be there."

Tia shook her head in wonder. *This guy doesn't quit. His own country has turned him down and barred the door, and he's still going for it.*

"You're amazing." She slipped her arms around him. "You just don't slow down."

"I can't," Ari said quietly.

That wasn't exactly the response she'd expected.

"Something in me keeps driving me forward, saying: there's too little time!"

He broke away and began pacing the narrow bit of grass in front of her. "Ever since my dad died I've had this feeling of urgency, like I never knew how much time I'd get, so I don't dare waste a bit of it. That's why I have so little patience for the mundane. I feel like I only have a short while to accomplish all that I can in this world."

His pacing stilled and he gazed back at the construction. Tia approached him and ran her hands gently along the long line of his back, in loving massage. He sighed, a long slow sigh, receiving her gesture. After a while he pulled her around into his arms, and his hand traced her cheek as if he were touching something very precious. She drank in his eyes, soft and dark and oh so alive.

"I love you, Ari."

He kissed her, tender and lingering, and the lingering meant more to her than anything else. *Precious moments of time. I treasure these beautiful moments of your precious time.*

(13.)

tdamek@lares.net
Barcelona is exhilarating. Without the U.S. resistance the atmosphere is very different than at other Conferences. The nations which are here want to be here, want to get something done, and are striving for new ways of working together. This is how I dreamed it could be. A.

tdamek@lares.net
My EU friends have pulled me into the alternative energy forum at the PrepCon. They can't acknowledge me as a U.S. representative, but when they learned I was here and the circumstances, they created an EU position to get me into the sessions, because they wanted my input on the material. I'm thrilled beyond words. A.

tdamek@lares.net
Other members of this renegade U.S. team kept referring the organizer of the side events to me for logistical questions. He's now calling me the 'Head of the U.S. Delegation,' which is a dark inside joke

since we are so painfully conscious of the absence of any official U.S. delegation. Nonetheless, we are heading into the final session of the preparatory committee with a sketch of a groundbreaking new international agreement. A.

adamek@lares.net
To: Head Delegate, United States
Dear Sir: take it and run with it, it'll look good on future Curriculum Vitae. Later, no one will know the history behind it! The first Lares units are now coming together. Steve has done beautiful work. Between Carl and Verity nearly all the units are spoken for. And Carl and Verity are now 'spoken for' as well, he proposed to her yesterday. All my love, Tia.

tdamek@lares.net
Congratulations to Carl and Verity! Carl had told me his intentions, but I was to keep it quiet. Celebrations here as well, we're moving into the official Plenary session with an awesome Framework agreement. The best aspects of Johannesburg – the diversity of representation, the breadth of issues – have been captured and transformed. Tia, in essence it's Factor 4: the nations who are party to this agreement are pledging to make their use of worldwide resources four times more productive! That encompasses water, energy, health, agriculture and biodiversity, economics, social and environmental issues, across the board! THIS is what I am in this business for! I'm so excited. A.

tdamek@lares.net
The main session is wrapping up the day after tomorrow. Most nations present are thrilled about this groundbreaking Barcelona Framework, the first major international milestone since Kyoto in '97. Prospects look good for adoption in many countries. I will be coming home via Washington, I have a meeting scheduled with Senator Alden. A.

(14.)

Ari stretched out on the sofa with Tia cuddled beside him, Annis already in bed.

"It will be great to move into the new place," Tia said. "Steve's made great progress, just wait until you see it tomorrow."

Ari heaved a big sigh. "I feel so satisfied with life right now. My lovely wife," he brushed her hair with his fingers, "a darling daughter, a new home in a few months, and man, what a successful trip!"

"It sounds like it was great." She forced a smile, the delight inexplicably draining from her.

"Alden loved the Framework. He and I ..." Ari shook his head in wonder, "we seem to think in the same wavelength. He really has an eye for the big picture. I'm glad he's in the position he is. There is renewed hope when there are minds like his running our country!

"I talked with him about the Barcelona Framework, but we also discussed the Moscow Treaty, the successor to Kyoto. Kyoto will expire this year, but that's pretty much irrelevant now. All the Kyoto countries, plus Australia and a few more, have already ratified Moscow and put it in force." His contented smile made him even more handsome.

"But of course the U.S. hasn't," she said automatically. His enthusiasm was somehow unnerving to her. She suppressed the urge to jump up and run.

"Not yet. But that's what Alden is pulling for. The amazing thing is, as the preliminary reports begin to come in from around the world, to a member, the Kyoto countries seem to have beat their Kyoto targets. They have managed to reduce emissions more than they were legally required to do! I'm sure most of them were striving to better the targets. A few, like Japan, relied heavily on trading emissions credits, but still they beat expectations.

"We have some semblance of a working relationship now between Northern Hemisphere and Southern. They've certified so many Clean Development Mechanism projects."

"Yeah, I saw Lori as the main page photo of some magazine." She watched for his reaction.

"Isn't that a marvel how she's managed to twist that MacKay thing into a publicity bonanza?" His eyes sparkled.

"A marvel?" She gaped at him. "You still admire her!"

He laughed warmly. "Well, just look at the free ride she's gained for these environmental projects. Magazine main-pages. You know we couldn't get that kind of positive press."

"You love it when she's on those magazines!"

"Sure I do." He grinned and raised one eyebrow suggestively.

Her eyes widened in alarm.

"Tia, half the men in the country love it when she's on those magazines."

She pulled away from him. "You saw her in DC, didn't you?" she said accusingly.

"Of course I did. We work together." He said it as if it explained everything.

She jumped up and backed away from him, averting her face, putting the distance of the room between them.

"You ... together ..." Suddenly she couldn't get an image of tangled bedsheets out of her mind. She couldn't say the words, her throat felt as if it were closing up.

He crossed the room to her. "Tia ..."

She tried to slip away into the kitchen, but he was too quick for her. His huge hand caught her shoulder and pulled her against his chest. She tried to push away, but his strong arms held her fast. He grasped her chin and turned her face to his. She wouldn't meet his eyes; the last thing she wanted to see were those eyes.

"Tia, I am not fooling around with Lori Fordon!"

Involuntarily she glanced at him. Those intense dark brown eyes were fixed on her face, the pain of her accusation clear in his expression. Then his lips were on hers. She tried to stiffen, to reject him, but instead with a little sob melted into it, hating herself for her accusations, hating his absences, hating the Treaties, Lori, Alden for all they got of him that she did not.

When she opened her eyes his face was inches from hers, the love and pain in his expression unmistakable. With a trembling hand she stroked the smooth skin of his throat, as if he might disappear in an instant beneath her touch. Her love for him felt overwhelming, terrifying – precisely the feeling that she had been running from all along.

(15.)

In the 2012 election, John Elliott was elected to the Presidency by a clear margin. President Elliott seemed determined to make up for the domestic inaction of Rafferty. One of the first social programs of

Elliott's Administration was the reestablishment of the 1934 Civilian Conservation Corps. Unfortunately – or was it truly an accident – in one of his early on-camera mentions of the program, the President slipped and called it the Creation Conservation Corps. The name stuck. Few save the lawmakers could recall the official name after that.

Some young people flocked to the ranks of CCC for the crusade in its recast name. Unemployed young people from the cities flooded it out of desperate need. Either way, the ranks of CCC quickly swelled.

Esperanza's Urban Forestry project with edible drought-tolerant species was embraced by CCC, not just in LA, but throughout the water-conscious West. Forest sinks were another CCC project, planting replicas of Sweden's willow forests around U.S. power plants.[62] Trees needed water, thus in many states greywater systems installations and swale building were a logical extension of CCC duties. CCC rolled back roads cut through the country's National Parks under the Bush Administration and repaired habitats destroyed by offroad vehicles.

CCC worked simultaneously to solve problems in both the natural capital and the human capital realms, providing both purposeful work and restoration of ecosystems. Select public lands throughout 50 states became managed wildlands, Permaculture zone 5s for the populace. City park spaces blossomed with an Eden-like bounty.

CCC had an immediate economic effect, yet it was only in the years to come that CCC's secondary effects became evident. By hands-on participation in the restoration of natural spaces, young people returned to the satisfaction of manual skills, returned to the great outdoors, returned to being literally 'in touch with' the earth and the spirit of life. This connection, in the millions of young adults who rolled through CCC programs, was far-reaching. CCC veterans emerged unwilling to return to the 'old ways' of sterile living in air-conditioned offices, packaged foods, and freeway driving.

Creation Restoration had begun, but the Civilian Evolution was pervasive.

(16.)

tdamek@lares.net
The U.S. delegates, newbies all, walked into this meeting for the Barcelona Framework where world delegates already know each other, and have had a working relationship for years. This is indeed the price tag of Rafferty's pulling the U.S. out of UN negotiations – we are out of harmony with the

nations of the world. I am the only Sustainability negotiation veteran on the team, and that is only because I so willfully crashed the gates in Barcelona! I'm an energy specialist, not a generalist, yet they have selected me as Head Delegate. A.

tdamek@lares.net
For there to be teamwork, there has to be a team relationship. The nations of the world have maintained it; with Bush and then Rafferty, the U.S. has abandoned it. Slowly we rebuild it, agonizingly slowly. And meanwhile, the clock keeps ticking toward the future, with little of this fantastic Framework ready for implementation. We have few results from these sessions except a multi-year schedule of future conferences. Frustrating. A.

(17.)

Steve's work was amazing, his style unique and refreshing. No two of the units looked alike, in part because of their original custom structure. Yet Steve's artful integration of found materials brought a delightful sense of individuality to each residence. Lares was no cookie-cutter condo complex.

At Ari's urging, Matthew and his family returned from San Diego to take one of the units. Matthew's business resources had been helped considerably by his work with Ari and Carl, but were still not adequate for his family needs. Following private discussions with Matthew, Ari declared the matter handled and there was no prying the details out of him.

Lauren Tilford, the educational speaker from the LA Future Fair, was considering moving to Lares, so Tia met her family for a tour. Immediately upon their arrival, eight year old Annis seized upon Lauren's daughter Janelle, who was a year younger. The two danced away for their own giggling version of the tour.

"These gardens will be delightful – Jana has truly done a masterful job with the layout!" These were meaningful words of praise from Lauren's husband Rhus, a professional landscaper. Rhus was a woodsy man, tanned, lean and muscular, with a full beard, and long greying hair which he swept into a ponytail.

"Jana began with what she learned at our old triplex, but the increased acreage here allowed her to explore ideas which were impossible over there," Tia explained.

"I heard about that triplex. Regrettably, I never got over to see it," said Rhus.

"The appearance here will be very similar," Tia said. "In overview the triplex looks like a country garden, bountiful and unrestrained, but on closer examination you would see that the plant material is herbs, edibles and beneficials. Here Jana used Permaculture zone layout and guild plantings, including spaces for children's play and community gatherings. Most of our produce will be grown on the premises, with some extra available for barter within the neighborhood.

"Over on this end of the property we have East House, a mansion that Steve split into a duplex. Carl Farren lives here. Ravyn Nurrish and his friend live in the other half."

"What a pretty little creek!" Lauren remarked. "I thought you used water conservation here."

"That pretty little creek is hard-working," Tia laughed. "That's our greywater filtration system. Steve and Jana decided it didn't need to look industrial, so they made it artful. It cleanses greywater from our washing machines and other primary sources, which is then used for irrigation of our orchards and ornamentals.[63] Shannon and Matthew Goodman and their family live in this little bungalow."

Shannon peeked out as they passed by, and Tia introduced them, then continued the tour.

"West House is in that direction, but here is our place, South House. We split this building with Ari's sister Jana and her husband Steve – he's the one who built out the Lares complex."

"Impressive sense of style, from what I have seen!" Rhus said.

"The elegance of upscale mainstream – quite unlike other shared housing we've looked at," Lauren added.

"That's just the exteriors – just wait until you go inside! Here we are at the bungalow we thought might work for you ..."

(18.)

"Tia, stick around a while, I want you to hear this." Ari sat with Carl at the Damek/Vernados table in the Lares South House. Tia eased into a chair and propped up her feet, weary from unpacking.

"Matthew's been going through the legal work for these places. If we are truly going to make them be CoHousing units, the best way to structure it legally is to put the properties into a Community Land

Trust.[64] The Trust would be a nonprofit organization, run by the members, and would own the land, so the residents would buy only the buildings, together with a long-term land lease. Requirements to sell at an affordable price assure that the Trust shelters homeowners from skyrocketing real estate prices."

"Sounds pretty good," Tia urged him on.

"We made a mistake. The Community Land Trust should have acquired the properties at the outset, rather than Carl and I. To achieve the CoHousing approach now, Carl and I should transfer the properties into the Trust."

"So?"

"The catch is, Carl and I bought the original mansions at rock-bottom, thinking we were going to make great profits in the traditional real estate appreciation way when values recovered. Buy low, sell high."

Carl's regrets were apparent. "If we sell them to the Trust now, it would be at zero profit. Not exactly how we thought it'd turn out."

"But a great deal for the Community Land Trust," Ari reminded him. "The Trust would be obtaining these properties at our exceptionally low price."

"Great for them," Carl said, crossing his arms across his chest. "I doubt we can find a deal this good elsewhere, to make our investment profits with appreciation."

"The thing is," Ari said contemplatively, "with what I've been reading, do we really want to? Drive the markets, I mean." He looked at Carl. "This is precisely why people have had to resort to Land Trusts. These appreciation games falsely and unrealistically inflate real estate values. When we talk of profiting on real estate what we're really doing is banking on the terribly unsustainable idea that values will skyrocket and we can sell out and make a killing. It is so contrary to the Sustainability concept."

"Sustainability in the financial capital realm?" Tia pondered.

"But, we're not in a Sustainable world yet," Carl argued. "We're in a Transition world. Why shouldn't we play the investment games of these unsustainable times? Need I remind you, you have a kid to send to college."

"Even in our financial capital transactions, at some point we're going to have to change to ways of investing our money which are more Sustainable – ways which don't rely upon slaughtering someone else," Ari said reflectively. "So what do we do? Do we go with the ethical high road, the wave of the future, and turn the properties over to CoHousing, or do we hold them as old-fashioned traditional rentals?"

Ari paused as the light of a new idea crossed his brow. "Hey, if we sell Brentwood to the Land Trust now, we free up our cash. We could then seed few more CoHousing projects elsewhere around the city, in succession, all with the same cash!"

"Well, that would certainly jump-start this model of housing for the future," Tia commented.

"We did it by mistake here at Lares," Ari said, "but perhaps we should be repeating it at different sites around the city. Others don't have the pool of cash to start something like this." Ari turned to Carl. "Do you want to go in on it with me?"

"I can't put in nearly as much as you've got, but sure."

Ari and Carl managed to create two other CoHousing locations, one in Hollywood and one in West LA, each of which were turned over to Community Land Trusts. Thus they created three unique versions of what came to be known as the eco-village concept.

Ari did not entirely sidestep real estate appreciation. At rock bottom prices he bought retail sites in several Westside neighborhood pockets, strategically located near the sites of future PLASE stations.

It truly was a Transition world.

(19.)

Ari was Best Man at Carl's wedding, a thoroughly Mainstream event. The ceremony was at a little church in Westchester, and the reception was in a Depression-ravaged hotel ballroom that looked more than a bit tattered in its decor. The reception struck Tia as a Who's Who of Legacy LA, yet Ari quickly tired of it.

"If I wasn't in the wedding party I'd have been out of here hours ago!" Ari paced in frustration, then flopped into a chair next to Tia.

A high school aged boy approached, whom Tia recognized as part of Verity's family.

"Dr. Damek?" The boy extended his hand with confidence. He had blond hair, blue eyes, and a very direct manner. "I'm Kegan Pearce."

Boredom still lingered around Ari's eyes but he stilled his impatient fidgeting.

"You're Verity's brother?" Tia asked. Kegan gave her a perfunctory nod.

"Dr. Damek, I've read your articles and many of your press clippings. I really admire your work."

Surprise registered on Ari's face. "You read this for school?"

"No, sir, we don't do anything like this in school. I read about the environmental crisis and global warming on my own. I can't believe, sir, how the U.S. never came on board the Kyoto Protocol. I think the claim that it would harm our economy is absurd – just look at our economy without it! I wish our government would sign its successor, the Moscow Treaty. I want to do something about it when I get older." Kegan's confidence faltered. "Like you've done, sir."

Ari's eyes were alive now. His face was serious as he reached out to shake Kegan's hand a second time.

"Kegan," Ari spoke very carefully, very firmly, "you seem quite wise for your years. The world needs your passion and your sense of purpose. Hold on to this feeling. Listen to it. This inner sense is what will show you how you can make a difference in the world."

"I ... I need a mentor, sir. Could I just hang out in your office sometime, see how you work?"

"By all means, Kegan, I'd be proud to have you with me. Here, I'll give you my card."

Ari pulled out his 4C and beamed his card to Kegan's cell. Kegan's gratitude was evident, almost embarrassing, as he slipped back into the party.

"That kid," Ari shook his head in wonder. "He's like a flashback to when I was young. Damn, I hope he makes it through. He's too intelligent to be caught up in the mainstream, but the Reactionaries can get so depressing, particularly when you're that passionate."

"You made it through," Tia said softly.

"Yes, but what a fight. Keeping the passion alive, keeping it undiminished by the bad news, the defeats, the naysayers – it's soulwork, it is. I think he's up for it, I just remember how tough it can get."

You're still doing it, darling, you're still working all the time to keep alive the flames of that great passion of yours. You've become used to the exercise, used to being different, used to rising above the humdrum and the everyday. But that doesn't mean you do any less of it, the discipline of filtering.

The image of Jana and her fruit trees crossed Tia's mind, Jana pruning the deadwood, removing the crossed branches, shaping, letting the sunlight in.

I see you, darling, you cull the mundane, you minimize the distractions, you prune that which isn't useful out of your life, to allow room for the passion to flourish. This discipline, this you can teach the Kegans of the world.

Or, perhaps ... you're not even aware that you do it?

Annis, age nine, flew by to check in, with flushed face and eager laughter as she related tales of new young friends met at the reception.

Ari was preoccupied and didn't seem to hear her stories. Annis chattered on, then hugged Tia, and bounded away to rejoin the other children.

Steve crossed the party, holding Jana's hand, with Esperanza following. Esperanza had clearly been crying and Steve looked agitated.

"There was a riot this afternoon in the camps downtown," Steve began, his face dark and hardened. "LAPD shot several of the homeless people. The National Guard were called in."

"This was on the news?" Tia asked in shock.

"Are you kidding? They're keeping a lid on it. No, one of Esperanza's associates called her."

Esperanza nodded tearfully. "These are human beings, *las familias*. The soldiers are gunning them down! It's not the first time they've shot into an uprising. These people are starving, they've been without work, some of them for years. The government agencies shift the blame to another level. Federal, state, county, city ... No one does anything, all they do is talk. And now, *¡están matando gente inocente!*"

Ben came by and pulled up a chair. Xavier appeared behind Esperanza, resting his hands on her shoulders.

Jana turned to Ben. "Whatever happened to your rail project? I thought you planned it so it could be installed with a setup like the old WPA of the 1930's? That would give these people work, and money for food."

"Ari, why is City Council delaying Ben's rail system?" Jana was firing questions without waiting for answers.

"Funding, political charade," Ari shrugged in answer.

"That's basically the same with my Recycling operation," Xavier put in.

Tia saw a glint of blond hair as Kegan seated himself off to the side within earshot.

"What's been happening with that RAI program, the Rebuild America's Infrastructure the President was touting?" Jana asked.

"I'm not sure it's come through yet," Ari replied.

"Well, what the hell are they waiting for?" Ben thundered.

The lights came on across Ari's face. He looked around the assembled group. "You mean, what the hell are *we* waiting for? I think it's time to muscle it through.

"First, RAI, we need to let them know we're interested. I'll call Alden's office. Steve, maybe you can get people from your other Sustainability groups to call their representatives too."

"Right," Steve agreed.

"But on the other end, we need to make it really easy for them," Ari continued. "If we have Sustainability-based projects lined up, ready to go, maybe we can get them earmarked as RAI projects when the program funding comes through. So, how ready are we? Ben?"

"The plans are ready. They've been through engineering and environmental approvals under the Haynes grant. The easements have already been acquired by the City," Ben answered.

"Xavier, do you have your plant locations selected?"

"Actually," Xavier looked sheepish, "I already hold options on the properties. I wanted to be sure we could get the right buildings. I'm prepared to turn the options over to the city as soon as the project gets underway."

"Wow, you're a bit ahead of it. Is retrofitting needed?"

"I can put RAI people to work immediately. The retrofit can be done by the same people. My plans follow the model of the school at Weedpatch Camp, giving these people practical training in a variety of skills. You see, it's not just about recycling," he confessed.

"The parks," Ari continued. "Jana, Esperanza, are the landscape plans ready?"

"Yup, I've drawn them up for all the locations Ben gave me," Jana replied. "Some will be for playgrounds, others soccer fields, some community garden spaces and some nature spaces. We could start on the community garden and nature space parks immediately. The soccer fields and playgrounds will have to wait until we get materials for the cisterns that will go in beneath them."[65]

"Great. Sounds like the one thing we are missing is the people angle. Damn, I need Verity. We need to mobilize all the citizen's action committees, to let City Council know we really want this to happen, and to happen fast. Once we get on the docket, we have to show a major presence in each of those Council sessions."

"I'll do it," Kegan said.

Heads swung around from the assembled group. Amused smiles flitted across the faces of Steve and Ben at the sight of this kid. Ari stroked his chin, considering this new development.

"Don't you have to be in school?" Ben asked rather tactlessly.

Lauren's lecture was in Tia's ears. *Immersion. How better to learn? How better to keep Kegan's passion alive than to surround him with action and possibilities?*

"If Ari thinks Kegan's right for it, we can solve that." Tia said.

Ari gave a curt nod. "Kegan, you're on. Oh … I neglected to tell you," he grinned to Kegan, gesturing toward the group in action, "I rarely use an office!"

"Somebody find Matthew, I thought he was here earlier. Let's get him in on this too. Monday we'll start in with City Council, this time for real."

"I thought you're headed back to New York?" Tia reminded him. Ari stared at her; he'd clearly forgotten.

"If Ari's gone, who'll lead the team?" Esperanza had become so hopeful and now looked crestfallen.

Ari looked at Tia, his deep brown eyes rich with the exhilaration of the project he was materializing before their very eyes. "You can do it," he said softly. "Will you?"

Saving the earth ... you picked the ultimate mission. I want it too.

"Yes," she whispered.

Ari didn't wait for Monday. Before the wedding reception ended he had contacted Alden's aides, revealing the shocking details of the riot shooting. City Council contacts were next on Ari's list, and by his flight time on Sunday, Tia's appointments were set. She attended none of the appointments alone, taking different members of the team to each.

Steve was frantically busy connecting with the citizen's action committees he had built and supported in other major cities. He reached out to his mentors at Sustainable Seattle, and to his associates in other cities across the country: Atlanta, Boulder, Pittsburgh, Portland, Santa Fe.[66]

The combined pressure from multiple major cities encouraged Congress and the President to pass the Rebuilding America's Infrastructure Act. It became widely known as the RAI Act, and was soon referred to by its acronym as the "Ray" of hope.

Cities with Steve's Sustainability support groups had, like LA, already lined up potential RAI projects that just so happened to further the cause of Sustainability. Program approval came quickly for these well-organized projects because they presented least-effort to the government bureaucrats.

(20.)

As the Lares orchard trees filled in and gave a suggestion of their future form, the gardens became a beloved outdoor room for the residents. In some areas – near the children's play area and the classroom – one could count on meeting up with other families for social interaction.

Jana had laid out the grounds in mandala patterns with cul-de-sac paths for the purpose of gardener access, but the residents had other ideas. These keyhole nooks among herbs and orchards created delightful retreats to curl up with a book or hold a private conversation. With benches added, they became favored hide-aways.

The paths were not of uniform material, Jana and Rhus using whatever salvage was on hand: sand, chipped tree trimmings, or the occasional gravel. The changing texture underfoot as one meandered through the gardens added tactile and auditory delight.

In the central children's yard, Steve hung a tire swing in one of the older sycamores and built a large rustic treehouse with scavenged materials. Firm decomposed granite paths around the play area made a bicycle highway. The children enjoyed roaming the general gardens in search of the chickens' newest location. A box turtle rounded out the menagerie, a useful addition because he ate slugs and other plant pests.

Birds and butterflies flocked to the garden, not limiting themselves to the designated zone 5 nature area. Lares seemed aptly named; the gentle spirits indeed smiled upon the homestead.

(21.)

"Ben, yes I know we already showed City Council the schedule for the rail installation. Now the RAI Administrator wants to see it. Tomorrow morning, if we can." Tia urged Ben via phone.

"Why can't these jerks get it together?" Ben exploded.

"Ben, cool down, if we want to make this happen, we have to give them all the dog and pony shows."

"We already did!"

"That was a different group of them."

"They're just feeding us delay tactics! And meanwhile they shoot!"

"What!?"

"You didn't hear? Esperanza called me. The National Guard fired into the riots again yesterday. Three dead, seven wounded."

"Oh God!" Tia put her head in her hands.

"The crowd got restless, they crowded law enforcement, a misunderstanding, and boom, it's escalated."

I try to stay positive, I try to keep this afloat, I try to lead this team. But we're getting nowhere, fast.

She paused a moment, fighting back her horror, then continued quietly, defeated. "I tried Alden's office last week. This is out of their hands. The law's on the books, it seems like that's the extent of their powers. Now that the ball's in the court of the RAI Administration, Alden can't help us."

"Somehow I knew that would be the story. We're still getting the runaround, Tia."

Don't I know it! And it's happening in other cities too. I hear the same story from Steve's other Sustainability groups.

"Ben, I know, but still, we need to make that presentation tomorrow."

"I'll be there, Tia. I'll meet you there."

"Thanks, Ben." Tia hung up the phone and sat staring into space.

Marginalized peoples – now we're killing them, treating them as a disposable commodity! We're never going to get a rail system in this town, we'll never get these fossil fuel burning cars off the road! We continue packing the landfills with items we could reuse or recycle while our youth turn to vandalism and gangs because they haven't a place to play, or a valid place to contribute in our society!

Ten year old Annis flounced in, tracking muddy footprints across the floor. Tia snapped. "What do you think you're doing!? Just look at that mess!"

"Wha-at?" Annis drew the word into two syllables with a considerable dose of attitude.

"Of all the careless, unthinking ...!" Tia ranted.

Jana flew out of her portion of the house. "Annis, go to Lauren's. Tia, count to ten until she's gone."

Annis shot Tia a triumphant look, slamming the door on her way out.

Jana turned to Tia. "You're all tied in knots about this project ..."

"Damn right I am!" Tia raged back, angry tears streaming down her face.

"You're carrying it with you, taking it out on all of us."

Tia turned her back to Jana, crossing her arms across her chest and glaring out the window.

"You need to let go of this, girlfriend. Go out and weed the garden or turn compost or something, at least that's productive!"

"Ben said they shot more of the people downtown. People are starving and dying, and we have a project where they could be working productively, but we can't make any headway! I've tried, I've really tried. I can't do it. It's impossible, it's never going to happen. I want to give up on the whole thing. We're getting everyone's hopes up, for what? Nothing. RAI. 'Ray.' Yeah, 'Ray' of Hopelessness!" Tia slammed out the door toward her garden assignment.

(22.)

Ari was home from the East Coast for the weekend, and he and Tia took Annis, Mark and Peter on a hike in Temescal Canyon. The young people delighted in bounding up the trail in the dusty heat of a dry spring. Tia enjoyed seeing the closeness between them as they laughed and joked together.

Ten year old Annis was at that gangly stage where limbs seemed too long for a still-childlike disposition. Her long dark hair had Ari's coloring. Across her face, mischief and invention sparkled in Ari's dark eyes, although her facial structure was clearly Tia's.

At almost fourteen, Mark could be taken for Annis' brother – tall and skinny with Matthew's dark hair and refined good looks. Yet there was a steeliness to Mark's nature that was all his own. Peter, on the other hand, had Shannon's short blond plumpness. He was the quiet one of the trio, content to ride in the wake of excitement created by the older two.

After the hike, Tia laid out a picnic at creek side. The young people quickly finished, setting off to explore the creek and the banks where fallen trees crossed. Tia and Ari languished in the hot spring sunshine.

"This consulting engagement with the Maryland environmental think-tank has about run its course; I'll have to be moving along soon. DC's been quiet politically, and that's frustrating, because while I know Elliott's for the Treaties, we can't get him to declare it publicly."

Ari struggled to find a comfortable backrest against a rock. "It feels like time is wasting. The signs of climate change are all around us now – we get strong El Niños now every three years, instead of every seven to nine. The Pacific Northwest is really hurting; their climate has vastly changed with rainfall far below their accustomed levels. Their summer wildfire season last year was worse than ever. It all seems to have become a recurring pattern."

"With our increased rainfall patterns here, the growth patterns on these hillsides have gone haywire." Tia picked up in agreement, gesturing to the Santa Monica Mountains around them. "Our fires last fall were no picnic either. We're in the midst of so many projects – PLASE, the Treaties – but my old fears are coming back, it feels like we're doing too little too late."

The delight of the spring outing drained from her face as she continued. "We've staked our lives on this, we're doing all we can, but what if it isn't enough? It doesn't seem to be getting out to the mainstream! The 2006 gas guzzlers are still on the road, we lack a good replacement for the internal combustion engine, we haven't advanced solar and wind power. We haven't done much to relieve the poverty in our own city, let alone worldwide. While Lares is great for us, not everyone can access housing solutions like it. The RAI committee has so many criticisms and hesitations on the PLASE plan. And I worry that we're not going to make it to the 2040 mark to turn the tide on emissions."

"I know," he said quietly. "I feel it too." He drew her across the picnic blanket to wrap her in a hug that pressed her firmly to his chest; whether it was in answer to her need or his was not at all clear.

"Sometimes I just feel so helpless," she began.

"Don't ever say that!" His tone began sharply, then eased off. "The answer is Action. We're never truly helpless in this cause, we've just lost hope. There's always something we can do. We have to keep on believing that it is possible, and looking for the next place where we can make a difference. The movement's growing; many people are now working toward environmental and societal changes."

He stopped to consider. "You know, I think you need to take someone under your wing, mentor them. Kegan's exuberant youthful belief carries me along. I can't stay down when he's all fired up for the next project. You've engaged in the learning, you're in the midst of the doing, time now to teach."

The voices of Annis and the boys carried up the creek, yet Tia was intent on her response. "I'll be teaching the Lares public classes beginning in two weeks."

"What I'm talking about is different. The Lares classes will teach the mechanics – how to achieve a garden, how to build the lifestyle. No, I mean find yourself someone eager to learn how to live a purposeful life."

"I'm not sure I know how to myself."

"Are you kidding?" he exclaimed, shifting her body so that he was now gazing into her face, mere inches away, his dark eyes at once serious and passionate.

"You're selling yourself short. You live with more focus than almost anyone I know. You build our home around it, you raise our daughter immersed in it, you pull our little community together. Your dedication to this cause inspires *me*!"

His face held an intensity of emotion that almost registered as pain. One big hand in her hair, he kissed her fiercely. Tia could feel the tension in the muscles of his body. She surrendered to the physicality, but the still-present fears gripped her heart.

He doesn't get it. He doesn't see how I falter at every step. It's he who has the dedication, not I. I just follow in his wake.

Even as the thoughts rolled through her mind, she knew them to not be true. Tears pricked the corners of her eyes.

The laughter of Annis, Mark and Peter was nearer now as it echoed in the channel of the creek. Tia tensed and tried to pull away. Ari held her tightly, just a moment longer, before releasing her.

She looked up to see Mark standing on the far bank of the creek some distance away, staring. Draped across Ari's lap and chest, Tia was suddenly self-conscious.

"Mark's watching us," she said quietly.

Ari's fiery eyes were still fixed on hers.

"Fine … let him watch. Let him learn that I love my wife!"

He crushed her to his lips yet again. This time Ari's fire penetrated her fears and she felt her own desire rising in answer.

But Mark is still watching!

She pulled away, trying to regain some sense of decorum, then nervously busied herself with packing the picnic.

Mark left his creekbank stance and rejoined the other two.

Ari stretched out on the picnic blanket propped on one elbow, his eyes tracking Tia's every motion. She reached to gather a fork from the blanket in front of him. He gripped her wrist, sending what felt like a surge of electricity up her arm.

"You know it's there. You're running from it." he said with steady gaze.

"What?"

"Your own fire, your own intensity, your sense of purpose. You're holding back. That's why the fears are returning."

She tore away from him and went to stand with her back to him, watching the cool waters of the creek.

No! It's not true! I'm not running from anything!

She wrapped her arms tightly around her own torso, suddenly feeling quite exposed standing on the creek bank. The water flowed at her feet.

An image of slipping underwater played in her mind, of looking up as the surface closed over her, reflecting the bright sunlight above. Slipping in too deep, getting too caught up in this environmental cause, felt like a very real danger.

I can't go in deeper, it'll close over my head. I'll lose myself in it!

The answer formed in her mind as if in Ari's voice. *But that is yourself, there on the other side. Surrender. You must let it overtake you, in order to fully arrive.*

The enormity of this realization left her gasping for breath. Her chest felt tight. She crouched down, huddled as she was accustomed on her breakwater rocks. She could feel Ari watching her but she wouldn't turn to look at him.

This journey I must make on my own.

She looked down at the creek waters and the sense of drowning swept over her again.

Ack, but I am not ready.

All in good time. Get used to the idea. Her mind answered using his voice.

She turned to look back at Ari; his smile was tender and loving.

(23.)

Tia took Annis and Janelle out to the Malibu Lagoon State Park to see the tidepools. Tia hadn't been there in years, and although they arrived at extreme low tide, the tidepools weren't there. A patrolling lifeguard answered her questions.

"Rising sea levels, ma'am. It's gradual, but over time, this is what happens." He gestured to the area where the tidepools had once been, and the sandbar separating creek from ocean. "Even though we rebuild the sandbar with bulldozers, we're having a terrific issue with salt water incursion into the freshwater marsh areas." He continued on his rounds.

The girls gleefully ran up the beach dragging long tendrils of kelp, moving toward the sandbar. Tia followed them. From this new vantage point the crossover was obvious: long-lived native shrubs were dying back from the increased salt exposure.

A sea level rise of a few inches didn't sound like much until you viewed it like this. The high tide marks on this gently sloping beach had advanced far more than a few feet. The rocks which had once been tidepools peeked through the outflowing waters, yet were no longer completely revealed. The ocean had cut the sand under nearby houses, and newly constructed seawalls were evident.

Tia looked out over the ocean. The intertidal zone, she knew, fostered the juveniles; it was a richly interactive breeding ground for the creatures of the Bay. *What happens to the critters of the oceans when this chain is broken?* The answers weren't in any scientific forecasts she had read but she could easily guess. *All up and down the California coast ... no, upon coasts all around the world!*

Tia had a sense of waters closing over not only the tidepools but over her own head as well, submerging her whether she was ready or not, a waking nightmare of an image. The tension in her chest made it tough to draw a breath. She crouched down on the sand and put her head in her hands. She couldn't even release her pain to tears.

Annis and Janelle chose this moment to tackle Tia, bowling her over on the sand. Tia tensed in irritation and anger, but the girls' delighted giggles were infectious. She rolled to her feet and chased the girls in pretended fury, the action cleansing the tension from her body. The young pair split, making an impossible quarry. Breathless with laughter herself, Tia sank to the sand in mock defeat.

Reality. The effervescent reality of these young lives, and the incredible trust they extend to us. Trust in us as their nurturers, trust in us as stewards of the world they are growing into.

They will never know a world with tidepools at this site. They will never know the cooler temperatures, the stable weather of my youth. Now is their carefree time, and they will treasure these memories, which to me are intertidal destruction, salt-burned marshes, beachfront erosion. This is all they know.

Love for how it was ... passion for how it ought to be ... love for you who inherit it ... ability to act ... they all come together in me.[67]

Tia covered her face with her arms as Annis and Janelle returned, shrieking with laughter, to dump seaweed on Tia.

Find someone to mentor, he told me.

Annis and Janelle ran down the beach. Behind them the bright sun glinted off the water's surface.

(24.)

Tia returned to the RAI committees with a clarity of mind and purpose that enabled her to rise above the frustrating details, to identify the big issues with laser-sharp perception, and to connect the right people to get the needed approvals.

Mired in bureaucracy a month before, the PLASE project now burst into fruition, seemingly overnight. Go-aheads came flying at Tia from all levels, from RAI administrators to LA City Council.

Tia's coordinating work was suddenly complete, the citizens action committees having filled their purpose. LA's comprehensive light rail system and Olmstead-inspired park plans were finally under way. People from the downtown camps were now employed on a regular basis, with a paycheck, albeit small, and the purchasing power to feed their families. Xavier's waste stream project advanced with similar speed, setting in place a highly sophisticated sorting, recycling and reclamation effort at several locations within the city's boundaries.

Thus the RAI programs simultaneously began to alleviate Depression unemployment and to jump start the move toward Sustainability.

(25.)

At the Lares gardens, apricots, peaches, oranges and lemons, limes and tangerines, pomegranate and avocado, grew bountifully in swales with Steve's greywater drip irrigation. The understory included thornless blackberries and native golden currants.

The air of the gardens was rich with seasonally evolving scent: wet earth and cool dampness in winter, heavy citrus blossoms in spring, sunbaked lavender, mustard and roses in the midst of summer.

Jana's predictions of public interest came true. The number of inquiries about the unique gardens and complex were astounding. The schedule of classes could hardly keep up with the demand.

Now with public classes to teach and children to school, garden time came at a premium, yet the self-reliant complex could not afford a drop in produce yields. Rhus came up with the idea of the Community Reapers Committee. Each household would contribute to the garden maintenance. Garden jobs were scheduled dependent upon the technical skill level of the workers available that day. Keeping the paths clear, the compost spread and the chickens fed could be done by anyone. Crop rotation calculations awaited Jana or Rhus' turn. Seedling care took place when Tia, Annis or Janelle were up.

Ari's skill at gardening was limited to hauling compost and moving the chicken domes. With his relative unavailability due to his travel schedule, Verity quietly suggested that Tia find other ways to meet the Damek household obligation. Thus Tia and Annis came to spend many hours together in the gardens among the growing things.

(26.)

Steve wanted publicity for the Lares project; he felt it would further the cause of Sustainability and showcase possibilities. In Depression depths, tales of do-it-yourself, reclaiming, adaptation, and the homestead mentality were quite popular. Lares stood as a shining example of all of these, yet conveyed a sense of art and style that was reminiscent of the pre-Depression good old days.

Tia expected earthy and green publications; she was not prepared for the appointments Steve sent her way. "Sunset Magazine and Better Homes and Gardens – what do they want with CoHousing?"

"They – er – don't exactly know about that aspect of it yet, but when they see it, they're going to love it," Steve replied.

He was right.

The beautiful photo layouts, the videos and the colorful narratives were a crown of laurels to the Lares team upon all the work it had taken to bring the project to fruition. The CoHousing angle was buried in the text of the articles. The glory of the final product and its gardens were the focus.

Yet eager readership didn't miss the reference. Within days of publication, the phone calls and email inquiries began rolling in, most of them interested specifically in the CoHousing aspect.

In more than a century as a printed magazine, Sunset Magazine had been the outlook on the mainstream Western States lifestyle. Now that it was, like all magazines, a fully online format, it was accessed by a far wider audience. Readers from Mediterranean climates around the world browsed its articles.

Thus, via the gleaming Lares project, alternative housing was catapulted to widespread awareness.

(27.)

A Megadrought was such a sweeping event and so new to the societal consciousness that weathermen and minor climatologists didn't have language or standards to measure it.

Certainly there were years when some rain fell in the Pacific Northwest – these the local weathermen proclaimed to be 'the end of the drought' that began at the turn of the century. Yet the big picture climate analysts knew better. Comparison with the historical record was pointless. It was a time of new history.

"Tia, honey, I'm going traveling." Cassandra's voice was bright over the phone. "I'm going up through the Central Valley, into the Oregon interior, perhaps into Washington. There's a meeting of the minds at UC Davis, people from agriculture. But this time a Union of Concerned Scientists representative will be there, speaking about warming and drought. I thought I'd go tell them about my seeds. Maybe this time they'll listen.

"Actually, it was Sahara's idea, we've been doing a lot more work together. She's integrating my drylands varieties into her biodynamic plans, a unique combination. It's been very exciting."

Sahara. I should be the one picking up as Mom slows down, it should be me there at Coyote Creek.

"So we're going to make the trip together. Of course Wade will come too."

"Have a good trip – keep me posted." Tia hung up the phone and sank back into the armchair.

194

Rhus' voice came from outside the open window together with Janelle's and Annis' bright voices, leaves rustling in the garden. "Here is the growth bud. We want to shape the plant, to keep its branches out of the path, so we place the cutting blade here. Then the new shoot will grow in that direction..."

She should be hearing this at her Grandmother's elbow, not that of a stranger.

How life takes us down a different path! We have expectations, we think we know how life should unfold, but then reality comes in. I thought I'd only live in the city for a short while and then return to Coyote Creek.

I always hated the city. But like it or not, it's somehow become a part of me. Lares, Legacy LA, PLASE, my place is here now. My roots are in Coyote Creek, but my mission is here in LA, to bring some essence of Coyote Creek's earthy ways, some essence of that connection, to the heart of this seething mass of humanity.

Purpose. It hasn't turned out at all like I thought it would. It's not some dreamy pretty concept. It's a tough, working tool. It's the steely threads deep inside my heart that hold me together. It's my drive, my power supply, it keeps me going. It's the windshield wipers that clear mists so I can see my way clearly. It's the source of my courage, the deep knowing that there is no other option for me.

Annis' laughter echoed in through the window.

No other option. For me, for her, for her unborn children.

(28.)

The man on the street would be hard-pressed to tell you how and when Lori Fordon became such a celebrity; her periodic appearances on newspages and magazine main-pages were now taken as accepted norm.

That the press still admired her was evident in the flattering shots they selected for publication and the absence of derogatory commentary.

As the MacKay angle ceased to be of interest, Lori Fordon cultivated the image of Champion of Worthy Causes, and used her paparazzi to maximum advantage. Glamour shots of her striking profile viewed through a thin-film solar power curtain wall on a Times Square skyscraper, photos of her emerging, Amelia Earhart style, from a prototype solar aircraft, video footage of her test drive of the latest electric vehicle on a well-known racetrack hit the major news magazines.[68]

In this way the charismatic Lori Fordon bestowed style and flair upon Sustainable choices.

(29.)

As Tia moved through the crowds before the Legacy LA meeting, she overheard Steve talking with Ben. "Have you heard about Esperanza's latest? She's now combined elder care with her inner city youth community gardening. She packs her baby on her back and goes out through mid-city to find seniors who can no longer maintain the garden around their homes. She organizes teams of youths to maintain the land as edible landscape. They call it FarmUrb, as in Farming the Urban spaces. They sell the produce at farmer's markets. With Jana's design approach, the appearance of these places is absolutely beautiful!"[69]

At the appointed hour, Tia met up with Ari and sat in the front row, as Kegan walked nervously onstage to bring the meeting to order for his first time. As he spoke, his eyes were on Ari, who nodded assurances.

"... Tonight we'll hear from Al Chapman about Consumer Values," Kegan finished the introduction.

"EXTRA VALUE! PRICE ROLLBACK! Two for the price of one! Only $3.99!" Al yelled, bounding out to center stage.

"The word 'Value' shares roots with 'Valuable.' I question whether, when you heard my opening line, it sounded Valuable. Probably, it sounded cheap. And it sounded urgent. Two essential ingredients that Madison Avenue has capitalized upon in our consumerist culture.

"Kegan said Consumer Values. I'll rename that. Tonight we're going to Remodel the Consumerist House of Cards.

"This is the WalMart-is-our-enemy show! WalMart, Costco, Target, 99¢ Stores, the epitome of the consumerist machine. Low cost, mass-produced, low quality disposable goods. Planned obsolescence. Excessive packaging. Single function, bulk pack, imported. And the ultimate: *fashionable*.

"Fashion drives it, boys and girls. That inner competitiveness, to have the latest and the new, more, more, more! The advertising industry has figured out how to latch into our insecurities and our competitive urges and combine these into an all-powerful, urgent *I want*. Gotta have it!

"Numbers are the scorecard. How many do you own, how much did it cost you, I got it for less. The scorecard, the almighty dollar, is fungible, it fits everyone: I got it for $4.99 while you paid $6.50, so it's clear that I won. The perfect entry for megacorp brand names and mass production.

"Let's take a breather here and wander over to the Green realm. Here I mean the Deep Ecology folks, not the green-cast corporate stuff. Deep Ecology says value is low footprint upon the earth: low eco-impact, reduce/reuse/recycle/rebuy. If you wander into a health food store you'll learn that food can actually be bought from bins, not just hermetically sealed plastic packages. In Europe, you'd better bring your own shopping bags because they don't hand out 'paper or plastic.'[70] Think back to your grandmother's days, the Little Depression times of the 1930's: goods had to be quality, they had to be durable, they had to be repairable. And 'refurbished' wasn't an ugly word. Multifunction, now there's a great word, my grandmother's favorite. She would never allow an appliance in her kitchen that served only one function. She refused to grant it the precious storage space.

"Our greenhouse gas and anti-oil friends are teaching us that 'local' is a significant concept. Locally produced, like your farmers market veggies, means less fossil fuels are needed to get it to market. In the case of those veggies, local also means greater nutrient value they're not deteriorating in warehouse storage, and local means a better match with the surrounding ecology and seasons. Handcrafted sounds like a throwback to the 1970's. But handcrafted means tender loving care. It means variety and interest, artistic and intellectual, both for the maker and the consumer, human capital brought into play. And for all of this wouldn't you expect to pay a fair price?

"But what is fair? What is local? What is low eco-impact? These are variable measures. Local for me might be different than local for you, if you live across town. Low eco-impact evolves through time as we get better and better at this stuff. It is a moving standard. Fair is subjective. The scorecard is wildly individual.

"Re-forming our consumer values is a mission for the Change Agents and Transformers. Redirecting the mainstream from a perception, spawned by the assembly-line mass-production of the Industrial Revolution, that 'value' means quantity.

"In our new era, 'value' must change to 'valuable.' It must mean quality.

"Our society is suffering. We have been in actual pain, from the illusive 'wealth' of accumulation. We have 'needed' bigger and bigger living spaces to house all our Stuff. Storage units and organizing services became big business. Landfill space became a huge problem. Families had to be dual income in order to finance it all.

"And despite all that, it was never enough. We felt a continual poverty of time, of space, and particularly of spirit.

"The hard Depression times we're currently experiencing are rolling back some of the consumerism. We're relearning the skills of our great grandparents: skills of reuse, of adapting things to multi-functions, skills of repairing things, and skills of selection, of picking more durable, repairable goods to start out with. Yet we still have the core problem and until we solve that issue, we have not achieved lasting change. The consumerism will simply return when the cash flow does.

"That issue we must solve is a matter of the spirit. A wildly individual scorecard, a satisfaction index, which only works when you have the maturity to really know yourself. It requires you to rise above the comparison with others, requires you to find the inner fortitude to step out of the keep-up-with-the-Joneses.

"This issue of satisfaction is one where we need to enlist the aid of our partners, the organizations who specialize in matters of the spirit."

Here Al paused and held out his hand to Matthew, who hopped up to join Al on stage.

"They must take the lead," Al continued. "They can lead the mainstream back to an inner satisfaction, back to the peace of wisely selected simplicity. What is most required at this moment is moral vision and leadership.

"You see, our coping skills for life, our coping skills for organized society, are like a house of cards. You cannot just remove a card and expect the structure to remain standing. But if you're wise in your selection and you operate patiently and carefully, you can slide out one card and replace it with another.

"We cannot just rip the Consumerism card from the card house of society. Gravity will operate to fill the gap, likely in a disastrous manner. We have to replace that Consumerism with something: a placeholder, another coping skill." Al turned to Matthew.

"Satisfaction," Matthew said. "Satisfaction comes from deep within. Not from how much Stuff you have, not from the brand of clothes you hang on your outside, or what model of car you wrap around you. Cultivate a rich inner life – get in touch with your non-material values and allow them to blossom and flourish, to fill you up. Gather around you a circle of companions who do the same. In this way Satisfaction becomes the norm within your social support circle, rather than consumerism being the competitive fashion."

Al returned for the summary. "The card on the table is Satisfaction of the Spirit. Whether this is a religious card for you, or whether it's purpose-driven, or a more earthy or nebulous definition of spirit, regardless of how you personally define this inner dimension, until we re-introduce it back into society, for each of our selves, and for each of the mainstream, we will make no lasting headway on a permanent switch away from Consumerism."

After Al's conclusion, Matthew jumped down from the stage and approached Ari.

"Back from DC? Hey, I've been wanting to hear your latest take on the China situation."

"Well, we had a lot of interest from the Chinese in the Framework we drafted in Barcelona." Ari began. "It's happening sooner than I dreamed it would: China's coming onto the world stage wanting to get competitive in the Sustainability movement. They were all over it in Barcelona, wanted in on everything from technology like solar and fuel cells, to wanting to be an early ratifier for the Barcelona Framework.[71]

"I'm thrilled that China's incredible drive to develop competitively is turning in this direction. One thing it means is, other countries will have to jump onto the Sustainability bandwagon in order to compete with China. In this way, China has stepped into a leadership position in the world; they're forcing the changes worldwide."

(30.)

To Los Angeles residents now buffeted by El Niño winter storms in three out of seven years, record rainfall and water conservation behavior didn't seem to go together. Most people had yet to reach the understanding that the supplies for water streaming out of the tap bore little relation to storm water streaming off the roof outside.

To supply LA's pipelines, rain and snows must fall hundreds of miles away in the High Sierras and the Rockies. As weather patterns shifted, abundant El Niño rains fell on Los Angeles and Orange County rooftops and freeways. With passing decades, as the weather patterns shifted, California's Northern Sierras and large portions of the Colorado River watershed received less snowpack each year. LA's human population grew, and thus water demand increased, yet the water supply to established aqueduct systems was declining rapidly.

(31.)

Following his reelection in 2016 President Elliott mounted an all-out campaign for Stewardship of the environment.

Elliott nominated a new Administrator of the EPA, Hugh Denley, a candidate highly praised in environmental circles. Ari was thrilled with the choice, knowing Denley from numerous conferences over the years. Denley set in motion a thorough housecleaning of the Agency. Seniority was no protection, in fact it was likely a detriment. Much to the chagrin of U.S. nationalists, Denley's new administration brought in experts from overseas – the EU, India – where environmental scientists had long been accustomed to working with an outlook to global issues.

Elliott threw Presidential support behind a Congressional bill for a long term Renewables Portfolio Standard (RPS), requiring that a growing share of the nation's power supply come from renewable sources by 2030. This long-term RPS provided the stable market environment that the renewable energy community had sought since the early 2000's. To kick off the RPS program and show Presidential commitment, Elliott had solar panels reinstalled on the White House.

The RPS programs included provisions for Public Benefit Funds where a small fee was collected as a surcharge on electricity bills; the proceeds went to fund renewable energy research.[72]

Ari was summoned to Washington for consultation on RPS proceedings. He then hopped between U.S. states: to Texas, Minnesota and Iowa to develop state level legislation in support of wind energy projects; to Arizona, New Mexico, and Nevada supporting solar enterprises. The blossoming solar and wind power industries on the heels of RAI and CCC further increased employment.

Elliott's social programs to increase employment brought him enormous popular appeal. Drawing on this political goodwill in his final years in office, he attempted to tackle the biggest hot buttons of all: the Moscow Treaty and the Barcelona Framework.

(32.)

It was an awkward transition, not unlike a teenager in a growth spurt, with feet and limbs suddenly too long for accustomed movement and operations. The city of LA was torn up, light rail being installed down major thoroughfares, yet the accustomed mode of transport remained individual automobiles. Traffic jams were nightmarish and tempers flared, as lanes closed to allow RAI construction workers to move massive materials into place.

Growing pains.

The searing summer heat didn't help one bit. The entire city seemed to be sitting on a powder keg.

Not much different from a 13 year old's tempers, Tia thought wryly.

Yet it was happening. Progress was unfolding before their eyes.

My city is growing up. LA has always been so childishly individualistic, to the point of narcissism. But the Depression times have altered people's consciousness. There is a new focus now.

When I first came to LA you didn't know your neighbor. Front lawns were sterile and unoccupied. Now the yards are the gathering places – the grass lawns themselves are becoming a thing of the past. Neighbors are connecting.

The focus is changing, from the childish all-about-me, to taking others into account. In the way our teens grow and stretch their perspective, our city is growing and stretching its consciousness as well.

If only our country would do the same.

(33.)

"Tia, I won't make it home this weekend," Ari phoned from Arizona. "I need to head back to DC. Elliott has something up his sleeve. Even Alden's office can't figure out what it is. Fordon has been called in, so I'm going back to join them."

"Oh Ari, we'll miss you terribly." This past year he had again been gone more than he had been home. *It's like 2009 revisited.*

"How are things in Arizona?"

"Well, the motivation's here, people really are behind the clean energy concept. Unfortunately, they want to assemble massive efficiency solar fields across open land, carpeting the desert, as if that open land has no value. I'm trying to get them to switch to rooftops – every rooftop they have – and to glass sheeting like has been done in New York City.[73] Installation would be more pricey, that's why they resist. It's cheaper to do large arrays across the flat desert. But long term, ecologically, the impact on the desert ecosystems, the loss of open land ...

"Also, they're still stuck in what I've come to call 'big think.' They are still thinking of big collection sources – New Mexico, Arizona, Nevada – and big grid trunklines to convey the power where it is needed. They still refuse to think locally, distributed energy systems, putting the collectors on buildings in cities where the power is needed. Local panels would eliminate the carrying losses along the way. It's not about the strength of the sun, even the turn of the century solar panels derived about the same amount of solar energy in Maine, let alone our contemporary technologies. The business world is still so stuck in factory and specialist mentalities that they can't see it's vastly more efficient to do it locally."

&

Disappointment wouldn't even begin to describe Annis' reaction to Ari's change of plans.

"He's *never* here!" Annis screamed with the full drama of thirteen. "He's *always* off on some trip or another! He doesn't care about us! Why can't he have a normal job like Steve or Carl or Matthew?

"And even when he is here, he hardly even knows I'm alive! He never does stuff with me, it's always work, work, work. If it's not his work he's not interested. Rhus does lots of stuff with Janelle. I wish Rhus was my dad!"

&

Ari phoned Sunday night from DC. "Tia, Elliott's sending an official U.S. Delegation to the UNFCCC Conference! Fordon's heading it up."

Please, tell me you're not going overseas right now.

"I don't know why he's doing it – it's been more than ten years since the U.S. sent any official delegation to the emissions conferences. I'm not at all sure anything productive will come of it. I decided to let Fordon handle it, I backed out. I'm sticking to this RPS schedule. There's a lot of good I can do right here in the U.S. I'll be flying to Minnesota on Tuesday for the wind power meeting."

Tia opened her g-news site Monday morning and sat stunned, staring at the screen.

ELLIOTT SIGNS MOSCOW TREATY
September 17, 2018. In a surprise move today, President Elliott ratified the Moscow Treaty, successor to last century's Kyoto Protocol. The Moscow Treaty is the international agreement that limits greenhouse gas emissions...

In the photo, among the beaming crowd behind President Elliott, were Ari, Senator Alden and Lori.

So that's what Elliott had up his sleeve!

"Annis, come look at this!"

"So? It's Dad on the g-news. Big deal."

Big deal!?

"Annis, your father and others have been fighting for this moment for more than twenty years." Tia's voice was quiet with her amazement at it all.

He was fighting for it when I met him. Twenty years of effort.

She stared at his picture on the screen.

And then it comes into being, so suddenly, with so little fanfare. An anticlimax.

Tia looked at Annis.

"You understand the significance of this."

Annis tossed her head in an I'm-not-listening-to-you gesture, but she didn't walk away.

"This means the U.S. is finally joining the other nations of the world to take action against global warming," Tia continued.

"We've got the Federal law, what do we need this for?" Annis tried to deliver it flippantly, as if she didn't care, but her pointed question belied her tone.

Yes! She's actually been listening all these years!

Tia pretended to be tidying her desk, as if the answer were of no importance.

"As the U.S. becomes part of the international Treaty, our country is stepping in to cooperate on the world stage. We're committing to this direction, making a pledge to the other nations, to their peoples."

In a very adult gesture, Annis studied her fingernails, then lapsed back into childhood and began biting them.

"Do you think he'll come home now, now that they've signed it?" Annis asked softly, mumbling around her fingers.

"I don't know honey, he said something about Minn ..." Tia cut off abruptly and turned to Annis. "Why don't you call him and ask him to?"

⚭

When Jana heard about the ratification she declared it was time for a party. She invited all the Legacy LA faces from the years of the Venice house and triplex, all the people who had supported Ari through two decades of effort.

"We'd better not make it a surprise party, Jana," Tia worried. "You know how he changes his travel plans."

Jana clearly preferred the surprise, but deferred to Tia's judgment.

"What are you doing that for?" Ari said when Tia told him about the party. But she could hear the smile in his voice.

CHAPTER 7:

A LOT OF COURAGE

2018-2025

In addition to being a celebration of the U.S. ratification of the Moscow Treaty, Jana let slip to the party guests that it was also within a month of Ari's fiftieth birthday. Shannon coordinated the food preparation, with Tia, Annis, Janelle and Jana as the cooking team. The menu was international hors d'oeuvres, Shannon's play on the nature of the Moscow Treaty.

The guest list was extensive, and filled South House. Party guests spilled out into garden areas and patios, as the event became yet another chance to share the delights of Lares living with others.

As Tia wandered through the party she overheard bits of conversation.

"Yes, I made a lot of the food for this party – I enjoy cooking and inventing healthy things that taste great," said Shannon.

"Ever think about starting a restaurant?" Ravyn asked.

"I've toyed with the idea, but haven't a clue how to start."

"You know that's what I do – new restaurant concepts."

"Oh, I had no idea!"

"Did you hear, Senator Alden has announced he's running for President in 2020?" Jana asked.

"Yes, what did Ari think of that?"

"Oh, I'm sure he's known about it for quite some time, they're very close."

The young people had taken over the office as their private lair.

"Have you heard this new music? Jeffrey Jubal – he's really dreamy!"

"Oh, it sounds so different! No processing."

"Yeah, he just gets up there and sings, his voice, his guitar. It's very old style, like way back when Grandma was young."

"I like it!"

"But listen to his songs, they're about trees, clean air, oceans!"

"Wow!"

"Oooh, look at his picture here on the grid!"

"Hey, I've seen that face before – I think my Mom knows his mom," Annis exclaimed.

"Have you seen Carl's CoHousing project in West LA? It's so beautiful! Rhus did the landscaping, inspired by what Jana did here," said Verity, quite pregnant with her second child.

"I hear Jana's writing a book now."

"Yes, about edible landscaping. It should be gorgeous – photos from here, the triplex, the Hollywood project and some of her projects downtown."

"Things are really bad in the Northwest. The megadroughts have been going on for almost nineteen years," said Cassandra.

"I thought they got some rain."

"Not enough to bring them back to their accustomed climate. The drought has hurt the massive bird migrations through the area. The salmon and steelhead populations have been dramatically lowered by warmer waters and lower streamflow. Now the cedars are dying. Shallow root systems, accustomed to moisture, you know."

"Cedar? That must be quite a big deal. I know the traditional native cultures were quite reliant on the cedar, spiritually and ceremonially."

"It certainly is a big deal! Also, many of the farms are going into default. They can't make it through climate change with the typical modern crops," Cassandra said.

"They need Cass's stuff," Wade laughed.

"Although the economy's recovering, the legal profession – well, it doesn't produce anything," Matthew admitted to another guest. "People just aren't willing to pay the magnitude of fees they did in the old days. And the whole litigious attitude, of suing everyone remotely connected to an event, that's gone now. People aren't lawsuit-happy anymore. They're much more realistic, willing to accept some responsibility for their own actions, no longer looking to the courts for compensation for something that resulted from their own choices. Good for society, bad for lawyers like me."

"Esperanza's going to help me with the site over in East LA. The girls came up with the project idea, and Peter and Mark were eager to join in. Even Seth's in on it now. It'll be a lot like the Community Gardens Jana and Esperanza did back in the early 2000s, gathering local people around edible landscaping," Rhus looked delighted at the prospect. "Sharing the knowledge – now into a new generation."

"I heard they've resurrected plans for high speed rail between LA and San Francisco."

"Well they're talking about it again." Ben replied. "Nothing concrete yet. Rail will cost less than half what expanding highways and airport runways would cost, to accommodate these same passengers. It would be a great thing to eliminate the air traffic on that short route, because airplanes can be especially fuel-inefficient over short distances. Plus it's a lot less destructive to use transportation down here on the surface where we can at least offset the greenhouse gas emissions with carbon sinks. For emissions up in the higher atmosphere where aircraft fly, there is little we can do about the significant CO_2 impact."

"Why is that?"

"Aircraft emissions at high altitude have an enhanced impact on the greenhouse effect, it's called radiative forcing. The carbon dioxide released up there by aircraft affects the atmosphere two and a half times more significantly than CO_2 released on the ground."

"I hear Steve's been busy."

"Yes, the popularity of eco-housing really took off when the economy began to recover. So Steve's retrofit and clean-remodel ideas have been in great demand. He's taken in several apprentices over the past year, to teach how it is done."

"Don't they go out and compete with him for business?"

"That's the thing about Steve. He says the important thing is converting to more efficient structures, and there is sufficient business for everyone. He loves to share the ideas."

"Oh, the recycling operations aren't RAI anymore, they're self-supporting," Xavier said proudly. "I should show you our input and output statistics some time. The product is paying for operations. Sure RAI built the places, but now ... We hired most of the people who built the setups – they have a fierce pride about it, really want to see it successful. Their work ethic is inspiring. Those people brought in friends, and now the originals are the foremen.

"Of the mixed material we process, only about 5% remains in the waste stream headed for landfills.[74] Our workers sort out every little scrap: metals, textiles, lumber. We can now reclaim five of the six major types of plastic resins. It all goes out the door as clean sorted raw material for the next product. Esperanza's brothers organized the raw materials sales force – now even the sales are fully handled by people who used to be RAI."

∽

Tia found Ari outside on the deck. He was facing out over the railing; his back made a smooth V from his broad shoulders to his trim waist. At fifty, his dark hair was now salted with grey, his tall proud form as noble as ever. He seemed to be focused out beyond the gardens, to vistas deep within his own mind. He glanced over at Tia briefly, then back toward the distance as he spoke.

"It's a fun party," he said to her. "I haven't seen some of these people in years. You and Jana really did a great job pulling it together."

"All in celebration of the incredible job you've done," she said, smiling and slipping her arm around his waist.

"It's not my doing, you know. Recall, I left the U.S. delegation after Buenos Aires. Fordon and Alden deserve the lion's share of the credit. I can't believe the U.S. has actually ratified. I was standing right there when Elliott signed it, but it still does not feel completely real. Kyoto was 21 years ago. I was so inspired by it at the time that I began working to join the UNFCCC negotiations."

He changed course abruptly.

"Have you heard the conversation in there?" He gestured behind him, toward the party through the windows.

"Why yes, isn't it delightful? It's like a roll call of successes!" Her delight in the magic of it all rang in her voice.

He glanced at her for a brief moment and then his eyes returned to far away. His voice was rich with emotion as he spoke.

"Tia, it's happening. The Transformation Wave. It's here, it's real, it's growing. It's in that gathering, it's in gatherings like that all over the state, the country, the world. I just can't believe it. I hoped for this for so long and it's actually coming alive. I hoped for it, but honestly, there were times when I didn't believe it would really happen."

You didn't believe it!? You, who wrote article upon article about the Transformation Wave, who made the speeches, who built this movement? You, who set up the groups that brought these people together, who rounded up and pulled together the teams, for Lares, for PLASE, for countless other projects?

"The U.S. on board the Moscow Treaty ... a comprehensive rail system in LA ... an environmentalist in the White House ... the grassroots green movement ..." He listed them in wonder.

"You made it happen, darling! Your victory, your accomplishment!" She smiled at him.

He rounded on her, his eyes hard reality. "Oh no, it's not my victory."

He turned her to face the large windows and the party inside the house. "It's their victory. They're the ones who have done it, with counterparts in countless other cities. They're not superhumans, just everyday people, each one doing his or her part.

"The amazing thing is that each one has made a conscious choice to guide this world toward what it ought to be. One at a time they decided: I won't accept this environmental degradation, I won't accept this denigration of people, I'm going to do something about it. I'm going to take action toward positive change. And before you know it, those efforts add up."

The whole is far greater than the sum of the parts.

He took a deep breath.

"But we're not done. We've just begun. The changes are beginning to touch the mainstream, which means that we now have the support to begin to work on the big things. The ink's barely dry on the Moscow Treaty but there's the Framework ... and the Alden campaign."

She stared at him in surprise. "You're going out on the campaign trail?"

"Oh God, no! I don't do that kind of thing well. No, if Barry gets into office ... *when* Barry gets into office ... He has some earth-changing ideas, Tia, milestone changes. He has a lot of courage." Ari's voice trailed off. "It's going to take a lot of courage."

"Why do you say that?"

"Because the United States needs to make some huge shifts, some enormous changes in the way we do things.[75] We need some new policies – we desperately need a new energy policy, for instance. We've needed it for decades. Rafferty wasn't going to do it – with the economy sinking, people didn't feel secure enough to make big sweeping changes. Elliott certainly couldn't find political support to do it, in the depths of the Depression. He did what he could by putting RPS in place.

"The big changes are long overdue, and they're more urgent than ever. The political status quo is going to fight them tooth and nail. I truly hope the next Administration is strong enough to make the changes we need to make."

Jana grinned out the door. "Oh, there you two are! It's cake time!"

⤌

"Land Trusts could preserve that open farmland," a party guest was saying to Verity as Ari and Tia followed Jana toward the cake table.

"We could prevent urban sprawl? With a Land Trust? Is that like Matthew set up here at Lares, so that the members own the land together?" Verity asked.

"Sort of. An Agricultural Land Trust protects open spaces, preventing shopping centers and housing developments from taking over our arable land. These trusts keep agricultural land values affordable, and preserve a critical mass of agricultural activity to support the farming infrastructure."

"Nice flat farmland is easy for developers to build on," Jana said wryly. "I wish they'd build someplace else, like on land that isn't prime for growing crops!"

"You can do something about those wishes," the guest continued. "Most of these Agricultural Land Trusts are charities. They collect donations, then buy an easement on the farmland. An easement is a right to the land; in this case, the easement limits the uses to which the land can be put."

"Limits those uses to agriculture, or perhaps wildlife conservation." Verity was catching on.

Ari had been listening to the interchange. "We're not buying the farmland, just the development rights? So that a developer doesn't get them?"

"Legally the approach is phrased differently but the result is the same."

"Hey, Matthew," Ari called across the party, "did you hear what Conrad is saying?"

Matthew joined the circle at the same time as Cassandra and Wade.

"Conrad is telling us that we could set up Agricultural Land Trusts to conserve farmland by buying easements," Ari said, clearly piecing together an idea. "This fits right in with what you were saying, Cassandra, about the drought hardships up north."

"Well, yes," Cassandra answered. "The farmers in the megadrought areas are defaulting and having to abandon the properties."

"There has to be a way to use these Trusts in coordination with the foreclosures, to acquire even more easements right now, at bargain prices," Ari declared.

"I'll look into it," Matthew promised.

"There are several Agricultural Land Trusts already in existence," Conrad said. "The Land Trust Alliance would be a good place to start."[76]

"I have some contacts up north who are working the land trust issue – I'll see if they have done anything with regards to foreclosures," Cassandra smiled up at Ari.

"Maybe Steve's Sustainability contacts up there can help, too." Ari added, looking around for Steve.

A small smile played across Tia's face as she watched Ari. *Even in the midst of his party he still keeps going.* His dark eyes were alive with excitement over his latest creation.

"Last night you said the abandonments worried you because the barren land was vulnerable to desertification," Jana said to Cassandra, cake knife poised in hand.

"Because it's farmland, it has been stripped of natural cover – trees and shrubs and such," Cassandra answered. "With the drought and abandonment, nothing much is growing there and the natural ecology of virgin land has not been reestablished. If too many patches of this occur in close proximity, we could be facing severe issues like the Dust Storms which stripped topsoil from agricultural lands in the 1930's."

"It's a shame we couldn't find a way to hold back the desertification with these Land Trusts," Jana mused. "Tell them they've gotta use Sustainable practices, polycultures, trees, native grasses …"

"The group in Oregon emphasizes Sustainable agriculture, and networks young growers for education and research, in addition to protecting rural and urban agricultural lands." Conrad said. "But your combination of techniques?" Conrad and Matthew shook their heads.

"It's an idea we should explore," Ari insisted.

The Transformation Wave – he said he didn't quite believe it, but he just cannot help himself, it just exudes from him.

Ari noticed Tia watching him. He hugged her to his side.

Annis appeared at Tia's elbow, a glint of merriment in her eye.

"Mom, what's Sahara's son's name? Isn't he Jeffrey Jubal, the singer?"

"I saw him in DC," Ari said.

"You DID!?" Janelle was right behind Annis. "Oh what is he like?"

"I've actually seen him a few times over the years."

Tia looked up, her interest encouraging the story.

"The first time was two, maybe three years ago. He was there with Wendell. Wendell's performance was awful, the bar was empty. Jeffrey was there as backup. We had a drink together and he asked what I was doing in DC. At that time it was a trip for the Barcelona Framework."

"Hey, he has a song about that Barcelona Framework!" Janelle squeaked. "The verses are about Factor 4 and Sustainability!"

Ari, did you catch that – Factor 4 and Sustainability – it's now part of the teen vernacular!

"Yes, he thought the global warming and climate change issues made great material for his work. It's quite interesting actually, to hear what he's done with it."

"Oh, Dad, he's sooo popular now!" Annis' eyes were star struck.

"It's thrilling that he gets this material out to such a wide audience of young people," Tia commented.

Verity overheard them. "Yeah, for so long American pop music was just about broken hearts, codependent relationships, dreary stuff, actually. It's great to hear something with some content."

(2.)

"Tia, I'm going to have a restaurant!" Shannon bubbled over with excitement as she and Tia chopped chard for a wild rice dish in Shannon's kitchen.

"Ravyn is trying out names. He's thinking of calling it Slow Food Fast, because it'll be fast pickup for the customer, in contrast with the fact that the restaurant prepares it slowly.

"It'll be all my favorite recipes. My slow simmered soups and stews. Clean meats and organic dairy. Vegetable and organic salads from healthy greens – not that iceberg junk. Fresh baked whole grain breads without the preservatives and sugars. Lacto-fermented condiments.

"We'll use locally grown produce, and seasonal foods, none of this imported off-season stuff. We've established some supplier connections through the Biodynamic Association of Southern California and Community Supported Agriculture.

"What we need now is a location. Ravyn wants to find a site near one of the PLASE stations."

"I'll talk with Ari and Carl – they might know of something," Tia volunteered.

Ari had a restaurant space vacant in his Westwood retail center. He liked the idea of Shannon's restaurant.

"I've always wanted to turn those retail centers into Sustainability Centers. This restaurant concept is a good starting place. It inspires me to find a property manager who can get me the kind of tenants I dream of having – Sustainably focused ones."

Verity heard about Ari's interest and introduced him to Troy Gaderian, a young, energetic retail property manager. Troy was thrilled at the opportunity. "I've long wanted to do something like this. But none of the other landlords I work with would risk something so cutting-edge."

"We have to be willing to take some risks if we're ever going to bring about societal change." Ari commented.

Troy brought in the EcoServ chain. EcoServ was not a store, but a connection point between businesses which under the old economy would have had to maintain stores and showrooms. A one-stop shop, here a customer could access any of a diverse selection of service businesses: carpeting services in the Interface Carpet leasing model; chemical services following Dow Chemical's lead; car services for short-term leasing of the most contemporary hybrid vehicles; furniture services leasing Sustainably produced furniture which reverted to the owner/manufacturer for rework or recycling at the end of the lease term. EcoServ provided wide market connection and sales force for these fledgling green businesses while supporting the cause of waste stream management and Sustainability.

Ari and Troy also began to remodel the buildings. Ordinary glass was replaced by solar efficient panes, roofs now included rainwater cachement systems, and plumbing was reconfigured to separate greywater for appropriate reuse.

As all of the sites were located within neighborhood pockets and within walking distance of PLASE stations, the strip mall parking lots for traditional cars could be removed and pared down to smaller scale Neighborhood Vehicle parking spaces with electric vehicle hookups. The solar arrays on the roofs powered battery storage for both the stores and the electric vehicles. The parking lots were surfaced with cobblestones to allow permeability for groundwater replenishment.

Jana and Rhus landscaped the freed-up land as tiny parks and greenbelts, each with fruit trees and benches over chipped mulch. Jana specified feijoas so liberally that Ari had them designed into his Sustainability Center logo just to tease her. Rhus began with citrus and olive trees, but soon discovered that he could adapt the landscaping to the particular tenant mix – a strip mall containing a laundromat yielded more greywater and an opportunity for lush tropical edibles.

Other landowners near PLASE station locations elsewhere in the city were interested in the Sustainability Center concept, yet Ari's frequent travels rendered him unavailable as a resource. Fourteen year old Annis seized the opportunity to be constantly at Ari's elbow when he was in town. She became 'press secretary' for the string of Sustainability Centers, maintaining an active grid presence listing materials information, subcontractors, construction photos, and conceptual explanations. Annis was interviewed about the Sustainability Centers by an environmental teens magazine. Ari was absolutely delighted.

(3.)

As the economy pulled out of 'sluggish' and became better described as 'blossoming,' it was with new and different vigor than in the old days, prior to the crash. In the old ways, economic vitality had been top down, first visible at the highest levels, in the global corporations, with claims the good times would trickle down. In this new era, vitality grew from the ground up, beginning with a rebuilding at the grass roots levels. Family businesses, family farms, ethnic neighborhood centers, here it began.

As the corporate world continued to flounder, economic advisors of the nation's highest levels, desperate for any good news to announce to the g-news, turned to figures and calculations they never considered before. One such alternative statistic was the Genuine Progress Indicator, or GPI.

When Depression times were at their depths, both the Gross National Product and the GPI depicted the country's agony. As recovery began, GPI, which included volunteer and household work, gave a more politically advantageous soundbite than the lagging GNP. GNP was heavily reliant on slow-to-recover traditional Wall Street industries, while GPI included home-based tasks and the significant environmental benefits wrought by CCC.

GNP was soon lost to the dusty archives of economics history lessons, where only first year business students learned about it. They groaned at its appalling inaccuracies and the distorted portrayal it must have given of the country's true economic picture.

(4.)

As a followup to the U.S. ratification of the Moscow Treaty, Senators Alden and Diamont teamed up yet again for a bipartisan bill which imposed a nationwide carbon tax, to assure that the U.S. would meet its new international obligations.

The carbon tax was based upon CO_2 taxes in Norway and Sweden.[77] The tax was designed to be an incentive to reduce greenhouse emissions, and to motivate businesses and private households to seek renewable energy sources. It was collected through utility bills, at the gas pumps and via airline ticket purchases. The revenues from the tax were dedicated toward federal backing of the RPS programs.

Senator Alden was wise in his selection of the spokesperson for the carbon tax public education campaign. Posed in stunning fashion in front of Arizona photovoltaic arrays or Minnesota wind turbines, Ms. Lori Fordon handled interviewer questions with charisma and technical knowledge. She won American public support for the carbon tax with pure charm.

(5.)

Prior to the early 1900s the High Plains were a semi-arid prairie region. Although the ancient Ogallala aquifer beneath Nebraska, Wyoming, Colorado, Kansas, Oklahoma, New Mexico and Texas had contained abundant water, this aquifer had been cut off from almost all of its natural recharging sources. Rivers drained rather than recharged it, as their water tables were well below that of the aquifer. Rainwater did not replenish the aquifer due to high evaporation and an impenetrable lime-like layer of caliche just under the soil surface.

The Ogallala aquifer was first drilled for irrigation purposes around 1911, leading to a regional dependence on groundwater for agriculture. By the 1960's, Water Management Districts were already concerned about the aquifer's water supply and began restricting the number of wells permitted. By the early 2000's, complex programs of "irrigation scheduling" were applied in weak attempts at conservation. Because the aquifer varied in depth throughout the area, water supply depletion was a more pressing issue in Texas than in Nebraska, thus local political infighting prevented any effective overall plan.

The uncertain rainfall of climate change placed farms in double jeopardy, without reliable source of water from either clouds or ground. Belatedly, interest arose in rainwater cachement and resource efficiency. Meanwhile, agriculture suffered. True to Cassandra's predictions, the massive industrial farms displayed the least flexibility in these times of change.

Yet powerful farm lobbies preserved valuable government disaster subsidies and the massive industrial farms remained highly profitable to their corporate owners.

(6.)

Ari came home from his RPS program travels for the holidays. His first night home, he and Tia took an evening stroll of the Lares grounds. They stopped in a garden niche to watch the brilliant winter sunset over LA. Ari flicked distractedly at the leaves of the olive trees as he paced. His dark eyes had been distant, his pacing perpetual, since he returned.

"I came back by way of DC. I stopped in to congratulate Barry. He's getting ready for the Inauguration next month," Ari paused. "Tia, he asked me to be his Secretary of Energy."

Oh Ari, you certainly do like to play this game at the high stakes level!

"What an honor! A Cabinet position!"

"Honor? Yes, I guess so. Surprise is how it hit me. I don't know why, but I didn't see this one coming.

"It's left me with some pretty tough decisions. Do I drop all I'm working on and switch to the national scene, or can I better serve the cause by continuing to work on the international Framework?"

"Ari, with your energy background and your RPS and UN experience, you're exactly what Alden needs in there."

"I know it," he said with a grimace. "It's big, Tia, it's big. Barry's right, there's a lot to be done. The Department of Energy needs a complete overhaul, a total re-think. Barry wants the DOE positioned for transition to the future. That means cleaning house, the way Denley did at the EPA under Elliott. It means a whole new energy policy, the likes of which this country has never seen."

"Ari, that's so exciting!"

"Yes, that it is. But it's limited to the national scene. Sure the U.S. carries plenty of clout worldwide, but I've had my sights on this international agreement for so long now!

"Before I talked with Barry, it was so clear. I'd planned to wrap up these state level RPS issues within the next few months. Then I would head to New York in time to begin preparation for the 2022 World Conference on Sustainable Development in Athens. That will be Rio+30. It's time to move the Barcelona Framework forward into a formal agreement. These next two years will see the Framework become an international treaty, one day legally binding like Kyoto became. And it's time to push for Factor 10."

"Factor 10? You don't even have a quorum of countries fully on board for Factor 4!"

"That's the thing – if I push for Factor 10, then Factor 4 becomes clearly the baby step, the compromise, no longer daunting. I need to showcase Factor 10 regularly and continuously, to make it a strong presence, so that the delegations of the world see it as something to strive for. Then Factor 4 becomes just a step on the path to the future."

"So then we won't see Factor 10 for …"

"… at least another decade." He finished her sentence for her.

"What did you tell Alden?" Tia asked quietly.

"He insisted that I not give him an answer until I'd given it serious thought."

(7.)

President Alden began his Inaugural Address.

"My fellow citizens, citizens of this noble country, and citizens of other proud nations around the world:

"Today I break with tradition and address not just the people of one country, but the people of one world.

"For in this year 2021 the issues before us are not bound by the borders of any one country. They are bigger than any one nation, any one people. They are not even bound by the mere surface of this planet.

"And in this year 2021, we Americans are truly willing to stand up and take our place with other citizens of the world, in setting in motion a new way of living together on this planet. A way of living which opens possibilities to all peoples, a way of living which paves the way for the hope of future generations of humanity.

"The issues before us are not simple. Today we face the tough road of adapting to massive changes unfolding in the patterns of the earth that surround us – changes in our global climate, changes in our sea levels, changes in our polar ice, changes in our water supplies.

"Today world peoples still grapple with extreme poverty, without the resources to adapt to these changes that affect us all.

"Today we face a new demographic – a migration of peoples, taking place worldwide, regardless of the artificial borders drawn between nations. In conjunction with this migration we grapple with basic issues – food supply, water supply, even the most subsistence level of housing.

"Today we face the toughest portion of a climb out of an addiction – our society's addiction to cheap, polluting, exhaustible fossil fuels.

"But we are not without solutions.

"We are, after all, empowered by God's grace with the ability to think, empowered by God's grace with the ability to act. And given such abilities, we have the responsibility to apply them to the issues before us.

"We are the change makers.

"Change is not always comfortable. But only through change will we move into that new way of living. Change will bring new opportunities, new industry, new jobs. Change can mean new harmony between peoples.

"Now is the time for new energy – both energy in the spirit between people, and new renewable energy resources to power our commerce and our homes.

"Now is the time to take our responsible place with the other nations of the world in bringing global solutions to life.

"Now is the time to bring new health to world agriculture and food supplies, thus bringing renewed health to all people.

"Now is the time for new modes of transportation, to replace the dated automobile; time to release the misguided worship of consumer goods; time to use our wealth wisely to end poverty once and for all.

"Now is the time to embrace a lifestyle that honors the miracle of the Creation around us. It is time to heal a divided planet, to forge a common bond of humanity, security and shared purpose across cultures and regions.

"We are the Transition Generation.

"In the eras to come our ancestors will look back on the people of today and say 'They did it! They made the change.' The generations of the future will look back on this time as a miracle of transformation, they will divide time into 'before' and 'after.'

"The power is in our hands. The duty is upon our shoulders. Now is the time for action."

◌

Tia stood at Ari's side on the stairs of the Capitol during the Address, her elbow against his through their thick winter coats. When the President's speech ended, Ari stood, eyes haunted, his mouth drawn up and twisted.

"I should have gone with it. This is one ship I want to be on! Man, this is going to be a special four years!" Ari watched wistfully as his friend, now his President, took the arm of the First Lady and descended the stairs to the waiting limousine. "He's going to nominate Reg Sherwin. I worked with Reg in Nevada on RPS. Reg has his head on right."

She put her hand on his arm. "You know he'll still be calling you."
"Yes, I'm sure he will."

Tia could have kicked herself for her prediction. The Presidential calls, which came at random times of day or night, abruptly extracted Ari from the flow of family life, and snapped him into attention to such an extreme degree that Tia came to resent any chirp of the Sliver.

There was no title to go with the obligation, unless it be that of 'trusted friend of the President.'

(8.)

The day the PLASE system opened, Tia hoped a page had turned to a new chapter in LA's history, yet in the weeks that followed she had her doubts.

The construction process had caused such upheaval in traffic patterns that media was unnecessary in getting the word out – everyone was overjoyed that the project was now complete, if for no other reason than the city flow would now return to 'normal.'

City officials created a citywide opening event, complete with media fanfare, political speeches and balloons at multiple PLASE hubs simultaneously. The system was more than just rail; there were the hydrogen fuel-cell bus lines radiating out along major thoroughfares from each PLASE station like spokes on a wheel, and hybrid-electric jitneys that circulated through the neighborhood pockets.

Construction jobs had eased back as each phase of the massive project completed. Yet the economy was rolling forward now, and workers who had previously relied on RAI now found better employment in other sectors. RAI had thinned the population of the homeless camps significantly.

᪻

Tia escorted fifteen year old Annis to her internship at the Long Beach Aquarium of the Pacific, for the first time using PLASE for the entire journey: a PLASE jitney through their Brentwood neighborhood, connecting to the bus line into Westwood, and rail from Westwood to Long Beach. Although it was unfamiliar and thus a bit awkward, the trip took about the same amount of time as sitting in freeway traffic in a cramped automobile.

The train had few passengers. Use of the system required a rethinking of travel habits. The population was making the adjustments slowly, loathe to leave behind the well-ingrained pattern of walk-to-automobile-insert-key.

Tia gazed out the window at the northbound tracks flowing alongside. *Habits. We build them up like tracks. We become accustomed to doing things one particular way. Our one way heads us in a fixed direction, with no variability.*

It's quite tough to jump the tracks, to break out of long-entrenched habits. Change requires conscious thought; you can't run on autopilot, and it's sometimes uncomfortable.

But if we don't break out of these habits, if we don't convince society to jump the tracks and change course – oh the destination we're all headed for! Ecological upset, polluting toxins, catastrophic global warming ...

Tia shook her head in horror at the thought. She looked over at her daughter in the seat beside her, Annis deeply engrossed in Frank Herbert's novel *Dune.*

Desertification! Massive bloodshed!

We have to persuade society to jump these tracks. I certainly hope it's not going to require a full-scale derailment.

(9.)

tdamek@Lares.net

The PrepCon here in New York is going well. I have been reconfirmed as Head Delegate for the U.S. team headed for WCSD Rio+30 in Athens. World representatives are motivated to see the Barcelona Framework transformed into a Treaty; there is very little resistance. It is exciting to think that the resource efficiency concept of Factor 4 will soon become a binding international law. A.

tdamek@Lares.net

As always when we get into the details of drafting these agreements, the flaws come to the surface. The concept of resource efficiency is vast. Becoming more efficient with one's resources is totally dependent upon what one's resources were in the first place. Thus Factor 4 will look different for each country of the world. That said, it is next to impossible to design a treaty that has any teeth to it. Unsolved, this could become a massive flaw in this agreement; it would be unenforceable. A.

tdamek@Lares.net
We leave New York with the WCSD agreement partially drafted, and one more PrepCon in Athens next spring prior to the Conference. The draft agreement is disappointing at best. The Barcelona Framework was a better document; it attempted to do less. The strength of the Framework, even though it was non-binding, was that it presented a set of standards, international goals if you will. That set of standards brought countries together, with a sense of shared direction and purpose, so exciting to behold. A.

(10.)

An overall sea level rise of a few inches may not seem like much, in the proportionality of the ocean's size. It may not seem like much in view of the wave action's ever-changing movement in the swash zone, where water and land meet. It may not seem like much when you live inland from the ocean's influence. But for shoreline communities the rising sea represented a subtle but definitive shift.

On beaches of gently sloping sands, the sea level rise of mere inches translated to a shift in the mean high tide line of several feet. Narrow ribbon beaches became significantly slimmer as foreshore overtook berm.

With the sea level rise, incoming swells now caught on rocks and shallows in different locations than before, shifting the surf zone, causing the full force of the waves' pounding to strike at new points along the shore. Waves pounding at newly accessed soft spots brought on significant underwater shifting of debris and sand. Shoreline erosion became a critical issue as berms and backshore crumbled.

Building firm barriers to slow the sea's assault on one bit of shoreline shifted the wave energy with powerful force toward other locations along the shore. Seawalls concentrate wave energy, intensifying erosion at the ends of the walls. As wealthy homeowners and shoreline businesses fortified their seawalls, erosion accelerated. Powerful longshore currents redeposited sediment in unprotected areas – public beaches, parks, wetland preserves.

Extreme high tide and storm waves, intensified by shifts in breaker patterns and steeper offshore profiles, now accessed new turf. Cliffed shorelines, at Santa Barbara, Point Mugu, Point Dume and Palos Verdes experienced landslides from undercutting. Older bulkheads, later in the queue for renewal, were breached. The ocean flung the debris of all this destruction at other coastline points with fury.

Increased El Niño frequency brought this seacoast battle to g-news mainpages on a regular basis.

(11.)

tdamek@Lares.net
As world delegations gather here in Athens, excitement is high. I cannot blame them, the thought of resource efficiency becoming an international treaty is certainly a thrilling concept. Yet I do not feel much excitement myself; I have a sense of foreboding that what we are creating here at the WCSD Rio+30 is little more than the opening play that Kyoto was. This Athens Accord is weakened in so many ways. I now realize that what we are so desperately lacking is an international organization to support this environmental effort – a World Environment Organization. A.

tdamek@Lares.net
We have a World Health Organization and a World Trade Organization, yet we have no world organization to integrate matters pertaining to the environment. It is clear, however, judging from the lack of receptivity to my WEO idea, that its time has not yet come. Progress continues on the Athens Accord. I am not campaigning against it; the international collaboration around it is a good thing. Yet I cannot see how it will be successful. Backtracking to another Barcelona-type Framework would be an equally weakening move. A.

tdamek@Lares.net
Another issue has come up which has me quite distracted from this Conference. Fortunately, the Conference itself is nearing a close. The Athens Accord is positioned for acceptance in many countries. Overall it will be good for so many nations to be committed to resource efficiency, although I still wish we had the full package in

place. The U.S. team will be heading to DC to push
for ratification. I hope they are successful. I will be
returning to LA in time for dinner Tuesday. A.

(12.)

Returning from Athens, Ari had barely walked in the door at
Lares, dropped his bags to greet Annis, when his Sliver began chirping.
Upon reading the screen, he came to attention, his shoulders squared;
he ducked into the office to take the call privately.

Tia stood disappointed in the living room – he hadn't even had
time to greet her. She picked up his abandoned bags and moved them to
their bedroom, then returned to finish preparing dinner: a Moroccan
tagine (stew) with apricots dried from the Lares trees.

Ari emerged from the office a half hour later, tucking the Sliver
back into his pocket. Tia looked up from washing Lares-grown mesclun
for the salad. His face was serious, his eyes intense and focused.

"Tia, let's take a walk," he said, in their signal for a private talk.

Ari was silent as they moved away from the house along the
garden paths. He lead Tia to their favorite of the garden nooks, the one
where the olive trees hung low over the lavenders. When he turned to
face her, his dark eyes were sparkling with life.

"Tia, I'm going to Washington. It's time."

"Secretary of Energy?"

"Yes."

"I knew it when I saw your message about the Treaty: I hope *they*
will be successful."

"You know I couldn't say more." He drew a deep breath, and
began a slow pace of the little garden nook. "The President needs me.
Sherwin hasn't accomplished what Alden wanted done."

"The restructuring?"

"Precisely. A major housecleaning at the DOE. Alden wants big
changes. Two years into it, Sherwin's pretty much maintained the
status quo. The President wants the DOE readied for the direction of
the future. So he's asked me to step in and do it."

His pacing intensified.

"It's time for a completely new energy policy. Alden and I have
talked about this for almost a decade, spun dreams together, how we
would restructure the country's energy policy, if we were given half a
chance. Accelerate renewables, phase out fossils, join forces
internationally ... I can't believe that day is really here!"

His eyes were blazing dark fire. A wide smile crossed Tia's face at the sight of him.

He's off on his next adventure. Oh, but it's a big one!

"The current department is all about fossil sources and nuclear. Renewables are a mere corner of it. I'll be turning it on its ear, decades of entrenched status quo, seniority, political pull. Alden wants original thinking, unorthodox, new approaches. He wants our policy positioned with a global viewpoint, not just a national one. I have barely two and a half years to accomplish it all."

Ari paused in his pacing and looked over at Tia. "Of course, I still have to go through Senate Confirmation Hearings."

"They finished your FBI and IRS investigations?"

"Just before Athens. We can tell the family now, it's no longer confidential."

"What about Sherwin?"

"He's with the President as we speak."

Tia gasped. *Alden's firing Sherwin in favor of Ari – oh this is big!*

"What about the Athens Accord?"

"The team is seeking ratification. I'll miss a few of the COP meetings, but it's only for two and a half years. My country needs me right now. I've never been much of a patriot, but the world needs the United States to progress. And I'm probably the best person to do the job." As he said it he drew his hand across his face as if still grappling with this idea. "I'll simply have to step aside on the Sustainability treaty and trust others to move it forward."

He cleared his throat. "Tia, there are some other details. You and Annis will have to unload that bit of your dad's stock you're holding. I'm sorry, I don't know a way around it."

"What does our stuff have to do with you?"

"It's all part of the conflict-of-interest rules."

The magnitude of this! Suddenly it's sweeping the whole family!

"I think I'll offer Kegan a job – I'm going to need an aide who I can trust completely.

"And Tia, I hope you'll consider coming East with me, or perhaps splitting your time between LA and DC." He looked away into the distance, his face set and troubled. "I'm going in to do the dirty work. I'm cast as the renegade before I even start. Alden knew what he was doing to pull in an outsider for this, but it's going to be tough to be that outsider."

She walked to him and hugged him. Automatically he wrapped his arms around her. He was clearly still miles away.

"If I can do this, if I can transform this department ..."

She looked up at him, putting her finger on his lips.

"No ifs, darling. When. Possibilities."

He looked down at her, and his dark eyes connected with hers.

Vision. Wisdom. Purpose. You can do it, Ari. Courage.

His face folded into a slow smile.

"I love you, Tia."

"Congratulations, Mr. Secretary!" she said warmly.

∽

At the dinner table with Jana, Steve and Seth, Annis didn't let Ari get a word in edgewise. "The community garden project in Carson went really well, it was lots of fun! The kids there are already planning another one! It was Mark's last project though, because now that he's got his firefighter's certification he'll be working."

"Strange that he never went to college, Matthew being so highly educated and all." Ari said.

"Matthew couldn't afford it," Jana said softly.

"He did City College," Annis protested. "He didn't want to anyway. Mark wants to help people, to save people's lives." She smiled as she finished, her eyes soft and dreamy.

Tia glanced at Ari. *Yes, he caught that too. It shocked him. She's growing up, Ari, she's now seventeen.*

Jana looked from Annis to Ari and switched the subject quickly. "How was Athens?"

Ari startled, then looked at Tia. Athens clearly felt very far away right now.

"Something else came up, since he's been home," Tia said, buying him a moment.

"The President is nominating me as the Secretary of Energy."

"Whoa," Steve said. "That's a Cabinet position, isn't it?"

"Yes."

"This is for real?"

"I fly back tomorrow to prepare for Senate Confirmation Hearings."

"Damn, Damek, you go after the big fish!" Steve grinned with pride for his friend and stood to shake Ari's hand across the table. Somehow that wasn't enough and Steve rounded the table to embrace Ari, clapping him on the back.

"What about Sherwin?"

Ari looked at his watch. "He's resigned," he said.

(13.)

The Lares youth had grown up together rather like a tumble of puppies. Eight years the families had now been in the complex. The spread in ages was considerable: Mark at twenty, Annis, Peter and Janelle clustered around seventeen and Seth at eleven. Yet despite the difference in ages, the junior crowd was amazingly tight-knit.

The week Ari departed for DC, a cleanup event was held at the Ballona Wetlands. Tia and Lauren joined the young crowd picking up trash along the roads and the bike path near the concrete-enclosed Ballona Creek.

They worked in pairs with the trash bags: Tia and Lauren, Mark and Annis, Janelle and Peter, with Seth insisting he would be the one to partner a stranger. *Under the quiet exterior a fierce self-reliance. It's no question he's of Ari's blood.*

As the participants spread out along the creek, Lauren gestured toward Janelle and Peter. "Cute, those two. She adores him, he barely knows she's alive!" Lauren laughed at her daughter.

But Tia's attention was on Annis.

Mark and Annis, clearly believing the attention of others was elsewhere, were parting from an ardent kiss. Tia watched as Mark's hand slid down Annis' body.

Take it easy, Mark! Tia flashed defensively. *That's my baby you're messing with!*

It didn't get to me when it was Jana and Steve. Tia thought back to the demonstrative lovebirds' early days. *I was delighted for them. Carl and Verity too.*

But it's quite a different thing when it's my daughter. I can see that Mark is altogether too familiar with her body. Oh Ari, have we done right by her? I don't want her to get hurt!

Annis shrieked in gaiety and ran playfully up the path. Mark dropped their trash bag and pursued Annis, laughing.

'All you need are pigtails.' Words echoed from the distant past, and the world seemed to smell once again like the warm earth and eucalyptus of Coyote Creek.

Ari, what happened to our youth? Now you're almost a Cabinet member, of all things, and I'm ... I'm on the threshold of Sage. How did this happen? Where did the years go?

Tia turned her head so that Lauren wouldn't see her tears.

On the PLASE bus back to Brentwood, it was a different group. Lauren, Janelle, Peter and Seth engaged in a lively discussion. Mark stretched out in the seat, arm around Annis, her head on his shoulder, in quiet conversation; Tia awash in the thoughts of her own private world.

(14.)

"Tia, these hearings are intense," Ari said over the phone. "Senator Magan is having a heyday with my activities in Bonn, Johannesburg and Montreal. He's brought out details about every turn in my career, every time I left the U.S. Delegation, worked for other nations, disputed U.S. policy. He's even hauled out transcripts of some of my UN debates. I have 'a history of blatantly opposing U.S. policies,' Magan declares. They didn't use the word 'traitor' but it's a tangible presence right there in the room."

"They didn't do this to Sherwin, he glided through the hearings!" Tia exclaimed.

"They must have known, even in the confirmation process, that they controlled him, they could keep their empire intact. Me ... with my background I present a significant threat.

"It really has nothing to do with what I did or didn't do in Bonn or Montreal. That's just the issue they've picked to try to hang me on, to block the nomination. Already the political sides are drawn. Big oil knows from my background what I've been sent in there to do. I'm scheduled to testify tomorrow afternoon. It's going to be tough." His voice shook.

"Do you want me to come back there? I could hop a plane tonight."

There was a long pause. Then a quiet "Yes."

⟡

By the time Tia arrived in DC the city was waking for breakfast. Ari was waiting when she got off the plane. He swept her into a hug that felt as if he hadn't seen her in weeks, as if he would never let her go. Perhaps, in the mental journeys of these past few days, it indeed felt like weeks to him.

"Tia, thank you for coming – I can't do this alone," he admitted quietly.

As they walked through the airport, morning news headlines were appearing on the airport screens. Ari wandered casually by to catch the headlines, then suddenly seized Tia's arm and directed her hurriedly away.

"Don't look at them," Ari's voice was low and tight.

"What's the matter?"

He didn't answer, instead bundling her into a cab.

Zipping along the Beltway, he finally spoke.

"I told you on the phone, they're out to get me however they can. The Reactionaries and the Resisters are fighting no-holds-barred. They don't want me confirmed, they don't want me in the position. They'll do anything to keep me out." He drew a deep breath.

"Tia, I love you. When you see this, I want you to know, it's all fabricated." His face was pinched and worried as he handed her the Sliver with the morning's headlines displayed:

ALDEN NOMINEE'S PASSION FOR LORI FORDON
Affair Spans Decades

Tia's hands shook uncontrollably at the sight of the g-news photo of Ari embracing Lori, both smiling and happy. She scrolled down to inset photos of them laughing together, shoulder to shoulder, perhaps a year or so ago. Another photo, of a young Ari kissing Lori.

The Sliver tumbled from Tia's hands as she covered her face. In her shock over the headlines, even the tears were stuck. Ari slid over and put his arm around her. It wasn't comforting; it chilled her and she wished he wouldn't.

"Tia, it's all contrived. This one's in the Oval Office, the day Elliott signed the Moscow Treaty. That one's likely some UNFCCC conference. I don't know where they dug up the old one – that's from before I met you."

Here it was, on the mainpage of the Post, the proof spread in stark media reality. Tia couldn't stop herself, she stared at the older picture. *Lori had brown hair back then, pretty and wavy. She looks soft and happy, not stiff and polished.*

It was torture to see her in Ari's arms.

Ari, younger than I ever knew him ...

Seeing his young image she recalled those first few months of their relationship, and her own twisted perception of the Johannesburg events. She'd accused him of it herself, and yet ...

She turned to look at the reality of Ari sitting beside her in the cab. His face was inches away from hers, his deep brown eyes solemn, unhappy. He tightened his arm around her.

'This man is his mission' Sahara told me once.

All the puzzle pieces fit together. Integrity.

"I'm so sorry they hurt you, when the attack is launched at me," he said quietly.

Oh, I'm one of his puzzle pieces too!

She buried her face into his shoulder and cried with the shock of the realization, cried for the injustice of the accusations, for her own jealousy over the years. Ari curled around her, his face pressed to her hair.

We're strong together, he told me. We'll get through this one too.

"We can't let them win," she whispered through her tears. The sound of her own voice strengthened her.

He slowly straightened, but not before kissing her hair.

"Where are we going?" she asked, looking out the cab window for perhaps the first time.

"A quiet little cafe, away from all this," he replied.

"Turn him around." She gestured to the cab driver. "Have him take us to one of the ritzy popular places."

Puzzlement added to the anguish of the past few minutes, written on his face.

"We'll fight fire with fire." She reached over and kissed him in exaggerated, drawn out style. His lips were dead beneath hers.

"Tia, I know what you're thinking – it won't work," he said miserably. "They won't print it. This stuff is driven politically. Power – that's how they decide what to print. Look, it was even timed strategically. They released all that garbage today, the day I testify."

She sighed. "I have a lot to learn about politics."

After a more few blocks it occurred to her to ask. "What else could they throw at you?"

He looked at her a moment, then his eyes widened in horror. "They wouldn't. Oh God, they will!" His hands made a fist, one doubled around the other, his eyes closed in torture. "Oh God, I never thought of that! Here I was worried about tapes of the Valdez speeches!" He curled forward, his head over his hands.

Power. She looked at him sitting wretchedly in the cab. *You need to look powerful by this afternoon.*

They reached the cafe. As Ari handled the cab fare, Tia's mind was busy.

Even his posture is caved. They're getting to him. They hit him hard today, it has really rocked him.

So much is at stake here: all that Alden wants to do, all that Ari can accomplish. The world is watching, hoping. He cannot fold!

Breakfast orders placed, she leaned over the table and spoke quietly, so that he had to lean in to hear her. Their faces were inches apart.

"Secretary of Energy," she almost whispered. "Let's work on that Energy."

She shifted her legs under the table so that her calf was touching his, at the same time sliding the Sliver out of his pocket.

She directed it to search for a moment, then handed it back to him. The screen displayed the text of Alden's Inaugural Address.

He gave her a long look from those dark eyes, then turned to read. As he realized what the document was, his shoulders straightened, almost as if his President was addressing him in person. When he had finished reading, he looked up at her, his face slowly breaking into a broad grin.

She took the Sliver back again, murmuring to navigate the device. Finding what she wanted, she handed the device back to him.

He drew a deep breath, staring at the screen. She knew what flashed before him: photos of the Culver City schoolchildren, which she had emailed him in Milan; photos of Annis as a baby; photos of Seth; photos of Jeffrey and of Carl's tiny sons.

"The U.S. energy policy is felt around the world," she said. "At this critical turning point, what you do here is possibly of greater impact on these children, and their children, than the rest of your career put together. My God, Ari, you have the chance to create a Sustainable energy policy! Just think of it!

"The President said it in his speech: The time is now. We are the Transition Generation. Ari, fight for it! They're putting up roadblocks but that won't stop you. You have a big job to do.

"You're a renegade. Alden knows it, you said it yourself last week. You're going to experience resistance every step of the way, for the next two and a half years. Steel yourself for it. You're accustomed to the uphill battle. You fought for twenty years for Kyoto. What's two and a half years?

"You are the master Change Agent. Time to do the ultimate translation, bringing Alden's new era ideas into something workable that mainstream people will live and experience in their everyday lives.

"Alden is trusting you to fight for what is sane and right. You're here to forge the way of the future, to help realize the dream in that speech. Go back to that Vision, carry it with you this afternoon, make it happen! Those kids are counting on you."

As she spoke she could see the brilliant fire come on in his eyes, the confidence return to his shoulders. He grinned, giving a short crisp nod of affirmation.

(15.)

For Immediate Release
The White House
Office of the Press Secretary
December 5, 2022

Remarks by the President and Secretary of Energy Ari Damek
in Swearing-In Ceremony
The Oval Office

THE PRESIDENT: I am pleased to welcome the Secretary and his family. I have known Secretary Damek for many years. We have worked together on numerous issues, both domestic and international.

Secretary Damek is a man of rare vision. He is well acquainted with the future direction of energy resources on the global playing field. It is high time that we reflect this future in our domestic policies and in our Department of Energy. Secretary Damek is equal to the task of making this milestone transition.

Secretary Damek is well aware of my strategy for our energy policy: First and foremost, that we operate in league with other nations of the world. Second, that we significantly boost our use of renewable sources such as solar, wind and clean hydrogen, and that we accelerate Research and Development in these areas. Third, that we wean ourselves off such unsustainable, polluting and hazardous energy sources as fossil fuels and nuclear. Fourth, that we increase the resource productivity of all our energy operations, not the least of which that we consider the impact of our energy policy on our environment, including greenhouse gas emissions.

My goal in this strategy is that we bring America's energy policy out of the dark ages, in order to participate in the new era of clean and sustainable sources of human activity.

Secretary Damek, welcome to the Cabinet.

SECRETARY DAMEK: Mr. President, thank you for this opportunity to serve the citizens of our great nation, citizens present and future. It is a great honor to be entrusted with this responsibility.

I have long dreamed that one day the official energy policy of the United States would reflect a sustainable direction such as the President has just outlined. It is my pleasure and supreme honor to be designated to carry this out.

(16.)

Tia alternated between Ari's apartment in Washington and the Lares house in LA where Annis was completing University of California applications and worrying a severe case of acceptance nerves.

Mark spent long hours at the Damek home, between his shifts as a firefighter. He continued living at Matthew's to save his money.

Saving his money, right. That's not all of it. This way he's right here with Annis.

Frequently now, the loud clash of male voices echoed through the Lares gardens, Mark and Matthew arguing. The voices would escalate, the door would slam, and Mark would quietly appear at the Damek/Vernados home, as if nothing had happened.

Here at South House there was also Seth, with a sort of younger brother hero worship that Peter never had quite adopted. Still skinny and lanky at twelve, Seth had Steve's hint-of-red hair and Jana's snapping brown eyes. Always the youngest in the Lares junior crowd, he had grown up shy and quiet, a nephew Tia felt she barely knew. Mark's now steady presence in their home had an unfolding effect on Seth.

In his years as a quiet observer, Seth had apparently been a raw sponge to the political intellectualism around him. Mark, by contrast, was fire and action. Seth brought out the contemplative side in Mark, while Mark spurred Seth to break out of his shell.

Seth taught Mark chess, into which Mark launched himself with lively competition, yet Seth consistently emerged the victor. Mark shared with Seth the long backpacking trails in the Santa Monica Mountains. The two frequently joined TreePeople on their intensive mountain plantings.

(17.)

The card was small, formally addressed to Secretary and Mrs. Ari Damek, carrying a New York postmark. Puzzled, Tia slit the envelope. Inside was a photo of a dark Indonesian toddler adrift in white taffeta in a proper studio setting. The enclosed engraved card, carrying a tiny pink bow, announced the adoption of Mireille Loralei Fordon.

(18.)

Slow Food Fast was a phenomenal success. Within a short time, Ravyn had persuaded Shannon to open two additional cafes near other PLASE stations.

Local produce and seasonality meant that the menu was never constant. Even the specific ingredients, and thus the flavor, of a given recipe changed with the availability of herbs, fruits and vegetables. Rather than building any concept of a standard menu, Ravyn wisely marketed the 'fresh flavors and vibrant variety.' The entire menu was a daily special, and customers loved it.

At Shannon's urging, Ravyn experimented with Sustainability Suppers, where takeout customers brought in their own reusable dish, rather than carry out food in waste-stream clogging disposable boxes and bags. The concept was too innovative for the health inspectors, so Matthew stepped in to engineer legal solutions. Thus solved, Sustainability Suppers gained media attention for their novel combination of packaging-free environmental consciousness plus healthy nourishment.

As the Slow Food Fast chain blossomed with health, burgers and fries slicked their greasy way toward oblivion.

(19.)

The reinsurance industry – the companies that insure the insurance industry – had been aware of the rising sea level issue since before the turn of the century. Now retail level insurance companies were feeling the pinch. Additionally, emergency services personnel saw significant demand for their services. The shorelines presented increasing hazard to the public. Insurance companies joined with emergency services in seeking solutions.

This unusual alliance commissioned a sophisticated University of California computer modeling of the Pacific shoreline: the U.S. and nearby portions of Mexico and Canada. Using updated IPCC forecasts of sea level rise, detailed maps were prepared, documenting for beachfront communities the inevitable shoreline land losses. This study defined Shoreline Elimination Zones, with gradients by decade, referred to as SEZ30 and SEZ40, lands that would be claimed by sea level rise through 2030 and 2040.

Insurance companies promptly refused to insure structures within SEZ30. Without insurance, banks refused financing. No building permits were granted. Thus the coastal communities quickly became odd shantytowns of diehard hermits and boarded up one-time multimillion dollar buildings.

LA's Westside, always so ocean-focused, reeled in shock. Many of its prized venues were deep within SEZ30: the Santa Monica Pier, the public beaches, Pacific Coast Highway and its glamorous oceanfront restaurants, the Malibu beachfront, Manhattan Beach and the Marina. The entire Playa Vista area, so newly developed at the turn of the century, was within SEZ40, as well as parts of Playa del Rey, Venice and Hermosa Beach.

In El Segundo, the Hyperion wastewater treatment plant and the Chevron oil refinery, while both raised upon bluffs, would experience serious operational issues under both SEZ30 and SEZ40 scenarios.

After the initial casting of the shadow of doom, change began. Insurance companies recognized a new liability in the abandoned structures as drifters moved in from the homeless population. Storm waves had disassembled some structures and flung the debris into others, creating obvious hazard. It soon became clear that all buildings within SEZ30 would eventually have to come down.

Over the next decade, funded by desperate insurance companies with little support from beleaguered States, building material companies mobilized teams of South American immigrants for careful disassembly and salvage of oceanfront structures. A new eco-business was born. The luxury materials used in seacoast mansions and restaurants were virtually free to any salvage company lucky enough to acquire a contract.

The SEZ designations carried long term economic effects. Employment among unskilled immigrants rose significantly, easing the burden on the State for RAI and similar relief programs. Construction materials were suddenly cheap and bountiful for an industry that had been particularly hard hit by the Depression. Property values rose significantly as a citywide building boom began.

Building with reclaimed materials required different thinking than the cookie-cutter mass-construction-think of the building booms prior to the 2000s. The huge building companies were gone now anyway, an early casualty of the market crashes. Small independent builders prospered. Their work product was as varied, innovative, and delightful as a diverse group of artists could produce. The building boom of the 2020s had character, style, statement and charm.

Recent California RPS legislation provided solar and energy efficiency credits, introducing incentives for environmentally conscious installations. Drought consciousness, spurred by g-news reports of the Northwest, inspired water-wise designs. The T.R.E.E.S. model for environmentally-aware retrofitting, created before the turn of the century by Andy Lipkis and TreePeople, became the sage model, upon which new innovations flourished. Thus the 2020 building boom marked a new era of environmental wisdom.

With SEZ areas redlined two decades into the future, and an unusual recent flurry of Land Trust easement acquisitions, building sites were confined in footprint, clustered mid-city around avenues of mass transit. Urban sprawl had reached its limit.

(20.)

"Tia, I'm glad you and Annis could come up here like this on such short notice." Cassandra and Tia sat on the veranda at Coyote Creek overlooking the gardens. The summer heat radiating from the earth warmed even the shade. The air smelled sweet with sage and eucalyptus. Cassandra cleared her throat.

"I'll talk to Annis about this later, but I wanted to tell you alone. I got the results back from the doctor about my leg pain. Tia, it's not my leg. There's a tumor in my spine pressing on the nerve so that my brain thinks my leg hurts."

"A tumor? Cancer?"

"Yes. And it has spread, metastasized, the doctors say."

"So, what are you doing for it?" Tia was afraid to hear the answer, knowing her mother's distrust of allopathic medicine.

"I'm counting my blessings and I'm saying goodbye."

"What do you mean?"

"I've had a good life, Tia. I don't want a hideous, drawn out end to it. I don't want all the surgeries and radiations and toxic drugs of Western medicine, and it's gone too far to be realistic about beginning any alternative treatment. I'm not going to get better. And I'm not going to wait until I'm some blob in a bed. I'm saying goodbye now."

The tears rolled down Tia's face and Cassandra's too.

"So you're going to ..." Tia couldn't wrap her mind around this, it was just too huge.

"I'm going to end my life, as gracefully and joyfully as I can. I can hardly walk now, Tia, the pain gets more intense each week. I don't want to wait until I can't walk out to the creek and my fields. I don't want to wait until I can't hug you and Annis. I don't want to wait until I can't make love to Wade. And I know all these realities are coming up, horribly fast."

Cassandra reached over and held Tia's hands. "My body's dying, Tia. I'm not going to ride it every excruciating bit of the way down. I don't believe it's meant to be that way. It's time to release my spirit, now, while I'm still able. I want you and Annis and Wade and Sahara to remember me as laughing and talking just like this. I want to still feel the joy of living right up until the end.

"My birthday is in two weeks. I'll be seventy-five. Sometime around then, when none of you are around so you don't get in trouble ...

"I've been hoarding the Western doctor's toxic pills – the painkillers and sleeping pills."

"You haven't been taking them?"

"Heavens no! They make me feel awful. No, I have my herbal ways for sleep and pain. But for poisons, I'll take their help."

I can't believe I'm having this discussion.

"They ration them, they count them out. But I've been saving them up so that I have plenty. A few sweet herbs so I won't feel it, throw in a good anti-emetic – it's good to know your plant friends for times like these!"

Tia slipped out of her chair and knelt to hug her mother, putting her head on her mother's bosom. Cassandra was shockingly small in Tia's arms. But her face held an other-worldly radiance.

"Tia, when it's all done, take my ashes up to the crest of San Marcos Pass and scatter them to the winds. That's what I did with Rick's. Let me be with the wild things like he is."

"You've never forgotten him, have you?"

Cassandra looked in Tia's eyes.

"Once in a lifetime we may get so lucky. When someone touches your soul like that – well, you know how it is. Tia, those murderers ripped him from my arms but never from my heart, he's with me always."

Tia stared at Cassandra's arms, at the long white scars from the burns.

"What about Wade?"

"Wade is – well, he's Wade. He's different. It's been nice, it's been fun. He's not Rick. I only hope Annis can find hers."

The question was in Tia's eyes.

"But of course, honey! I knew it the first time I saw you two together. I was so glad for you." Cassandra looked away. "I wish I could say goodbye to Ari too. But I can't do this on the phone. And I'm not all that sure he'd understand."

"I think he would. Do you want me to have him fly out here?"

"No, don't bother him."

Tia eased back and sat on the floor at her mother's feet, like a small child.

"Tia, my papers, my data. Sahara's too busy with operations to go through it all. I wish you'd consider going through it, or organizing some interns to do it. I think it will be valuable some day when the world is ready for it."

A sudden sob raked Cassandra.

"I tried. I tried to help them see. I tried to have it ready for them when it was needed. The droughts are here now, but so few are willing to accept that reality, they're not willing to change. They persist in trying to grow the water-fat hybrids. It's going to come to a crisis point. Unfortunately, this physical body of mine won't make it that far. I never thought I would have to leave my project so unfinished. I thought I'd see it implemented. It's such an odd feeling to create something that will go out beyond you – it's a different feeling than having a child, even."

Cassandra reached out and tenderly stroked Tia's cheek, sobbing again.

"But I never thought I would leave it like this, it's like it's a small child and I meant it to be a young adult by now. I hope that, somehow, their eyes get opened in time. I hope someone finds a way."

"Sure, Mom, I'll take care of your papers. When I go back I'll ..." Tia stopped in realization.

When I go back ... when I leave ... leave Mom forever ...

It was Tia's turn to sob now.

"Honey, it's not like that," Cassandra said soothingly. "It's not such a great sadness. Think of it as a completion."

&

The afternoon before Cassandra's birthday, Tia received the call from Wade.

"Tia, she's gone."

"Oh, Wade, I'm so sorry. I'll be up there in the morning."

"We found her in her favorite chair under the oak tree, my hound dog standing guard." Wade sounded empty without her.

(21.)

The days Tia spent in DC were lonely as Ari worked long hours in the DOE offices. Ari had selected his apartment for location; a brisk walk of a few blocks placed him in easy access of mass transit to the government offices. He enjoyed the walk, saying it cleared his head for the next rush of ideas. The apartment itself was on the third floor – removed from all contact with the earth and growing things. Tia felt trapped and isolated, and terribly homesick for Lares.

Yet the quiet apartment provided the perfect atmosphere for sorting Cassandra's papers. Tia hauled several boxes of them across country, cursing her mother's lifelong distrust of computer systems.

Tia was astonished to see the data, the variety of locations in which Cassandra had maintained test fields under various associates and interns. Phoenix, Santa Fe, Tucson ... the list went on. Piles of documentation, recorded painstakingly by the hand of numerous growers.[78] *And not a computer run among them.* Somehow the handwritten records better conveyed the passion, the love these unseen people had for what they were doing.

Her travels – I didn't know those trips were for seed trials! I thought she was off collecting her crazy Indian fetishes. She used to come back and rave about how 'spiritual' these places were!

An image flashed across more than forty years, herself as a young girl watching Cassandra and an older bronzed woman. The woman pressed something into Cassandra's hands, a small bit of leather and feathers. Cassandra opened a pouch at her waist and trickled something into the woman's hands. *Connecting.*

I thought they were coins! But they didn't jingle. I'll bet anything the leather bundle contained seeds too!

Tia thought of Cassandra at the Legacy LA meeting, opening a cloth bundle and trickling beans between her fingers. *Sensual.*

Her hands. Tears pricked in Tia's eyes at the thought of them. *Some people have worry beads, Mom always had seeds. Bean seeds, squash seeds, amaranth, corn. Sunflowers, onions, cilantro.* Tia could see each one clearly. The black angular onion seeds, buried within the lifelines of Cassandra's palm. The fat beans, which trickled over white-scarred knuckles. The slim cucurbits which slipped between her fingertips. *Life. Every one of them a miniature capsule of Life.*

Tia looked at her own hands in wonder. She began to tremble at the shape of them, the very curve of the little finger. *Here they are, Mom's hands. What have I done with them? Deadened paper, computer devices. Where is the Life?*

Mom, I don't know how to hold Life like you did. The tears began to fall.

Through her tears she watched her hands – Cassandra's hands. She moved them in the air in front of herself, in slow torment to her grief. The downward funnel motion of Cassandra's fingers trickling bean seeds. The horizontal push-push motion of Cassandra's palms kneading bread. The tender scooping motion of Cassandra's hands planting a delicate seedling.

My hands can go through the motions, but my hands don't hold that life-sprouting magic.

◆

As the weeks of sorting progressed, Tia classified Cassandra's notes into broad categories: irrigation techniques, water conservation techniques, drought tolerant species and varieties, dry farming methods, political efforts. *She attacked the problem from all sides!* Cassandra's quiet passion for her chosen mission radiated out from the scraps of paper and scrawled handwriting.

Focus. Purpose. Tia recalled Cassandra on that final weekend, weeping over her unfinished life work. Tia's tears began falling again. She vainly tried to keep them off the papers. *Your legacy, Mom. It goes out beyond you. I'll see that it gets out to the world.*

She reached for a bundle of papers and froze.

Mom's hands. Mom's papers.

Tia laid her hands in ceremony upon the stack of papers. *I must bring them to life. I must bring them out to life. Mom's power to sprout Life is in these ideas. My hands will take her message out to those who need it, our nation's farmers, so that they may sprout Mom's ideas and produce life-giving crops for the people.*

Sitting on her knees on the floor as if in ceremonial offering, Tia raised a sheaf of papers in her hands, Cassandra's hands, delivering the message to an imaginary recipient.

That life-sprouting power is in my hands too.

(22.)

Tia had been sorting Cassandra's illegibly scrawled documents on the floor all afternoon. A click at the door and Ari walked in, his face jubilant mischief. He tossed a substantial glossy bound document onto the carpet in front of her and eased himself out of his overcoat and suit jacket.

"There it is – it goes out to the press in the morning!" he announced triumphantly, flopping into an easy chair.

Ari's energy policy – Tia never could bring herself to think of it as the Alden Administration's – was shockingly different. It was a brazen departure from DOE policies of the past.[79] The introduction laid out goals that sounded remarkably like President Alden's Oval Office comments with a banner head that blatantly stated the goal:

To Position U.S. Energy Resources for a Sustainable Future

Tia's heart skipped a beat just seeing the phrase in print in an official government document. A pair of bold definitions followed: Renewable and Transition energy sources.

"The oil agenda of prior decades has muddied the definitions so that Big Oil can keep their grubby fingers in the pie." Ari sat back in his chair, removing his tie and undoing his shirt collar. "They came up with many blended fuels and energy sources where petroleum slips in behind the scenes. They called the whole hodgcpodge Alternative so that it sounds progressive. What a green-washing publicity stunt!

"We're phasing out the use of the term Alternative. Everything is either Renewable, Transition, or part of the fossil nightmare. Those we've termed Sunset Sources meaning they're fading into the sunset!

"Part of our policy is public education about what Renewable really means. In my opinion, any connection with fossil yanks an energy source out of the bounds of Renewable. The reality is, our technology isn't far enough along for us to use pure renewables yet, so we have to use these blends. Thus we coined the term Transition Sources so that everyone understands that they're temporary, and they're not the ideal end-goal.

"Renewables are things which in the future will be fully sustainable: solar; wind; Cellulosic Ethanol; biomass when it's pure combustion as contrasted with blends; hydrogen when it's clean sourced, meaning it's been isolated using other renewables to power the process; tidal and wave energy.

"Transitionals are the in-between world. They're not quite so evil as big oil, but we'll want to get off them eventually, because they're not Sustainable: CNG and LNG; LPG; Biomass co-fired with coal; Ethanol blends, because those include gasoline; Corn Ethanol, because of its greenhouse gas impact; hydrogen when it's derived using petroleum to fuel the extraction process. We put hydropower under Transitionals because with rainfall unpredictable due to climate change, many dams may fall short of adequate river flow to do the job. Biomass from landfills is another tough one because I don't think we'll have the landfill sources forever."

"You're thinking about Xavier."

"Yes, there are hundreds of Xaviers out there, all rushing to be the first with new waste management technology. Talk about resource efficiency – whew! But in the meantime, biomass from landfills is a good Transition energy source.

"These definitions become very important as we make choices into the future, choices about where to invest infrastructure. The infrastructure we build now will outlast any kids Annis has. I'd hate to see us throw copious resources behind Transitional sources when we could be funding Renewable ones instead."

The section on Renewable energy sources comprised well over three-quarters of the entire document.

"This is only a small fraction of your department!" Tia protested.

"For now," he said with a jaunty tilt to his eyebrows. "And it's the lion's share of our policy."

"What are you doing about the fossil fuels?' Tia asked.

"Every sentence of it shows fossil sources as history. In phase-out. Alden's certainly put his political neck on the line. He's well aware of what's in there. He's wanted an official energy policy taking this position since I met him well over a decade ago. So I delivered.

"Conventional oil, unconventional oil, oil shales, coal – all are headed into the sunset. We'll stop licensing any further oil and gas exploration, and program subsidies and tax benefits for oil and gas will end.

"The coal industry has made a lot of noise about carbon sequestration in conjunction with their IGCC processes. I'm not at all convinced they know what they are doing. But years around Cassandra have taught me there's huge sequestration potential in those agricultural soils. We'll be recommending major changes in the agricultural sector to increase wise land management practices as well as carbon sinks in the form of tree cover, particularly trees native to the planting area.

"Nuclear is already a Sunset source – most of the licenses are expiring; we won't be renewing them. The only expansion under Nuclear will be our recommendation that Advanced Nuclear Waste Decontamination Techniques be explored to clean up the radioactive waste dumps of the past: Brown's Gas-Metal Matrix Process, ZIPP Fusion, RIPPLE Fission, LENTEC Processes, PIT Processes, Kervran Reactions, the Monti Process, Higher Group Symmetry Electrodynamics, and Photoremediation, each one appropriate for a slightly different angle of the radioactive waste issue. There are so many possible solutions out there.

"It's a full ten year plan," he finished with a satisfied smile.

"Ten years? Alden's term is up in less than two!"

"That's the curious thing." Ari stood, and walked to the window to look out at the city. "Not all presidents write a new energy policy. I think that Alden's trusting that his successor, whether that be in 2024 or 2028, will see the wisdom and will carry forward with this plan."

"Isn't that bit optimistic?"

"Perhaps. Or, he's holding a vision for the future, a vision which outlasts us." His admiration for his President was written across his face.

After a moment's pause he continued outlining the plan, pacing the room as he did so. "The Energy Plans of other administrations included Energy Efficiency – ways to streamline ordinary operations so that we use less energy. While we do have plenty on that topic, we place even more emphasis on citizen education toward a new concept: Energy Alternatives.

"As we move from a fossil-dependent world into this array of renewable sources, and simultaneously move into a lifestyle oriented toward Sustainability, we will in fact be using less energy. Sustainable practices have their own energy. In the long term, for example, rather than fossil fuels to power trash trucks, very little in the way of outside energy input is needed for on-site and local composting, rebuy and reuse. Thus most Energy Efficiency ideas are really for the Transition period."

"This all sounds like you're sneaking in a bit of Factor 4!"

"I'm easing them into Factor 4," he corrected. "And I'm showing them what lies beyond it."

He's like a kid in a toy shop with this stuff. It's almost as if it's not real to him, he's playing.

No, it's very real to him, she corrected herself. *And that's why his delight – that he's been handed the power to make the changes. He's known for decades that these things needed to happen.*

"What about the departmental structure?"

His pacing stilled and the merriment drained from his face.

"That's a lot tougher than moving words and figures on a policy document. But I have to do it, my orders from the Commander in Chief were to position the DOE for the direction of the future.

"Legacy Management is a department originally formed to handle Nuclear phaseouts, but I'll fold the entire Sunset programs in there – all Fossil, all Nuclear – so everyone knows they're doomed and in phase-out.

"What used to be one small Energy Efficiency and Renewable Energy department will be exploded – each category will rise to Assistant Secretary level. Solar, wind, hydro, hydrogen, biomass. In Energy Department meetings these departments will be the active chairs. Fossil energy will no longer be an Assistant Secretary level position; Fossil and Nuclear will only be observers."

Ari came to sit beside her on the floor.

"That sounds like a UNFCCC members-only structure!" Tia laughed.

"Blatant plagiarism." His eyes glinted.

Then his face became solemn. "Once these changes begin to unfold, once this policy and restructuring are all set in place, I'll be on a fast plane back to California. So many heads will have rolled, so many power strongholds will be in shambles, that no one will want me in Washington. I'll certainly be persona non grata.

"It's a good thing Fordon's become such a force. She will have to move the international treaties forward without me. After this outspoken

Policy, I'll likely become a significant political detriment to the Treaties, possibly for years to come." Ari closed his eyes and averted his face.

A single word loomed large in Tia's mind: *Sacrifice.*

She put her arms around his great shoulders and hugged him. He rested his head upon her breast. She stroked his hair, his face.

He came here at Alden's summons, to do what was required for his country. And in doing so, he can no longer serve the cause so dear to his heart, the cause that he has championed for decades!

The personal cost of being a Change Agent of this magnitude is so very high!

"You did it, Ari," she said softly. "Thanks to you, the United States now has a policy supporting renewable energy. You're amazing!"

The gestures of comfort and caring became warm and sensual, then more heated and focused. And the country's first effort toward a Sustainable energy policy rolled on the floor atop designs for a future arid-lands agriculture.

(23.)

In LA, Steve Vernados & Associates had won a major contract from the City of Los Angeles for the eco-remodel of all city buildings. Many of the innovations with which Steve had experimented at Ari's Sustainability Centers jumped into large scale application. Solar sheeting, contemporary high-efficiency ventilation, energy efficient window panes, insulation made from recycled materials. Rooftops became photovoltaic solar fields and rainwater collectors.

The landscaping designs provided by Vernados & Associates' expert Jana Damek eliminated lawns, ivy and thirsty non-native plants, replacing these with California natives and a diverse selection of productive edibles.

The changes happening at city buildings and schools were a powerful model for building owners throughout the metropolitan area. Building codes were amended to promote energy efficiency. Water conservation was encouraged, to a degree that surpassed even the conservation campaign of the 1970's. And LA City Council finally passed Rhus Tilford's pet motion to prohibit lawn irrigation.[80]

(24.)

It took time. Time for people to see the PLASE trains in operation, time for the city to get over the disruption the construction had caused, time for the populace to experiment and adapt to new ideas and new ways of getting around the city. But above all, it took time for LA to grow, an inner growth, a journey that began with shedding the cosmetic consumerism of 'I am the car I wrap around myself.'

The PLASE trains took LA citizens on this journey, from decades of all-about-me, through an acknowledgement that I-am-part-of-a-whole. A whole city, a whole populace. Unlike in a personal vehicle on a freeway, in a PLASE train one could not remain isolated from one's fellow citizen. Sharing a train car meant sharing a portion of life – a small portion of life, yet an enormous step for Los Angelinos.

Sharing a ride meant I-am-no-longer-higher-and-mightier-than-thou, West LA versus East versus Central. It meant growing beyond 'you are brown so I am scared of you' and 'you are white so you are out to get me.' We are people together, we are united in this moment in a shared train, united in place in this shared territory of a city. And as such, we are united in the problems we face as a society: pollution, safety, water supply. We are united in our dreams: raising our children to see better tomorrows.

PLASE was the place it happened in LA.

(25.)

In May 2024 the Athens Accord was ratified by Italy, the last country necessary to meet the quorum requirements to place the treaty in force as binding international law. If Tia hadn't read about it on the international g-news she would scarcely have known about it; Ari was so nose-down in DOE issues that he scarcely noticed.

"Did you hear about the Athens Accord?" she asked when he had made no mention of it.

He continued flipping reports, madly dictating notes into the Sliver.

"Yes I heard." He didn't look up.

"Ari, the Athens Accord. Factor 4. Resource efficiency. Doesn't it matter anymore?"

He looked up over the top of the eyeglasses that were the Sliver's new remote video display.

"I'm thrilled." His voice was flat and strained. "I'm thrilled for the world." He returned to his work.

She closed her eyes in silent pain. *This job has so completely eclipsed him. His big dreams no longer matter!*

As if in answer to her thoughts he pulled off the glasses. "The Athens Accord means more to me than you can believe. It is the direction of the future. We have to get on board. The U.S. is so far from it right now."

He pursed his lips and shook his head slowly, then gestured to his work. "This is the next step for us, this is the best I can offer. We need to get on board that Treaty, but first I need to position the U.S. so that we're *ready* to get on board that Treaty — with the reorg and by implementing the recommendations we made in the energy policy."

He sighed. "Some day. Maybe in Annis' generation, maybe beyond ..."

"You think the U.S. will hold out on signing Athens for that long? Like they did on Kyoto?"

"I don't know what we'll do about the treaty document. Probably Fordon's better connected to answer that for you. I meant Sustainability, a truly Sustainable existence.

"We won't see it in our lifetimes, Tia. Perhaps even Annis won't. I hope her children will. But just because we won't see Sustainability now, that doesn't mean we shouldn't be trying, trying with everything we have, to move steadily in that direction. What we do now, every step we take to move in that direction, every bit of it brings us one step closer. We have to start now if we're ever going to get there. We have to do the work now to turn the mainstream, so that then, humanity will make the mark."

Tia's eyes widened. He had never said it like this. He'd talked about future generations for as long as she'd known him. But he'd never admitted that he wouldn't see the changes. It was a huge admission.

"I don't say it that way very often. Because even the most farsighted Change Agents stumble and begin to have difficulty with it at that point. Not many people can keep going, passionately pursuing something for which the results are beyond them. Sometimes it is better not to know. The hope stays stronger that way."

"But you know, darling," she whispered.

"I've always known." He paused and his eyes got that faraway look to them. "And somehow, I just can't explain it, that has strengthened my resolve. It's driven me forward, harder, faster, as if everything I can manage to accomplish in my lifetime brings that magic date sooner. Maybe by my efforts, Annis will see it, not just her grandchildren or her children. Every step we take now shortens the transition timeline. It feels so incredibly urgent.

"Time is slipping through my fingers. The clock is running, fast and furiously, toward 2040. If we don't make that mark, we may never achieve any of this. To hell with paper Treaties, we need action steps *now* in the right direction, to change our societal course.

"Time is slipping through my fingers," he repeated. "Time, to get these changes in place, and my own lifetime for what I can accomplish."

With a harsh gesture, as if to wipe away that thought, he jammed the glasses back on his face and returned to work.

Tia sat staring at him with amazement.

He's known all along that the timeline's just too long. His entire career he's been passionately dedicated to this battle, and he knows he won't see the outcome. This is truly what it means to devote oneself to a greater cause!

The sounds of the DC city bustle outside the apartment cascaded in upon her in her silence. She directed her feelings at the anonymous populace outside. *They can't even make the changes for their own lifetime, let alone if they knew.*[81]

President Alden's image flashed before her. *"We are the Transition Generation!"*

Brilliant rhetoric, Mr. President, but listen to your Cabinet. This generation won't ...

She stopped in mid-thought.

Alden did listen to his closest advisors. Ari wasn't in the Cabinet yet, but the President was listening to him. Ari, the Change Agent, would have written the speech exactly that way: hope, inspiration, enthusiasm, enrollment. Suddenly deep within her heart Tia knew that Alden knew.

And the Resisters know too. Her blood chilled. *That's precisely why they resist: because it means giving to a greater good than their own lifetime interests. They can't do it. They cannot, will not, reach beyond.*

Her focus returned to Ari, dictating frantically in his work.

We are the Transition Generation. Not because we will accomplish it, but because we have dared to begin it.

(26.)

"Shit, Tia, this leaves me in quite a bind." Ari and Tia spread the paperwork from Cassandra's estate attorney across the DC apartment kitchen table.

"Ari, I'm sorry, what was I to do?"

"Nothing, there was nothing you could do. Cassandra did what she did," Ari shook his head. "I'm glad it was quick, not all drawn out leaving her helpless like my dad. But now ..."

"Now Annis and I are inheriting all of Dad's stock."

"Which is a major holding of stock in a company in the energy field, so is thus a conflict-of-interest for me when I'm making policy recommendations to the President."

"But if we sell it ..."

"If you don't sell it, I have legal problems. If you do sell it, I still have press problems."

"It's almost a controlling interest in the company, so it's a major decision to sell it," Tia said hesitantly. "Unloading that much stock would be a huge hit to the company's stock price and the whole industry would reflect it. There would even be SEC limitations on how we do it. Not to mention the takeover potential. It's not wise to do it."

"I give it a week until some reporter finds out about it."

"Well what was I to do? It wasn't like we knew the stock was coming our way! Who knew Mom was going to die?"

"That's another thing. Get yourself ready, get Annis and Wade and Sahara ready, to see Cassandra's name and the whole gory story in the news. It's going to be a mess. Damn it! I have photoremediation in my recommendations too! Oh, the media are going to have quite a time with this one. They'll claim I was lining my family pockets."

"But you recommended photoremediation because it's a possible solution to the nuclear waste problem, regardless of who invented it, relative or not!"

"You know that and I know that and a handful of scientists across the country know it. But to my political opponents that's irrelevant. There is a significant power base in the fact that Nuclear needs to be controlled, monitored and policed. Where is the incentive to neutralize it, to render all that accumulated waste harmless? Why would my political opponents get behind something that erodes their power? No Tia, it doesn't matter whether it's the sanest and wisest solution in the world, they will fight it because they are protecting their power base.

"They are Resisters. They will use any weapon they can. Here we're handing them something huge to use against us, the fact that we stand to gain financially if the process is used.

"Don't you see that even if we had no connection to it, they would still fight photoremediation? The unfortunate thing is that the mainstream has little ability to evaluate whether the process is scientifically valid, but the media blitz about conflict-of-interest will be something they can understand. The mainstream will follow the Resisters. It will be very difficult for Alden to stand firm. Shit, why couldn't Cassandra have waited until I left office!"

"Waited until you left office?"

"Sorry Tia, I said it in frustration, I didn't mean it."

"No, wait, that's the thing." Tia tried to explain. "You see, I don't actually have control of the stock yet. It's still in the estate. If we leave it in the estate, leave the estate open until you're out of office ..."

"I'd better get an attorney. Even if we manage to solve my legal problems, we're still going to be hit hard in the press. Steel yourself – remember what they did last time, with the Fordon story."

The press, clearly fueled by Ari's opponents, capitalized upon this opportunity. To Tia, it seemed as if they managed to slide the scandal into every g-news section except the sports pages. Mainpage splash, OpEds on conflict-of-interest and death with dignity, Business articles panning Rick's company, in-depth Special Reports on the dubious ethics of the Secretary of Energy. The attacks were unrelenting.

Ari's face acquired a certain grimness that never quite left him even in the middle of a grin. "The silver lining is, no one will ever forget that the photoremediation process exists. Some day, when I am gone, they'll remember. And they'll try it."

(27.)

As the DOE reorganization crossed over from theory and policy into practice, Ari's pace became even more frenzied. Tia had been commuting between California and DC; now she rarely left Washington. Ari was so focused on work that he relied on her completely for every detail of ordinary living.

The reorganizations meant program simplification, thus demotions and firings, in departments which had long been the power class of DOE elite: fossil sources and nuclear. The week arrived when Ari held the first Department meetings in which the one-time Assistant Secretary for Fossil Energy was limited to observer status. That week Ari's face carried a perpetual grin of delight, despite his obvious fatigue.

Yet as that week passed on the calendar, Ari's complexion became greyer, worried. His work calls increased in number, the Sliver frequently chirping in the middle of the night. Ari now had periods of sleeplessness, and he would often get up in the wee hours of the morning to return to his work in the other room.

Lying awake one night, her own sleep disturbed by Ari's rising, Tia heard the Sliver's rude mid-night chirp. Ari answered it, swore, and slammed it onto the table. An hour later, she heard the cycle repeat.

These aren't work calls. And this has been going on for a while.

In the morning he looked pale and exhausted. She questioned him about the odd calls.

"It didn't sound like you spoke with anybody."

Ari glanced at her, then looked away, his hand tracing a nervous path between coffee mug and chin, lap and table edge. His habitual languid body-stretch into conversation had completely vanished.

"I didn't. Don't let it bother you."

"But it clearly bothers you."

"Okay," he admitted with a little venom in his tone, "they're harassing me."

"Are you doing anything? Have you reported them?"

"Yes, yes," he waved her off in annoyance.

"Ari, are they threatening you?"

His eyes met hers for a moment, stony and resolute. A look of determination came over his face and he pushed back from the table.

"I have work to do."

His hug of parting contained a certain fierceness this morning. He drew a deep breath, squared his shoulders and departed for the DOE.

(28.)

President Alden ran for reelection in 2024. His opponent was clearly an oil and gas man, with the full force of that industry's support. The mudslinging was one-sided and brutal. But somehow the voters saw through it and President Alden was reelected by a narrow margin. *Perhaps they crave a noble hero*, Tia thought.

The election campaign was the easy part; the real difficulties were soon to follow.

Greenhouse gas emissions reporting for the Moscow Treaty was submitted on an annual basis. Reports came from various sectors of industry, up through the Department of Energy's Office of Policy and International Affairs, prior to being forwarded to the UN's expert review team.

This year, there was a catch. An investigative reporter, a known consumer bulldog, latched on to the greenhouse gas emissions reporting process, determined to manufacture a story if there wasn't one to be had. As it turned out, little manufacture was necessary.

The story broke on major grid sites in late November: fraudulent reporting, by several major plastics manufacturers. Greenhouse gas emissions statistics had been blatantly understated for several years running in order to achieve sufficient emissions 'decrease' to obtain clearance to open a large new factory operation. Plastics being one of the few remaining growth industries that purchased outmoded petroleum products, it was clear who was behind the fraudulent reporting.

Investigation revealed that the fraudulent reporting had been compounded when DOE staffers complied the country's figures. To achieve U.S. goals under the Moscow Treaty, parties deep within DOE had 'adjusted' the figures.

And it was clear who was on the receiving end. As the head of the Department, it was Secretary of Energy Ari Damek whose signature graced those glowing reports. It was Secretary Ari Damek who spent long days testifying during the Congressional investigation.

And it was former Head Delegate Dr. Ari Damek who fielded the incredulous calls from EU and Indian delegates he had worked with for decades.

(29.)

As the drought years unfolded, agriculture yields in water-thirsty hybrid varieties declined severely. Before the turn of the century, U.S. farm subsidies had been built upon the premise that a surplus of crops had lowered crop prices too far, and farmers needed subsidies to recover lost income. The federal government's solution had been to offer subsidies that increased in amount as a farmer planted more crops; more crops meant more subsidy dollars. In the past this had created even greater crop surpluses, to the point of overproduction and dumping.

Excess harvest was in some cases dumped on the world marketplace, reducing commodity prices for crops which were the mainstay of some third world countries. The U.S. government-subsidized overproduction had served to prevent these countries from supporting themselves.

With declining harvests during the drought crisis and erratic weather patterns during the 2010s and 2020s, what had previously been dumped overproduction now became essential farm produce for the nation's food supply. While U.S. farmlands continued to yield plenty for the country's own people, the days of substantial exports, of excess and dumping faded into the past.

The U.S. farm subsidy system, founded upon supposed excessively-lowered crop prices, could no longer be justified. Agricultural subsidy payments were placed on a schedule of phase-out. Since three-quarters of farm subsidy dollars had gone to the top ten percent of subsidy beneficiaries, almost all of whom were large industrial farms, the disbanding of the subsidy system severely undermined the profits of the industrial farms. The medium and small sized farms, most of whom did not qualify for subsidy payments, felt little impact from the shakedown.

(30.)

More than a decade after California's state greenhouse gas law had come into effect, capping emissions for new vehicles, millions of inefficient gas guzzling, greenhouse-gas-emitting pre-2009 vehicles still remained on the road. In the early 2020s, California again braved new legislative ground by imposing a Fossil Fuel Carbon Car tax which came to be known as the FFCC tax.

No vehicles were exempt, and there were no tiered systems. Legislators wisely concluded that all vehicles – trucks, busses, heavy equipment, pickups, delivery trucks, as well as cars – contributed to global warming, thus all must pay the tax. The FFCC tax increased in magnitude as the decade stretched on. Since energy efficient vehicles such as hybrids suffered a lower FFCC tax than traditional engine cars, the market for hybrid and electric retrofitting blossomed.

The revenues from the FFCC tax went toward carbon sequestration programs, funding reforestation and native vegetation projects statewide. By the mid 2020s, other states were passing carbon taxes, following California's Transformer leadership.

(31.)

Midmorning, Tia's DC phone chirped; it was Kegan. "Tia, Ari's been in an accident."

Oh my God, Ari!

"He was hit by a car when he was crossing the street. He's in the hospital now, but he should be okay."

When Tia reached Ari's hospital room, the man guarding the door checked her i.d. against his handheld, then admitted her and closed the door.

Ari turned to greet her. The side of his face was bruised and his arm was heavily bandaged. But his right leg had clearly taken the worst of the impact, his knee now encased in thick bindings at a fixed angle.

"Tia! I'm so glad you're here!" He tried to sit up in bed to greet her. A wave of pain crossed his face. As she approached the bed he held out his arms to her and folded her into a hug.

"Careful! My ribs!"

Despite his own warning, he held her tightly. She could feel a long, cautious, trembling sigh.

"And I'm glad you're ... okay," she said. It was a relative term. He looked awful. "How bad is it?"

He released her, only so far as to allow her to sit up; he maintained a tight grip on her arm. His dark eyes met hers – serious, with a hint of something she didn't dare acknowledge.

"It could have been worse, far worse. My knee is smashed, they'll do a knee replacement surgery when it stabilizes, no big deal. A few cracked ribs. They tell me I'm lucky there's no head injury. But that's not the worst of it." He glanced at the closed door.

She made the chilling connection. "Ari, why are you being guarded?"

He held her arm even more firmly; it seemed he needed that touch.

"Tia," he looked deep into her eyes, "they accelerated."

His voice was trembling.

"What do you mean?" She smiled in denial and shook her head.

He reached out and held her chin.

"Tia, it was supposed to be far worse. I'm not supposed to be here."

"No. No, Ari."

"Tia, they knew my route, they knew I'd be alone, they were waiting. They floored it. I don't know how I managed to get out of the way."

No! She began trembling uncontrollably. *No!* Her hands flew to her face. Then to his, to touch him, to assure herself he was really still here. *They couldn't! This isn't real!*

"They're very serious about this. They don't want me doing my job. They couldn't get Alden voted out. I didn't cave under their threats. But they're determined to stop this Policy."

Determined to stop ... you, Ari.

She grabbed for him, curling against his chest. She'd forgotten about the ribs and she could hear his sharp gasp of pain. But he held her tightly nonetheless.

"Be ready, there will be lots of questions. Lots of discrete questions."

Just like after Dad, only ... he didn't survive!

"But what I just told you doesn't leave this room, do you understand? To the rest of the world, it was a simple hit and run accident."

Ari, they tried to ...

The sob escaped her with a tight little squeak as the rush of tears came. She raised her face to his and kissed him desperately.

Assure me you're still here. Please, tell me this is all a bad dream.

He raised his head. His voice was icy steel.

"They're not going to win. They fucked up, I'm still here. They're really going to regret it now."

(32.)

Kegan was quite busy, ferrying paperwork between the DOE offices and the apartment. The knee surgery went well, although Ari refused to heed doctor's orders and stay off it.

He even finds a way to pace on crutches!

His pacing habits had intensified, along with the determination in his eye. Every waking moment he was working, an organizational chart or DOE report propped on the table beside him as he ate, his video display glasses perched on his nose.

He was an intolerable patient, demanding and harsh in his pain. He refused medications because they clouded his mind and he couldn't work. Tia phoned Shannon for a care package from Lares, and Shannon sent herbs for poultices and infusions, salves, and detailed instructions. Ari's improvement began immediately. The swelling and bruising reduced and the lacerations healed quickly. Soft tissue injuries healed steadily. The doctors declared the knee surgery successful, but it was never quite right. Ari resorted to a cane anytime he needed to walk further than to cross the room.

But there were no herbs for the deeper injuries. A government agent now accompanied Ari every time he left the apartment. Ari insisted on a security service for Tia and for Annis in California as well.

"They're *deadly* serious, Tia," he said with emphasis when she objected. "I'm not going down. And I'm not taking any chances with you or Annis. Sorry."

(33.)

Tia stood on the bare workshop pad. It glowed eerily in the moonlight. Yellowish. *Odd moon*, she thought. Now reddish. *Fire!*

She tried to run, but her feet wouldn't move faster than a stumbling pace through a landscape now fiery red. Everything was red and flickering, the trees, the buildings around her, everything the color of the flames of the Malibu hills. She was at Coyote Creek, at the creek bed. A few more steps, and she was in the gardens of the Santa Monica triplex, all bathed in flickering firelight. It was hot, oh so hot! Where was everybody? And still she walked, a stumbling, dragging step. Why wouldn't her feet move? Now the gardens were those of Lares.

Five year old Annis was crying, "Daddy, Daddy!" Blood dripped from a gash on her forehead. Tia couldn't reach her to wipe it off. *Oh the blood!* It mingled with the firelight. There was blood on the ground now, everywhere. She looked down at it in odd disbelief. Dad's blood. Nooooooo ...

A dark form lay on the ground ahead. The light was dim and flickering but Tia continued forward. She couldn't see well, so she bent down and crawled on hands and knees through the blood. She reached the still form – a body – ripped apart in the explosion, the eyes open, dead and staring, the torso blown open by the pipe bomb. Fire lit the sky. She saw the face – *Ari!*

She tried to scream and nothing came out of her throat. Again and again she tried, without a sound. Her chest ached from the effort. And from the bloody hole ripped in Ari's stomach a baby's head was crowning. Tia reached out to catch the baby.

Gathering the newborn to her, looking into his wizened face, she knew that the baby's name was Kyoto. It began to rain, great sheets of orange rain, a horrible rainstorm in a fiery world.

There will be no world for this baby, Tia realized in panic. *The emissions – they're accelerating! They've floored it! The world is on fire, because they didn't reduce emissions in time! At first they wouldn't agree, and then they cheated! They cheated!*

A bolt of lightning cut the flaming sky and flashed in Ari's lifeless eyes. Still holding the baby, Tia screamed and screamed.

Covered with sweat, Tia was now awake in bed, the scream still in her throat, her heart pounding, Ari hugging her with his great arms.

"Tia, Tia, wake up, everything's okay, you're having a nightmare."

She sobbed into his chest. He rocked her gently, kissing her hair and soothing.

It's not okay! We're living a nightmare!

(34.)

As the agricultural subsidy system phased into the twilight, powerful political pressure was mounted by farm lobbies to claim disaster payments for this upheaval.

At the turn of the century, money dedicated for agricultural conservation programs had been shunted to fund agricultural disaster payments. Now, in the mid 2020s, the lasting impact of President Elliott's Civilian Conservation Corps came to the forefront, as citizens campaigned Congress heavily to preserve conservation funding for conservation purposes.

The General Accounting Office reviewed agricultural disaster payment recipients and determined that disaster aid of the past had been concentrated among a segment of chronically 'disaster-prone' recipients. One-third of all disaster payments were going to farmers in Texas, Oklahoma, the Dakotas, Kansas and Missouri. This statistic was particularly amazing when reviewed in conjunction with the decline of groundwater sources from the Ogallala aquifer.

The industrial farms, having established themselves in a semi-arid geographic area where their operations were based completely upon the limited and non-replenishing resource of the ancient aquifer, had been fully supporting their corporate profits with federal disaster funding.

(35.)

Tia's phone rang one November evening in the DC apartment.

"Tia, it's Jana." Jana's voice was brittle and strained.

"What's the matter?"

"Tia, you'd better come home, as soon as you can."

"What happened!?"

"It's Mark. Tia, it's terrible. Mark's dead, he's been killed. Annis is beside herself, she's absolutely lost it."

"Mark ... killed ... what ..."

Oh my God, they went after Mark!?

But that wasn't it at all.

"In all the storms, down at the coast, the waves are breaking up the remaining structures. Some hermit was in one, wouldn't come out. The fire department went in early this morning to rescue him, Mark's unit. It was Mark who got the guy out."

Jana broke down crying. It took her some time to recover sufficiently to finish the story. "Part of the building collapsed into the storm surf. Mark didn't make it out.

"We're all a mess here. Shannon's beside herself. Annis is not much better."

"Let me talk with her."

"Tia, she won't talk with any of us. She just sits and stares."

"I'll catch the next plane out of here."

❧

Annis sat on the couch, simply sat. Her eyes were glazed, staring into the distance. She refused to interact with anyone, including Tia.

Sitting long hours in the Lares living room with Annis, Tia half expected to overhear Matthew and Mark arguing, the usual door slam, and the quiet appearance at the garden door, of the figure who would never again grace their lives.

Periodic rainshowers drenched the gardens beyond the windows, each one a reminder of the storms that had taken Mark. It was as if even the world beyond shared their waves of sorrow.

❧

Ari flew in a day later. He went immediately to see Annis. Tia followed him to the living room doorway, unsure how he would take Annis' isolation.

Ari sat on the couch beside Annis and began talking to her in a low voice. Tia couldn't catch his words. He kept talking for several minutes. Then to Tia's amazement, Annis slowly raised her head and turned to face Ari.

Tia started forward but Ari gestured for her to stay back. Ari kept up the low, steady stream of talk directed to Annis.

Annis blinked, her eyes becoming alert now. Her face lost its stupor, her facial muscles coming alive again. Ari kept talking. Now Annis uncurled her body, ever so slowly.

Tia yearned to run and hug them both but knew it was not yet time.

Annis' face drew back into a look of anguish. Staring at Ari, her expression changed to revulsion.

"Get away from me!" Annis hissed like a coiled snake.

Ari drew back in surprise.

"Heroes!" Annis said with scorn. "I'm done with all you damn heroes! I don't want any part of you. I had to have a hero, and look what's happened, he's dead, he's dead, he's dead!" Her shrieks filled the house.

Ari moved to hug her, to console her.

"Don't you touch me, you're the worst of them all!" Annis swung at him and her fingernails slashed his cheek.

"Go back to your crusades!" Annis launched herself, screaming at Ari. "I don't need you!"

He put up his arm to shield his face from her blows. Annis' fists were ineffective, she was too weak from mourning. Yet her ear-piercing shrieks of anguish more than made up for it.

Jana and Seth came running at the sound of Annis' screams. They halted in the doorway of the living room, frozen in inaction, like Tia, at the horrifying sight of Annis attacking Ari.

"Always so noble, high and mighty with your grand causes!"

Ari just sat there, whether stunned or by intent, his arm shielding his face, Annis' fists pounding him.

"I didn't get a real dad! I got some fucking legend!"

Annis collapsed, sobbing, onto Ari's lap.

Ari stroked her hair, then bent over her in a hug, his great shoulders all that were visible.

Tia ran to them and knelt by the couch, attempting to hug both of them. Annis' face was hidden beneath a mass of tumbled dark hair. Ari's cheek bore long scratches from Annis' attack; several of the wounds were bleeding.

Tia's touch roused Annis. Annis tensed and sprang from Ari's lap, suddenly realizing where she was.

"Let me go!" she hissed at Ari, recoiling from him, her dark eyes furtive like a wild animal's. She tried to stand, to run, but almost collapsed. Tia caught her, supported her, half carried her, down the hall to her room.

Jana brought a nourishing broth. "Go to Ari," she said to Tia in a low voice. "I'll take Annis."

Tia returned to the living room but Ari was gone.

"Garden." Seth indicated with a jerk of his head.

Tia searched the rain-drenched garden. Ari was in none of their usual nooks. She found him at last, far from their typical areas, sitting on a dripping wet bench with his head in his hands, his cane fallen to the ground beneath.

Tia sat down beside him.

"You shouldn't be here, you should be with her," he said despondently.

"Jana's taking care of her," Tia said. "I'm here with you."

It began to drizzle but Ari didn't seem to notice the rain.

Tia looked at his face. The long scratches were raised and reddened, leaving a ghastly appearance. She reached out to stroke his damp hair, half expecting him to push her away. Instead he curled into her shoulder and cried, great big retching dreadful sobs.

(36.)

Tia and Ari straggled in from the garden amid sheets of rain, to find an empty house. Even Annis was gone. Tia was on the verge of panic when Lauren came in, bringing dinner; Lauren, Verity and Ravyn were cooking in rotation for the stricken families.

"They're all over at Shannon's," Lauren explained.

"Annis?"

"Oh yes, she's there too, comforting Shannon. Annis looks so much better today." Lauren sounded quite relieved.

Tia looked over at Ari, standing in the shadows of the room, haggard and bent over his cane, dripping from the rain. Lauren's glance followed Tia's. At the sight of Ari, Lauren's eyes grew round, and she hastily made her departure.

Tia lead Ari back to their bedroom. He flopped on the bed atop the covers, still wearing his rain drenched clothes, not caring. Tia changed into dry clothes herself, then, since he was taking no action, she moved to help Ari. He sat up and removed his wet shirt, waiting like a small child for her to hand him a fresh one.

"Maybe she's right, Tia." His voice was quiet and broken as he sat shirtless on the edge of the bed, his head in his hands, his huge shoulders curled round in defeat. "I guess I have been on some insane crusade, trying to make the world a better place."

"Ari, she was very upset, out of her mind, don't read anything into it!"

He didn't seem to hear her.

"I'm no hero, I'm not strong enough. I tried to hold fast through all the scandals, everything they threw at me." His shoulders heaved. "But damn it, it hurts like hell. Every … single … attack."

Tia reached out to touch his shoulder in comfort but he moved away, turning his back on her.

"Fucking bastards." His head came up, his fist suddenly pounding the bed. "Bastards! They don't care about a better life. We want the old ways, they say. We want our power. Fuck the better world, fuck the future generations! To hell with anyone who's trying to make it better. They get off on the denigration, on the destruction of anything worthwhile, in destroying anyone trying to do some good!"

His voice became a vicious sneer. "They don't want heroes. They need them desperately, and seek them out. But then they rip them to shreds, tear them down, denigrate, attack, mutilate, grind them into the filth.

"They're fighting me tooth and nail, Annis!" he yelled to the empty house. "They're fighting for their petroleum and their nukes, with everything they've got! They've ripped me down with every scandal they could throw at me, everything they could do to me! They shredded my character over photoremediation, slandered my name with their Congressional Investigations. They gouged my hopes and my dreams by falsifying greenhouse gas emissions, they've broken my body …"

He paused, his eyes haunted, his voice twisting into a tortured whisper.

"That gutter, oh that filthy stinking gutter. Lying there, bleeding, helpless … me, helpless! …" He curled inward on himself upon the bed.

"… Asphalt against my face, my blood running into the street … This is how it all ends, helpless in the street … the Treaties incomplete, the Policy … Annis, my little one … Tia … Tia …"

Even as he called to her, she was afraid to touch him. His shuddering shook the bed.

"The calls … that chilling distorted voice, they're going to try it again. I can't go back, I can't!" His hands clutched the sides of his head. "I'm a fucking helpless weakling." His groan of inner agony was hideous to witness.

The wind outside blew sheets of rain roaring against the windows.

"Mark, you were brave to the very end … so young, his whole life before him … Climate change, it's killing our children! I can't stop it. I'm fucking helpless to stop it."

He lay still now, eyes glazed and unseeing, the stillness more horrifying than the trembling. Tia collapsed over his big shoulder and wept.

(37.)

The death of firefighter Mark Goodman galvanized the West LA populace. The odd phrase GOODMAN 07632, Mark's name and badge number, began appearing around town: on buttons pinned to the chests of young people, on flyers in Sustainability Center windows, on stickers on bicycles and Neighborhood Vehicles.

It spread like wildfire through the youth of the city. More than a show of support for the bravery of a young hero, GOODMAN 07632 became an statement about the natural forces that had claimed this young life, about global warming and its resultant sea level rise. GOODMAN 07632 became a declaration: I am doing what I can to curb global warming.

There were GOODMAN 07632 grid pages, the 2025 equivalent to *50 Simple Things You Can Do To Save the Earth*.[82]

The campaign ceased to be about one individual. "Goodman" was no longer a surname, rather an affirmation of values of the individual citizen: I am a good man, I'm an activist, I'm working for change.

The Lares adults puzzled at how long and how far the grassroots campaign had carried. Annis certainly wasn't leading it, being in no shape to be more than a tearstained image on the grid page.

The day the LA Times g-news carried a photo of LA City Mayor Justis Carlyle wearing a GOODMAN 07632 button, the campaign mastermind revealed himself. A victory shout echoed from the Lares office, and Seth appeared, his face glowing triumph.

(38.)

After Mark's funeral, a despondent Ari packed a single slim bag for Washington. He was leaning very heavily on his cane these days.

"I won't be gone long, Tia. Just long enough to clean out the apartment. My resignation letter is already drafted." He tapped the Sliver in his pocket.

His weary face still bore the long reddened scratches, slow to heal.

"It wasn't for nothing. Alden got his policy – the policy of his dreams."

Your dreams, darling, yours too.

"The reorganization has happened. He only needs to find someone strong enough to hold it together, he doesn't need to find someone gutsy enough to do it."

He already did that, Ari. You were the one gutsy enough to do it.

"My hat's off to whomever can take it on. It was too much for me."

Don't say that! You did it, you pulled it off, the great transition, the beginning of the transformation!

"Actually," Ari looked up and a glint of the old calculating look returned, "if I handle this right, I can hand Alden his scapegoat so he doesn't get tagged with the emissions scandal."

"Ari," Tia began in objection. This was too much, his taking the fall for it.

He raised his hand to still her.

"Alden knows the score. I know the score. I'm quitting anyway. Why not use it to his advantage? Spin it to the positive, so that the country still has its hero."

"You're putting your neck on the chopping block, your reputation, so that your friend can be the hero?"

"Precisely," Ari said with resolve.

A little while later, Tia noticed Ari in Annis' room. He was holding Mark's picture from Annis' bedside, scanning it into his Sliver.

CHAPTER 8:

HEALING THE EARTH

2026-2032

What was I seeking here at Coyote Creek? Tia pondered as she roamed the fields. The outdoors comforted her far more than the house. The late spring air already smelled of sun-drenched chaparral: white sage, artemesia, dusty earth. Tia's walk took her out to the old eucalyptus grove.

Several months before, the emptiness of Coyote Creek had become too much for Wade; he moved into an apartment closer to his son. While Sahara continued to run Cassandra's experimental fields with an abundant staff of interns, the house remained empty. With all the tension in their lives, an extended visit to Coyote Creek had seemed the perfect solution. Yet now that they were here, Tia wasn't so sure.

Perhaps I'm just running from the reality of life right now ... Annis mostly grown ... Ari so strange ...

At the thought of Ari, the tears welled up. Tia leaned her head against a broad tree trunk and sobbed. Ari withdrawn into a shell, Ari spending long hours sitting on the porch simply staring into the distance, Ari taking solitary walks through the fields limping heavily with his cane. His dark eyes were listless and the noble orator was silent; he now had little to say to the world.

Ari, what they have done to you! She cried for the fears of the long months in DC, for the loss of Mark, for the pain of Annis, but mostly for that fierce fire, now stolen away. The rough bark of the eucalyptus scratched her face harshly, yet she leaned into it, welcoming the physical bite. *Reality.*

He's changed, it's all changed. DC was not even three years, yet I hardly know where to pick up our life again. Big dreams we had then, and what has come of them? She picked at the tree and the bark fell away in long strips exposing the tender honey-pink trunk beneath. It looked naked and raw. *That's me, too.*

(2.)

"I had to wait until Duane was in the shower to talk with you, it seems I never get the chance," Tia said to Annis as she poured tea at the Coyote Creek breakfast table.

Annis wouldn't meet Tia's eyes.

"How are things? How are classes?"

"I was taking one class this session, but I dropped it."

"Honey, why?"

"I didn't like it." Annis picked lamely at the tie of her bathrobe.

"Then you're working?"

"Sometimes. For Ravyn."

"At the restaurant?"

"Yeah."

"This friend, Duane, did you meet him at school?"

"Mom, I don't want to talk about it." Annis stalked out the door to sit on the stairs of the porch, the screen door slamming behind her. Tia sighed and followed her out.

"Annis, we need to talk about this. Two weeks ago it was Kaden and the visit before it was Emilio. It's never been the same face twice."

Annis turned away from Tia. "So?"

Tia continued talking to the back of Annis' head. "Annis, this isn't wise. It's not even safe ..."

"They're all such jerks. Like Dad."

"Have you said one word to your father since you've been here?"

"Why?"

"Because he's your father, and a human being in this house."

"I don't want to. I don't need him."

Tia winced. "I think you do. And maybe he needs you."

"That's his problem."

"Annis, honey, have you seen him, have you seen what all this has done to him?" The words tumbled out with a little shriek, the perfectly wrong thing to say, yet Tia couldn't contain it.

"I don't care!" Annis jumped up, barefoot and in her bathrobe, and ran a few steps down the path toward the gardens. She turned and shouted at Tia. "You're so caught up in him. I don't care about him. It's always about him. If it's not his work he doesn't want to hear about it. He's self-centered, egotistical, arrogant, just like all the corporate idiots!" She turned and ran a few steps further into the garden.

Then she stopped and marched back toward the house. "You know, I came out here to see you Mom, but this is no fun. We're leaving. I'm going to pack."

"Honey, please ..."

Annis flung open the screen door and gasped. Ari stood in the doorway, unmoving. His jaw was hardened, his posture tense.

"Yes, you go pack." His voice was low and sinister. "Get out of this house."

"Ari!" Tia began to protest. He glared at her.

Annis' eyes welled up with tears. She turned and ran out into the grounds. Tia watched her in horror. Annis looped around to the other side of the house and they heard the far door slam.

"Ari, you can't kick her out!"

"I can and I will." He stepped out onto the porch, his cane clenched with white knuckles.

"We can't send her out on the streets ..."

He snorted. "She'll go back to Lares and lick her wounds. I can't stand any more of this under my roof." He gestured toward the bedrooms.

"How much did you hear?"

"All the parts that count. Let's see." He tallied on his fingers. "I'm egotistical, arrogant, self-centered, did I get them all?"

His face folded. "She doesn't get it. I did it all for her! For her and her children and her grandchildren ... and Seth and Jeffrey and Mark..." He sighed deeply, closing his eyes in silent pain. "What's the use."

Tia jumped to her feet to hug him. "Ari, don't say that!"

He pulled away from her.

Damn it, you won't touch me anymore, not since DC!

"It didn't do any good. The emissions continue to climb, the Policy's not implemented, the Framework ..."

"The Athens Accord is ratified overseas, the Policy is in process – they won't move quickly," Tia debated.

"It's no use. I can't fix it." He limped down the garden path. "The world's going to hell." He swung his cane viciously at a rose blossom in the full of bloom. It exploded in a burst of peach-colored petals. "The planet's falling to pieces, just like she is."

(3.)

Ari perched on the footstool of the chair under the sweeping avocado tree. His forehead pressed to his folded hands atop the crook of his cane, his shoulders curled, he appeared to be huddled in the cold, yet the spring temperatures were already soaring.

Tia brought him a glass of iced borage tea and automatically ran her hand across his shoulders. He shook her hand off with a sharp twitch of his shoulder blade. The rejection stung and the feeling added to the heavy lump of similar rejections aching in the pit of her stomach. She willed the tears to stay put.

"I told Sahara not to come for dinner, it seemed you didn't feel like having company."

His shoulders raised slightly in answer.

"Ari, you seem to be getting worse since we've been here at Coyote Creek. These silences..."

He heaved a deep sigh.

"You've always been a man of such profound words, and now you have nothing to say about what's going on inside?"

"I don't want to hear it." His voice was muffled yet sounded odd from disuse.

"Ari, darling," she crouched down in front of him in vain effort to see his face, "out here," she cast around for anything to say to draw him out, "the breeze will carry it away."

He slowly lifted his head.

She bit her lip. He hadn't shaved in at least two days. His brown eyes were dull and glazed and seemed to not even register her presence. He had aged nearly a decade in the four months since leaving DC. But the past week, these tortured silences had been unbearable.

"I can't do it," he said.

"Yes you can, darling, just whisper it."

"The problem is just too huge."

"The breeze will carry it away." She needed to hear it again, to convince herself it could be true. Looking at him she felt no confidence it was possible.

"I knew when I took it on. I talked myself into believing it could be solved. I've been kidding myself all these years."

Tia stared at him in horror as she realized what he was saying.

"I'm ... helpless to stop it." He closed his eyes. "Helpless." His heavy sigh was heartwrenching. "I tried, I can't fix it. There's no point in trying."

Carry his words away, she begged the breeze as tears rolled down her cheeks. *I don't want to hear this. Not from him!*

A chill feeling crept upon her. *What if he ... doesn't get past it?* Her mind hardly dared form the despairing words.

"Tia, help me up." His call sliced through her thoughts. His disinterested expression hadn't changed, but he extended his hand to her. "My knee's swollen again." His hand caught hers with a desperation that exceeded the needs of the action.

She pulled him to his feet. "Can you walk?"

"Yes." He still held her, his fingers wrapping her wrist.

Then he withdrew his hand, the moment was gone, she was left drifting alone again. The tears came to her eyes as the chills returned.

"I'll pick some plantain for a poultice." She ran down the path blinded by her tears.

⌒

Steve, I'll call Steve.

Despite work pressures at a critical portion of a contract, Steve arrived at Coyote Creek after dinner. He and Ari talked long into the night, while Tia huddled in the far bedroom. Words didn't penetrate the walls, but Steve's steady tone did, together with occasional quiet responses from Ari. By morning, Steve was gone, Ari silent, grey, looking worse than ever.

"Is he coming back?" Tia asked hopefully over breakfast.

Ari shook his head slowly. *No.*

She turned from the table and busied herself with the dishes to hide her tears. *He might never* ... She scrubbed dishes furiously, soap suds flying as if she could scrub the thought away.

(4.)

After cleaning up her mess in the kitchen, Tia looked around for Ari. He was gone, together with his cane. She put on her sunhat to go out to the garden. From the porch she could hear the sound of heavy work, someone chopping firewood perhaps. The sound didn't come from the direction of the neighbor's property; oddly, it came from the creek. *Sahara doesn't have interns here today.* Tia walked out the path to investigate.

As she approached the creek, the sounds were more distinct. A gasp of exertion, a heavy thud accompanied by a groan of pain, repeated again and again.

She parted the buckwheats on the bank of the creek. Ari stood in the dry creekbed, shirtless and running with sweat. He had positioned himself alongside a sharp boulder, a chunky section of eucalyptus branch in his hands. She watched in horror as he swung the branch overhead, slamming it against the boulder. His cry was anguished with each blow, as his body shuddered, the branch splintered, chips flew.

Shaken, she turned away, leaving him alone.

꒳

Ari didn't reappear at lunchtime, but occasional noises from the creek revealed his whereabouts. Mid-afternoon Tia heard him enter the house and take a shower. She found him later, sitting on the porch, looking quite exhausted and in pain. He couldn't lean back in the chair. She brought ice water and aloe vera without even asking.

"Take off your shirt," she directed, gesturing with the dish of crushed plant pulp. He groaned as he complied. His back was scarlet and searing under her hand as she eased the aloe onto his sunburn. "You'll need some yarrow too, you have a fever."

He didn't say anything, simply opened his palms, a mass of raw blisters.

She gasped. "Okay, calendula. I think Mom had some here somewhere."

The purposeful action was cleansing, gathering the herbs, making the infusions. The plants under her hands seemed to speak to her. Aloe, soothing, healing. *It will be okay*, its cool minty smell called to her as she crushed its fat pulpy leaves. *A vase in the kitchen*, the lavender begged, *you are the one who needs me, not he. Balance will be restored*, the yarrow promised, *in time*. The sunny calendula flowers beamed their effervescent message: *Hope*.

(5.)

Tia's meanderings brought her out to the little creek. Today, in late spring, the creekbed was already dry and hot. She sat on the ground in the middle of the creek, idly poking the fine sandy silt with her fingertips.

Out of the corner of her eye she could see the rock where Ari had proposed to her, so many years ago. She wished she hadn't picked this spot to sit, she didn't want to see it. She swallowed hard to stuff down the tears that seemed so everpresent these days. *He's healing. But oh so slowly!* Logically, she should be rejoicing; three weeks ago she didn't think he would ever turn the corner. Yet her heart felt heavy, aching. The days of caring for Ari had been busy, full of household and nursing tasks. Now that he was recovering, the reality of life was returning as well.

Involuntarily she glanced at the rock, her erstwhile pedestal. *Marriage. What has it been? Survival, all those traveling years. Survival, the DC nightmare. Survival, this worry-filled spring.* The leaden feeling filled her stomach and burst out in tears.

A rustle of bushes, a footstep on the path and Ari appeared, parting the branches with his cane. Tia hastily wiped her face.

"I thought I might find you here." He sat beside her on the ground, his knee carefully outstretched.

"How are you feeling today?" she asked.

"A lot better. You're a good nurse." He looked at his palms, the blisters now healed. He hadn't helped them much, that first week, reopening them almost daily with return trips to the boulder. The activity had cleansed him: his posture was straightening, the swelling gone from his knee. His sunburnt skin had peeled off in great sheets but now he was tanned. Yet his eyes remained flat, devoid of that lively fire.

She looked away quickly. She couldn't meet those eyes without crying.

He caught her chin, saw her tears and puffy face, then pushed her away roughly.

"Looks like we both need to be out here." He drew a deep breath. "Out here with the sun and the elements, but mostly here with this." Making a cup of her hand, he scooped a handful of fine soil from the creekbed and pressed the soil into her hand. He closed his hand around hers.

"Did you know, Damek means earth." In his weary eyes a small spark of the old fire glimmered.

His focus drifted away, to far landscapes beyond the physical scenery. "I was away from it for too long. Planes and offices, computers, policies ... My dad used to warn me about this. You get too far from it and you lose touch he'd say. Damek. By our very name we are people of the earth. A constant reminder of our duty. Heal the earth." He squeezed her hand around the little lump of soil.

"When he lay there helpless it was dreadful. I made a vow, I would never be like that. When I faced the environmental issues, I felt the helplessness, deep inside. I feared it might overtake me, so I worked harder. I dove into the work with passion, and that sense of purpose gave me strength.

"These past months have been humbling. Helpless under the wheels of a car, helpless to save Mark, powerless to get that Policy in place, defeated in emissions by my country, useless with my own daughter.

"But one thing I've figured out, with rock and stick and quite a bit of insanity is, floundering helpless doesn't have to be the end. I'm not afraid of it any longer. I survived it, and I will find a way to go on." He lifted his head a notch higher, his eyes seeking hers.

"I'm sorry for dragging you through all of this. You have been so devoted and patient. I can see in your eyes the unhappiness I've brought you." His hand still held hers around the little lump of creek sand. His dark eyes were intent upon her.

Don't! I can't bear it! Her yearning for him was physical pain.

"I love you, Tia."

She couldn't restrain it now; she folded against his chest, sobbing. She cried for the deadened times, the lethargy, the silences. The rejections, the awful loneliness. He held her tightly, his arms strong around her, as if once again, anything were possible.

His hand was now in her hair, guiding her lips to his. After the long months, her rush of desire frightened her with its intensity.

She had forgotten about the little pinch of earth in her hand; as she reached for his shoulder it showered both of them in fine silt. He looked at the golden shower. "That's precisely what we need."

He pushed her to the ground, his eyes alight with an unfamiliar heat. He rolled over on her, and the small stones and plants of the creekbed dug into her back, bruising her, cutting her, but she didn't care.

She clung to him fiercely, in the process splitting her own lip against his teeth. His hands were like fire upon her body. She gasped as he yanked her shirt off over her head.

"Naked against the earth," he commanded.

Her urgency matched his as he stripped her roughly, then tore off his own clothing. His eyes were wildfire.

(6.)

The weeks now passed quickly at Coyote Creek. Tia spent the days compiling her mother's papers for publication. She took odd pleasure in sitting outdoors, barefoot to the earth, editing in the shade of the young oak tree.

Cassandra's flowing dresses still hung in the house closets. Wider and shorter than Tia would have worn in the city, in the heat of early summer here in Coyote Creek it felt deeply satisfying to wear them with little underneath. *Senses. I can feel again.*

That creek bed did something to us, she realized.

She clearly remembered the feeling of the sunbaked grit upon her body, together with the cruel bite of the creek's discomforts. *Reality. I am of the earth.*

Cassandra's papers spread around her were further reminders. *Life. Life sprouting forth.* An urgency filled her, to finish the project and share it with the world.

Among Cassandra's china, Tia discovered a tiny crystal salt dish that had been Saffi's. This she placed on the kitchen windowsill, to hold a pinch of sand from the creekbed, where she could touch it daily. *Damek means earth. Healing, empowerment, a return to life. A focusing of purpose.*

⊷

Ari selected tactile projects, building a solar oven and hauling an old model solar array into the workshop to disassemble and resurface. The solar oven came in handy as the weather warmed into summer; the kitchen no longer heated up with dinner preparations, and it gratified Tia to cook using such environmentally-conscious methods. At first she dismissed his old solar panel project as idle tinkering. Days into it, she began to see its purpose.

"I never worked this end of it," Ari gestured with tools in his hands. "I always worked the theory and the politics. This is very satisfying."

He carried that satisfaction on his frame, his shoulders and back proud once again. His expression came alive with curiosity and contemplation. His grin unfolded easily and sunshine graced his dark eyes.

He came to her one day. "Help me make a garden."

"What?" she blinked, not sure she heard him properly.

"Seeds, growing things. I've never done it before."

They selected a sunny spot in the old vegetable patch. Tia started him with the easy plants, beans, mesclun, onions, nasturtiums, pressing the seeds into his huge palm.

Ari planted his garden with fastidious care. Watching him burrow his hands into the deep brown earth, Tia was transported to the community garden patch where she had met Jana. *Damek means earth. He feels it too.*

⊷

Sahara dropped in frequently, and it was through her that Ari learned the politics of the valley, its vulnerability to development. Suddenly Tia heard phrases like 'Agricultural Land Trust' and 'Citizen's Action Committee' echoing through the family room.

"Who runs the Town Hall meetings?" Ari badgered Sahara. "Get me an introduction, and I'll come explain how a Land Trust works. We could pull it together easily with the help of my attorney friend in LA. I'll get you in touch with some people in Marin who are already doing it."[83]

The valley residents began calling, and the Sliver reappeared from the drawer.

Coyote Creek had filled its purpose.

(7.)

In early autumn Tia and Ari returned to a different Lares. Their first evening back they lingered with Jana and Steve on the South House patio, catching up with the news.

"Shannon never recovered," Jana explained from her place curled within Steve's arms. "She turned to her family down in San Diego. Began spending more and more time there, deeply distraught, blamed it all on poor Matthew. Meanwhile, Matthew was here, and well ..."

"He got sick of her absences, felt he needed to go on with his life. He sold everything he had," Steve said. "Very freeing, he told me."

"Ravyn bought Slow Food Fast, snapped it up quick as could be," Jana interrupted. "He's been franchising it. There are so many of them now!"

"Matthew sent Peter to Harvard," Steve continued. "Shannon moved to San Diego permanently. Matthew didn't want to be here alone, so last month he quietly left. I think he first went East to see Peter. After that – well – he used to talk about seeing the Holy Land..."

"I miss Shannon so much, she doesn't return messages. She really cut us off." Jana said. "And with you gone too ... I'm *really* glad you're back!"

"You had Annis here," Tia began.

Steve and Jana looked at each other. "Sort of," Jana said quietly. "Tia, she doesn't spend much time here. And when she does, she kind of sneaks in and out. She really hasn't let us wrap her into the family."

The hard knot formed again in Tia's stomach. She looked to Ari. He crossed his arms across his chest, his face set.

"Hey, we have a new vehicle," Steve went for the distraction. "It's all electric, fully charged off the extra solar I put on the garage, completely free of fossil fuels! You'll have to see it. It's sleek, and it's fast!"

Ari barely smiled in acknowledgement.

"What's the news on your landscaping book?" Tia asked Jana.

"It's out now, I've been traveling a lot for book signings and lectures, plus we got tons of interest in the Lares gardens. Rhus handles some of it, but it's quite a load. Gavin has returned from Goleta, Gavin Duer, he's one of my students from a few years ago. He used to work for a CSA but now he's been doing Lares-type gardens up the coast. He helps with the classes here now." She turned to Ari. "I hope you don't mind – I let him camp in the vacant Goodman unit when he teaches, so that he doesn't have to travel so much."

&

A week after they had returned to Lares, Ari came out to where Tia was weeding the garden.

"I'll be leaving for Geneva next month ..."

Yes! Tia bit her lip to contain the scream of joy. *He's back on course!*

"... Fordon just called. She's putting together the team for the UNFCCC meeting, and wants me aboard. They're ready to tackle the Developmental Assistance issue. It's time."

Tia dropped her garden tools and stood to hug him; she couldn't keep the delighted smile from her face. *It's time.*

(8.)

CHINA RAINS: 80 DIE, WORSE TO COME

GROWING DESERTS 'A GLOBAL PROBLEM'

The g-news headlines cascaded at Tia in overwhelming array. In Coyote Creek they hadn't paid much attention to the news. The headlines now screamed out at her, an undeniable pattern revealed.

NEARLY 200 DIE IN INDIAN HEAT WAVE

EXTREME WEATHER ON THE RISE

(9.)

On the g-news, the new Secretary of Energy, Richard Willard, looked to Tia to be weak-chinned. Yet every time Ari saw Willard's image, he touched his brow and murmured some variation of 'my hat's off to you.'

The Recommendations from the Alden Administration's landmark Energy Policy were gradually set in motion. Subsidies to fossil energy sources were revoked, renewable energy industries flourished, and the organizational structure at the DOE remained as Ari had revised it.

With Ari out of the public eye, Secretary Willard wisely waited a few months to allow the photoremediation crisis to settle down, then launched a full-scale government experiment with photoremediation and other processes to clean up the accumulated nuclear waste dumps of decades. Secretary Willard clearly had backbone.

As the U.S. began to put action, not just lip service, behind transition to renewable energy sources, other countries around the world took notice and began to change over as well. Australia, an emissions treaty laggard since the Kyoto days, while at the same time being a hotbed of the Permaculture concept, jumped into world leadership in demonstrating how renewable power sources were only the beginning; clean energy was part of a matrix of converting to a more Sustainable existence on the planet.

China, realizing the U.S. move was the seal of confirmation on the world direction, redoubled its efforts to become the world's sharpest competitor in this, the renewable energy, marketplace as well. China streamlined manufacturing processes on photovoltaic solar and wind turbines, undercutting prices.

Cheaper photovoltaic panels meant accessibility for impoverished countries in East Asia, South Asia, and Sub-Saharan Africa. The Alden Administration's policy of unconditional relief of foreign debt helped considerably, and outreach from NGO's and religious groups oriented the third world toward an increasing standard of living along Sustainable pathways.[84]

(10.)

"Have you seen how our growing season is adjusting?" Rhys commented. He poured over garden records as Tia and Jana sorted seeds at the South House patio table. Ari reviewed legal documents for the new Land Trust in the nearby shade.

"I've seen it evolving for decades," Jana said sadly. "Back at the Venice gardens I used to plant cool season peas around the time of Ari's birthday. Now I wouldn't dream of it, we still have several weeks of dry summer heat left at that point. We're already pushing the limit on chill hours; soon our peach and apricot trees won't set fruit well."

"Seasonal changes, drought tolerance. Those are going to be the story everywhere," Rhus said grimly. "On my tour up north it was very clear. The odd rainfall patterns are affecting the irrigation sources. They're having terrible problems with water salinity. The major irrigation inlets built prior to the turn of the century were at points in the river where, at that time, water was fresh. Now, with sea level rise, the salt-to-fresh crossover is at a different point, and the irrigation inlets are drawing water that is too salty. Farmers are going to be hard-pressed to maintain their accustomed productivity without the irrigation."

Jana's assistant Gavin approached the patio, trying to catch Jana's attention. Gavin was tall and lean, with sandy hair and hazel eyes, just under thirty. He was not familiar with the Lares crowd, rarely socializing with them, usually doing his business with Jana and going on his way.

"I'll be right with you," Jana called to Gavin. "Let me finish this batch."

"Do you think we'll see another round of foreclosures like we saw through Washington and Oregon eight years ago?" Ari asked in mild curiosity.

"I think it's inevitable," Rhus' face was grim. "The industrial methods of those huge farms just don't have the flexibility and adaptability to cope with all these variations in rainfall and temperature."

"That sounds like something my mom forecast," Tia said reflectively. "She focused on creating options: alternative varieties, water-conserving techniques. She called it an insurance plan.

"I found some unexpected things among her papers. Climate change forecasts, lots of them. The fine-grain models, which show regions within our country rather than just our country as a single whole, agree that different sections of the country will experience vastly different results. Some areas will gain in productivity and others will lose terribly. But as to which sections with gain and which will lose, the studies don't necessarily agree! Most models show losses to the Corn Belt, Southern Plains, Southeast, Northeast and Appalachian regions, some moderate, some extreme. But for the Pacific region, some models predict benefits, while others predict losses. The one clear answer they all give is: things are going to change. A lot."[85]

"You mean rainfall change," Steve asked. He had been listening from the doorframe and now joined the gathering, straddling the bench behind Jana to rub her shoulders.

"Not only water supply. Mildly increased CO_2 levels have a fertilizing effect on many crops. Mild increases in temperatures will cause quicker growth. Barley, oranges and tomatoes flourish in the mild increases. Potatoes, hay and winter wheat suffer. But these positive effects are based on *mild* increases in CO_2 and temperature. If we get into more *significant* increases, production will drop off tremendously, in the U.S. and worldwide."

"What is 'significant'?" Rhus asked.

"Temperature rise beyond 7.2°F," Tia answered. "That's the point at which crop yields begin to fall significantly. California predictions for 2090 are for a temperature rise of 4° to 6.5°F under lower emission models, 8° to 12°F if we don't control emissions. We don't have a lot of margin."

"Wait ... 8° to 12° ... that's way more than 7.2°," Steve calculated. "You're saying that the 2090 forecast is for temperatures which will severely impact our agricultural production?"

"Yup, that's exactly where we're headed if we don't control emissions," Tia said grimly.

"All the more reason why that new energy plan was so urgently needed," Steve said pointedly to Ari. "If we had just waited around in inaction, we'd be past that 7.2° in no time."

"Don't I know it," Ari said quietly with a humorless smile.

"I know that the mild temperature increases we've already experienced have hit the California wineries hard," Rhus offered. "The ripening season comes earlier now, and higher temperatures during ripening reduce grape quality. Further temperature increases and we'll see significant losses in that sector of the state's agricultural economy."

Jana paused in her sorting. "Isn't it weird that we have all these solutions here at Lares – building the natural richness of our soil, waterwise growing, symbiotic and guild plantings, varieties selected for our microclimate – a whole mini-ecosystem that produces food for humans. Yet the industrial farms don't seem to be able to use these same Sustainable techniques."[86]

"Of course they can't!" Rhus retorted. "Look at what it takes. Hands on care, observation, responsiveness, not to mention knowledge of all these specialties. You can't do that on an industrial farm. It'd take massive manpower!"

Jana laughed. "If Esperanza were here she'd jump on you for that one. We've got massive manpower, sitting idle in the camps downtown! Most of them accustomed to agricultural lifestyles."

"They're not trained in things like biodynamics, Permaculture, and drylands techniques." Rhus' protest was not too convincing.

"Clearly, that's just a matter of some education," Jana replied scornfully.

Ari sat listening to the debate, then suddenly broke in. "Rhus, put me back on the Community Reapers roster to work the Lares gardens. I think everyone in the community should be on there. Otherwise we get out of touch."

Jana stared at Ari, her eyes wide with amazement. She glanced at Tia, who couldn't hide her knowing smile.

"Now, why weren't we putting these things together before?" Ari's voice became crisp and businesslike.

"What things?" Rhus looked blankly at Ari.

Ari stood, surveying the group, then gestured to people with his cane as he spoke. "Megadroughts, foreclosures, drylands and biodynamic techniques, hands-on manpower, education, put them together. Problem solved."

"You're crazy!" Gavin exploded out of his silence, striding the few paces to the table. "It doesn't work like that. You don't just blast in there and fix it overnight. You city folk don't know what you're talking about. I worked with a CSA in Goleta, my uncle farms in the Cuyama Valley, my buddy's entire family farms in the Fresno area. People have been trying to change this industrial trend in American agriculture for more than my entire lifetime and nothing's ever come of it! You don't understand politics!"

Ari began pacing the flagstone patio, yanking an autumn leaf from a peach tree. He smashed the yellowed leaf in his fist, yet his voice was carefully controlled. "So they tried before and didn't succeed, so what? We don't give up. We keep on trying. Maybe our approach is a little bit different, maybe we find a more advantageous political climate, maybe we just get lucky. There could be a million maybes and a million differences between our approach and those that failed. Maybe ours will fail too. But that doesn't mean we shouldn't try. If we have a passionate desire to see this dream happen, we have to go for it. Not just dream it and sit quietly on that dream, but put it into action, bring it alive in the world. Someday, sometime, someone will be able to bring about the changes."

He paused, looking at the leaf in his palm. His face contorted as he straightened and flattened the leaf, his voice quiet now. "It's not up to us to complete the task, only to do our part. Even if my efforts don't come to fruition, my failure will become the mulch, the compost for the next man's attempt to bring this dream alive."

He set the peach leaf down on the table in front of Gavin, then turned and limped down the garden path, leaning heavily on his cane. Tia looked anxiously after him.

In stunned silence, Gavin slumped into a chair, staring at the leaf. The breeze lifted it and he instinctively reached out to prevent its flying away. Once he had touched the leaf he didn't seem to be able to release it, smoothing it with his fingers repeatedly as Ari had.

"So he's saying ..." Rhus tried to comprehend.

"That we should pull together an educational program!" Jana said in delight. "We already have experience with this, we've been doing it for years, here and at the triplex. Now it's just slightly different students. Just wait till I tell Esperanza!"[87]

"For something this big, we'd probably have to set up a formal foundation or a nonprofit organization," Tia said.

"Maybe Carl can locate a grant to get us started," Steve said. He gave Jana a final squeeze and left the patio.

"We need a good name. Andy Lipkis' organization calls themselves T.R.E.E.S. We could be R.O.O.T.S.: ReVisioning Opportunities for Open Territories through Sustainability. Roots hold the topsoil, prevent wind erosion and desertification." Jana grinned.

Tia heard commotion from the house doors behind her. Annis joined the scene, on the arm of a skinny, pale looking boyfriend. She kissed Tia and did a brief round of introductions. "This is Oran."

Ari's garden pacing brought him back toward the patio. He spotted Oran and Annis, a dark look came over his face and he abruptly changed course, vanishing into the house.

Gavin stood, watching the new arrivals across the table. The peach leaf had vanished, but Tia found a glint of yellow peeking from Gavin's pocket.

"Who are you?" Annis eyed Gavin scathingly.

"A guest of Jana's, we have business," he replied coolly, meeting Annis' glare.

"You could get on with it," Annis snapped.

Oran looked very uncomfortable, hands shoved in pockets.

"And you could use some manners," Gavin said. He took his time sitting back down, turning to Jana to ask her a technical question about their class series. Jana began a lengthy reply.

Annis shook her head in irritation. "Seeds. Boring."

"Annis!" Tia began.

Annis tossed her hair, draping herself around Oran. Her eyes were on Gavin. "Come on, Oran, let's take a walk in the orchards."

(11.)

Later that evening, as Tia entered their bedroom, Ari was reading on his Sliver. She closed the door firmly, although Annis was not in the house, still being out with Oran.

"Ari, we need to talk about Annis."

"What about her." His voice was flat, darkness descending upon his expression.

"You know what about. You intentionally didn't come back to the patio."

He didn't answer, curling his fist around his crippled finger, the scowl now firm upon his face.

"Why do you do that?" It burst out of her. "What is it about your hand!?"

"It's life's permanent reminder of what can happen when I get out of control."

"Don't talk riddles to me. What happened? All these years and you never would say!"

He met her eyes, his face was cold, his eyes dark and stony. "I nearly killed a man once."

"You what!?"

"You heard me. I lost control."

"Enough of the secrets, out with it!"

His eyes were directed toward her face but she could tell he was seeing a very different scene. "I would have killed the bastard, if Jana hadn't stopped me. She was screaming, eventually it got through to me. But I was still full of it. So I started punching the wall. Pounded a big hole in it, until my fist was bloody raw, broke my finger. If it hadn't been for Jana that would have been him, his filthy little face."

Tia's blood ran chill. *Ari just wasn't violent, he wasn't*, she insisted to herself.

"So there it is," his jaw set, he stared at his hand, pressing the cursed finger into submission, "the reminder of what I did to another human being, of the despicable acts of which I'm capable. When I get pissed, and I make a fist, the damn thing clicks inside, it doesn't work right, it gets my attention."

"What did he do to you?"

"Nothing."

Her eyes widened.

"Then why did you ..."

"He hurt Jana."

"What did he do to her?"

"Beat her ..." he winced. His voice dropped to a whisper. "Raped her."

He continued tearing at his hand, more and more viciously, as if he could wring the memories out of it. "She called me crying for help, she was in terrible condition. He came back before I got her out of there.

He took a swing at me." His hand flew to his jaw. "I lost it. I just saw Jana's face, all bruised and bloody. I hit him, again and again. I couldn't stop pounding him. He went down, I followed him. He was begging for me to stop, pleading, and still I ... I couldn't stop!" He closed his eyes, his face tortured.

"But you did stop, Ari," she whispered.

He shook his head, deep within the pain of the memory. "She was screaming ..."

"The guy, what happened to him?"

"I have no idea. I took Jana home, left him lying there, bawling on the carpet.

"I tried to get Jana to report it, but she denied it all. He never reported me – sure could have, but with what he did to her, I guess he was afraid to. Yet all that time at DOE, I expected this story to come out, somehow it never did.

"Jana was a mess. And now I fear the same thing could happen to Annis!" He crushed his hands to his face with such power his shoulders bulged. "She's doing exactly what Jana did, all these men. She's not being smart, who knows what they might do to her?"

"Why would Jana ..." Tia began softly.

"My dad, it all started when Dad died. I guess she just needed him."

His head raised slowly and he looked at Tia, his eyes wide with realization. "Her dad. Oh God, that's me."

Then he deflated, sighing and shaking his head, his shoulders curled in defeat. "She doesn't want anything from me," His voice broke. "I'm that fucking legend."

(12.)

Ari's messages from the Geneva Conference were more frequent and soul-searching than any set of conference correspondence Tia had ever received from him.

> tdamek@lares.net
> The Pre-Sessional Consultations begin tomorrow. I see now that Fordon was courageous and perhaps a bit reckless, to have included me on the U.S. team. My tarnished reputation precedes me, and I have a long journey ahead of rebuilding trust, particularly with long-standing associates. Some avoid me like I have a dread illness, others seek me out privately

trying to learn the inside story. To all I say: examine my track record, look at my actions, judge for yourself. I can't make it better by slathering it with some pretty story. I'm living the consequences of my choices. But through it all I am here to do a job that is much bigger than all of those history reviews, a job with a view toward the future. A.

adamek@lares.net
Ari, darling, Lori Fordon may have been reckless, but it's clear that she knows your value. She's wise at negotiations and I'm sure she knows what you will contribute. You have always been so able to look forward rather than back. This talent will get you through these trials as well. Carry on, the world is waiting for you. All my love, Tia

tdamek@lares.net
Do I hear the ice melting on your opinions of Fordon!? She is a clever leader and is pressing for a solid agenda here. Meanwhile, Kegan is wide-eyed at his first foray into international sessions. A.

tdamek@lares.net
I understand now why Fordon wanted me on this team. Developmental Assistance has become the major issue in the realm of emissions treaties negotiation, yet it overlaps substantially with what we are trying to accomplish in the Sustainability treaty negotiations. The time has come to merge the two. Back in 2002 a South African Minister suggested such synthesis but the world was not yet ready. The Sustainability treaty, particularly resource efficiency, is the perfect umbrella under which to bring all these issues together. A.

(13.)

The morning Ari returned from Geneva, Tia was harvesting plums. He joined her in her walk to the orchard, carrying the harvest baskets for her.

"Geneva was quite interesting. International treaties before Barcelona had been a problem-defined approach: a CFC problem lead to a CFC treaty; a greenhouse gas problem lead to Kyoto.

"Barcelona and the Sustainability effort was our first venture toward solving the underlying issues, rather than just doing damage control on the symptoms. The Sustainability effort became solidified around the concept of resource efficiency: how efficiently did we use each resource, how little waste, how little pollution." He stopped, watching her. "Why aren't you removing the plums the birds left half-eaten?"

"I'm hoping those ones will distract them. Maybe they'll return to the ruined plums instead of ripping apart more good ones."

He continued. "Just prior to Geneva, Fordon and a few others on the international emissions teams realized that as emissions negotiations became less about infighting and carbon caps, the new effort in emissions control – Developmental Assistance – had a lot in common with our Sustainability efforts."

"Developmental Assistance is those projects in underdeveloped countries?"

"Exactly. Helping less developed nations grow their standard of living in a cleaner, less carbon-based route. But the wealthy nations kept sidestepping their funding obligations.

"Over in the Sustainability arena, poverty can be viewed as a resource inefficiency. With the wealthy nations already committed to Factor 4, it's all part of the same package, not a separate item for negotiation. So the hope is to merge the efforts toward a successor to Moscow with the Athens Accord Sustainability treaty."

"Aren't the parties to these two treaty efforts different?"

"Not really. The players are pretty much the same nations. Countries who wish to work together to create one unified world seem to participate in international efforts, whether that be emissions or Sustainability. Certainly there are a few impoverished nations who cannot afford to send delegates to either."

"But nothing like the U.S. overt resistance of the turn of the century."

"Thankfully that nightmare is nearly behind us. Elliott brought us back to the table, and everything Alden has done has built international connections ..." He lapsed off.

"How was that aspect of Geneva?" she asked quietly.

He drew a deep breath. "Tough, really tough. A few angry words. Many more barbed silences. The U.S. cheated on emissions, I was the designated fall guy and then I show up at emissions negotiations barely a year later. The U.S. is still distrusted, a legacy of the Bush era which the efforts of two Presidents have been unable to fully erase. I was the recipient of that distrust … and even hatred …" He shrugged, and gestured to the ruined plums still in the tree. "Decoys, distractions."

She picked another plum, only to discover it was a bird-opened one, its tender insides exposed and vulnerable.

He drew his shoulders back, his jaw hardened with resolve. "It worked. President Alden is making fine progress in regaining the U.S. position as a world leader toward a greater good. By the end of the conference a few of them saw my true intentions." He set the baskets down and limped slowly down the path alone.

(14.)

By the late 2020s the huge industrial farming operations were in deep trouble. Governmental subsidies were no longer forthcoming, and petitions for disaster aid were being delayed.

The aquifers were depleted in many locations, and clearly a limited resource in others. Weather patterns had changed, leaving these farms without the rainfall to which they had been accustomed. Shifts in the jet stream brought differing growing season temperatures – warmer in some areas and cooler in others.

A super strain of verticulum wilt developed in eastern Tennessee, wiping out tomato crops for several years running. Locust swarms, commonly known as grasshoppers, a pest typical of drought conditions, were sufficiently problematic to merit study by NASA. Hybrid varieties of main crops proved intolerant of the changes in growing conditions.

Industrial crop yields were dismal and financial losses mounted. GMO royalties went unpaid, so lawsuits erupted. Peripheral industries such as shipping and packing experienced layoffs.

As the foreclosures and abandonments began, dust bowl circumstances and desertification threatened the vast stretches of untended lands.

(15.)

tdamek@Lares.net
Here in New York at this MOP meeting for the Athens Accord I realize how long I have been away – it's been nearly half a decade, four years of MOP meetings, and so much has changed. Geneva raised the issue of merging the emissions issue with the

Sustainability negotiations. Now delegates are considering bringing in other international treaties as well. It seems so logical to consider Sustainability – particularly the resource efficiency concept of Factor 4 – to be the 'umbrella' under which most international agreements reside: environment, health, trade. It seems that this umbrella concept will be the big issue for the WCSD in 2032. Through it all, I have never given up on Factor 10. A.

(16.)

Tia awoke to a strange sound, muffled sobbing, from somewhere out on the Lares grounds. The sound of someone's quiet pain continued, so she slipped out of bed, quietly so as not to disturb Ari, and went to investigate. She followed the sound on paths well lit by moonlight.

Annis! She was squatting in the middle of the path, fetal-like, with Jana's assistant Gavin, of all people, sitting silently beside her.

Tia hurried to Annis and wrapped her in a hug. Annis buried her face in Tia's shoulder and her sobs intensified.

Gavin hadn't moved, and in hugging Annis, Tia could feel the oddity of Gavin's presence – not close enough for lover, but too close for stranger. Tia looked over at him and in the moonlight his expression certainly seemed like solemn concern.

"Come on, honey, let's go inside. It's 2:30 in the morning." Tia guided Annis to her feet and down the garden path toward the house.

Gavin followed them at a respectful distance. Tia glanced back at him as she reached the door of the house. He silently turned and headed away.

Ari was standing in the hall blinking sleepily as Tia opened the French doors into their private suite. Annis' sobs were silent now, but she was still crying desperately. Ari pulled his robe tighter around himself and held open the door to his daughter's room for them to pass. Tia sat with Annis on the edge of the bed. Annis was quieting down now. Tia stroked her hair.

Ari stood uncomfortably in the middle of the room. Annis had been so averse to his presence these months, yet it was clear he was loathe to leave them in this emotional scene. He shifted his weight and a floorboard creaked. Annis startled and looked up, her face tearstained. Tia felt Annis' body tense. Tia braced herself for the shouting bout.

It didn't come.

Tears streamed anew down Annis' face as she held Ari's gaze. Tia suddenly felt like an indecent observer, even as she sat alongside Annis, the connection between father and daughter across the room was so powerful.

Go to her, Ari! Tia's voice screamed in her head but she didn't dare make a sound. *Go to her! Swallow that pride and go to her!*

Ari squared his shoulders and stood taller, his dark eyes on Annis, full of pain and love.

No, no, no! Not more pride and distance!

But it was more as if he were steeling himself for what he had to do. Slowly, agonizingly slowly, he lifted one foot and took a step toward Annis.

That was all it took.

Annis flew across the room to him, curling into his stomach, hugging him, crying raw emotion. Ari looked down at her, his face contorted. His arms raised slowly as if to hug Annis, yet froze in mid air filled with the strangeness of it all.

"Hug me, Daddy, just hug me!"

Thus instructed, Ari did. He hugged Annis for all he was worth, his great shoulders hunched over, his face in her hair. Annis cried desperately, her broken heart unfolding.

Tia closed her eyes, in her mind feeling Ari's great hug as if it were around herself. Tears streamed down her face, tears of thanksgiving, of gratitude; tears of love for Ari that he found a way to do this.

As Tia opened her eyes, Annis was still crying, deep within Ari's arms. Tia thought back over the time since Mark's death, thought of Annis' helter-skelter path through recent life: the broken studies at college, the endless stream of young men. Her eyes rested on Annis' nightstand. Nearly a year and a half, and Mark's picture was still there, with a dried rose beneath it. Tears rolled down Tia's face as she stared at Annis.

Annis quieted and straightened. She drew her arms up around Ari's neck and kissed his cheek. In that moment, Ari's eyes connected with Tia's. His eyes were rich satisfaction, before he closed them to take in his daughter's hug.

Instinctively, Tia stood and made way for them, as Ari tucked Annis into bed, tenderly, as if she were five, not twenty-one. He straightened and turned, his hand fumbling to grasp Tia's hand as they left their daughter's room.

(17.)

The next morning, Tia awakened alone; Ari had already risen. Tia dressed and started down the hall. At the sound of low voices from Annis' open doorway she paused, afraid of what she might discover.

Ari was sitting on the edge of Annis' bed, his arm around her shoulders, in mid-conversation.

"… Look for it. Some problem that calls to you, for you to make it your own to solve. When you find it, and dedicate yourself to it, it will help you make your choices. It will point the way."

"But Dad, I've made such a mess of things! School …"

"I know you'll be able to straighten that out."

"… and, well … other things…"

Ari drew a long breath, his jawline tensed, his head held a notch higher. His eyes flitted to the doorway realizing Tia's silent presence. She nodded assurance to him and slipped silently back into the shadows of the hall.

"Annis, a long time ago someone I love very much was doing what you are doing right now. All these boyfriends, fooling around. One day one of them attacked her. He beat her, he…"

"It was Jana, wasn't it," Annis cut in. "She told me about it a few years ago. I wondered, why was she telling me this? But how did you know about it, Dad? She said she never told anyone but Steve!"

"She didn't tell you that part?" Ari took his arm from Annis' shoulders, and leaned forward, his elbows on his knees, clenching and unclenching his fist.

"She told me he hit her, he was violent. What does this have to do with me? I never had anything to do with the violent ones."

"We all are," he said quietly, "at some level. Annis, I knew about Jana because I was there; she was hurt so badly she called me for help. It seems she kindly didn't tell you my part in the story. Annis, I beat him. I beat the crap out of him for what he did to her. I nearly …" Ari seized Annis' hand and put it across his crippled one. He slowly made a fist against her palm, "Feel it? It's real. It took Jana more than ten years to get back to normal life." He kept flexing his hand, looking at it in revulsion.

"We think our choices are all ours. But in truth our choices affect many others around us." Suddenly, Ari grabbed Annis in a huge hug, sweeping her against his chest. "Annis, Annis…" he rocked her slowly. "I believe in you. You're going to do great things with your life."

"I love you, Daddy." Her voice was muffled against his shoulder.

Tia silently slipped down the hall.

⋙

Jana was mixing batter for zucchini bread as Tia entered the kitchen. "Oh, thank goodness you're here! These need to get baking and I have to prepare for our 10 a.m. class."

Just then Gavin entered at the glass door. His eyes met Tia's briefly, his face unsmiling, almost pained. He looked as if he hadn't slept. He sighed deeply and sat down at the table with Jana to go over class materials.

Ari and Annis soon joined Tia in the kitchen, Tia handing them cups of peppermint tea.

Annis caught sight of Gavin and froze. "Oh no! Mom, what's he doing here?" she whispered.

"Working with Jana, I believe," came Tia's automatic response.

Annis stared at her teacup. A look of horror crept across her face. "I'll eat breakfast later." She dashed back up the hall toward her room.

Gavin's eyes were glued to the doorway through which she had fled.

(18.)

"Esperanza absolutely loves the ROOTS idea!" Jana declared, flying through the South House kitchen. It was now early spring; the days were warming yet the winter season harvest remained plentiful.

"We need to look into other organizations doing this," Tia washed spinach in a strainer over the greywater sink as Ari brought in another basketful from the garden.

"That's easy." Seventeen year old Seth already had a pile of tangerine peels in front of him and was reaching for more of the tiny fruit. "There are apprenticeship programs through ATTRA, SAREP, Mariposa, Ecology Action and Snakeroot."[88] He shrugged in response to Tia's inquiring glance. "I did a little research. Dad's already called some of them. You know, you really don't have to do much teaching, you could just network the resources which are already out there."

Tia gaped at him.

"Steve told me this morning the Land Trust people have contacts where more skilled farmers are needed." Jana said over her shoulder as she joined Gavin at the table.

"Terrific! We'll end up supporting and supplementing efforts that already exist, rather than fragmenting people's efforts with something new," Tia said.

"This is all great but you still have the industrial farms, the remaining farming subsidies, the agricultural disaster relief system," said Gavin.

"And ..." Ari waited.

"Someone has to deal with the political issues!" Gavin insisted. "There shouldn't be subsidies at all – look at New Zealand, how well they do without them. The agricultural disaster relief should be tied into the climate projections so that our government's not funding the drought-doomed areas into perpetuity."[89]

Seth looked from Ari to Gavin, grinning, shoving another tangerine in his mouth while watching the show.

Ari raised one eyebrow, still looking at Gavin. "Sounds like we need to take a little road trip, learn what we are dealing with. Gavin, how about it? You know the technical end. And I know a thing or two about what can be done with the politics."

(19.)

Tia lounged at the railing of the South House deck sipping a glass of limeade; somehow she couldn't drink limeade without thinking of her mother.

The spring breezes fluttered Tia's skirt and she had a sudden memory of the wind of San Marcos Pass, the feeling of its gusts pressing her body and whipping her skirt, the fragile ashes disappearing from her fingers. *Goodbye Mom, Dad. You're together again.* She had whispered to them. *Together forever.* Tears filled her eyes.

She relived the final time she had seen her father: his last hug, casual, with the presumption that they would see each other again soon. *Never. Never again.*

She hadn't even seen his body. "There wasn't enough left," an ashen faced Cassandra had told Tia.

I can't even imagine.

Ari approached behind her. "Willard's latest push is for soil sequestration ..." He continued but Tia wasn't listening.

DC. Brutal attacks, yet we got off easy, darling. You're still alive.

Alive. A relative word, that. Particularly in those days at Coyote Creek. He was barely alive. We're still regrouping.

She snuggled up against him, desperately needing to feel the solidness of his touch.

"... so he's working with the Secretary of Agriculture ..."

Soil sequestration. "Sounds a bit like ROOTS," Tia murmured.

"Willard's approach is policy based ..."

Policy. What it cost us to get that Policy. Tia's mind returned to the DC days, the horror of the accident, the waves of scandal. *Emissions, photoremediation ...*

"... but then the plans for ROOTS could be said to be policy-forming ..." Ari seemed to be agreeing.

Photoremediation, ROOTS, soil sequestration. That's it!

"Ari, I'm giving Dad's stock to ROOTS."

"You're what?"

"If you don't think I should, please advise me. But if I give it to ROOTS, it can do some good out in the world."

"That's a sizeable chunk, particularly after Willard's contract."

"Yes, but, well, we have enough." Tia gestured to Lares around them. "Sufficiency."

"This is your dad's company. Are you sure you want to let it go?"

"What is more fitting? Dad's stock funding Mom's seeds."

"I think it's a wonderful idea, particularly when you explain it that way."

The Permaculture Flower... She suddenly realized the answer to the puzzle of decades. *They worked different petals toward the same goal. The ties that bound them together!*

"Shared purpose," her thoughts crossed her lips in a whisper.

"Yes!" he said in excitement. "Precisely." Ari wrapped her in a warm hug.

"I wish I had thought of this back when you were still in DC – it could have saved you some of that ..."

Ari pulled away from her, turning to look out across the gardens, his arms folded across his chest. It was a long moment before he spoke.

"But then the world still wouldn't know that there are solutions to nuclear waste, the answers would still be swept under the rug. Their slander campaign backfired, you realize. They meant to oust me, but along the way they publicized the very secret they didn't want the public to know."

But then they would have thought of something else to stop you. We know how they escalate. We're so lucky you got out in time.

Tia walked to him and rested her cheek against his shoulder. He automatically stroked her hair, his focus still distant across the gardens.

After a while he pulled her around to face him. "Tia, it's an incredibly generous gift. It will fund ROOTS for many years, the way Carl manages finances. It will make great things possible." His eyes were rich and tender, inches from hers.

(20.)

The call came from Alden's staff, not from the President. That, Tia knew, was crushing in itself. Ari's face in an instant had regained that drawn grey expression.

"He wants me there for the signing, Tia."

Shouldn't this be joyous? He's ratifying your Athens Accord, Ari!

But she knew it was the return to DC that he dreaded.

"Should I go with you?"

He waved her away trying to say with a gesture what he couldn't bring to his lips. Still he boarded the plane alone.

The Sliver was busy. Tia loathed the video phone, feeling it to be such an invasion of privacy. She usually turned off the screen, unless it was Ari. Even then, it was small comfort, because in the grainy display she couldn't read his face like she did in person.

"I hate this, Tia. I'm holed up in a hotel room, I have no appointments, no business here. I shouldn't be here. I don't belong anymore."

She could see the background whizzing by behind his face as he paced the room.

"It's only for another day, Ari. The signing is tomorrow. Stick it out. You'll regret it if you don't go."

"You're right, but it's the between times that are killing me."

⁓

Tia didn't hear from Ari after the signing, to the verge of worry. He arrived home on schedule, however. On his first evening back at Lares, they took a walk out through the grounds along the delightful little pond and brook, the reeds of which quietly filtered the complex's greywater and rendered it pure.

Ari was walking briskly now and swung his cane as a punctuation mark to his conversation points. "For the signing, I was across the room, not like for the Moscow Treaty. I suppose they didn't want the press to catch sight of me. But afterward ... the President called me in." A small smile played at the corner of his mouth. "It was good to see him." The smile split his face in a broad grin. Ari squared his shoulders and stood that much taller.

"Alden helped me understand a lot about my time in DC. He reminded me that we all work together in this battle. No one person can do it all, although I gave it one hell of a try. Rather, we each do our part and pass the baton to the next guy. In the end it's the sum total of all the individual efforts that makes the big difference."

Ari stopped and turned to face Tia on the path, his voice rich with sincerity. "You did your part too. You weren't out there in front of Congress, your name wasn't on the org chart. But you contributed so much to the cause. You kept me going through all the insanity they sent my way. I couldn't have done it without your support."

He took her into his arms, his eyes very dark and glistening in the setting sun. "That Policy – our nation's new direction – it's every bit as much your doing as it is Willard's and Alden's and mine. Thank you."

He kissed her, and her silent tears rolled down her cheeks, down her neck.

As they resumed their walk, at a slower pace now, his strong arm held her close. The first stars appeared, together with a slender moon. The silhouettes of the fruit trees made beautiful filigree across the sunset sky, and the air was full with the sweetness of Life.

(21.)

Annis' study materials for her American Art History final were spread all over the South House office. Since the night in the garden, the night of reconciliation with Ari, Annis had refocused on her studies, and, to Tia's relief, there had been no more young men appearing on her arm. Tia picked up the photos and books, carrying them to Annis' room to pile them neatly on the nightstand.

Exiting, Tia reached the door of the room before she realized the nightstand had been empty. Mark's picture was gone. She sighed in relief.

Her heart lighter, she went out into to the garden to transplant the new batch of tomato seedlings. The warm May sun felt delicious, and the cool soil around the baby plants presented a tactile contrast as she eased them into the circular bed. Bees hummed in the blanket roses at the corner of the path, and the air was full with the flowers' fruity scent. With Annis back on track, Ari contemplating another thrilling mission, Cassandra's manuscript now on the publisher's desk, and ROOTS coming into being all around her, Tia breathed in deep satisfaction with life.

Sufficiency.

Lines from the old Donella Meadows essay came to Tia, mingled with images from Annis' Art History materials.

Scarcity. The Dorothea Lange photo, the woman grasping her infant, hungry children in the background, a haunted, helpless look on her face.

Abundance. The rosy cheeks and plump roundness, opulent plenty of the Norman Rockwell Thanksgiving. America has internalized this as its theme song. It is fantasy, yet we regard it as the norm, the standard, the expectation.

Who is the artist of Sufficiency? Among the pile of visual images Tia had gathered from the office floor, not a single one seemed to fit. *We have no image for it, we don't have a vision we can embrace. No wonder it is so difficult.*

Enough of the dark angst, the gnashing teeth and grinding innards. We need something noble, that inspires, that embodies the joy of it. Where are the Change Agents and Transformers of the art world?

Tia breathed in the air of roses again, feeling the sunshine on her arms, hearing the mockingbird in the nearby peach tree. She felt again the joy of her family and the purposefulness of her circle of friends. She smiled, a gentle smile that embraced all of these things, and life's wonder in general.

(22.)

"What can we city dwellers do to support these agricultural changes?" Lauren stated as she chopped chard at a furious pace in the South House kitchen. "That's the part of ROOTS which I want to focus on: consumer education."[90]

"There's so much that people in the cities can do about it," Tia replied as she broke fresh Lares eggs into a huge bowl. "Look, we already know the value of organics to our children and our health. That's simple."

"Explain the subsidy inequities and people will get behind that effort with letters to their Congressmen and their votes," Jana joined in.

"And farmers markets and CSAs – don't forget that one," Jana continued. "Many small farms support themselves through farmers markets or Community Supported Agriculture programs. Sometimes they sell subscriptions so they can assure a steady income to be able to stay in business. Consumers can participate in these different market routes rather than buying the industrial produce at the chain markets. And they can create farmers markets where none exist." Jana resumed washing dishes at the blackwater sink.

"We need to educate the city people to expect to pay a bit more for the small farm produce," Tia said. "People have become accustomed to paying so little for their food, with prices artificially brought down by agricultural subsidies, water subsidies and financial capital maximization by the mega-corp farms." She added feta and pinenuts to her bowl.

"And from those industrial farms we get what we pay for: little," Jana grumbled. "Little flavor, little nutrition, little variety ..."

"Supporting Land Trusts is another one," Tia continued. "Most Agricultural Land Trusts are nonprofit organizations, charities. They rely on contributions. People from the cities can give donations to support the preservation of these arable lands. That's going to become a big issue in a decade or so as climate change limits which areas will be productive. It would be horrible to have the land all taken up by urban sprawl in those few areas where the climate is good for agriculture!"

"Again, choices. City dwellers can make such a difference with their choices in financial capital," Lauren said quietly.

"There are now several urban agriculture programs like Esperanza's," Jana dried the large baking dishes. "City folk can help support those efforts through volunteerism, purchasing, contributions, and through participating in the community garden projects, like our kids did."

Lauren heaped the chard into Tia's bowl for mixing as Jana buttered the baking dishes.

"We raise the awareness of the city people, while Steve brings in the networks..." Tia grinned as she scooped the contents of the mixing bowl into Jana's baking dishes. Lauren held open the oven.

"Together. We'll get it done together."

(23.)

"We've been having fun," Ari announced over the videophone. Even through the annoying display, Tia could see his grin. "We've been up through Washington, Oregon, hooking around through Idaho, Montana, Nebraska, Kansas and Oklahoma. We met with people from the Environmental Working Group and the Kerr Center, and more local farmers than I can count. Tomorrow we're taking a minor detour over to DC."

"DC!? What's there?" Tia exclaimed.

"Education, my dear. I'm giving the boy a bit of education about how the political process works. He seems to be under the mistaken impression that results are impossible. We have lunch tomorrow with Diamont. Gavin will learn."

Tia laughed aloud. "You're beating him over the head with this."

"Now I wouldn't say it that way," Ari's voice was rich with humor. "I'm just bringing him up right. It seems that he needs to learn how to believe."

His tone became serious yet the joy was still in it. "He'll come home with some pretty powerful contacts. And just between you and me, I think the political climate is perfect for this campaign. Gavin's going to realize results beyond his dreams."

(24.)

Mature fruit trees meant abundant harvests. In the Lares kitchen, Tia and Annis prepared peaches for the dehydrator racks.[91] As Tia rinsed the peaches, rubbing to remove the down, her eyes rested on Saffi's crystal dish with its contents of light brown creek sand. As always, the sight of it brought a smile to her face.

Annis sliced peaches as she spoke.

"I'll finish with a degree in Marine Biology, but all the courses I took in Political Science won't hurt. I'm applying down in San Diego at Scripps for my masters, I hope to get into their fall 2028 program. Meanwhile, for this semester I'm trying to set up an independent studies on the intertidal drift with sea level rise. There's a group of us trying to get approval for the project. I'll do the wetlands; there are others doing the tidepools and the land use aspects."

"This doesn't sound like a single semester's effort," Tia commented.

"Oh, but of course it's not! We're just starting there. It'll be easier to make something more of it, get grants and stuff, once we have the teams working together and the class on our curriculum vitae."

Tia's jaw dropped in amazement. *She clearly is Ari's daughter. She already has that long range vision.*

"With the change in shoreline from sea level rise, the old lines between sea and marsh, and between freshwater and saltwater wetlands, are all changing."

Tia thought back to the salt-burned shrubs nearly a decade ago at the Malibu Lagoon.

"In a perfect world, nature would adjust slowly, sediment accretion would take place, and new plants would seed in the appropriate places, forming fertile new wetlands as the sea advanced. But with climate change, the whole timeframe speeds up. Plus humans are in the way, with roads and buildings and seawalls and breakwaters and artificial marinas."

Don't you mess with my breakwater! Tia joked privately.

"Sure, the SEZ30 and SEZ40 designations will help pull back the human activity, but we've messed it up pretty good. So our team wants to build artificial wetlands and tidepools as sea level rise progresses – breeding grounds for the creatures of the Bay. Eventually we want to push the State to build manmade salt and freshwater wetlands forward of the sea's rise.[92] That means fighting the land use battles, working within the SEZ designations, and getting some kind of funding for the restoration. Mom, the pits go in the compost, the fruit goes on the rack!"

In her amazement at her daughter's discussion, Tia had reversed the process her hands were following.

"Mom, do you think he even knows I'm alive?"

Unprepared for the change of subject, Tia swung around to look at Annis. Gone was the proud and purposeful lecturer. Annis' hands were shaking as she put down her paring knife, her downturned face hidden in her shoulder length dark hair.

"Gavin talks to me, just like to any of you around here, but that's it. He's never done anything more."

You mean he hasn't hopped into bed with you, like all the others, Tia thought bitterly.

"This is a good thing, honey. Give it time." Tia paused, then asked the question that had been eating at her for months. "Honey, what happened between you two that night in the garden?"

Annis' eyes became distant, losing herself to the memory. "Well, I was kind of crazy back then. He was staying in the vacant unit – in Mark's room. I couldn't stand it. It felt disrespectful, indecent!

"I wanted to – I don't know what – drive him away, destroy him or something. I went over there in the middle of the night to ..." In unthinking motion she reached for the next peach in the bowl, fondling it sensually.

She dropped the peach suddenly, its sweet ripeness bruised and abandoned on the counter. "No. Not like this, he told me. It won't be like this. He walked me home like some little child. Oh God, what a mistake!" She burst into tears and ran to her room.

(25.)

Ari and Gavin returned from their national tour in late autumn. The leaves of the Lares peaches and pomegranates were again yellow and while the afternoons were warm, the evening's chill drove the families indoors. Annis cooked the meal this evening, a lively Jamaican chicken dish with the season's first collards, sweet and fresh from the gardens.

"It's a full life," Steve declared in cheery satisfaction. He pushed back from the table, intertwining his fingers behind his head, his sandy red hair now heavily silvered. "This City remodel contract has been extended to the County. We'll be on it for another two years at least. Between that and ROOTS, I have my hands full."

"ROOTS – let's hear from our travelers," Jana invited, curling into Steve's arms.

"Gavin, would you care to give them your version?" Ari asked.

Gavin was seated a bit apart from the others, not particularly focused on the group conversation. *He's focused on the cook!*

Gavin pulled himself to attention and began. "Well, the blossoming of the Great Plains that took place as a result of the aquifer will become merely a history lesson. Much of what we have become accustomed to there will no longer prosper: industrial farm crops, water-rich cities. We will be forced to remember that it truly is a semi-arid area.

"It's also becoming obvious that climate forecasts don't guarantee smooth sailing. While the computer projections might show a given area will get water, it may come in the form of severe storms: hurricanes, tornadoes. We just don't know.

"Add to all this mix a bunch of unknowns: pests and plant diseases. We're already seeing the mosquito population shift, and there have been some grasshopper invasions."

"Tell them about DC, too," Ari prompted.

Gavin reddened slightly. "Here's where I eat my humble pie. I learned a thing or two about making big changes. I had no idea who I was dealing with." His eyes turned to Ari. "Thanks, for a life lesson."

Ari smiled and gave him a slight nod.

Gavin continued reflectively. "This trip was a chance for me to take a look at the resources I have. I didn't realize I knew so many people, or knew people who knew so many people. Our circles of influence can be surprising, if we just pause to take count of who we know. The vast number of lives we can touch, in spreading an idea, the power we wield to bring change to the world – it's truly incredible.

"I'm not sure how it came to be that I met up with you all, you city movers and shakers, me from the farm areas and all. It's like I'm the connection point between two huge worlds. And because of that, well, there's a tremendous amount I can do. A tremendous amount I have to do. The changes have got to happen. And it's up to me to do something about it." His voice eased off into thought.

The others let him sit with the moment. Most of them had felt this at one point or another.

Tia looked over at Annis. She was poised in the kitchen, gazing longingly at Gavin, hanging on every word he said. Her cheeks glistened with tears.

(26.)

FRENCH HEAT TOLL 'COULD TOP 5,000'

EL NIÑO SPURS RISE IN GLOBAL AVERAGE SEA LEVEL

SEVERE FLOODS KILL 127 IN INDIA

NATIONAL PARK'S NAMESAKE GLACIERS – GONE!

(27.)

Moss Bainbridge, the new owner of what had previously been the Goodman unit, drew Community Reaper duty with Ari and Tia. On this mid-summer day Tia collected lettuce and leek seedheads which Rhus had tagged earlier in the season, then Ari and Moss bundled drying stalks and foliage into carts to be chipped and composted, bringing mature compost back on the return trip. As they worked, Moss told them about water issues in California.

"Until recently the water districts made their plans based on historical supply figures. They didn't figure climate change into their calculations at all."

Tia gasped. "They didn't even consider it?"

"Yup," Moss nodded grimly. "They figured more storage and conveyance facilities would solve all our water supply problems.

"We in the NGOs fought their plans tooth and nail each step of the way – each massive new dam or aqueduct project proposed.[93] Sure these projects made sense if historical supply were going to continue. But it was ridiculous to invest in such expensive fixed-location long-term projects when climate change scientists were predicting changes in rainfall patterns, season length, warming trends, shifts in snowpack.

"On paper our LA water comes from three main sources – from the Southern Sierra Nevadas via the Owens River Valley and the Los Angeles Aqueduct; from the Rocky Mountains via the Colorado River and the States Water Project; and from 'groundwater.' But that last one is misleading, although we do pull water from the ground beneath LA. With so much LA land covered in concrete and asphalt, we've had very little local collection despite all our El Niño storms. For decades now, we have replenished our 'groundwater' with imported water from Owens or Colorado."

"So it's not really groundwater, is it?" Ari confirmed.

"Not in the traditional sense, no, it's really warehoused imported water. And now with sea level rise, the balance has to be very carefully managed: if we don't maintain sufficient fresh water in the underground aquifers, seawater comes in and contaminates our groundwater. They've been fighting this problem in Hermosa, San Pedro and Los Alamitos since the 1950s, but the intrusion issue has become far more significant now with sea level rise."

"If seawater gets in there, it salts our soils, right?" Tia guessed.

"Yes, agricultural issues, urban forestry issues, plus salt can cause health problems as well." Moss stood to mop his brow and reseat his wide-brimmed hat. "In the earlier decades of this century, we had significant wet weather patterns here in the southern part of the state. Now those are shifting, and projections for the 30s through the 90s are for much dryer times.[94]

"We already pull the maximum we can out of Owens. LA had to pay them remunerations for drought hardships, when we pulled too much out of there. So Owens is maxed out as a source.

"Colorado river water has been in dispute for decades, as Arizona grew. At this point, very little water reaches Mexico. Yet the States Water Project is heavily dependent upon that as a source. And they're predicting that with temperature rise, the Colorado watershed will yield far less streamflow.

"Up in the Central Valley they have relied on multiple streams and minor rivers coming off the Sierra Nevadas. Now the snowpack is shifting to the south, and their supply will be severely curtailed.

"In the Sacramento-San Joaquin River basin, we're seeing more winter runoff with flooding, and less summer runoff with resulting drought conditions. As climate change progresses, this situation will intensify, plus higher temperatures will increase evaporation, reducing streamflow and lake levels.

"It's not only supply problems," Moss continued, reaching for the shovel. "We have had an appropriation system which contains outdated features. There are beneficial use standards which severely limit the way water can be used because the state has narrowly defined the uses, with heavy biases in favor of historical uses like agriculture and ranching.[95]

"Additionally, we have a provision that water rights can be lost if they are not put to use, often called the use-it-or-lose-it rule. Clearly this type of requirement discourages conservation. Add to that our agricultural water subsidies and it's quite a complex issue."

"So what do we do about it?" Ari bundled dry stalks into the wheelbarrow.

"Lots of folks are pushing for water markets, a system whereby property rights to water can be bought and sold. Proponents claim it will balance supply versus demand, and will promote water conservation."

"You sound hesitant," Ari observed.

"Back in 2002 in a World Conference in Johannesburg," Moss paused as Tia and Ari looked at each other, "I see you've heard of it."

"I was there."

"Oh wow! Well, in the side sessions they discussed the problems of privatizing the world's water supplies. Worldwide, privatization has proven lucrative for the corporations, and disastrous for poor residents who can't pay privatized rates. By setting water as a property right, we completely reject the idea that water is a common property belonging to all living creatures.[96]

"So yes, I'm cautious about water markets. Although trading water rights sounds like a great way to solve some of our water issues in California, if the system isn't wisely designed, we've only created another problem."

(28.)

In late May, the approval came through for Annis' wetlands project. She was thrilled, and invited her team of fellow students to Lares for a celebration on the large patio.

Turning house and kitchen over to the young people, Tia took a book out to one of the garden benches. She could see the young people at a distance through the dainty branches of the currants, yet the sounds of their carefree laughter made Tia feel melancholy.

The Lares youth had grown up here together. Janelle was now off to college, independent, not likely to return; Peter, gone permanently; Seth, likely soon to fly. Even Verity and Carl's sons were entering their teens.

Tia recalled fondly the children searching the gardens for the chickens, the strawberry hunts, tiny hands planting fat bean seeds. The children lined up on chairs in the big Damek/Vernados kitchen, dishtowels clothes-pinned for aprons as they learned to cook. The deep satisfaction of a young head pressed against her arm as she read *The Garden in the City* to the youngers, or *The Secret Garden* to the olders.

I need to bring children back to Lares, to share the knowledge, to share the wonder.

Who is sharing with whom? Adults with children or children with adults? We need each other.

I'll ask Lauren. Perhaps we can do it together.

Tia heard the crunch of footsteps on the path. Gavin strode across the garden, toward South house, his path purposeful, as if he were headed for a meeting with Jana or Steve. Yet as Tia watched, Annis, laughing with her friends, ran to him, dragging him by the arm into the celebration.

⁓

That night, Gavin was absent from the South House dinner table. Annis babbled happily about the wetlands project and her celebration, but Tia saw her several times glance longingly toward the garden door.

As they cleared the dishes there was a knock on the glass garden door. Hands behind his back, Gavin formally waited for admittance, quite unlike his usual familiarity with the house. Annis flew to the door to open it.

Gavin smiled to her warmly. "*This* is how we begin." He pulled a rose from behind his back and handed it to her. Offering Annis his arm, he escorted her out into the moonlit garden.

Ari's eyes met Tia's across the room.

"He certainly has style," Ari said, grinning in approval.

"I remember a certain Legacy LA meeting. I know someone else who has a lot of style." She crossed the room to sit on the arm of Ari's chair.

Ari looked up at her, still grinning, his eyes deep and warm. "You had rather a delayed reaction, but it worked!"

He pulled her down onto his lap and kissed her, the sweetness of memory, the richness of years in his gesture.

(29.)

Tia and Lauren's children's classes were immediately popular. Parents participated along side their children, so that the knowledge could be brought to life at home. Tia's choice of subjects varied widely, from planting seedlings to cooking. With Lauren, participants observed wildlife and made nature journals. Each class finished with storytelling in the shade of the orchards.

Today they visited Jana's Permaculture zone 5, the wild zone of Lares. They sat on the ground, a thick carpet of natural leaf fall beneath them. At eye level the world looked different. The Tidy Tips towered overhead, their bright lemon daisy flowers waving gently in the breeze. A Buckeye butterfly frisked by. The air smelled fresh, of pungent white sage and delicate monardella mint. A hummingbird visited the deep tubular orange and red throats of the native lobelia.

"All of these plants are California natives," Tia said. "We selected them because they are the types that we think would have grown here before there was a city. That way the birds and butterflies and bugs have a place to call home."

Tia plucked a handful of mature seed from the Encelia, its fresh flowers the Blackeyed Susan of the canyons. A petite blond girl helped her. "Kaia, we look for seedheads that are dry and brown like this. Then you crumble the seeds into your hand and toss them to distribute." Nine year old Kaia eagerly imitated. "That way, more of these lovely flowers will grow in this area. Let's do the same with the fennel. Now, smell your hands."

"Licorice!" Kaia grinned. She returned to her mother's side, still savoring the plant oils on her hands.

Beneath the shelter of the drooping sycamore and malthocarpus it seemed unbelievable that they were sitting in the middle of the sixth largest city in the world.

"Now, be still; let's listen to the birds."

(30.)

Ari repaired a chicken dome, stretching wire with Carl's twelve year old son Walter, simultaneously answering Walter's questions about global warming. Tia attempted to salvage ruined young cabbage plants nearby.

"The CO_2 molecules – actually there are six targeted greenhouse gasses, but we usually focus in terms of CO_2 because it's the largest percentage of the problem – are released down here at the surface of the planet, say by an internal combustion engine. These carbon molecules had been contained, or sequestered, for millennia. They were last exposed to the atmosphere when they were part of some dinosaur's body. Now we burn the fossil fuel and release those previously sequestered carbon molecules. If the carbon molecules aren't sequestered again, say by growing trees – called a forest sink – or by agriculture that is intensive in the use of organic materials – called soil sequestration – then these CO_2 molecules rise into the upper atmosphere. It takes decades for the molecules to rise to the point where they do the ultimate damage.

"So in answer to your question, that's why planetary temperatures will continue to rise for quite some time even after we control emissions. That's why we need to curtail our imbalance of carbon emissions sooner rather than later – to allow for the time lag, without approaching a disastrous level of warming."

"Imbalance?" Walter asked.

"You caught that. Curtailing CO_2 emissions doesn't mean that we cannot emit anything, that's impossible. Life itself is a carbon flow. No, what we need to do is reach a point of *balance* where, when we release these previously sequestered carbon molecules – for instance burning a log on a campfire – we simultaneously sequester similar amounts.

Ari gestured to the nearby greywater garden hose. "Say I'm filling a bucket with water. The bucket is our model for our upper atmosphere; the stream of water is our CO_2 emissions. With a big sponge, I could soak up some of that water and prevent it from reaching the bucket. That sponge equates to carbon sequestration, in forests and soils.

"When we speak of 'decreasing emissions,' we're talking about turning down the valve so that we reduce the volume in the stream, simultaneously bringing out those big sponges, the net result being less water reaching our bucket. Right now the world continues to open that valve further; the stream of CO_2 emissions is still increasing. The big hope is that soon we will reverse that direction, tighten the valve, decreasing the volume of water streaming into the bucket by the year 2040.

"Sometime after we begin decreasing emissions, perhaps a few decades later, we should observe that the level of water in the bucket is no longer increasing; the atmospheric concentrations of CO_2 will have plateaued.

"If we can reduce emissions by 2040, the IPCC believes we should see a plateau in CO_2 concentrations around the year 2100, at which time temperatures will also plateau. Hopefully we can achieve all of this before that water level in the bucket gets so impossibly high that life on the planet cannot cope with it. There." Ari stood back from the repaired cage. "No more escapees."

Tia looked ruefully at the bed of young cabbages where yesterday the escaped hens had gleefully scratched and pecked, mutilating the tender plants.

Balance. The chickens are an essential part of our garden balance. We use their droppings, we use their eggs, we use their labor. They scratch through fresh spread compost to further break it down, distribute and turn it for us. But out of balance – too many chickens too long in one spot, or chickens roaming loose among tender seedlings – wreaks havoc.

Natural systems strike a balance: the food chain, the water cycle. When man interferes – by domesticating chickens, or unearthing fossil fuels – we must consciously re-create the balance by designing caged rotations, carbon sinks.[97]

A system out of balance is chaos and destruction. But ah, a system designed by man's ingenuity to allow the balance of nature to reestablish itself ... that indeed is Restoration.

(31.)

By the late 2020s the PLASE mass transit system was in widespread use. Small electric neighborhood vehicles recharged from local solar panels were used for short distance transportation within neighborhood pockets.

Carbon taxes and FFCC taxes had sent most of the older model automobiles to the recycling or retrofitting services. High-efficiency contemporary hybrid cars were used for longer trips, yet it was clear that even these would soon be replaced by the MagLev high speed rail.

Boulevards were quieter now, with no engine noises and significantly decreased vehicle volume. Parking lots, having been re-striped for the more compact neighborhood vehicles earlier in the decade, were now only partially used. Land was precious within the city's footprint and people began to question the amount of earth covered by blacktop.

Parking lots became mixed use buildings, small businesses below, with residential units atop. Boulevards were narrowed, to fewer traffic lanes. Esperanza's FarmUrb veterans became community leaders in encouraging the people to reclaim the land, teaching the power of human connection with the earth. The land regained from streets became community garden spaces and edible landscaping.[98]

Bike paths were no longer an afterthought lane pressed between rushing automobiles and parked cars. Bikes merited a separate roadbed, divided from the busses, jitneys and electric vehicles by foliage berms.

Roadway narrowing did not stop with the Boulevards. The latter portion of the 20th century had seen massive projects to widen Southern California freeways. Now, the late 2020s saw this land reclaimed. These massive stretches of land became landscaped CoHousing and FarmUrb greenbelts.

Decreasing asphalt coverage meant better permeability so that storm rains could replenish local groundwater. And decreasing blacktop meant less heat absorbed by acre upon acre of the earth's surface.

(32.)

Even Ari was surprised at the speed at which Gavin embraced the ROOTS political scene. Following the nationwide tour, Gavin worked with the Environmental Working Group campaigning to curtail federal agricultural disaster relief funds to chronically disaster-prone large farms.

Internal Revenue Service Hobby loss definitions for more than a half a century had delineated between a valid business and a pursuit unworthy of serious attention. These definitions required valid businesses to show a profit in three out of five years. In a unique crossover of federal provisions, these guidelines were now applied to agricultural disaster payment applicants. Farms unable to prove that they were a viable business enterprise were not permitted to apply.

Climate change forecasts were utilized and disaster aid was limited for farms located in areas forecast to become less productive in the coming decades. Non-qualifying applications were rejected. The massive corporations which had been major recipients of disaster aid checks in the past no longer qualified for federal funds.

These restrictions on system abuse freed up federal disaster funds for the truly needy farms: those subject to the whim of nature in areas where climate change forecasts were unclear.

(33.)

Construction of the California high speed rail system was well underway by the late 2020s.[99] There had been great debate at the turn of the century over the type of rail vehicle, advocating conventional high-speed trains, dismissing the MagLev induction motor as 'untried technology.' In the intervening years, MagLev trains had been performing brilliantly in Germany, Japan and Pennsylvania. California citizens turned to the future rather than the past.

MagLev construction meant special tracks, thus another overhaul of downtown LA around the crowded Union Station hub. Again, the City of Los Angeles was torn up with construction debris. Yet this time, few automobiles were displaced from the roads; so many travelers were now opting for mass transit. This in itself was proof that times had changed.

(34.)

Ari leaned on the pitchfork, his forehead dripping sweat. As he wiped his face, his dirty hand left muddy smudges. "I think Jana's giving assignments with a vengeance here, making up for lost time!"

"You said you wanted to work the gardens again," Tia teased, parking the wheelbarrow.

"It is good to be out here, but turning compost piles is heavy work."

Tia watched him as he returned to his labor. In contrast with the time in DC, his muscles had firmed again, his knee was no longer giving him trouble. His cotton shirt stuck to him, revealing the strength of his shoulders, the long line of his back. She suddenly yearned to run her hand down that long sweaty back.

"Look at all the earthworms, the critters in there." He moved his pitchfork and the soil wriggled with life.

She peered into the pile. "They don't get it, those corporate industrial operations. This soil life, it's every bit as important as the plant life in producing the crops. These critters can't survive with the toxic fertilizers, the chemical residues, the salts remaining as the chemicals degrade."

"Hey, pour on enough water and you'll wash those chemicals away down the rivers." His sarcasm was biting.

"Together with the topsoil," she added grimly. It didn't feel like a joking matter.

"Factor 4 efficiency, right there." He poked the compost to make it squirm again. "They recycle garden wastes, we avoid the chemical applications, the plants love it ... Isn't that what it all comes down to, these agricultural changes we need to make." He gestured to the writhing pile.

"What do you mean?"

"Life. A return to a fuller picture of life, and what that means. Humans re-integrating with other lifecycles on the planet. Rejoining it, rather than 'doing-to' it. It's not just agriculture. This stuff's soil sequestration, it's the carbon cycle as well. We're removed from it, we need to re-engage in it."

She looked at him in amazement. Ari, of jet planes and offices – this sounded more like something Jana or Rhus would say.

"We feel it so profoundly here in the garden." He bent and extracted a ball of long red worms, writhing together in a thick knot. "Raw fertility."

His expression of wonder was boyish, in marvelous contrast to his tousled greyed hair, the strong cords of his neck, his full chest. She could no longer resist. She drew closer as if to look at the worms, running her hand up the muscle of his arm.

"Look at how they burrow together, all wrapped around each other." He was captivated by the worms in his palm.

Her hand reached his neck, wet with sweat, she could feel the bits of dirt along his skin. He looked down at her; her desire was written upon her face.

He tossed the worms back into the pile, wrapping his arm around her. She writhed against him thinking of those worms. His mouth upon hers, his hand traveled her outstretched side, sliding under her shirt. She could feel the grit against her skin. The front of her shirt was now damp from the sweat of his chest.

His eyes traveled the garden nook they had been working, and she wished he would drop with her right there, but the voices of other Lares residents were audible through the fruit trees.

"Damn, this is no Coyote Creek," he laughed. "The disadvantages of living in a community!"

Tia giggled.

He ran a coarse finger across her throat, down between her breasts. "You, my dear, need a shower. With me."

(35.)

Annis and her fellow edgelands conservationists formalized their efforts into an NGO called REGROW, Restored Environment Graded Rebuilding of Wetlands.[100] More than two hundred people joined REGROW's Community Work Day at Ballona Wetlands this month.

The beginners team cleared non-native plants on the landward side of the expanding freshwater marsh. The intermediate team followed, planting divisions of native freshwater grasses. Tia's team, the veterans, carefully picked their way through a designated central band, where the salt water was invading the seaward edge of the freshwater marsh. Here, the team planted small starts of the salt-loving species.

After an hour's work, stooping under the late morning sun, Tia stood to stretch aching muscles. As she removed her broad-brimmed hat and shook out her long grey hair, she looked out across the wetlands.

She recalled the wetlands at the turn of the century, wide multi-laned blacktopped boulevards crossing it, noisy carbon monoxide polluting vehicles whizzing by at incredible speeds, the vain attempts to block developments on the very land on which she now stood. Now those developments had vanished, cleared with the SEZ delineations a decade ago. She recalled the pitifully small freshwater marsh the development had begrudgingly installed – territory insufficient for more than a scant few pairs of nesting blue heron.

She looked around her at the vast open space, now free of roadways, the limited-access Tongva Trail being the only human extension onto the cleared plain. Several pair of blue heron circled low overhead. *At one time we feared losing them!*

Up and down the Pacific Coast, along the Pacific Migratory Flyway, Tia knew through Annis, REGROW and affiliate groups were organizing similar restoration projects, rebuilding the wildlands in advance of the sea. Locally, at Malibu Lagoon, Madrona Marsh, Bolsa Chica Ecological Reserve. Tia had attended events at each of these in support of Annis' work.

Tia looked back at the crowd of volunteers. At work days at the turn of the century, turnout would be counted by the tens, not the hundreds.

They understand the importance now. We humans are interwoven with these other living things on the planet. Our survival depends upon theirs. The balance of ecosystems we need to survive is dependent upon the balance of edgelands such as these. In her imagination the microscopic plants and animals breeding in the wetland territories around her flowed bountifully back out to the Bay.

Replacing her hat, she bent to pick up her shovel. *Interdependence.* She turned the grey-green salt grass division in her hand. *My existence, that of my daughter and her future children, depends on you.* She plunged the little tuft into its hole and proceeded to plant another.

(36.)

With a recommendation from Professor Carl Farren, Seth secured early entrance to USC. Seth took a smattering of courses in Political Science, Business Law, Sociology and Architecture, but after a brief two years he was done.

"They don't teach what I want to learn," Tia overheard Seth telling Ari one evening in the Lares living room. "I'm going back to work with Dad."

"What's missing?" Ari inquired.

"The classes are all about the distant past. Not even the recent past, as in the changes that have taken place since I was born. I want to be part of the future direction."

Seth leaned forward toward Ari, his broad shoulders curled as he rested his elbows on his knees. "Architecture was useless – we won't be building new structures on empty land in the future – it will all be remodeling and retrofitting like my dad does. Under Factor 4, even teardowns will be minimized unless we really can recycle the materials. Skyscrapers are a thing of the past. They're extremely inefficient, as are single story buildings."

Ari looked out the window at the Lares community, all but one of the buildings single story. "What about this?"

"This is low density. In a few years, you'll see, we'll be adding additional stories to the buildings.

"I think Dad started something here that will be the launching-off place into future directions. That's where I come in. It's not just the structures he designed. We'll have new ways of working together, new ways of living together, we will have to evolve. Our legal agreements, our social configurations – we have to accommodate a much greater population on a smaller footprint."

"Explain that."

"Well, as climate change makes certain lands unusable, whether by sea level rise or desertification, or relocated agricultural spaces, we'll have less prime land. As displaced populations migrate here from places where the climate has become unliveable, the population density is going to intensify.

"Sure we all need some private spaces, but that historical stuff about the open range, me and my horse, 'don't see no one for miles,' we have to get past that. Even these mansions you and Dad redid into Lares held an aspect of that. These wide open floor plans and huge lawns were originally built for just one family."

Seth's voice became quieter. "Dad knows this stuff, at some intuitive level. I wish he could teach it, like Carl, but Dad doesn't have it all organized neatly in his mind like Carl. Dad teaches by working, by you working at his side. He's had so many apprentices over the years, but that's a very slow way to spread this concept.

"The world is hungry for it. It's not just the physical structures of the buildings, it's Dad's whole Sustainable Seattle community-rallying bent too. That combination is the unique edge Dad has. Eco-remodeling, CoHousing, shared spaces, cooperation, with life and growing things woven between all. There's really no name for it."

"Vernados and Son," Ari suggested with a smile.

Seth waved him away. "He tried that. I told him Vernados & Associates fits us both just fine because the Associates are such a big part of it – the network, the cooperation, the interrelation of all."

"You seem to have a pretty clear picture of it."

"You and Dad made it clear for me. You two are a pretty big act to follow. But I'll find a way."

(37.)

As the candidates emerged for the 2028 Presidential election, polls reported that the conservative candidate Congressman Arthur Newell had an early lead.

After Tia's years of battle for environmental and social change, the label 'conservative candidate' was heart-stopping; it typically meant moderation, cautiousness, and signaled an end to forward motion in the trend of change. Yet it was deeply shocking to realize that media was now applying the term 'conservative' to a candidate who favored renewable energy sources, advocated wisdom in the use of natural capital and pressed for international cooperation. After sixteen years of environmentally conscious political leadership the meaning of the term had changed.

Newell didn't have the courage and heroics of President Alden, but a vote for Newell would clearly be a vote for continuity of policies. His opponent, Senator Magan, who had lead the opposition to Ari during his Confirmation Hearings, was now perceived as the radical candidate, a departure from the current course, a departure from the status quo. The Transformation Wave had clearly reached the mainstream.

(38.)

Weather patterns in LA shifted again, the wet years of the 2010s and 2020s bygone. Reduction of northern Sierra snowpack became news reports rather than Union of Concerned Scientist forecasts. Twentieth century aqueducts carried less volume with each passing year.

Water markets received their first real tests, at times needing renegotiation and legal action to correct design flaws. Most significantly, the Factor 4 consciousness blossoming within the population brought out innovative conservation and re-use applications which were thrilling to behold.

(39.)

Tia and Ari relaxed on the Lares patio, late upon a summer evening.

Ari had been reading a UN report on the Sliver's interactive eyewear display. "Finally, we're putting through the international poverty tax."

"That's the tax on international currency transactions?"

"Precisely. It will help fund Sustainable agriculture, basic health, education, power, transport and communications services, safe drinking water and sanitation in underdeveloped countries."[101]

Annis and Gavin came tumbling in from the garden in high spirits. Annis' fingertips entwined with his, Gavin approached Ari.

"Sir," Gavin began formally, to Annis' giggle, "I would like to marry your daughter."

Ari slowly drew his glasses off, the smile rising on his face. "And what does she think of this idea?" Ari looked to Annis and the grin overtook him. Ari opened his arms and she ran to hug him.

"Take good care of her, will you," Ari said to Gavin, his voice choked with emotion.

(40.)

True to Seth's prediction, ROOTS did indeed become a networking and teaching organization. The ROOTS educational and apprenticeship programs attracted a wide diversity of students, from city families yearning to change to a more rural lifestyle yet previously unaware of how, to climate refugees from foreign lands eager for a place within the panorama of America.

For lands which had gone dry and were forecast to remain unproductive, ROOTS via Gavin and Carl coordinated with other conservationists to exert pressure in the state governments and the U.S. Department of the Interior to acquire these lands at foreclosure prices. Agricultural researchers leased some portions for experimentation. In select microclimes a combination of Steve Solomon's drylands techniques and Cassandra Chandler's low water varieties yielded some harvest, but rendering these lands productive on a commercially practical scale was clearly an issue for study over future decades.

The predominance of these lands fell to the care of CCC. Restoration was not simple under climate change. Native varieties which had previously flourished were now less successful under drastically altered moisture conditions, season extensions and contractions. Researchers attempted to introduce natives from nearby microclimes. In some areas this was successful with respect to the botanic population, yet wildlife suffered; the crossover of species was no longer the particular mix for which they had evolved. Habitat maintenance under climate change became an enigmatic challenge in need of urgent answers.

It was in the areas which had been lush and productive, which now were beginning to feel the pinch of reduced rainfall, that ROOTS and its associates had the most impact. It began with the small and medium-sized farms, where owners were intimately familiar with their land. Looking to the areas already decimated by megadrought and realizing the changes descending upon them, the small farmers eagerly embraced the techniques and varieties offered by ROOTS. Permaculture, polyculture, biodynamics and drylands varieties came alive in combinations as varied and unique as the plots of land.

As the decade came to an end, larger farms floundering in their inflexible industrial practices noticed the success of their smaller neighbors. The corporate conglomerates now realized that subdividing their massive operations and subcontracting to managers trained in the new techniques was the only path to survival.

(41.)

In 2028 when the greenhouse gas emission reports were complied by the United Nations' expert review team, the results were startling. CO_2 emissions had barely increased over the prior year. When the reports came in for 2029, UN officials hardly dared hope. Again, emission levels remained unchanged. Emission reports for 2030 confirmed a clear trend: world CO_2 emissions had reached a plateau. Not yet a decrease, but a definite plateau.

In the United States, meanwhile, President Newell quietly continued implementing the Alden Administration Energy Plan in its full and precedent-setting glory.

(42.)

tdamek@Lares.net

I saw Barry yesterday here in NY. Life post-Presidency seems to be a rough adjustment. I told him he needs to find a good cause to champion!

At these meetings the issues being considered for the 2032 WCSD in Seoul are increasing in number. It is clear that Sustainability will become the guiding principle, the 'umbrella,' under which many erstwhile separate issues will now fall. Every day the future of the Sustainability treaty grows closer to the breadth and completeness depicted in the Permaculture Flower. While I am delighted with this idea I still believe we have insufficient institutional framework to make it truly fly. A.

tdamek@Lares.net

I cringe at the memory of my DOE reorg days, yet that experience is so valuable now. Considering the operational necessities of this umbrella-treaty concept, we must strengthen the world political structure to accommodate and enforce these policies.

The Commission on Sustainable Development has always been focused on the 'Development' in its name. I believe instead, that we need some sort of a Commission on Sustainability, to assure that the ball remains balanced upon the ruler.

In its support there would be international organizations for the 'triple bottom line': environment, economy and society. We have a World Health Organization, we have a World Trade Organization, and I have been campaigning for a World Environment Organization.[102] The trio would work together, coordinated by the overriding principles of Sustainability. I am staring with disbelief at the diagram I have sketched on my screen – plain and simply, it is an org chart for the world. A.

(43.)

Annis' wedding was at a small rocky alcove on the beach in Santa Barbara, an intimate gathering, with a choice handful of their dearest friends. Annis wore Tia's wedding dress, with Lares flowers in her hair. Despite the nontraditional setting, Annis wanted traditional staging; she entered the ceremony on Ari's arm.

The Ancient within the New.

Tia thought perhaps she had never seen Ari stand so tall. His grey hair heavily streaked with white now, at sixty-two he still looked dashing in his dark suit. Solemn and proud, he gave Annis' hand to Gavin. Tears of joy and bittersweet coursed down Tia's face. Ari returned to Tia's side and slipped his arm around her. He seemed to need the touch as much as she did.

As the minister spoke of the Creation around them, amid the crashing of the waves against the ancient rocks, Gavin gazed at Annis.

"With this ring I thee wed."

His grandmother's ring. Binding the New with the heritage of the Past.

As Jeffrey sang of love and connection, Tia looked around at some of the familiar faces gathered on the beach. Jana and Steve, Lauren and Rhus, Carl and Verity. Tia thought of Annis in her growing years, surrounded by this close little circle of families. *We didn't do it alone. Every one of them had such a role in her growing. It truly does take a village.*

Tia watched Annis holding Gavin's hand, Janelle and Seth part of the wedding party.

This is our 'village' ... our tiny village within the bosom of the enormous city. The age-old social structure of the small group, within the modern reality of the metropolis. We are re-forming the social structures to cope with the new world, reforming the Ancient amidst the New.

PART THREE

Most of the things worth doing in the world have been declared impossible before they were done.

Louis Brandeis

CHAPTER 9:

IMPOSSIBLE

2032-2041

tdamek@lares.net
Here in New York at the PrepCons, the process of moving from individual treaties to integration under Sustainability is quite a feat. The tension between factions, the desire to protect the status quo, the reluctance to reorganize political power-bases, is incredible. I try to remain positive and keep my team focused on the larger agenda, but in the details, particularly after a day like today, resolution seems impossible! A.

tdamek@Lares.net
Between these frustrating sessions I have been doing much reflection and writing. I am attempting to capture my ideas for this World Sustainability Commission, as I have come to call it. It must be flexible, able to use and respond to change. It must integrate rather than segregate the varied functionalities of the World Health Organization, the World Environment Organization I know we will one day have, and the troublesome World Trade Organization. The WSC must be able to intervene to redirect these organizations from the course of danger, yet must promote self-regulation and balance amongst the nations of the world. And it must be able to grow the concept of Sustainability as this evolves with circumstances of the future. A.

(2.)

Ari had just arrived from New York when the call came from Gavin. "It's time!" Tia announced with glee, dragging a travel-weary and reluctant Ari out to the PLASE jitney to make the trip to Gavin and Annis' unit in the Hollywood CoHousing cluster.

Gavin met them at the door, beaming in excitement. Ari shook his hand formally as Tia pressed by them to see Annis.

"How are things on the legislative front?" Ari asked Gavin conversationally.

"Huh, the what?" Gavin was too distracted to follow the question.

"You were just in Washington, weren't you?"

"Uh, yes … but …"

Ari gave Gavin an irritated look.

Tia crossed the living room bearing the small bundle. She took one look at Ari's aloof stance.

His head is still in New York! He doesn't get it!

"Ari, come here," she insisted. "You have to hold him."

Ari resignedly sat on the couch and Tia passed the newborn to him. Ari accepted the bundle dutifully.

Then baby Edan opened his unfocused brown eyes and stared at his grandfather.

"Oh, man …"

Ari's whole demeanor changed. He suddenly couldn't take his eyes off the tiny scrunchy reddened face.

"I was not prepared for this …" Ari passed his hand across his face. "A grandson. Oh, this is intense."

Tia curled over Ari's shoulder watching Edan. "*Our* grandson, Ari!"

"He is incredible. What a miracle!" Ari's hand came up to brush his cheek again.

Tia looked over at Ari. His cheek glistened.

Hours old and Edan's already working magic.

She hugged Ari with one arm, reaching out to touch Edan at the same time.

Ari was still staring at Edan's now-sleeping face. "It's a great world out there, little fellow. We've worked hard to get it ready for you. You're going to have a great life."

(3.)

tdamek@Lares.net
The greenhouse gas emissions treaty issues have been smoothly integrated into our draft for the new

Sustainability agreement, the successor to the Athens Accord. It is a milestone achievement in international negotiations. Fordon and her associates should be quite proud of themselves, they have worked hard. Kegan, as well. A.

tdamek@Lares.net

An exciting shift has occurred. As critical greenhouse gas emissions issues were resolved, France and Germany suddenly joined my campaign for a World Environment Organization.[103] It is really going to happen, Tia! The WEO will coordinate the emissions aspects of the new treaty. WEO will be a global environmental watchdog and an international resource for expertise in environmental law, policy and management. In short, it is everything I had hoped. A.

tdamek@Lares.net

Even as delegates discuss the creation of the WEO, they are becoming aware of our need for a coordinating entity, an organization which can carry the vision of Sustainability forward and guide the WEO, WHO, and WTO to integrate their efforts. I think the world is finally ready to consider the World Sustainability Commission. A.

tdamek@Lares.net

We depart from Korea with a new milestone: the Seoul Accord. I even like the name of it. I yearn to spell it 'soul' rather than 'Seoul,' it so completely captures my hopes and dreams. Sustainability is now the official goal, and greenhouse gas emissions control is considered to be management of a resource inefficiency. The WEO is now a reality, a sister organization to the WHO and WTO. And our team has received the go-ahead to develop a plan for a World Sustainability Commission! A.

(4.)

In 2033 the California state MagLev train system was completed. A marvel of ground transportation, it was fully interconnected with metropolitan systems such as PLASE. One could now leave a West LA location and arrive in San Francisco or San Diego within a scant few hours, all without the use of a single automobile.

Between the MagLev system and EcoServ short-term leasing of the latest high-efficiency vehicles, few families owned a long range vehicle anymore. Even the local transport Neighborhood Vehicles were typically owned in vehicle pooling rather than individually. Reduced need for vehicle storage further freed up land within the city footprint. Driveways and garages quickly converted to gardens and residential units.

As consumer habits evolved and more food was produced within the cities, the need for long range trucking significantly declined. Some freight could be moved in off-peak hours on the rail systems, but the vast quantity of freight was an issue of the past. Goods produced and materials recycled within neighborhood pockets and within city limits provided local jobs and family businesses. Rather than the enchantment of the past, 'imported' now was understood for its detriment to human and natural capital. The colorful and individualistic villages within the city footprint thrived.

(5.)

Ari's pace quickened through the streets of Brentwood as he hauled the cart of Lares vegetables to the Neighborhood Barter Market with Tia. There they would exchange Lares autumn abundance for other items grown or made by neighbors and local tradesmen.

"It was great seeing Edan yesterday. He's running now," Ari grinned with pride.

"If he takes after his grandfather he'll never stop!" Tia trotted a few paces to keep up with Ari.

"Coming home from the meetings to a day with my grandson – it's amazing the places my thoughts ran to. That WCSD in Seoul barely two years ago was truly a milestone. The Seoul Accord brings together several international treaties under the Sustainability umbrella. Already, enough countries have ratified, including the U.S., that we have a legally binding international agreement.

"We have come such a long way, Tia. I think back to the time when the United States wouldn't even ratify Kyoto. Now we have reached a point where greenhouse gas control is truly accepted as a 'must do' part of existence on the planet. Do you realize what a shift in consciousness that represents? Thirty years ago it seemed this was impossible!

"The urgency with which countries ratified is amazing as well. It took seven years for sufficient countries to ratify the Kyoto Protocol. Now we're already into MOP meetings on the Seoul Accord, barely two years out from its initial release.

"Resource efficiency has changed life all around us. Look at the way in which we use the land." He gestured to a Lares-type CoHousing project as they sped by it.

Tia's pause to look necessitated her jogging to catch up to Ari's dashing pace.

"When we lived at the triplex, this area was 2,500 square foot single family mansions, with sprawling water-thirsty lawns." He gestured to the main street as they approached. "San Vincente was a 60 mph high speed thoroughfare with two or three lanes in each direction!" They waited for a clean emission bus and several bicycles to pass, then pulled their cart into the gathering of neighbors, greeting familiar faces.

At 60 mph I didn't know my neighbors. They were strangers around me. Connections between people are precious resources too. Human capital? Perhaps. But certainly something you never would have seen on a Roberts & Warner financial statement. We were so estranged from this valuable asset that we didn't know we were missing it!

On the return trip, the cart now laden with honey, goat's milk, feta cheese, and other exchange goods for the Lares community, Ari resumed his thread.[104]

"I was there with Factor 10 again, Tia. My associates laugh now. They say 'Damek, your day is coming, keep at it, we'll catch up soon!'" Ari laughed, his face capturing the warmth of the afternoon sunshine, the delightful babble of the market, this thrill over the international negotiations. "A decade ago they told me Factor 4 was impossible!" He laughed again, his joy and satisfaction contagious.

"We're still deep in a Transition world, Tia. We've seen so many changes, yet we still have plenty of areas which need work to bring them to efficiency. But Edan ... Edan and his children are going to see it. The end of the Transformation Wave."

"The end!?"

"But of course! Society won't be in this Transition forever!"

Her confusion showed on her face.

He laughed at her expression. "Tia, the Transformation is the *between* part, not the destination!"

"All these years we've been working to ..." she hesitated.

"To get the ball rolling, to get change in motion, to get the process started. The changes are happening, they're coming to fruition all around us.

Restoration, resource efficiency, new connections between nations and between people. We're well on our way back to some form of ecological balance. Remember my lecture years ago? Or have you forgotten?"

He dropped the handle of the cart, spun around dramatically in the path, and pointed at her, his dark eyes no less fiery than that long ago day.

She burst out laughing at the sight of him. His gesture was identical to that long ago day, but the white hair, the age lines made the picture surreal.

What I should have done then!

She walked boldly to him, slipped her arms around his neck and kissed him. *For the preciousness of that long-ago gesture ... for the fullness of the years between ... for the joys of the years ahead ...but most of all, for this moment, right here, right now ...*

He hugged her, pressing her head to his heart, sighing deeply.

Oh, to make this moment last forever!

"Sustainability," she whispered.

He gave her a tight squeeze and released her to look excitedly into her eyes. "Precisely!"

The question mark was written on her brow.

"As the Transformation Wave completes, *then* we'll be ready to truly begin Sustainability." He retrieved the cart handle, then slipped his arm around her waist to complete the walk home.

(6.)

As the UN's expert review team collected Greenhouse gas emissions reports in the early 2030s, the world anxiously awaited the results. CO_2 emissions statistics had shown a distinct plateau in the late 2020s, but a true decrease was yet to be proven.

When statistics were compiled in 2033, United Nations officials checked and rechecked their calculations. Countries around the world were discretely asked to confirm their reports. No one could quite believe the news. CO_2 emissions had dropped off significantly.

In 2034, apprehension was high as reports rolled in. Again, the news was incredible. For the second year in a row, CO_2 emissions showed a staggering decrease.

ॐ

Ari leaned back in the chair in the Lares living room, spinning his new Venture headset in his fingers. He sighed deeply, then ran his hand across his brow. "Tia, the 2035 emissions figures are in."

"No! Not good?" she gasped, noting his quiet body posture and deep sighs.

"Lower than ever – the lowest in the past 10 years."

"Oh, Ari!" She ran to him in excitement, then halted, "What's wrong?"

"Nothing, nothing at all." He still sat, hand to forehead. "I guess I'm in shock. I ... I always hoped it could happen, but, oh man, it's really here. Not just a wave of ideas but real physical changes. And it's happened a half-decade ahead of the IPCC's 2040 target."

She threw her arms around his shoulders. "You did it, darling! You and all your teams, over all the years."

He pressed her arm to his lips. "Yes, I believe we did." His voice was hushed. "All the millions of people who worked to make this possible, all the Change Agents who fought for this, all the Transformers who lead the way, all the Mainstreamers, who changed their habits. Just look at what we've accomplished!"

He broke away from her hug and began pacing the room. "We've actually changed the course. The world is pumping less CO_2 into the atmosphere. I hope it holds. I think it will, there is every indication that the trend will continue. We have so many renewable sources in place, and so many sequestration techniques.

"It will be decades more before we see the results; the IPCC now estimates that atmospheric concentrations of CO_2 should plateau around the end of the century. If the CO2 concentrations plateau and then taper off, temperatures will stabilize and begin to come down. I think they will, I have confidence that they will, call it my confidence in the planetary systems."

He sighed deeply again. "It's not our duty to complete the task, only to do our part. This is the point at which I pray. We've acted, to the fullest of our abilities; I pray that it is enough. Now we must turn it over. We must trust a power more unfathomable and mysterious..." He nodded quietly to himself. "Edan's children will see those incredible results. I just know it."

⊰

Renewable energy sources were now providing a significant portion of many nations' power needs. Forest sinks planted with the early days of the Kyoto Treaty had grown into mature trees, sequestering carbon. Agricultural methods worldwide utilized native vegetation for soil sequestration rather than bare fallows, and other sustainable farming methods were becoming commonplace.

With carbon trading systems in place for more than thirty years, rainforest destruction was now virtually unheard of. Third world countries counted their carbon trading income, rather than worrying how they would meet their World Bank interest payments. The international poverty tax on money transfers was helping to boost education and genuine development, and the Third World standard of living was vastly improving along Sustainable pathways.

(7.)

Wildflowers bloomed exuberantly in the Santa Monica Mountains after the 2035 El Niño rainy season, and the Hollywood CoHousing complex was similarly in grand display when Tia arrived to pick up Edan. Annis was pacing the gardens in the easier stages of early labor, Gavin at her side.

After a short ride on PLASE across town, Tia and Edan reached Lares, to Grandpa Ari's eager hugs. Then Tia and Ari followed Edan's mad dash to the central children's area and the swing in the old sycamore tree.

"It's so deceptively simple," Ari said reflectively to Tia as he pushed Edan. "His tiny body goes hurtling from me, away into the air and back to my arms. Carefree and joyous Trust.

"They trust us so completely. They trust us to feed them and shelter them and teach them the truth about life. They trust us with every aspect of their beings, including their future. They trust us to hand them a liveable planet.

"We're doing our best to hand them a better world than we were given: biodiversity, emissions control, resource efficiency, restoration, saner consumption habits, solutions to poverty. But sometimes it feels like we've just scratched the surface. There's so much more to be done."

Edan now clamored to see the chickens, so Ari scooped him out of the swing, holding him for a brief moment in tender embrace. "I can still craft him a better legacy than this," Ari murmured, his eyes half closed.

Edan scrambled down the path in search of the chickens.

⌀

Daughters. Daughters of our daughters. The chain of generations.
It was nearly a physical sensation, of links in a chain, backward through time – *Cassandra, Saffi* – and forward through time – *Annis,*

and now Linnette. Tia looked down at the new pink bundle in her arms. *I'm a link in a chain, forward and back, woman to woman.*

Dear little Linnette, as women we carry the torch, we carry the light, the vision in our hearts. We the torchbearers must point the way, toward a future of more links in the chain, daughter to daughter, forward in time.

A Sustainable lifestyle, dear little one, that is our only option if we are to see those links fulfilled. We're doing it, Linnette. For you, for your daughters and your daughters' daughters, torchbearers all.

(8.)

tdamek@Lares.net
As Sustainability becomes positioned as the umbrella principle for world agreements, the World Trade Organization rears its ugly head. The idea of placing its economic policies under the Sustainability portfolio is staggering. Globalization of the past has worsened both environmental and social issues, by increasing corporate power and reach, stimulating environmentally detrimental industries such as transportation and energy, overriding traditional local controls on resources, basically increasing the spread between wealthy and poor. Instead, we must invent a globalization which is consciously managed for people and the environment, Sustainability in both human and natural capital realms. A.

tdamek@Lares.net
Kegan and I have been drafting a fine proposal for the World Sustainability Commission, attempting to design a forum which will balance economic, social and environmental policies. The WSC must be able to do what one person cannot: it must transcend the course of a given human lifetime. It must carry that long-term view of Sustainability into the future. I guess my mind runs to the limitations of a lifetime, because they've now called in Hospice care for Barry's wife.[105] I'll make a trip out to see Barry and Marian instead of to LA this weekend. A.

(9.)

It was a rare stormy day in Los Angeles, in this La Niña year. Steve and Seth rushed to check the rainwater cachement systems around the Lares property and other Vernados & Associates projects around town, to assure much of the downpours would be captured. Jana turned to garden recordkeeping. With Ari away in New York, Tia took the opportunity to clean out some of the old papers stored in the office.

Misfiled amongst financial paperwork, Tia discovered a copy of the Permaculture Flower diagram from Jana's lectures. Tia recalled that long-ago Legacy LA talk, her first exposure to the Flower's ideas. *I thought Ari was trying to do it all!* She chuckled.

Impulsively she began writing on the diagram, listing projects around its edges.

Land & Nature Stewardship: *That was Mom's entire career. The Lares gardens, the triplex gardens, Esperanza's FarmUrb and President Elliott's Civilian Conservation Corps. Annis' wetlands come in here too.*

Built Environment: *Steve's eco-remodel movement, Seth now, too. Lares and PLASE, the Sustainability Centers.*

Tools & Technology: *Dad's inventions, Wade's. The RPS and CDM projects, new solar devices, contemporary wind turbines. The greywater filtration – that sure has changed. MagLev technology. And the resource efficiency innovations everywhere!*

Culture & Education: *Our garden classes here at Lares and back at the triplex. Lauren and my children's classes. ROOTS. The LA Future Fair. Legacy LA and Steve's Sustainability groups in other cities. Jeffrey and his songs with a message.*

There's not a clear place for it on this Flower, but I mustn't leave out our long term Sustainable relationships between people, our marriages!

Health & Spirituality: *The healthy eating Shannon taught us all, and Slow Food Fast, her extension of that to the general public. Matthew's lectures. Our connection with the earth. Herbal healing, Jana's homebirth, Mom's conscious death.*

Finance & Economics: *I remember feeling so unsustainable on this one! Natural Capitalism has really come of age. Even the staid AICPA came around. The RAI programs. Moss' water negotiations. Emissions trading credits. The Sustainability Centers and our neighborhood Barter Markets. Our economy has so completely transformed!*

Land Tenure & Community Governance: *Gavin's subsidy elimination. The Land Trusts, both Agricultural and CoHousing. Factor 4 fits in so many places, so I'll just drop it in here. President Alden's sweeping changes, President Elliott setting the stage. The international treaties, the whole succession of them, both emissions and Sustainability, now merged into one. Ari's entire career.*

Tia looked in amazement at the wealth of notes on the diagram.

We are doing so much! I had no idea!

She looked more closely at those items with which she was personally involved. *My goodness, I have been busy! It hasn't been Ari trying to do the entire Flower – yikes, it's been me!*

(10.)

Tia walked with Ari the short distance to the PLASE jitney, as was their habit. He carried his single slim bag for his stay in New York.

"Remember when you used to drive me to the airport in an automobile to drop me off?" He laughed at the ridiculousness of it. "This trip I'll finally get to ride one of those new ultra-efficient planes, at last they're placing them in use on major routes on a test basis.[106] All these years of travel on those horribly unsustainable aircraft. It is a relief that they have finally engineered better solutions! Tia, one of these trips you'll have to come to New York with me, it has changed so much, just like LA has."

Tia looked around the Brentwood neighborhood: the small stores along the greenbelts, artistically dotted with community garden plots. An occasional neighborhood vehicle swooshed silently by, the tire traction and the laughter of occupants the only noise it made. The bike paths were always full now, except in the middle of an actual downpour. Other neighbors were out walking, and smiled greetings. The fresh air, sweet with blossoms from the plantings, cooled her cheeks.

We are so accustomed to walking, she realized. *The intimate contact with our surroundings, the satisfying self-sufficiency, the clean alive feeling of it.*

The cool on her cheek brought back memories of air-conditioning-cooled polluted air, idling in traffic in individual automobiles. *Oh, the poisoned, trapped, frustrating times! We couldn't imagine getting by without our cars!*

She looked over at Ari, moving at a brisk pace toward the jitney stop, and thought back to the gyms of her youth and the preoccupation with fitness even as the populace grew into obesity. *Living in closer relationship with the land we have a 'doing' lifestyle rather than a sitting lifestyle. Our foods are closer to their original state – vegetables, fruits, eggs, so few processed foods. We no longer hear about an 'obesity problem' in the nation!*

Impulsively, she took Ari's bag from him to free his hand, and slipped her hand into his. He strode purposefully, his posture proud at seventy-two, his face gently tanned from garden hours. After fifteen years without it, the cane had returned to his life as he aged.

"I can't believe it: Rio +50, the preliminary organizing meetings," he continued, in eager anticipation of his trip. "I remember after Johannesburg there were doubts there would ever be another World Sustainability gathering. Now we're at fifty years, have international treaties on the subject, and soon a World Sustainability Commission!"

"Where's the 2042 Conference going to be?" she asked. It was unusual that he hadn't mentioned it.

"We'll be deciding that this week in New York. I've been working on a little surprise." He gave her a mysterious smile. "I sincerely hope this Conference will see Factor 10 into action; once we get to the PrepCons I will certainly be pushing for it. We've been with Factor 4 for two decades now. I think the world is finally ready to take on the new step."

∽

Three days later her Venture chirped for attention. Ari was visible in the tiny video screen, grinning broadly.

"Get ready, Tia. I'm bringing it home!"

She didn't understand.

"Rio +50 is going to be in Los Angeles!" he announced in triumph.

∽

At PrepCon1 at the United Nations headquarters in New York the 2042 WCSD Chairperson was selected: Dr. Ari Damek of the United States. Ari spent long weeks in New York working on Conference arrangements.

In Los Angeles, selection of venues began, planning for the arrival of thousands of delegates, vendors, journalists, companies and NGOs. Tia joined the committee organizing the side sessions, and was soon asked to be the committee's Assistant Director.

(11.)

Ari came home to Lares for a short visit. Tia had been working with her new helper, Kaia, the same Kaia who had grown up through the Lares classes. WCSD paperwork was now stacked in piles around the office.

Ari laughed at the sight of the room. "What a whirlwind! It has caught both of us, it seems!"

"More than just the two of us," Tia told him. "I took some of the foreign committee members for a tour of various sites around the city, including the wetlands. They insisted that the restoration be presented at WCSD, so Annis will be speaking for REGROW."

"Incredible! I am so proud of her achievements. It's great that others will get to hear about her work."

"And it's looking like Gavin may be part of the session on subsidy elimination."

"The whole family," he grinned. "And what will the kids be presenting?"

They strolled in the twilight through the Lares grounds, these walks precious now amidst their busy schedules. Tia brought a basket to gather jasmine blossoms along the way for their evening tea.

"It's thrilling that we're all doing this together," he said. "You haven't been part of a WCSD before. They're quite exciting."

"The side session registrations have been amazing," she commented. "I can't wait to see them unfold."

Their walk carried them to the nook beneath the spreading olive trees.

"Tia, this meeting we began the draft agreement," he revealed in quiet excitement. "The terms take it to Factor 10! It's incredible. Factor 10 in an international treaty. I have worked for so long to see this day." His eyes glistened with joy.

"Ari, darling, that is thrilling! I'm so happy for you – and for the world! " She slipped her arms around his neck and reached up to kiss him. The heady sweet scent of the jasmine encircled them.

Tia thought back to Johannesburg, to his description of those long ago debates, his fury at the policies of the U.S. Delegation. "The U.S. has come so far, to actually be hosting a Sustainability Conference!"

"Oh, yes, recall how Rafferty boycotted Barcelona?" He grimaced at the memory.

"Oh, I remember," she buried her face in his neck. "I remember how you crashed the session!"

"That I did." He laughed, his posture proud and tall. "Ah, the impulsivity of youth."

"That 'impulsivity' brought us Factor 4," she said warmly. "I'd say it was a little more like 'forward thinking'!"

"Or bullheaded determination!" His face was mischief. "And now that determination has just about got us Factor 10. At one time they said it was impossible."

His dark eyes inches from hers, a determination of a different sort suddenly clear within their depths. His kiss took her by surprise with its fire.

He eased himself onto the bench, pulling her down on top of him. His hand caressed her thigh through the thin fabric of her skirt. The mere thought of it, here, in the gardens, under the olives, left her warm and trembling. She pressed herself against him, feeling his body come alive.

The basket of jasmine tumbled to the earth, its sweet blossoms bruised and potent in the garden air.

(12.)

By the early 2040s, CO_2 emissions were in steady decline, at a rate even more rapid than the IPCC models had hoped. As expected, atmospheric CO_2 concentration levels and global temperatures continued to rise in time-lag reflection of the emissions increases prior to the 2030s, while sea levels rose steadily. Yet the world remained hopeful.

The SEZ delineation system adopted for U.S. coasts was set in place for other nations: the Netherlands, Italy, Egypt. As an extension of developmental assistance, SEZ studies were extended to lesser developed countries: Bangladesh, Indonesia and small island nations. With the certainty of inundation and the understanding of the emissions curtailment and time lags, came acceptance, and the beginnings of multinational solutions.[107]

(13.)

Ari was up early to make the trip downtown to open the final set of PrepCon sessions in Los Angeles. Tia made whole grain muffins in the Lares kitchen, serving them with fresh grapes from the arbor. Ari was impatient and a little cross over the breakfast preparations.

"We open the session at 9:00 and I want to be there early." He winced as he raised his arm to adjust the Venture's eyepiece. "Oh man, I woke up feeling so stiff. My arm and my back ache."

"Too much gardening?"

"Perhaps. It doesn't feel like that though." He waved it off and picked up his teacup. "Over the next week at this final PrepCon we'll finalize the agreement, get it ready for the Plenary session next May.

"As Chair of the Conference I'll have plenty to do. But it's odd. As far as negotiations, my job is done. Factor 10 is being written into this agreement. The WSC is well on its way. I'm not sure what else there is to do."

"What?" she laughed.

"Yes, it sounds funny doesn't it." He laughed too, but his expression was sober. "I've worked for it all of my life, and now it's done.

"They're asking me to head the WSC, get it off the ground. The thought of developing a whole new organization, at my age – I'm getting too old for this stuff, Tia."

No! Don't say that! Don't even think that!

He winced again as he pushed back from the table.

"Would you like me to go downtown with you?" she offered, suddenly concerned.

"No," he said, looking at her fondly and shaking his head. "You have your own schedule to attend to. Gil is coming with me."

Ari stood to leave. He seemed to be leaning on his cane a little more heavily this morning. Yet at full height he still looked every bit the senior statesman. His white hair was a crown of authority. He straightened his suit and kissed her goodbye.

(14.)

"Mrs. Damek," it was Gil calling. "Dr. Damek's been taken to the hospital, he collapsed in the meeting!"

The hospital? Ari, no! Tia's hand trembled so violently she could hardly hold the phone. "Which hospital?"

"UCLA."

Ari was in the CCU, surrounded by bustling nurses and aides. His eyes were shut, he was lying horribly still, and he was very white. He was a mere shadow of the man who had walked out of the kitchen this morning. Oxygen masks and IV tubes, monitors and techno equipment surrounded him, all so foreign and strange.

Gil was sitting in the hall, looking quite scared.

"Mrs. Damek, he went ashen and collapsed on the floor, sweating like crazy. Oh, it's horrible!" Gil looked to be on the verge of tears.

The doctors used scary words like Cardiogenic shock, Myocardial Infarction, Congestive Heart Failure. Tia learned that Ari had been put on multiple medications to sedate him and ease the pain.

Tia tried to reach Annis but couldn't get an answer. She had better luck with Jana, who promised to come to the hospital right away.

A haze of mechanical motions set in, from phone calls, to doctor's reports. Tia moved through the process woodenly, losing all sense of time. She remembered Jana forcing her to eat something, and a nurse urging her to rest.

Gil disappeared sometime in the spin of events, and Annis appeared for a while. Annis drifted away and Jana reappeared. Attendants scurried through, adjusting this and that, changing Ari's IV, changing his oxygen mask to a smaller nose device.

"Tia, you need to come home for the night," Jana insisted. "Come on, I'll take you home. They'll call you if there's any change."

Tia looked at Ari, lying so still and grey. She gripped his hand, then his arm. His hand responded, faintly, then he opened his eyes. His focus was glazed with the drugs.

I can't leave him, Jana, I can't.

Tia bent to kiss him, and she could feel him answer her. His eyes cleared for a moment and the familiar light was there again.

His eyes are clearing. He's going to be okay. It's just like the accident in DC. In a day or so we'll have to tie him down on doctor's orders!

"I love you, Ari."

He smiled slightly.

"Love you," he whispered.

She hugged him awkwardly across the hospital equipment.

Jana took Tia's arm and lead her away.

(15.)

When Tia returned in the morning, Ari looked to be sleeping. His tall body beneath the covers filled the length of the hospital bed, but his presence in the room felt very small. She moved to the bedside and looked down at him quietly, not wishing to disturb his rest.

He opened his eyes, his dark eyes clouded with pain or the medications, she didn't know which. Gone was that desperate intensity, the passion for life.

"Tia, hold me," he whispered.

She reached for his arm, caressed his hand.

"Hold me," he repeated, weaker this time. If she hadn't been so close she would have missed it.

Tia looked in confusion at the array of hospital monitors, the bedrails, the devices. She looked around toward the nurses station – no one was in view. She sat on the bed beside him, and swung her legs up, the maneuver cumbersome and awkward. He watched all this in stillness, with horribly distant eyes.

She lay down beside him, atop the covers, wrapping her arm around his stomach, pressing her head in its accustomed niche at his heart. He was so still. She could hear his heartbeat; it seemed far away, so faint.

Ari sighed, the faintest of little sighs. *Silence.*

The room was suddenly full of people. Tia felt like she was watching it all from within some distant tunnel, all was grainy and slowed around her. She held Ari, his frame the only solidness she could feel. There was lots of activity, outside in that haze that spun around her, many voices, urgent tones, hands reaching toward Ari, pulling at him, pulling at the bedclothes. Someone's hands worked her arms free of Ari and she felt herself being lifted and carried.

The grayness spun around her and she longed for the darkness to win over the bright reality. But it was the darkness that receded instead, and she felt cold, desperately cold, as if she would never be warm again. Her muscles ached, her bones ached, and the lights and motion around her were altogether too much. She wanted to scream, but no voice came through her throat. She curled into a fetal position, rocking herself.

Awareness of the reality around her was coming back into hard sharp focus. She was on a bed, and there were lots of strangers bustling around, but they weren't paying attention to her. Deep in some critter-sense, she knew.

An icy calm washed over her. She uncurled her body, and sat up, dangling her feet over the edge of the bed. Something inside her solidified, into a cold, hardened, concrete feeling. She could feel her breath, and her heartbeat felt far, far away, in some distant small chamber reserved within the concrete form. She pulled her shoulders back, took a deep breath, and stood up.

A stranger approached her; all she registered was the white uniform.

"Mrs. Damek, I'm sorry, your husband has ..."

Don't say it. I know. She brushed the person aside.

"I want to see him."

He lay motionless on the bed. Her every sense recoiled from the bed, he was not here. The room emptied and someone gently closed the door. She went to him, knowing it wasn't him. She sat on the edge of the bed and picked up his hand; it was limp and cool. She couldn't bear not to touch him, but to touch him was no comfort whatsoever. She looked at his still face.

Was it a minute ago that you whispered to me? Or was it an hour?

Already it felt like ages. The tears began to fall. She put her head on his lifeless chest and sobbed.

Oh Ari, you said to hold you ...

It felt as if his life had slipped out somehow, between her very fingers.

... I never could hold you.

Rather than the still form within her arms, she felt the sandy wisps of time, their time together.

Together. What did we have together? It feels like a brief moment, when you balled it all up into one. All the little moments. Because they were always little moments. Just a brief taste, even a tease, of life together. And then you were off, on the next plane, to the next meeting or appointment. And now you are gone on your final journey.

Oh darling, how I ached to hold you. But there was never time. And now there never will be time.

She surrendered to the tears, the tears that felt like they might never stop.

(16.)

DR. ARI DAMEK
1968-2041

Former Secretary of Energy Ari Damek, 73, died Wednesday at a Los Angeles hospital, of massive heart failure. In recent months he was serving as Chairperson for the United Nations World Conference on Sustainable Development, scheduled for Los Angeles next May.

Dr. Damek was Secretary of Energy under President Barnett Alden from 2022 to 2025 and developed the Alden Administration's landmark Energy Policy, the first United States policy to emphasize renewable energy sources.

Dr. Damek was influential in several international treaties which have been instrumental in control of planetary climate and environmental changes. He lead the United States delegation for the 2022 Athens Accord and the 2032 Seoul Accord Sustainability Treaties.

Locally, he will be remembered as the founder of Legacy LA, the group which jumpstarted the Sustainability effort in Los Angeles.

Dr. Damek is survived by his wife, daughter, two grandchildren, and a sister.

Annis finished reading Kegan's draft for the obituary and crushed the paper to her bosom with a sob. Tia crossed the living room to hug her, their slender arms poor substitute for the great hugs they each ached for.

"I can't believe he's gone!" Annis' voice was a bare squeak amidst her tears. "I never thought he wouldn't make it!"

I never thought he wouldn't make it, either.

"I thought he'd be up and around in no time, just like always, off to still more meetings, on yet another global campaign. He was always so strong, so full of energy, so alive. It was never possible ... that he could d...d...die." Annis couldn't say any more, the sobs were too overwhelming.

Tia held her tightly. The tears were contagious. After a long while they recovered the ability to speak.

Annis gestured to the now crumpled and tearstained narrative. "He sure accomplished a lot of great stuff. He was always so motivated, so driven. He just never stopped."

He did stop. Yesterday.

"I just don't know how he did it." Annis said.

Tia willed her tears to pause. "Annis, your father loved you very dearly. You and Linnette and Edan, even the thought of your grandchildren. You were his motivation to go on. He was always fighting to make a better life for all of you. Come here, let me show you something."

Tia went to the bag from the hospital and brought out Ari's Venture headband. She slipped it on, directing it to shift files.

"Look what he called it, honey. 'Inspiration.' This was how he did it."

Annis took the Venture. Tia knew what scrolled before Annis' eyes: old images, the photos from the Milan trip, of Annis as a baby, and the Culver City school. The photos of Linnette and Edan, wrinkled and new. The old photo of Mark, from Annis' bedside. Annis at Coyote Creek, Annis with Seth. Jeffrey onstage. Kegan, age eighteen or so.

Kegan as an adult, holding toddler Terry and infant Cody. Annis with Linnette and Edan in the Lares gardens last month.

"He carried them with him always." Tia spoke as much to herself as to Annis. "When things would get tough, in the negotiations, he told me he would bring these up on his screen, have them open before him so that he could carry on. You were why he did all the impossible things that he did, you and your children and grandchildren and their grandchildren.

"Annis, he was a very special man. His heart didn't hold just one child. Your dad had the incredible ability to think in terms of generations. He had the gift of being able to share his vision with people, the ability to rally the fighting spirit in others, to get everyone focused in a single direction to make that vision come true. He dreamed impossible dreams, and then he found a way to make them come true."

Impossible dreams.

Oh Ari, the dream wasn't supposed to end like this! Tia's grief returned.

"Dad did some incredible things," Annis stared out the window. "And he encouraged me to. People said it was impossible to get REGROW funded and get State approvals. Dad always believed it could be done. He taught me to believe. He'd give me one of those incredible hugs and tell me to go at it again. 'There's always a way,' he'd say. Damn, I'll miss those hugs!"

"You'll have to teach Gavin," Tia tried to smile through her tears but somehow it didn't work.

"Mom, after Mark, that terrible time, all I really needed were Dad's hugs."

"Now you have your Gavin. And Edan and Linnette …"

And I have my memories. Empty arms and memories.

"Yes," Annis smiled a watery smile. "We'll pick up and go on. Great things, just like he did."

How will I go on? I have no magic file of photos to keep me going. All these years what kept me going were those dark eyes. One look from you and I knew, I could do whatever impossible task we had before us. The triplex, Lares, PLASE, ROOTS, WCSD ... How many times did I pick up the reins to drive on with the team when duty called you prematurely to the next project. Just one look at the passion in your eyes, the mission, the purpose, and I could do anything. You were my inspiration.

Tia cried for the unresolvable 'forever' of it all.

Now those incredible eyes are gone from me, forever. Never again will I see that intense gaze. How will I go on? It's impossible.

CHAPTER 10:

SUSTAINABILITY

2041-2045

Jana took on the project of arranging the memorial service. Ari's death seemed to have thrown her into a mad fit of activity. With Gil and Kegan, she deftly coordinated arrangements for the service and the cremation, made announcement calls and directed out of town visitors.[108]

"It's going to be rather large, Tia, get ready for that. You know he touched a lot of people."

Tia recoiled from the thought of a huge gathering. If it had been up to her it would have been small, intimate. *I don't want to share him. I always had to share him. I don't want to share him now.*

She turned inward in her grief. Jana and Annis had to beg her to eat, tell her to sleep. Phone calls went unanswered. Tia sat, for hours at a time, beneath the old olive trees in the nook of the Lares gardens, not speaking to anyone.

The day of the service, Tia moved through the process woodenly, doing whatever Jana directed: Get dressed. Sit here. We're leaving now.

Tia had a vague sense of being in a huge hall with far too many people, Annis on one side, Jana on the other, holding her hands. Speeches in turn from the front of the room felt like one continuous stream. All that she heard from it was Ari... Ari... Ari...

Seth took his turn, reading at the podium, but Tia hardly noticed through her tears.

> "This is the one true joy in life, the being used for a purpose recognized by yourself as a mighty one; the being a force of nature instead of a feverish, selfish little clod of ailments and grievances, complaining that the world will not devote itself to making you happy. ...."

Someone touched Tia's knee, an invasion into her wooden world. Linnette was attempting to climb across Annis to get to Tia.

"... I am of the opinion that my life belongs to the
whole community and as long as I live it is my
privilege to do for it whatever I can. ..."

Linnette began to whimper amidst Annis' restraint.

"Let her come," Tia whispered, holding out her arms to the
wiggling six year old.

"... I want to be thoroughly used up when I die, for
the harder I work, the more I live. I rejoice in life
for its own sake. Life is no 'brief candle' to me. It is
a sort of splendid torch which I have got hold of for
the moment, and I want to make it burn as brightly
as possible before handing it on to future
generations."

Linnette snuggled into Grandma's bosom and Tia clung to her.

*Oh, it feels good to hold her. The warmth, the snuggle. I needed
this, more than you can imagine, Linnette.*

Now a man was speaking, forthright, commanding, familiar. Tears
still coursing down her face, Tia's focus cleared.

"After his heroic forty-year leadership of his
people, Moses was not able to enter the Promised
Land with them. So too, we do not need to enjoy
the fruits of our longing, as we see them taking fruit
in others who will come after us. We are part of a
great chain of big-hearted people who care about
the Earth, about the life that gives it fruitfulness,
and about a world where rights would be respected,
children cherished, and peace prevail. We have to
be part of something larger than ourselves, because
our dreams are often bigger than our lifetimes."

Oh, it's Former President Alden! Tia looked to Jana. *What have
you done here?* Jana smiled back, watery, she was crying too.

Tia looked around the hall. Alden's inevitable bodyguards. Press
cameras flashing. Vast numbers of people. Tia recognized faces, but
names escaped her. Instead, it was a roll call of nations: EU ... Russia ...
South Africa ... Canada ... Australia ... India...

I had no idea!

The reception that followed was equally massive. Still Tia drifted in and out of her private world. Images filtered through.

Nine year old Edan standing at her side, drawing himself up as tall as he could. *He has Ari's stance.*

President Alden, shaking her hand, paying his respects. "He was a noble man, a brilliant mind, a valued friend." His pale eyes were warm and sincere. "Now, if you ever need anything, you just let me know, we can still pull the connections together." Tia nodded mechanically and he was gone.

A woman, tall, like herself. Elegantly coiffed white hair. *I know those grey eyes.* "Mrs. Damek, Lori Fordon..."

You can call me Tia now, just Tia.

"I never had a chance to tell you what a difference you made in my life," Lori said. Her grey eyes were warm now. "Thank you, for getting me back on course."

Lori shook Tia's hand. Impulsively, not quite knowing why, Tia folded Lori into a hug. A sob coursed through Lori as Tia held her. As she pulled away, Tia could see Lori's tears.

Steve wrapped Tia with an enormous bear hug. His huge frame shook. "We'll go on, Tia, we will. We'll miss him terribly, but we'll carry on."

Kegan approached, his family in tow, Terry and Cody teens now. Tia hardly recognized them. "Tia, we're carrying his mission forward. It doesn't end here," Kegan said.

"It doesn't seem possible." Tia could barely whisper.

"Tia," Kegan held her arms and gave her a gentle shake, his blue eyes intense and sincere. "It's always possible! Just think of how many earth-changing things Ari accomplished, he just set his mind to it. He rallied the teams and made it happen. And he taught us how to do it. We'll miss him, certainly, but we'll still go right on with that very possible dream!"

An elderly Ben overheard that. "Tia, remember at Carl's wedding, how impossible it all seemed? LA was a mess back then. Just look at it now! The impossible seems to happen every day around here!" Ben's familiar chuckle was warming.

(2.)

"His ashes," Jana said gently. "Tia, you must make a decision about his ashes."

That long ago day at San Marcos pass returned to Tia, her mother's ashes filtering through her fingers as the wind carried them. *Back to the earth she loved.*

But Ari? *Ah my traveler, to be eternally in one spot, so unlike you in life. You were never of one place, never of one country, even. The years of EU affiliation, the international treaties, one spot just won't do for you.*

Through the silent tears, everpresent upon her cheeks these days, she thought of their youth, their early relationship, the breakwater walks … the ocean.

The oceans of the world are really one. We name them differently, artificial divides, like the borders between countries. Through the oceans we can truly see that it is just one world, one small planet we all share.

She thought of the ocean conveyor, the massive current flow that wraps the globe and stabilizes the climate, the shut down of which scientists had warned about in the uncontrolled emission days. With CO_2 emissions now stabilized it was so much less of a possibility. *The conveyor carries currents around the planet. The lifeblood of the planet.* It all became one in Tia's mind: international negotiations, the atmosphere, that massive current. *The circulatory system. Your heart failed and you are gone from me but I will deliver you to the Heart of the planet you loved.*

"The ocean," she murmured to Jana. As Jana moved quietly away, Tia called after her. "Arrange for a sailboat – wind energy."

∽

The flowers from the Lares grounds looked so odd bobbing upon the ocean's surface. Annis, Linnette and Edan clustered in the boat next to Tia, with Jana, Steve, Seth and Gavin standing close by.

This is the private part. Tia thought of the massive funeral. *You were of the world but you were very private as well.* She felt the preciousness of those private times with Ari so powerfully now. *One love, one powerful sharing of our hearts, our minds, our bodies, our souls. A spark of you will always be with me, darling.*

She watched the ocean currents carry the flowers. *Onward you go, on your forever travels. I never traveled with you.*

But one day I will.

She turned to Annis. "When I'm gone, bring me out here like this, to be with him." The tears overtook her.

(3.)

Late afternoon, a week after the ceremony, Tia found her way back to the Marina breakwater. She hadn't been down here in years. Things had changed, a lot. She knew the rising seas and the increased storm activity had necessitated breakwater rebuilding all up and down the coast, but it had never occurred to her that the changes would be so complete.

They had razed all the buildings where her apartment had been. The channel entrance was completely reconfigured, the breakwater border with the sea had been moved landward. The Playa del Rey portion was still visible across the channel, but it looked completely changed as well. There was still a pathway atop the new rock arrangement and Tia walked carefully.

There were benches here now. She eased herself into one, realizing that perching on a rock probably wouldn't be a good idea anymore.

The place felt so different, nothing at all like the old days when she had walked here with Ari.

It's the same spot on the planet, but so very different. I'm the same girl I was then, but so very different. You're ... not at all the same, you're gone forever now.

Forever is such a crazy long time. It will never be the same.

The grief welled up inside her and spilled out in tears.

The rocks might be rearranged, the shoreline reconfigured, but the waves feel eternal. Some things never change.

Change. That's what it all comes down to. We think we can build some sort of stability, a sense of sameness, but we're fooling ourselves. Living is change. Life with you was always about change. Changing times, changing Treaties, changing lifestyles, changing paradigms, changing the world.

Yet this change I just cannot take. Life without you, it feels impossible. I can't go on without you, darling.

But you did so much without me.

It felt just like he was talking to her.

Just look at all you did, Tia. The LA Future Fair, you did that with Steve. Legacy LA and PLASE, you took those on too. You were the one who publicized the Lares project, that wasn't my doing, the Lares children's program, too. And now the WCSD side sessions call. You can do it, Tia. Will you?

I can't, not without you here to guide me. Ari, I need your strength. She ached for his arms hugging her.

Tia, whatever do you mean? You were my strength! You kept me going in Johannesburg. You turned me around in Milan. What about Mark's death and the crisis with Annis? You were my sanity through all the horrors of DC!

We're strong together, you told me.

Together. Remember I said that part of it? I meant what I said, I always did choose my words carefully. I needed you. Certainly, you miss me now. But I am here, you have all these years of collected memories. You can do it. Will you?

Collected memories? Of what? Scraps of time. I guess I always held the delusion that one day you'd come home, to some Rockwell image with the cottage and the turkey and all the happy glowing faces.

Didn't we have happy glowing faces? Yes, indeed we did, Tia, but over such bigger things. International treaties, and massive social reforms.

She twisted her ring on her finger. *Marriage. How differently it had all turned out.* There was smooth gold in her fingers, but in her memory there was another band.

What ever happened to that?

When she arrived home, she nearly ran to the small box of treasures collected over a lifetime. Deep in the corner, she found what she was looking for. Amazing that after all these years it survived. It had not decayed nor crumbled, the thin circlet carefully handwoven from the grasses of Coyote Creek, now dusty and pale, but intact.

'I give you this as a symbol of our commitment, and a symbol of our joint purpose.'

Joint purpose? Ari, darling, I never understood what you meant! What could possibly be more sacred, through all this time, than our shared purpose, our shared legacy into the future? Isn't this in fact the deepest intimacy of all?

All these years, I have worn the wrong ring!

She slipped off the gold wedding band. Later she'd look around for other odd gold pieces and have Jeffrey's artist friend melt them down to form a locket, to house the grass ring. After all these years, she would wear the right ring.

I am here, in your heart, all these years of collected memories. You can go on. I left much incomplete when I died. Someone needs to pick up the pieces, someone who has the courage.

You can do it. Will you?

You have incredible courage.

And you have a job to do.

She knew then that she would carry on. She would pick up the pieces he had left, carry them to fruition, and beyond.

His and her own, legacy woven together over time.

(4.)

The PrepCon was now over, a new Chairperson chosen, the agreement readied for the Plenary sessions. The world delegates had disbanded, and UN officials had returned to New York until the beginning of the Conference. But much of the organization of the side sessions remained an LA issue.

The Director of the side sessions kept calling Tia periodically with updates and gentle concern. "Tia, there is much to be done," he said in rich Nigerian accents. "You know this city, you know the venues. Come back to the committee, try it out for a day or so. ..."

Come back to the living, you mean.

"... We need you."

She froze.

Ari, you told him to say that!

Those fiery eyes, that intense gaze. 'We' wasn't just you, it was the world. You called me then to a purposeful life. And you do it again today. You are right, darling, the world needs me.

"I'll be there in the morning," she promised.

(5.)

At the World Conference on Sustainable Development in Los Angeles, delegates launched a new international institution: the World Sustainability Commission. The first Director-General of the new WSC was an American, a veteran in matters of policy, organizational structure and international negotiation, a man well acquainted with the vision under which the WSC had been created: Dr. Kegan Pearce.

The WSC was a small organization, flexible and fluid in its functionality. It encouraged the World Trade Organization, the World Health Organization and the World Environment Organization toward self-reliance and balance, toward creating stability through diversity. It became the coordinating organization assuring that the globalization of the future would work for the environment and for the world's people, including its poor.[109]

Modeled on the two hundred year forestry plan of eighteenth century Britain, its initial charter set forth goals which exceeded any single human lifespan. Because, after all, Sustainability was a plan for generations.

(6.)

Tia knelt beside the greywater reedbed, planting a memorial grouping of red and white tea roses. She wished she could plant them in her favorite olive nook, but their water needs dictated this placement in the carefully zoned Lares layout. As it was, she'd had to campaign for their planting space, space which would more efficiently be used for edible crops.

The WCSD had been exciting, a milestone and recognition for the city. The side sessions had been fascinating, showcasing the new efforts in resource efficiency and sustainability from around the globe. Yet something had been missing.

Tia recalled stories from Johannesburg of political messages written across flags, of fiery floor debates between members of the same delegation. She thought back to the days of Barcelona, renegade teams, government boycotts, scientists country-hopping so that their message could be heard. She gazed at the little reed stream, its flow so slow as to be almost indiscernible. And then it hit her.

WCSD has reached the Mainstream.

Resource efficiency, even with the increased challenge of Factor 10, is an accepted norm. It's no longer just a brave few trying to bring the rest along. We have not arrived yet, not by a long shot, but we move closer every day.

Tia brushed the dirt from her hands and headed back toward the toolshed. She paused beside a chard plant bolting to seed, its tall stalk shooting six feet in the air, towering above lowly vegetable fellows.

It took a lot of courage to be a Change Agent with that message, to stand up and boldly point in this new direction so foreign to the Mainstream course. Courage to stick up for one's values. Courage to stand up and be vocal, to get shot down and to get up and go on again. Pushing, pulling, prodding, getting the message out anyway they could.

Tia slipped into the nook with the lavenders and the olive trees. She reached for the circular golden locket on the long chain around her neck. Its smooth surfaces were comforting in her hand.

Ari, you and your fellow Change Agents got us past the fulcrum. The balance has tipped. Now the momentum carries us forward toward Sustainability, no longer toward destruction.

(7.)

With the support of California small farms, the renewable energy industry and the citizens of the changing cities, Gavin Duer won his 2042 campaign for a U.S. Senate seat.

Meanwhile, Annis' REGROW presentation at WCSD had leapfrogged her to international recognition. Suddenly the world was calling: Australia and Canada, Columbia and England, all clamoring for her to share the concept.

Thus Edan and Linette spent many joyful hours at Lares with Grandma. South House was full of happy activity again: Lares garden adventures, planting fat bean seeds, feeding the chickens, visiting the wildflowers, learning to cook at the big counter, all in generational replay.

Kaia, too, appeared at Lares often. Even though the WCSD work had been completed, she continued to be a cheerful presence at the South House patio. Rhus found her enchanting, and lingered to soak in her young laughter as she plied him for details of harvest scheduling, varietal selection, and the intricacies of crop layout.

Kaia was patient beneath that cheery sparkle, Tia decided, because it took weeks for her presence to gain its intended attention. But finally Seth noticed.

Once he noticed, Seth fell hard. After years of never revealing any clues about his dating life, his devotion to Kaia was clear to all. Tia and Jana giggled together about the young couple. Kaia's curly head barely reached Seth's strong shoulder, yet it seemed that it was now positively glued there. When Seth finally figured out that he might propose, the entire complex was delighted.

(8.)

Tia took PLASE down to the beach early this Saturday morning. Here, periodically, regardless of weather or season, she would walk barefoot through the chill waters at the edge of the ocean waves.

In the old days, the beaches were all named and predictable, they had unique character attributes: Sunset, a surfer's beach; Mother's Beach, gentle waves and broad sands for small children.

Tia recalled the government studies of the cost of replenishing beach sand at favored locations. *A ridiculous exercise that was. The sand comes and goes with the storms, at the whim of the ocean currents. As soon as the bulldozers deposited it, the oceans redistributed it.*

Now, we clear the man-made features in advance of the SEZ forecasts, and the ocean chooses its course. Now we invest the State funds in REGROW and sister restoration programs in advance of the sea.

This morning was foggy and cool. Tia abandoned her shoes and towel to the sand, hiked up her dress and waded into the cold waters up to her knees. The sea wind cut through her wool sweater as she sloshed along the beach, the water alternately ankle deep and thigh high with the surge of the waves. Her sodden dress floated on the waters, then plastered itself to her legs.

She stopped walking to watch anew with dizzied wonder as the water rushed back to the ocean leaving foam scallops around her ankles. The next wave crashed and sent its surge forward to caress her legs again. She reached for the locket on the long chain around her neck. *Connection.*

I'm here, Tia. I'm here. Another wave came out to greet her. When she came down to the ocean like this, it was as if he spoke with her again.

Sustainability. Ari, my darling, I've been thinking about Sustainability this week. It seems there's more than just one meaning.

I told you, international delegations couldn't agree on a meaning! The clatter of pebbles rolled by the receding waves sounded like laughter.

When you spoke of Sustainability, you always meant Sustainability of physical resources. Your definitions meant the resources we took were in moderation, in balance. No more taken than could be regenerated. And you said this lifestyle was in the future, something perhaps Edan and Linnette would see.

That I did ... you're living in the Transition, a time of changing habits, and of Restoration, moving toward an ecological balance which can support that Sustainability.

But I see a certain Sustainability around me now – a Sustainability of the spirit, of Purpose and Service, a change in the hearts of the people. There was a time when the inertia seemed impossible to overcome. In your time, darling, the Change Agents had to drive the movement, they had to instill the energy, overcome the inertia. I used to watch the people in the cars idling on the freeway and say: when will they get it, when will they act!?

The answer was when they no longer felt alone. That is the beauty of the Transformation Wave, that's why the wave works. People see that they aren't the only one. They aren't renegades, they are part of a Movement, with a direction, a future, a hope. And at that point they begin to act. They are now willing to step forward and make the changes.

Stepping forward, Ari, I must do it now. Life with you was exhilarating. What a whirlwind, what a deep connection we shared. It truly was more than I ever dreamed possible.

The ocean wind whipped her long white hair and chilled the tears on her creased cheek.

Three long years it has been. I miss you darling. I will never forget you.

She pressed the locket to her lips as the waves swirled around her ankles.

I am gone, Tia. But you are still very much alive.

Alive. What is alive if not mission, service, purpose? I still have more to do, Ari.

She trudged back to her towel and shoes, cold, alone in the chill wind.

Tomorrow a plane to DC for the presentation to WSC. Then we're off on the second world tour for ROOTS International. Soil sequestration. Rainwater harvesting. Indigenous varieties. Traditional techniques. President Alden certainly pulled the connections together to make it possible. He has taken quite an interest in this venture; he has become the international spokesperson.

He's a good man, Tia.

This time he announced he would join the tour. Venezuela, Columbia, Brazil. He's on a mission, too, of a different sort. Forging connections between people, he tells me. He's been pressing me to drop the formalities and call him Barry.

She watched the breakers roll into foam.

His eyes are pale blue, Ari, like the ocean of Santa Monica Bay.

(9.)

In the politicians' drawing rooms he lead the sessions. Tia listened with renewed amazement to the power of his vision, the strength of his leadership. Here she saw the pure brilliance of Barry Alden, undistilled by speechwriters and press agents, as he encouraged local organizers to work together toward Sustainable agriculture under climate change.

But in the fields of the villages, with the common people, it was Tia who knelt in the raw earth and, through an interpreter, told of earthworms and fungae, soil porosity and composting, native grasses and tiered food forests. The elders nodded, recalling their grandparents telling tales of such, before the disastrous days of the "Green

Revolution" of hybrid patented seeds dependent upon the dreadful chemicals, and the related indebtedness to the big American corporations.

At first he stood aloof from these earthy discussions, until the day when she took a handful of the rich soil of Venezuela and pressed it into his palm. His pale eyes widened in astonishment. Holding his hand she drew him down to bury his fingers in the soil of the field. He glanced at her, but then bowed his head over his hands, rubbing them together to savor the grit.

Later, at her elbow on the path back to the village he said simply, "I had no idea." His face was alight with wonder.

"You needed to know it … Barry."

He smiled at her first use of the familiarity.

When she planted beans with the children of a Columbian village, pressing flat indigenous varieties into tiny palms, she found his palm extended as well. Press cameras rolled as he planted beans alongside the children, but in the expression on his well-lined face, Tia could see that his intention was no publicity stunt.

Visiting a Brazilian field where people had been coached by the first ROOTS tour, he took the coarse shovel from the villager and with his own hands opened the compost pile for her demonstration. The soil was rich, teeming with life. He bent to examine it, coming away with a knot of worms which he extended in his palm in boyish innocence. She looked from the writhing worms to his pale blue eyes, his face familiar from a decade of newscasts, yet so unlike Ari's. Tears stung her eyes and she turned so that her audience would not see.

After the formal meal with village elders, he took her arm in the style of a grand ballroom promenade, formal in front of his entourage but tender in his touch. They walked the short distance to the small houses given them to stay. When they reached the houses, he paused, the world suspended in the midst of his aides and bodyguard. He slowly pressed her hand to his lips. His eyes were a summer's sky clear of clouds. And hers held the answer he had long been awaiting.

(10.)

Her first evening home at Lares, Tia's Venture chirped around ten o'clock. Barry's confident voice was in her ear, his proud face in the display.

"I called to wish you goodnight, dear."

She nearly dropped the Venture in her surprise.

"Tia? Are you there, Tia?"

"Yes, Barry, I'm here – it's just …"

"He didn't call you at bedtime?"

"No…"

"Ah, but I will."

⤴

With Ari, Tia had rarely traveled. Now she saw the world, accompanying Barry on his trips as dignitary to London, New Delhi, Beijing, as well as further ROOTS trips to Africa, South America, Australia. An occasional mention in the press called her the Former President's companion, but for the most part she enjoyed peaceful anonymity, much to Annis' relief.

⤴

In Los Angeles, the Sepulveda Pass, now clear of roadway except for the MagLev and a PLASE line, was restored as the Benton Tremain Nature Preserve of native plants and small wildlife. Here Barry bought a small condo for his frequent visits to LA.

"Why did you become President?" Tia asked as they planted a tangerine tree in his courtyard.

"Because I knew I could make the world a better place." He said it simply, unpretentiously, while forming the tree's basin with his bare hands.

As she dug in slips of yarrow, desert mint and sage, she thought of his Administration's policies. The energy plan, his support of Sustainable development, the third world debt relief, and the strides made toward an enlightened globalization, a world where nations worked together for the benefit of all peoples.[110]

"You have, Barry, you have," she said softly.

"Oh, I'm not finished yet."

(11.)

The faces of Lares were changing. The Tilfords moved to Wisconsin to join Janelle and her family. The Bainbridge daughters were growing, now approaching their teens. Carl's sons had moved on to adult lives, Walter beginning a family of his own.

With the vacancy in the Tilford unit, to Tia's delight, Gavin decided to move his family closer to Grandma. Edan and Linnette, now nine and twelve, needed only to cross the gardens to visit.

With Seth's marriage to Kaia, and the impending arrival of their firstborn, Tia made the heartwrenching decision to relinquish her wing of South House. She moved into Seth's old room in Jana and Steve's wing, now rechristened the Seniors' Wing. And Kaia and Seth prepared their new home for the next generation of Lares.

(12.)

From the window of Barry's Sepulveda condo, Tia could see the native ceanothus and elders of the nature preserve. This winter the ceanothus flowers were unremarkable and the elder was late to releaf; the rains had again been insignificant.

Barry approached behind her and kissed her shoulder. She turned to him and smiled.

The glint of the gold locket caught his attention. He lifted it from her breast. "I just noticed – this has little continents on it, look, there's South America! What is it? You don't ever seem to take it off." He fumbled with the catch to open it.

She wrapped her hand around his; the locket remained closed. "It's ... my wedding ring."

A shadow crossed his face.

He gently took her left hand, touching her ring finger. "I hope you'll allow me to replace it with one here."

In her mind the native plants Restoration of the hillside merged with an image of a youthful Ari, cradling a toy ball tenderly in his palms. *'Save the El Segundo Blue Butterfly!'*

Barry, this between us is Conservation. Without the supporting ecosystem...

Still holding her hand, his pale eyes moved to hers.

"Tia, will ..."

She put a finger gently to his lips, his words better left unsaid.

(13.)

Kaia delivered at home, her midwife in attendance. Steve couldn't endure the laboring, and disappeared to Gavin's unit to be called when it was over. Jana paced, her pacing heavier and slower than Ari's used to be, but reminiscent nonetheless. Tia looked out at the afternoon sunshine over the gardens, thinking of Seth's birth and the terrible storm that night. Kaia's cries of delivery were audible throughout the house, but strangely did not upset Tia the way they did Jana.

The high pitched cry of a newborn cut the air, and Jana froze. Tia smiled. *Another generation, another leaf on the family tree.*

After a while, Seth came through the French doors, carrying the tiny bundle. "Mom, meet Genia. My daughter." His voice shook.

As he handed the baby to Jana, tears welled up in Seth's eyes. Tia hugged him, his massive shoulders heaving in her arms. "I'll get your father," Tia offered. Seth broke away to compose himself and Tia went to summon Steve.

When Steve and Jana had their turns, Tia at last met Genia.

Genia, whose name means 'generations.' Tia held her, gazing into her impossibly tiny face. Genia looked exactly like Seth had in those first hours, with those same dark brown eyes. Ari's eyes, brown like the earth. Damek eyes, rich and alive, healthy soil.

We are turning the planet over to our children and grandchildren. It's a process, not a point in time, but a gradual unfolding. They reach out with eager hands and we transfer the Trust, the Trust that future generations extend to us.

Genia gazed up at Tia in full-hearted vulnerability.

We reached out our hands to receive it, long ago.

Tia thought of her reading after her father's death. *I still remember my horror at what had been placed in my hands.*

But oh, what we did with it! Restoration, transformation, paradigm change.

Tia looked into Genia's large brown eyes.

Ah, little one, what a Legacy we are handing to you!

CHAPTER 11:

THE TRANSFORMATION WAVE

2005

In the United States, more than thirty thousand nongovernmental organizations, foundations, and citizens' groups are addressing the issue of social and ecological sustainability in the most complete sense of the word. Worldwide, the number of organizations exceeds one hundred thousand. Together they address a broad array of issues, including environmental justice, ecological literacy, public policy, conservation, women's rights and health, population, renewable energy, corporate reform, labor rights, climate change, trade rules, ethical investing, ecological tax reform, water, and much more. These groups follow Mahatma Gandhi's imperatives: some resist, while others create new structures, patterns, and means. The groups tend to be local, marginal, poorly funded, and overworked. It's hard for most not to feel palpable anxiety that they could perish in a twinkling. At the same time, a deeper pattern is emerging that is extraordinary.

If you ask all of these groups for their principles, frameworks, conventions, models, or declarations, you will find that they do not conflict. This has never happened before. In the past, powerful movements such as Christianity, Marxism, and Freudian psychology started with a unified or centralized set of ideas and then disseminated them, over time creating power struggles as the core mental model or dogma was changed, diluted or revised. The sustainability movement did not start this way. Its proponents do not agree on everything, nor should they ever, but, remarkably, they all share a basic set of fundamental understandings about the earth, how it functions, and the necessity of fairness and equity for all people in partaking of the earth's life-giving systems.

These groups believe that self-sufficiency is a human right. They imagine a future where producing the means to kill people is not a business but a crime, where families do not starve, where parents can work, where children are never sold, and where women cannot be impoverished because they choose to be mothers. These groups believe that water and air belong to us all, not to the rich. They believe seeds and life itself cannot be owned or patented by corporations. They believe that nature is the basis of true prosperity and must be honored.

This shared understanding is arising spontaneously, from different economic sectors, cultures, regions, and cohorts. It is indisputably growing and spreading throughout this country and the world. No one started this world-view, no one is in charge of it, and no orthodoxy is restraining it. It is the fastest and most powerful movement in the world today, unrecognizable to most American media outlets because it is not centralized, based on power, or led by white, male, charismatic vertebrates. As conditions continue to worsen socially, environmentally, and politically, organizations working toward sustainability increase, deepen, and multiply.

– Paul Hawken

Because you comprehend the changes our civilization must make, because you glimpse what lies before us if we don't change course, you have a job to do. You can't remain on the sidelines. It'll drive you crazy with fear and worry. Or else, you'll try to blind yourself to it, and shut down a part of your innermost self. The only way out of this is by doing, by stepping out into the lead, by doing your part to help transform this society as you realize it must.

– Ari Damek

It's time for you to choose your place, to select what you want to do. What part do you want to play? Choose your petal of the Permaculture Flower. What problem do you want to embrace and make it your own to solve? What issue do you want to devote yourself to? It's time to act.

– Jana Damek

Become a Change Agent: Seek out new restorative and Sustainable technologies. Translate them into something that others can embrace. Engage others in the conversation of how to refine solutions. Support the entry of these new technologies into mainstream life.

Become a Transformer: Make Sustainable practices come alive in your own life. Massage the solutions into practicality and model them for others to see. Little by little, show the Mainstream, through your actions and everyday living, that environmental change is possible, it is enticing, it is desirable and it is fun.

– Steve Vernados

If you try to interest the apathetic, or convert the opposition, you are in for frustration and perhaps failure. But if you quietly attract the curious and the open-minded, and those hungry for something that addresses a nagging worry they have, you will start building critical mass. And that critical mass will tug the rest of ... your organization, community, or society at large ... in a new direction.

> – Alan AtKisson
> Author of
> *Believing Cassandra*

One thing is clear: the needed changes will not simply happen. No hidden hand is guiding technology or the economy toward sustainability. The issues on the global environmental agenda are precisely the type of issues – long-term, chronic, complex – where genuine, farsighted leadership from elected officials is at a premium. But we have not seen this leadership emerge, and we have waited long enough. What we need now is an international movement of citizens and scientists, one capable of dramatically advancing the political and personal actions needed for the transition to sustainability. ... It is time for we the people, as citizens and consumers, to take charge.

> – James Gustave Speth
> Environmental advisor to
> two U.S. Presidents

I didn't realize I knew so many people, or knew people who knew so many people. Our circles of influence can be surprising, if we just pause to take count of who we know. The vast number of lives we can touch, in spreading an idea, the power we wield to bring change to the world – it's truly incredible.

It's like I'm the connection point between two huge worlds. And because of that, well, there's a tremendous amount I can do. A tremendous amount I have to do. The changes have got to happen. And it's up to me to do something about it.

> – Gavin Duer

The notes on the following pages identify many of the nonfiction portions of *Legacy*. These exciting discoveries, inventions, ideas, and events, were created by ordinary people, like yourself, who dedicated themselves to making a difference. Set forth in a single list, what an enormous contribution they have made to environmental change. What a profound legacy to you, and to the generations of the future.

These are the *real* Transformation Wave. It is happening, right now, all around you.

Come with us, work with us. Let's make the list even longer, until the Mainstream cannot ignore it, until they follow in our footsteps. Together we can change the world, for the benefit of future generations.

We need you.

---

[1] In 1992 most of the world's countries, including the United States, signed and ratified the United Nations Framework Convention on Climate Change, acknowledging the need for a global agreement about greenhouse gas emissions. In subsequent meetings, including a 1997 meeting in Kyoto, Japan, a Protocol agreement was developed to implement the world's first global treaty for control of greenhouse gasses. In the ensuing years, more than 141 of the world's countries – including all the developed nations with the exception of the United States and Australia – ratified this Kyoto Protocol.

The Natural Resources Defense Council and the WorldWatch Institute do an excellent job of ongoing documentation of the environmental and social crisis we face. http://www.nrdc.org/ and http://www.worldwatch.org/

[2] The Monterey Bay Aquarium offers a wallet sized card which guides consumers to wise choices in seafood purchases. Free online at "Seafood Watch: Make Choices for Healthy Oceans," http://www.mbayaq.org/cr/seafoodwatch.asp

[3] Bountiful edible gardens are accessible even to apartment dwellers. McGee and Stuckey's *Bountiful Container* is full of ideas on container gardening of edible plants, and Adam Caplin's *Urban Eden* provides inspiring photographs.

[4] The Union of Concerned Scientists has published a clear and readable report entitled "Climate Change in California: Choosing Our Future." This PDF report is available free online at http://www.climatechoices.org/

[5] Although *50 Simple Things You Can Do To Save the Earth* is an older book, its suggestions are no less valid today. While 'reusing envelopes' sounds laughable, most of the recommendations are not, particularly if undertaken by large segments of the population. Its action items are very much grassroots in approach, and most are quite appropriate for incorporation into mainstream life. Additional grassroots action items are included throughout *Legacy*.

[6] The Photoremediation process, also known as the photodeactivation process, a technique for rendering some types of nuclear waste harmless, was invented

by Dr. Paul M. Brown. Dr. Brown also invented a resonant nuclear battery which would last 25 years. Dr. Brown's company, Nuclear Solutions, Inc. (NASDAQ: NSOL) continues, and in June 2005 announced that it had filed for an international patent for one aspect of nuclear cleanup, remediating tritiated water. http://www.spiritofmaat.com/archive/feb2/nuclear.htm , http://users.erols.com/iri/Pauleulogy.htm and NASDAQ news for symbol NSOL, accessed July 18, 2005.

[7] "Some 26% of American adults have adopted a new worldview in the past 40 years that is largely consistent with the values of sustainability." WorldWatch Institute, *State of the World 2001*, New York: WW Norton, 2001, p.195.

[8] We must become "jacks of all trades and master of one." David Holmgren said, quoting a German permaculturist. "Permaculture Solutions Around the World," workshop sponsored by the Santa Barbara Permaculture Network, Santa Barbara City College, August 2, 2005.

[9] Bill Mollison and David Holmgren are the founders of the Permaculture movement. Their joint publication, *Permaculture One*, has become a Permaculture classic. Mollison went on to publish *Permaculture: A Designers' Manual*, and Holmgren published *Permaculture: Principles and Pathways Beyond Sustainability*. Holmgren's garden can be seen online from his webpage or from his *Melliodora ebook*. Alan Chadwick was a British practitioner of biodynamic agriculture. John Jeavons has refined many of Chadwick's ideas. Jeavons' best known book is *How To Grow More Vegetables on Less Land Than You Can Imagine,* and many of his techniques are described throughout *Legacy*. Masanobu Fukuoka is a Japanese agricultural innovator, whose 'do nothing' gardening involves intercropping of multiple species, including orchard trees, grains, vegetables and legumes, on the same untilled plot. His concepts are described in his many books, including *One Straw Revolution*.

[10] Much of Europe has already passed legislation to become GMO-free. Select U.S. counties are similarly becoming GMO-free. See GMO Free Europe, http://www.foeeurope.org/GMOs/gmofree/ and http://www.foeeurope.org/GMOs/explore/whats_wrong.htm , GMO Free Alameda County, http://www.gmofreeac.org/environment_htm, all accessed June 25,2005.

[11] The United Nations' definition of Sustainability reads: "Sustainable development meets the needs of the present without compromising the ability of future generations of humans and other species to meet their own needs while restoring local and global ecosystems." http://www.un.org/esa/sustdev/index.html

The WorldWatch Institute's definition of a Sustainable economy requires "a population that is stable in balance with its natural support systems, an energy system that does not raise the level of the greenhouse gases and disrupt the

Earth's climate, and a level of material demand that neither exceeds the sustainable yield of forests, grasslands, or fisheries nor systematically destroys the other species with which we share the planet." Lester R Brown, Christopher Flavin, and Sandra Postel, *Saving the Planet*.

This webpage includes a diverse selection of Sustainability definitions: Sustainability Measures, "What is Sustainability, Anyway?" http://www.sustainablemeasures.com/Sustainability/DefinitionsDevelopment.html accessed Aug. 12, 2005.

[12] "Because we live in such a dramatically depleted world today, it is not enough to seek merely to sustain it. Sustainable systems may be a reasonable long-term goal in a regenerated world, but for now we need to tip the scales toward *restoration* to regain the subtle equilibrium that is the nature of nature." Kenny Ausubel, preface to *Restoring the Earth*, Tiburon, CA: HJ Kramer, 1997. (emphasis his)

[13] Well-written books about living from purpose and finding one's direction include Richard J. Leider, *The Power of Purpose*, New York: Fawcett Gold Medal/Ballantine, 1985. (Seek the older edition, ISBN 0-449-12840-7 rather than the newer one.) Ram Dass, *How Can I Help*, New York: Alfred A Knopf, 1988 contains stories and reflections about living a life of service.

[14] Native Seed/SEARCH is a seedbank for Native American vegetable varieties. http://www.nativeseeds.org

Steve Solomon's online book details techniques for growing vegetables under extremely low-water situations. Accessible with registration at http://www.soilandhealth.org

Desert Harvest by Jane Nyhuis describes drylands techniques for larger scale farming, including crop calculations for diverse indigenous crops.

[15] "It's essential that we stop growing crops and start growing soil instead. The wonderful thing is that in the process of growing soil, we'll wind up with healthy crops we can use. If we feed the soil, we feed Mother Nature, and in turn, she will feed us abundantly." John Jeavons, quoted in *Gardening for the Future of the Earth*, Howard-Yana Shapiro, New York: Bantam, 2000, p. 79.

Woodbury County Iowa offers a tax incentive to farmers if they switch from conventional production to organics, and is one of the first local governments to do so. "Long Overdue: Tax Breaks for Farmers Who Shift to Organic Agriculture," by Amigo Cantisano, http://www.organicconsumers.org/organic/taxbreak071805.cfm accessed July 18, 2005.

[16] In 1992 in Rio and again in 2002 in Johannesburg, representatives of world nations and NGOs met for a World Summit on Sustainable Development. "WSSD may increasingly be seen as the coming of age of new ways of

addressing sustainable development at the global level. ... [The NGO activities and side sessions] generated numerous new commitments, ideas, allianaces and activities – as well as allowing organizations to learn more about each others' work and take stock of what has happened in different parts of the world ..." Tom Bigg, "The World Summit on Sustainable Development: Was it worthwhile?" International Institute for Environment and Development, PDF available at www.iied.org/docs/wssd/wssdreview.pdf accessed Aug. 16, 2005.

[17] The Bioneers conference is a regular gathering focusing on solutions to restore the earth. Stories from the bioneers are available in two books edited by Kenny Ausubel, *Restoring the Earth*, and *Nature's Operating Instructions*, or through the Bioneers website www.bioneers.org

[18] Alan AtKisson explained the spread of new ideas in terms of Change Agents, Transformers, Reactionaries and Iconoclasts. It is notable that Change Agents and Transformers create new dynamics through positive action. Alan AtKisson, *Believing Cassandra.*

[19] The myriad of examples in Paul Hawken's *Natural Capitalism* can be read as a long list of instances in which Green has inspired Business.

"... the hunt for carbon savings could become a major new source of competitive advantage." WorldWatch Institute, *State of the World 2001*, New York: WW Norton, 2001, p. 101.

[20] "As the scientific evidence of climate change has mounted, so has congressional activity. The number of climate change-related legislative proposals increased from seven introduced in the 105th Congress (1997-1998) ... to nearly 100 in the 108th Congress (2003-2004). Legislation to have the largest emitters of greenhouse gasses disclose their emissions has passed the Senate twice. And in October 2003, the bipartisan team of Senators Joseph I. Lieberman (D-CT) and John McCain (R-AZ) won the support of 44 Senators in the first vote on their bill to cap U.S. greenhouse gas emissions." Pew Center on Global Climate Change, "Q&A: Russia and the Kyoto Protocol," www.pewclimate.org/what_s_being_done/In_the_world/russia_kyoto_q_a.cf m accessed Aug. 12, 2005.

[21] The 1994 Declaration of the Factor 10 Club states "current resource productivity must be increased by an average of a *FACTOR of 10* during the next 30 to 50 years. This is technically feasible if we mobilize our know-how to generate new products, services, as well as new methods of manufacturing." (emphasis theirs) "1994 Declaration of the Factor 10 Club," www.techfak.uni-bielefeld.de/~walter/f10/declaration94.html accessed Aug. 12, 2005.

[22] Activists protested General Motors' destruction of EV1 electric vehicles as described in the text. Meanwhile, after six months of similar demolitions, Ford Motor Company announced a plan to return its surviving electric Ranger

pickups to owners. "Vigil an Outlet for EV1 Fans" by Patricia Ward Biederman, LA Times, Mar. 12, 2005. "Electric Pickups to Keep Truckin'," by Eric Bailey, LA Times, July 19, 2005.

[23] Forest gardening techniques, guilds, and integration of edible plants within a home landscape are explained in detail in Toby Hemenway, *Gaia's Garden: A Guide to Home-Scale Permaculture*; Patrick Whitefield, *How to Make a Forest Garden*; and Robert Kourik, *Designing and Maintaining Your Edible Landscape Naturally*.

[24] Sally Fallon gives detailed information on avoiding toxins and building health through nutritional choices, in extensive sidebars in her book *Nourishing Traditions*. Robert S. Mendelsohn, M.D. discusses the allopathic medical system's orientation toward medication and surgery in *How to Raise a Healthy Child in Spite of Your Doctor*. For ways to treat the whole body rather than just the symptoms, see Alice Likowski Duncan, *Your Healthy Child*. Annie Berthold-Bond's *Clean and Green* tells how to clean house without toxic chemicals.

[25] Cooking straight from the garden is emphasized in cookbooks such as Renee Shepherd's *Recipes from a Kitchen Garden* and *More Recipes from a Kitchen Garden*, or *Twelve Months of Monastery Soups* by Victor d'Avila-Latourrette. Conventional cookbooks often require imported or out-of-season ingredients, but cookbooks such as these are designed for garden-harvest-to-kitchen; virtually all of the ingredients called for in a given recipe ripen in the same seasonal timeframe, under similar growing conditions.

[26] The Intergovernmental Panel on Climate Change is a worldwide body of scientists who have developed numerous climate change projections. The projection curves referred to in *Legacy*, including the 2040 target date for greenhouse gas emissions decrease, are online at http://www.ucsusa.org/global_environment/global_warming/page.cfm?pageID=967

[27] Oasis Design creates greywater systems and maintains a website full of concrete information on greywater. Art Ludwig, "Common Grey Water Errors and Preferred Practices," Oasis Design http://www.oasisdesign.net/greywater/misinfo/index.htm

[28] La Leche League International has provided breastfeeding support, information, and public policy since 1956. http://www.lalecheleague.org/

[29] Europe's 'Efficient and environmentally friendly aircraft engine' project "aims to reduce CO_2 emissions by as much as 20 percent and NO_x emissions by an impressive 60-to-80 percent, while, at the same time, cutting engine life cycle (repair and maintenance) costs by nearly one-third." European Commission, Research Aeronautics, "EEFAE – efficient, eco-friendly aircraft engines," March 25, 2005

http://europa.eu.int/comm/research/aeronautics/info/news/article_2327_en.htm
l accessed July 30, 2005.

[30] Connecticut, Delaware, Maine, Massachusetts, New Hampshire, New Jersey, New York, Rhode Island and Vermont are already part of the Regional Greenhouse Gas Initiative. Maryland, the District of Columbia, Pennsylvania are close to being on board. California, Georgia, Illinois, Oregon, Texas, Washington, and Wisconsin have some form of state level greenhouse gas legislation. New Mexico and North Carolina have action plans. Refer to the *Legacy* website for specific web references.

[31] Seattle Mayor Greg Nickels formed a Green Team of cities committed to the 'intent and spirit of Kyoto.' On February 16, 2005, the date the Kyoto Protocol came into effect, his goal was 141 cities, to match the number of countries which had ratified the Protocol. By late August 2005, 178 cities were a part of the declaration. Seattle Office of the Mayor, "U.S. Mayors Climate Protection Agreement," http://www.ci.seattle.wa.us/mayor/climate/

[32] BettyClare Moffatt wrote a delightful piece which artfully captures the process of manifesting a vision. BettyClare Moffatt, "How to Make a Miracle," *Opening to Miracles*, Berkeley: Wildcat Canyon Press, 1995, p.210.

[33] The Path To Freedom project of Pasadena, CA provides invaluable inspiration in urban homesteading and edible landscaping. http://pathtofreedom.com/

Victory Gardens were a grass-roots self-reliant response to changing times embraced by nearly 20 million Americans in the 1930s -1940s. Gardens produced up to 40% of produce consumed. www.victoryseeds.com/TheVictoryGarden

"Most indigenous and traditional people recognize that, if their culture is removed from nature, land, food and other practical expressions, its most valued aspects – language, kinship, spiritual beliefs – become a disconnected and eventually a dead tradition." David Holmgren, *Permaculture: Principles and Pathways Beyond Sustainability*, Australia: Holmgren Design Services, 2002, p.211.

" I remember the time that I spent with the Karok Indians of northern California – whenever I presented one of them with an unfamiliar plant, the inevitable question was 'What's it good for?' Certainly the Indians love nature as their home, but rather than merely holding an aesthetic viewpoint about it they combine a sincere appreciation for its beauty with a functional attitude." Michael Tierra, *The Way of Herbs*, New York : Pocket Books, 1998.

[34] Numerous examples of service economies, including the Dow Chemical and Interface Carpet examples, are presented in *Natural Capitalism*, Paul Hawken and Amory Lovins, chapter 7. Also, in "Natural Capitalism: Where the Rubber

Meets the Road," by Amory Lovins and Hunter Lovins, *Nature's Operating Instructions*, Kenny Ausubel, editor.

[35] R. Lal says soils could sequester 5%-15% of our carbon emissions, in his article "Soil Carbon Sequestration Impacts on Global Climate Change and Food Security," Science magazine 11 June 04. Guy Dauncey uses the higher figures 8%-17% in his book *Stormy Weather*, p. 127.

[36] Seattle Public Utilities is launching an initiative called Wasteless in Seattle, "moving beyond recycling to preventing garbage itself," to drastically reduce the need for landfills and to lower disposal, transportation and energy costs. Debera Carlton Harrell, "'Zero waste' is Seattle's new garbage mantra." Seattle Post-Intelligencer, July 18, 2005.

A "Zero Waste California" concept is posed by the California Integrated Waste Management Board, encouraging citizens to reach beyond "reduce, reuse, and recycle" into efficient use of our natural resources. www.zerowaste.ca.gov accessed April 5, 2005.

[37] *The Art of French Vegetable Gardening* by Louisa Jones could perhaps be called the coffee-table book of edible gardening. Full of gorgeous and inspiring photographs, it shows how edible gardens can be every bit as visually enticing as ornamentals.

[38] TreePeople has a forestry program called "Fruit Trees to Combat Hunger" distributing fruit trees to community groups, schools and churches. http://www.treepeople.org/vfp.dll?OakTree~getPage~&PNPK=28 accessed May 25, 2005.

[39] Gary Gardner encourages environmentalists to work with religious thinkers in his article "Invoking the Spirit", WorldWatch Institute Paper #164, December 2002 available as a free PDF.

[40] The examples of religious environmental thinking given in the text are nonfiction. Refer to the *Legacy* website for specific source information. While the examples in the text are largely Christian, due to the context set by the Lynn White essay, this same rethinking is taking place in non-Christian religions as well. Discussion, and illustrations of multiple world religions, can be found at Dr. J.R. Thorngren, "Religion and the Environment," http://daphne.palomar.edu/calenvironment/religion.htm accessed Aug. 12, 2005.

[41] The California greenhouse gas bill, Assembly Bill 1493, passed July 22, 2002. It directs the California Air Resources Board to develop and adopt regulations that achieve the maximum feasible and cost-effective reduction of greenhouse gas emissions from motor vehicles. It will be effective for vehicles manufactured in 2009 and beyond. Pace Law School, http://law.pace.edu/globalwarming/california.html accessed February 20,

2005. In August 2005, as this book was going to print, Oregon and Washington were on the verge of adopting terms similar to the California bill.

[42] In 2005, UPS, FedEx and the United States Postal Service each had a limited number of fuel cell vehicles operating on a test basis. FedEx had a small percentage of its Tokyo fleet, UPS had three delivery vans, and the USPS had one fuel cell vehicle. Refer to the *Legacy* website for specific web references.

[43] A few of the many Sustainability support organizations include: San Francisco, Monterey Bay, the Santa Barbara Permaculture Network. Oakland has a Sustainable Community Development Initiative, Long Beach has some specific sustainably-focused park and greenbelt areas. Additionally, Santa Monica's Environmental Programs Division recently celebrated its 10th anniversary. Refer to the *Legacy* website for specific web references.

[44] The Bradley Method is one technique for natural childbirth. *Husband-Coached Childbirth*, by Robert A. Bradley and *Natural Childbirth the Bradley Way* by Suzanne McCutcheon.

[45] The lecture on poverty and environmental issues has been presented in terms of immediate action available to citizens of U.S. cities, namely consumption control. For excellent discussion of world population issues, see Jeffrey D. Sachs, *The End of Poverty*, New York: Penguin Press, 2005, particularly "Saving Children Only to Become Hungry Adults?" at Chapter 16. Also, "Population" within Chapter 6 of James Gustave Speth's *Red Sky at Morning*, New Haven: Yale University Press, 2004.

[46] The American Institute of Certified Public Accountants is presently reviewing guidelines for the reporting of greenhouse gas emission credits and sustainability reporting, which would cause these natural capital items to be included in conventional financial reports. www.aicpa.org/innovation/baas/environ/gaq.htm accessed March 2005.

[47] The Trust for Public Land is attempting to identify sites in LA's most under-parked communities, secure them access to park designated bond funds, and create 25 new parks in Los Angeles County. Trust for Public Land, "Parks for People – Los Angeles," www.tpl.org .

[48] The John Randolph Haynes Foundation supports social science research for Los Angeles. They have given several grants for projects relating to the topic of Sustainability. http://www.haynesfoundation.org/

[49] A staggering number of individual light rail lines are currently in various stages of proposal in the Los Angeles area. For LA citizens, living in a city with minimal mass-transit, this will come as a surprise. City politicians do not dare use any term like "comprehensive system" for fear the citizenry would balk at the price tag. Many of these lines are described in "LA City

Councilman and MTA Director Tom LaBonge Offers a Bullish Agenda for Rail" per Metro Investment Report Dec-Jan 2005. The bus lines and jitneys connecting with the light rail are also part of the vision of Councilman LaBonge. Refer to the *Legacy* website for specific details and web references.

[50] Trans-Agency Resources for Environmental and Economic Sustainability (T.R.E.E.S.), a project of Los Angeles based TreePeople, constructed demonstration sites, best management practices, design charettes and a planbook, "designed to work with nature's cycles of flood and drought (not to fight them) and to heal the damage we have done to our environment and to ourselves by paving the earth with concrete and asphalt." www.treepeople.org/trees/demo.htm accessed Feb. 20, 2005.

[51] Permaculture zone layout is explained nicely in Toby Hemenway's book *Gaia's Garden: A Guide to Home-Scale Permaculture*, White River Junction, VT: Chelsea Green Publishing, 2001 and in Linda Woodrow's *The Permaculture Home Garden*, New York: Viking/Penguin Putnam, 1996.

[52] Biodiesel fuel for a standard diesel automobile can be made from vegetable oil, animals fats, or even from recycled fast food deep fry fat. http://www.biodiesel.org/

The Los Angeles Department of Water and Power has a goal of 20% of its energy sales to retail customers coming from renewable sources by 2017, with an interim goal of 13% by 2010. Los Angeles Department of Water and Power, "Renewable Energy Policy," http://ladwp.com/ladwp/cms/ladwp005864.jsp accessed Aug. 12, 2005.

[53] "I have always believed that I could help change the world because I have been lucky to have adults around me who did – in small and large ways." Marian Wright Edelman, *The Measure of Our Success*, Boston: Beacon Press, 1992, p. 9.

[54] University of Idaho ran Biodiesel Workshops in September 2005, for school bus, urban truck and other diesel fleets. Source: "Biodiesel Utilization & Production," Biodiesel Workshop 2005 flyer, University of Idaho.

[55] The University of California (9 campuses) in July 2003 adopted a Green Building Policy and Clean Energy Standard. These policies are felt by 208,000 students and 120,000 faculty and staff. Additionally, there is a California Student Sustainability Coalition active at many of these campuses, whose objective is "to implement environmentally sound practices in the UC system."

[56] Thank you A.B., J.B., C.B., S.B. and D.B. (children from two Los Angeles families), who in 2004-2005 really did have birthday parties requesting contributions to Heifer International as described in the text.

Heifer International is a charity which fights poverty and hunger by donating productive animals (chickens, goats, water buffalo) to needy families worldwide. http://www.heifer.org/

[57] Efforts are underway to use manufacturing practices that recover, recycle and reuse materials and minimize energy conservation in the manufacture of silicon integrated circuits and in the manufacture of solar photovoltaic modules. Y.S. Tsuo et al, "Environmentally Benign Silicon Solar Cell Manufacturing," National Renewable Energy Laboratory, July 1998. http://www.nrel.gov/ncpv/pdfs/tsuo.pdf accessed Aug. 20, 2005.

[58] Bill McKibben writes about seeking deeper meaning in lieu of additional consumer goods. His book *$100 Holiday* uses the Christmas season as the example, yet his message extends far beyond that season.

[59] Several companies manufacture neighborhood electric vehicles. California Energy Commission, "Neighborhood Electric Vehicles," http://www.consumerenergycenter.org/transportation/urban/nev.html , March 8, 2005.

Energy Control Systems Engineering of Monrovia, CA has converted a Prius to achieve 150 to 180 mpg, "by replacing the Prius' batteries with a more powerful array and recharging it using a standard outlet at home. ...The car can deliver 150 to 180 mpg for up to 35 miles of low-speed, around-town driving and can average 70 to 100 mpg on longer trips at higher speeds." John O'Dell, "Plugged-In Hybrid Tantalizes Car Buffs," LA Times, June 25, 2005.

[60] Chickens can live happily in the city. See extensive website, photos and articles at Katy Skinner, "The City Chicken," www.thecitychicken.com or http://www.angelfire.com/falcon/thecitychicken/ and Linda Woodrow's *The Permaculture Home Garden*, New York: Viking/Penguin Putnam, 1996.

[61] The Forest Stewardship Council encourages the responsible management of the world's forests and certifies lumber as to sustainability of source forest management. http://www.fscus.org/

The Green Building Resource Center in Santa Monica, CA collects resources for chemical-free and environmentally-friendly building resources. http://www.globalgreen.org/gbrc/

[62] The town of Enkoping, Sweden plants willow trees around their power plant to offset carbon dioxide emissions. Fred Pearce, "A Most Precious Commodity," NewScientist.com, January 8, 2005

[63] Read about John Todd's advanced wastewater treatment systems called Living Machines, in Chapter One of Kenny Ausubel's *Restoring the Earth*, Tiburon, CA: HJ Kramer, 1997.

Description and photograph of a greywater filtering artificial wetland which looks like a natural pond can be found in Toby Hemenway's *Gaia's Garden*, White River Junction, VT: Chelsea Green Publishing, 2001, Chapter 5.

The City of Arcata in Northern California maintains a marsh and wildlife sanctuary which is an integrated wetland wastewater treatment plant. California Wetlands Information System, "Map of Arcata Marsh and Wildlife Sanctuary," http://ceres.ca.gov/wetlands/projects/Arcata_map.html accessed Feb. 26, 2005.

[64] Community Land Trusts are membership organizations which acquire land for community residences. Learn more about them through the Institute for Community Economics, "The Community Land Trust Model" www.iceclt.org accessed March 16, 2005.

"The ethic of earth stewardship provides a moral imperative to continue to work out more creative ways for vesting control of land in collective structures, rather than taking as natural the individual ownership of land that goes with our Western industrial culture." David Holmgren, *Permaculture: Principles and Pathways Beyond Sustainability*, Australia: Holmgren Design Services, 2002, p. 5.

There is one eco-village in LA, the Los Angeles Eco-Village, http://www.ic.org/laev/

[65] Treepeople installed a 110,000 gallon cistern under a T-ball field at the Open Charter Elementary School in the Westchester area of Los Angeles. The new main branch of the Santa Monica Public Library will include a 200,000 gallon cistern. Rainwater collected in these cisterns is recirculated to water landscaping during the dry months. Refer to the *Legacy* website for specific web references.

[66] Santa Fe has a Sustainable Santa Fe Commission. Atlanta holds a regular Sustainable Atlanta Roundtable. Pittsburgh holds a Smart Growth Conference. The City of Portland has an Office of Sustainable Development. Refer to the *Legacy* website for specific web references.

[67] "In fighting back we find a meaning, an identity, a sense of what is of ultimate value about ourselves. This meaning is both spiritual and social, both transcendent and as grittily earthy as can be. All the dissolution of ego praised by the great spiritual teachers occurs; it occurs, however, not as an escape from a social situation that is just too painful to face, but as an embrace of all that surrounds us." Roger S. Gottlieb, *A Spirituality of Resistance,* New York: Crossroad Publishing Company, 1999, p. 177.

[68] In New York City, "4 Times Square … features a thin-film solar power curtain wall extending from the 35th to the 48th floors on the south and east walls, which replaces traditional glass cladding material." Caption and

photograph at U.S. Photovoltaics Industry, "Our Solar Power: U.S. Photovoltaics Industry Roadmap Through 2030 and Beyond," PDF, Sept 2004, p.10.

Bertrand Piccard and his team are working on a prototype solar aircraft, hoping to complete it in 2006. Solar Impulse, "A New Project," http://www.solarnavigator.net/solar_impulse.htm, July 30, 2005.

[69] The Community Food Security Coalition is operational in 41 states "We are dedicated to building strong, sustainable, local and regional food systems that ensure access to affordable, nutritious, and culturally appropriate food to all people at all times." They promote community gardens, backyard gardens and urban commercial farms. The Neighborhood Urban Agriculture Coalition in Philadelphia reclaims abandoned inner city land for urban commercial farms. http://foodsecurity.org and http://www.greensgrow.org/

[70] Smart shopping strategies are outlined by Kenneth R. Berger at "Consumer Choices can Reduce Packaging Waste," University of Florida IFAS Extension, ABE328. First published September 2002, http://edis.ifas.ufl.edu/AE226 accessed Aug. 8, 2005.

The California Integrated Waste Management Board has published an article emphasizing Reduce, Reuse, Recycle, and Rebuy (or buy Recycled). "Grocery shopping with the four Rs in mind," California Integrated Waste Management Board, www.ciwmb.ca.gov/WPW/Coordinator/Articles/ShipPack.htm accessed April 5, 2005.

[71] China unveiled plans to make offshore wind farms a key part of its renewable energy program by 2020-2030. "China to build wind farms offshore," CNN.com International, May 16, 2005, http://edition.cnn.com/2005/WORLD/asiapcf/05/11/china.seaturbines.reut/ accessed May 30, 2005.

[72] "By August 2000, 21 US states had set up [Public Benefit Funds] ... By 2010 they will have channeled $1.7 billion into the development of renewable energy." Per Guy Dauncey, *Stormy Weather: 101 Solutions to Global Climate Change,* New Society Publishers, 2001, p. 183.

Denmark leads the world in wind power, with more than 20% of its electricity coming from wind sources. Mattias Akselsson, "The World's Leader in Wind Power," Sept. 2004, Scandinavica.com

[73] The Moscone Center in San Francisco has a 675kWp rooftop solar array, installed in Nov. 2001. Approximately 15% of the power needs of the Staples Center in Los Angeles are provided by solar panels installed as a shade over the parking garages. Refer to the *Legacy* website for specific web references.

[74] The City of Los Angeles has a goal for 2020 of 70% waste diversion from the waste that is currently landfilled. In 1995 the city documented 45%

diversion, and 49% in 1999 (It should be noted that these figures do not include private waste haulers, and thus exclude over 140,000 businesses and 34,000 multi-family apartment complexes). Sources: City of LA, Bureau of Sanitation, "SR Fact Sheet," www.lacity.org/SAN/factsht.htm accessed Mar. 31, 2005; and Judith A Wilson, Director, Bureau of Sanitation, City of Los Angeles Inter-Departmental Correspondence to Ellen Stein, June 6, 2001, available as PDF.

[75] "What are the choices that we must make if we are now to succeed, and not to fail? ... One of those choices has depended on the courage to practice long-term thinking, and to make bold, courageous, anticipatory decisions at a time when problems have become perceptible but before they have reached crisis proportions. This type of decision-making is the opposite of the short-term reactive decision-making that too often characterizes our elected politicians – the thinking that my politically well-connected friend decried as '90-day thinking,' i.e. focusing only on issues likely to blow up in a crisis within the next 90 days." Jared Diamond, *Collapse?*, New York: Viking Adult, 2004, p.522

[76] Learn more about land trusts through the Land Trust Alliance. "About LTA," Land Trust Alliance, http://www.lta.org/ .

The Marin Agricultural Land Trust acquires agricultural conservation easements in order to preserve open space. MALT also emphasizes agriculture that uses virtually no pesticides or chemical fertilizers. http://www.malt.org/ .

Oregon Sustainable Agriculture Land Trust protects rural and urban agricultural lands, networks apprentices, and promotes research and education into sustainable production. http://www.osalt.org/ .

[77] "Carbon and energy taxes have been frequently advocated by economists and international organizations as a policy instrument for reducing carbon dioxide emissions. In the practice of environmental policies an increasing number of Western European countries have implemented taxes based on the carbon or energy content of the energy products (Sweden, Norway, The Netherlands, Denmark, Finland, Austria, Germany and Italy). Several other countries, like Switzerland, France and the United Kingdom, are currently discussing proposals for their implementation." Per Regional Environmental Center for Central and Eastern Europe, "A Review of Carbon and Energy Taxes in EU," http://www.rec.org/REC/Programs/SofiaInitiatives/EcoInstruments/GreenBudget/GreenBudget6/carbon.html accessed Aug. 12, 2005.

[78] Drylands agriculture experimentation with indigenous edible plants continues. "...we are evaluating or experimenting with fifty useful plants native to the Sonora and Chihuahuan Deserts. We have roughly tripled the number of desert plant species that are growing on that degraded plot of land. Our runoff catchment basins, arroyo diversions for flood irrigation, and drip

systems have multiplied, as we work to conserve water. Our goal of a rainfed, desert plant community restoration seems more and more plausible. ... We hope to make better use of the ecological adaptations that allow certain native crops to function in extreme heat and drought. Tepary beans. Sonoran panicgrass. Murphey's mescal. Land races of prickly pears from the Chihuahuan Desert. The annual crops have produced plentiful seeds in our small field trials this season, and the perennials have grown well, despite above-average heat and little rain." Gary Paul Nabhan, *Enduring Seeds*, University of Arizona Press, 1989, p.192-193.

[79] Detailed nonfiction source information for all aspects of the fictitious Alden Administration's Energy Policy is available at the *Legacy* website under Resources.

Organizations such as Environmental Entrepreneurs (E2) circulate information about fuels of the future. SERA, a UK based environmental network, has compiled a description of energy sources and their CO2 impact. "What comes after oil?" Environmental Entrepreneurs Update, June 18, 2004, http://www.e2.org/ext/jsp/controller?docId=5444&section=afteroil accessed Aug.25, 2005. SERA, "Changing the Future of Fuel: The Green Fuel Challenge," http://www.sera.org.uk/publications/briefings/briefing_future_of_fuel.htm accessed Aug 25, 2005.

[80] In five years, between 1999 and 2004, the city of Palo Alto cut energy use by 17%, began a switch to biodiesel in their heavy equipment, and switched to low- or non-toxic cleaners, pest control systems, and printing chemicals. Paraphrased from Alan AtKisson, "Watch Out! Here Comes the Amoeba," The AtKisson Group, April 21, 2004.

Food Not Lawns is an Oregon based group whose name is somewhat self-explanatory. http://www.foodnotlawns.com/

[81] "Most of us who have children consider the securing of our children's future as the highest priority to which to devote our time and our money. We pay for their education and food and clothes, make wills for them, and buy life insurance for them, all with the goal of helping them to enjoy good lives 50 years from now. It makes no sense for us to do these things for our individual children, while simultaneously doing things undermining the world in which our children will be living 50 years from now." Jared Diamond, *Collapse?*, New York: Viking Adult, 2004, p. 513

[82] Several organizations have made lists of actions grassroots citizens can take to help curb global warming. Michael Brower and the Union of Concerned Scientists, *The Consumer's Guide to Effective Environmental Choices,* Three Rivers Press, 1999; The Natural Resources Defense Council's Global Warming page http://www.nrdc.org/globalWarming/default.asp ; The New

American Dream http://www.newdream.org/ ; Guy Dauncey, *Stormy Weather: 101 Solutions to Global Climate Change,* New Society Publishers, 2001.

[83] The Ojai Valley Land Conservancy works to preserve open spaces and natural habitats, and to educate youth in stewardship. http://www.ovlc.org accessed June 16, 2005.

[84] "… even the best-intentioned humanitarian aid can have negative consequences if the recipient government is based on elite local and foreign interests. An immediate step that we as citizens can take is to tell our representatives that the best use for our money is not supporting the status quo but alleviating the largest economic barrier to true development in the third world – its foreign debt." From *World Hunger: 12 Myths,* by Frances Moore Lappé, Joseph Collins and Peter Rosset, quoted at http://www.globalissues.org/TradeRelated/Poverty/FoodDumping/USAid.asp accessed July 20, 2005.

"It is time for the debts of the highly indebted poor countries to be cancelled outright as part of the financing package for the Millennium Goals-based poverty reduction strategies." Jeffrey Sachs, *The End of Poverty*, New York: Penguin Press, 2005, p. 281.

[85] Forecasting of climate change impacts on U.S. agriculture are being prepared by many sources, including: National Assessment Synthesis Team, "U.S. National Assessment of the potential consequences of climate variability and change, Sector: Agriculture," U.S. Global Change Research Program, 2000; Richard M. Adams et al, "A Review of Impacts to U.S. Agricultural Resources," Pew Center on Global Climate Change, February 1999; the Goddard Institute for Space Studies, the Geophysical Fluid Dynamics Laboratory, the United Kingdom Meteorological Office, and the National Center for Atmospheric Research.

[86] "Integrated farming systems [employed by smaller farms] produce far more per unit area than do monocultures. Though the yield per unit area of one crop – corn, for example – may be lower on a small farm than on a large monoculture farm, the total production per unit area, often composed of more than a dozen crops and various animal products, can be far higher." Peter Rosset, "Small is Bountiful," The Ecologist, v.29, i.8, Dec99 www.mindfully.org/Farm/Small-Farm-Benefits-Rosset.htm accessed May 3, 2005.

The Kerr Center for Sustainable Agriculture in Oklahoma is a nonprofit policy organization. It has produced "Seeds of Change: Food and Agriculture Policy for Oklahoma's Future" and also has identified "Steps to a Sustainable Agriculture: Priority Areas for Oklahoma Producer Grants." Both documents are available free at their website http://www.kerrcenter.com/ accessed Aug. 8, 2005.

[87] "...to go along with growing soil, we have to grow people as well – not more people, but rather people who understand the importance of growing soil." John Jeavons, quoted in *Gardening for the Future of the Earth*, Howard-Yana Shapiro, New York: Bantam, 2000, p. 79.

[88] ATTRA, the National Sustainable Agricultural Service runs sustainable farming internships and apprenticeships. The Mariposa School for Biodynamic Agriculture offers an Organic Agriculture Apprenticeship Program, as does the Center for Agroecology and Sustainable Food Systems at the University of California, Santa Cruz. SAREP (Sustainable Agriculture Research and Education Program) is a statewide program through the University of California. John Jeavons' Ecology Action works with people worldwide teaching sustainable agriculture. Snakeroot Organic Farm has published online an extensive Farmers' Retirement Plan including an apprenticeship program. Refer to the *Legacy* website for specific web references.

[89] New Zealand is well into its second decade of subsidy-free farming. Laura Sayre, "Farming without subsidies?", The New Farm, from the Rodale Institute. http://www.newfarm.org/features/0303/newzealand_subsidies.shtml. accessed July 20, 3005.

Organic Consumers works toward consumer education about the inequities of agricultural subsidies. www.organicconsumers.org/ofgu/subsidies.htm accessed April 12, 2005.

The Environmental Working Group is very active in policy formation, legal action, statistics accumulation, and public information regarding agricultural subsidies. www.ewg.org

[90] The city dwellers suggestions in the text are from The American Farmland Trust and the Kerr Center for Sustainable Agriculture. Both organizations are active in consumer awareness.

[91] Eliot Coleman and the Gardeners & Farmers of Terre Vivante have compiled numerous techniques for preserving garden abundance in *Keeping Food Fresh: Old World Techniques and Recipes.* Coleman encourages us to renew our trust in the food preservation techniques that served generations of people.

[92] In Newport, Oregon at Quarry Cove there are man-made tidepools. "Newport, Oregon," www.spectacularoregon.com/coast/central/newport.htm accessed April 12, 2005.

In Ormond Beach, Ventura County, CA, the Coastal Conservancy has secured conservation easements on farmlands adjoining marshland and dunes in anticipation of sea level rise. "The Meaning of a Foot: Looking out for the Wetlands," California Coast & Ocean, Volume 19, No.3, Autumn 2003.

Philip Williams Associates is projecting the impact of the next 50 years of sea level rise on such projects as the Redwood Creek watershed in Golden Gate National Recreation Area, and the Cargill Salt tidal wetlands and managed ponds in the San Francisco Bay area. "The Meaning of a Foot: Looking out for the Wetlands," California Coast & Ocean, Volume 19, No.3, Autumn 2003.

[93] Gary Bobker, Program Director, The Bay Institute testified before the Committee on Resources, House of Representatives in opposition to dams and similar hardscape, on June 28, 2003. He advocated conservation, efficiency, markets and improved technology rather than new dams and surface storage infrastructure. A PDF transcript is available online.

[94] Jay R. Lund and associates at the University of California, Davis have created models projecting California water availability, deliveries and scarcities through 2100 under climate change. Select data from these CALVIN models are available as a PDF. Jay R. Lund et al, "Climate Warming and California's Water Future," Feb. 23, 2003, Civil & Environmental Engineering, University of California, Davis.

[95] Clay J. Landry has created "How Water Markets Can End Conflicts: A Guide for Policy Makers." This PDF, available free online, explains such water issues as Beneficial Use Standards and the Use-It-Or-Lose-It rule.

[96] In side sessions ("shadow summits just down the street") to the 2002 WSSD in Johannesburg, "thousands of anti-globalization activists and environmentalists ... [called] attention to the dangers of privatizing the world's water supplies." For a brief introduction to worldwide water issues, see Ginger Adams Otis, "A World Without Water: Advocates Warn of Thirst and Turmoil for a Parched Planet," Aug. 21, 2002, The Village Voice, www.villagevoice.com/issues/0234/otis.php accessed Aug. 15, 2005.

[97] "Permaculture involves the transition from dependent consumer to responsible producer, but it is just as important to acknowledge that it is our energetic creative side trying to control and manipulate nature that is the root of the environmental crisis." David Holmgren, *Permaculture: Principles and Pathways Beyond Sustainability*, p.241

[98] Phytoremediation is the use of plants to remove pollution from the soil. Alpine pennycress *Thlaspi caerulescens*, pigweed *Amaranthus retroflexus*, thale cress *Arabidopsis thaliana* and pumpkins *Cucurbita pepo* – plants known as hyperaccumulators – have been used to clean up zinc, cadmium, nickel, DDT and PCBs. Rufus L. Chaney, "Phytoremediation: using plants to clean up soils," USDA Agricultural Research Service, http://www.ars.usda.gov/is/AR/archive/jun00/soil0600.htm accessed Aug. 12, 2005, and "Please Don't Eat the Pumpkins," World Ark Magazine, September/October 2004.

[99] The California High Speed Rail was in draft Environmental Impact Report stage in 2005. The tentative route runs from Sacramento to San Diego, with a line to the Bay Area. California High Speed Rail Authority, http://www.cahighspeedrail.ca.gov/route/default.asp accessed March 25, 2005.

[100] The Wetlands Action Network has been active in stalling development across Southern California wetlands properties, and taking legal action against polluters. Heal the Bay is active in citizen awareness, beach and creek cleanups and political policy to preserve the ecology of the Santa Monica Bay.

[101] Taxes on international money transfers, known as Tobin Taxes, are advocated by many groups. http://www.ceedweb.org/iirp/factsheet.htm Guy Dauncey proposes Tobin Taxes to create a Global Climate Fund or Energy Modernization Fund. Guy Dauncey, *Stormy Weather: 101 Solutions to Global Climate Change*, New Society Publishers, 2001, p. xii and Solution #93.

The list of poverty-reduction goals found in the text is from Jeffrey D. Sachs, "On-the-ground solutions for Ending Poverty," Jeffrey D. Sachs, *The End of Poverty*. It is a distillation of the U.N.'s Millennium Project.

[102] Creation of a World Environment Organization is described by James Gustave Speth in Chapter 9 of *Red Sky at Morning*. He proposes several models, including one which groups WEO with WTO and WHO under jurisdiction of the United Nations. Strengthening the United Nations is also a recommendation of Jeffrey D. Sachs, chapter 18, *The End of Poverty*. The 'triple bottom line' is a paraphrasing of James Gustave Speth, *Red Sky at Morning,* p.180. The ideal attributes of a World Environment Organization are summarized by James Gustave Speth, *Red Sky at Morning*, p. 178-179.

[103] "The leaders of France, Germany, and other countries have called for the creation of a World Environment Organization." James Gustave Speth, *Red Sky at Morning*, New Haven: Yale University Press, 2004, p. 177.

[104] Jim Montgomery and Mateo Rutherford of West Berkeley keep goats successfully in a 6,000 square foot urban yard. John Fall, "Urban farmers produce nearly all their food with a sustainable garden in their backyard," San Francisco Chronicle, July 23, 2004.

[105] The Hospice Foundation of America provides comfort-oriented care and support to family and patient in the final stages of terminal illness. http://www.hospicefoundation.org/

[106] "The Advisory Council for Aeronautical Research in Europe (ACARE) proposed very tough environmental targets for, primarily, emissions and noise levels in 2020. The EU has adopted these targets and is endeavouring to put them into international legislation through the International Civil Aviation Organization (ICAO). Commitment to sustainable aviation will mean an international R&D agenda of massive proportions. Research into advanced

aerodynamics, materials, more fuel efficient and cleaner engines, and more electric aircraft, the production of lighter structures, and decisive improvements to Air Traffic Management (ATM) technologies, are just a handful of the key areas of research and development needed to meet these targets." Per QuinetiQ corporation, "Sustainable aviation for 2020," http://www.qinetiq.com/home/defence/air/paris_air_show/age_of_sustainable_ aviation.html accessed July 30, 2005.

[107] "… a special effort of world science, led by global scientific research centers of governments, academia, and industry, must commit specifically to addressing the unmet challenges of the poor. Public funding, private philanthropies, and not-for-profit foundations will have to back these commitments, precisely because market forces alone will not suffice." Jeffrey D. Sachs, *The End of Poverty*, New York: Penguin Press, 2005.

[108] Several organizations, mostly outside the U.S., are active in bringing our burial customs to a more Sustainable form. The Natural Death Center works on a panorama of issues, including woodland burials. http://www.london21.org/articles_item.php?id=1013class=pageblue Ecopod creates recycled paper, paper mache sculpted coffins http://www.tve.org/ho/doc.cfm?aid=1453&lang=English A British sustainability group is studying ways to achieve more energy efficient cremations http://www.idea-knowledge.gov.uk/idk/core/page.do?pageId=72893

[109] James Gustave Speth presents various proposals for an "international polity … as robust as the international economy" in chapter 9 of *Red Sky at Morning*. Attributes of the fictitious World Sustainability Commission outlined in the text are in part from the political observations of James Gustave Speth, embellished with the nature-based philosophical reflections of David Holmgren, *Permaculture: Principles and Pathways Beyond Sustainability*, chapters 9 and 10.

[110] Jeffrey D. Sachs discusses enlightened globalization in Chapter 18 of his book *The End of Poverty*. Sachs makes the point that the multinational companies are not the problem, but can be part of the solution. Other Sachs ideas in the fictitious Alden Administration's policies include international cooperation, redeeming the role of the U.S. in the world, and Sustainable development.

There is an international initiative for a Nobel Prize for Sustainable Development. www.sustainable-prize.net accessed Feb. 20, 2005.

Please refer to the Legacy website

for further Resources:

www. LegacyLA.net

THE BREADTH OF CHANGE

Legacy is far from a scientific treatise. While it showcases the panorama of solutions available today, its intention is breadth, not depth. Thus any given corner of society (CoHousing, agriculture, national politics) is illustrated in *Legacy* with a sketch rather than a fully developed oil painting. It would take volumes of books to achieve the latter. Instead, *Legacy* is the sweeping big picture, the overview, the vision, all in the palm of your hand.

The fully developed oil painting, filling volumes of books, already exists. These volumes are not found on the fiction shelves of your bookstore. By means of the preceding notes, and further notes online, you will find today's expert thinkers outlining real developments – technologies, techniques, theories – a complete how-to covering every petal of the Permaculture Flower. These ideas paint the way to a Transformation of every aspect of today's society.

Because we can indeed craft a better *Legacy* than this.

CREDITS

Permaculture Flower diagram reprinted from *Permaculture: Principles and Pathways Beyond Sustainability*, by David Holmgren, Copyright 2002. Used with permission of David Holmgren.

Chapter 3, Section 10: "I take a look at the world …": Alan AtKisson, "When the World gets Weird, Get Creative," online article, Aug. 6, 2003. Used with permission of Alan AtKisson.

Chapter 4, Section 2: Paraphrased explanations of Innovator, Change Agent, Transformer and Iconoclast from *Believing Cassandra*, by Alan AtKisson, Copyright 1999. Used with permission of Alan AtKisson.

Chapter 4, Section 5: Series of quotations on Scarcity, Abundance, Sufficiency from Donella Meadows, "Living Lightly and Inconsistently on the Land," *The Global Citizen*, copyright 1991.

Chapter 5, Section 17: "Soil is being literally strip-mined": Howard-Yana Shapiro, *Gardening for the Future of the Earth*. New York: Bantam Books, 2000. p.77.

Chapter 5, Section 23: Simplicity quote is from the Message of Pope John Paul II for the 1990 World Day of Peace. Ecologic destruction/folly quote is from the National Council of Churches, "God's Earth is Sacred: An Open Letter to Church and Society in the United States," 2005. Responsible stewards quotation is from the Statement of H.E. Archbishop Renato R. Martino, Apostolic Nuncio, Head of the Holy See Delegation to the United Nations Conference on Environment and Development, Rio de Janeiro, Brazil, 4 June 1992. No single solution quote is from the United States Catholic Conference, *Renewing the Earth*, 1991. Gary Gardner quotes are from "Invoking the Spirit," WorldWatch Institute Paper #164, December 2002.

Chapter 6, Section 1: "Poverty is the greatest polluter …": Indira Gandhi, first UN Conference on the Human Environment, June 1972, Stockholm Sweden, quoted in "A Framework for Action," handout for the World Summit on Sustainable Development, Johannesburg, 2004.

Chapter 6, Section 1: "It is manifestly unjust …": Pope John Paul II, "Peace with God the Creator, Peace with All of Creation," Message for the 1990 World Day of Peace, 8 December 1989.

Chapter 6, Section 2: "contemplation of natural scenes": Frederick Law Olmstead, quoted by Anne Whiston Sprin in "Constructing Nature: The Legacy of Frederick Law Olmsted," *Uncommon Ground: Rethinking the Human Place in Nature*, William Cronon, editor. New York: W.W. Norton & Company, 1996. p.93.

Chapter 6, Section 7: "a constantly moving standard": Rabbi Arthur Waskow, "And the Earth is Filled with the Breath of Life," online article, 1996.

Chapter 6, Section 9: "Wealth of selection …": Ayn Rand, *Atlas Shrugged*. New York: Random House, 1957. p.736.

Chapter 8, Section 10 and Chapter 9, Section 6: Not ours to complete the task, paraphrased from Pirke Avot 2:21, various sources and translations.

Chapter 8, Section 26: "completely reject the idea…": Maude Barlow, chair of the Council of Canadians, quoted by Ginger Adams Otis, "A World Without Water: Advocates Warn of Thirst and Turmoil for a Parched Planet," Aug. 21, 2002, The Village Voice.

Chapter 10, Section 1: "This is the one true joy …", "I am of the opinion …", "I want to be thoroughly used up…": George Bernard Shaw, in part from the 'Dedicatory Letter' in *Man and Superman*.

GENEALOGY OF TIA'S FAMILY

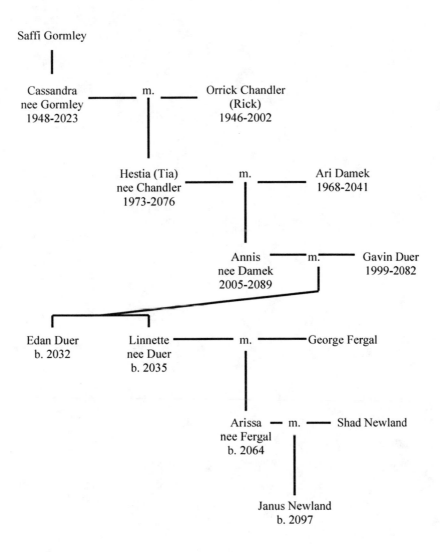

GLOSSARY

AICPA   American Institute of Certified Public Accountants, the nonfiction organization which guides financial statement presentation

Athens Accord a fictional international treaty focused on Sustainability

Barcelona Framework   a fictional international pre-treaty standard, focused on Sustainability

CCC   Civilian Conservation Corps, also known as the Creation Conservation Corps, a fictional social project under fictional President Elliott, a rejuvenation of the 1934 nonfiction social project under President Roosevelt.

CDM   Clean Development Mechanism, a nonfiction provision under the Kyoto Protocol

CO_2 Carbon dioxide, a gas that has significant impact on the greenhouse effect. Nonfiction.

COP   Conference of the Parties, nonfiction conferences of the nations who were party to the 1992 United Nations Framework Convention on Climate Change.

CSA   Community Supported Agriculture, a nonfiction membership program often used by small farms.

CSD   Commission on Sustainable Development, a nonfiction division of the United Nations

DOE   Department of Energy, a nonfiction bureau of the U.S. government

EPA   Environmental Protection Agency, a nonfiction bureau of the U.S. government

EU   European Union

Factor 4   a nonfiction theory of resource productivity, challenging participants to increase their resource productivity by a Factor of 4, to be four times more productive in using resources than they are today.

Factor 10   a nonfiction theory of resource productivity, challenging participants to increase their resource productivity by a

Factor of 10, to be ten times more productive in using resources than they are today.

FarmUrb   a fictitious urban agriculture program, managed by inner city youth. The program's name comes from Farming the Urban spaces.

feijoa   a bush bearing edible fruit, botanic name *Feijoa sellowiana,* also known as Pineapple Guava. Yields successfully in low-water locations.

FFCC Tax   Fossil Fuels Carbon Car tax, fictional tax on carbon emitting vehicles.

GNP   Gross National Product, a nonfiction standard measure of the economy.

GPI   Genuine Progress Indicator, a nonfiction alternative measure of the economy.

g-news   grid news, the fictional term for newspapers on the grid.

Grid, gridsites   intelligent hub successor to the internet and world-wide web, currently nonfiction in test cases.

IPCC   Intergovernmental Panel on Climate Change, a nonfiction multinational gathering of scientists examining climate change data

LA   Los Angeles

Lares   Los Angeles Restoration and Sustainability, pronounced "Larry's," a fictional alternative housing development

Moscow Treaty   a fictional international treaty, purported successor to the nonfiction Kyoto Protocol

MOP   Meetings of the Parties, nonfiction meetings of the nations who have ratified the Kyoto Protocol. Countries which have not ratified have observer status only. In fictional projection, the MOP term/process is applied to future agreements as well.

NGO   Non-Government Organizations, a nonfiction general term for environmental and social change organizations

NY   New York

PrepCon   Pre-Sessional Consultations, working sessions that take place prior to the main events. Nonfiction term used for United Nations events.

PLASE   Plan for a Los Angeles Sustainable Environment, pronounced 'place.' A fictional city plan including a comprehensive rail system, mass transit and park spaces. The individual rail lines attributed to the fictional comprehensive PLASE system are nonfiction lines currently in planning stages.

RAI   Rebuild America's Infrastructure, also called the 'Ray' of hope, a fictional social program under fictional President Elliott. Similar to 1934 nonfiction WPA program under President Roosevelt.

ROOTS   ReVisioning Opportunities for Open Territories through Sustainability, a fictional NGO networking education and apprenticeship programs in biodynamic dry-lands agriculture.

REGROW   Restored Environment Graded Rebuilding of Wetlands, a fictional NGO restoring edgelands (wetlands and tidepools) along the California coastline.

RPS   Renewables Portfolio Standard, a nonfiction standard requiring that a growing share of the U.S. power supply come from renewable sources

SEC   Securities and Exchange Commission, nonfiction.

SEZ30, SEZ40 Shoreline Elimination Zones, fictional mapping of seacoast areas soon to be lost to sea level rise. The number refers to the decade of anticipated loss.

Sliver   a fictional clean-chip recyclable electronic device, substitute for laptop and communications devices, with the added features of voice recognition and miniscule size. Purported successor to the 4C. In later decades it is accompanied by a video display mounted upon eyewear. Such components are currently available separately as pioneer models, although nonfiction does not include the recyclable aspects.

T.R.E.E.S.   Trans-Agency Resources for Environmental and Economic Sustainability, a nonfiction coalition of government agencies and environmentalists founded by Andy Lipkis and TreePeople, to solve drought, flooding, air and water pollution, landfill closures, high energy costs, youth unemployment, and urban blight. T.R.E.E.S. publishes a planbook describing environmentally conscious retrofitting of existing buildings.

UN   United Nations

UNFCCC   United Nations Framework Convention on Climate Change, the nonfiction international committee that negotiates the details of the Kyoto Protocol

U.S.   United States

Venture   a fictional clean-chip recyclable electronic device. Self-contained headband, with full computing and communications capabilities, purported successor to the Sliver. A headband video display is currently available as a pioneer model, although nonfiction does not include the recyclable nor the self-contained aspects.

WCSD   World Conference on Sustainable Development, a fictional world conference series. In 2002 a nonfiction World Summit on Sustainable Development was held in Johannesburg, South Africa. Political theorists suggested in retrospect that the side sessions were more valuable than the Summit of world leaders. Thus the fictional series is based upon the Johannesburg side sessions rather than the Summit portion.

WEO   World Environment Organization, a fictional organization guiding world environmental policy, equal in stature to the WHO and WTO. The idea of a WEO is proposed by nonfiction political theorists.

WHO   World Health Organization, nonfiction.

WSC   World Sustainability Commission, a fictional organization coordinating the efforts of WHO, WTO and WEO. The idea of such a coordinating organization is proposed by nonfiction political theorists.

WTO   World Trade Organization, nonfiction.

4C   Clean Compact Communications Center, a fictional electronic device, purported successor to cell phone, and palm pilot combined. Its technical abilities are nonfiction in premium technology markets, however its clean chip, recyclable aspects are fiction.

Do not retreat into your private world,
That place of safety, sheltered from the storm,
Where you may tend your garden, seek your soul,
And rest with loved ones where the fire burns warm.

To tend a garden is a precious thing,
But dearer still the one where all may roam,
The weeds of poison, poverty, and war,
Demand your care, who call the earth your home.

To seek your soul is a precious thing,
But you will never find it on your own,
Only among the clamor, threat, and pain
Of other people's need will love be known.

To rest with loved ones is a precious thing,
But peace of mind exacts a higher cost,
Your children will not rest and play in quiet,
While they still hear the crying of the lost.

Do not retreat into your private world,
There are more ways than firesides to keep warm;
There is no shelter from the rage of life,
So meet its eye, and dance within the storm.

Kathy Galloway

CPSIA information can be obtained at www.ICGtesting.com
Printed in the USA
LVOW080846050112

262488LV00002BA/185/A